Rod

. . . a two-mile s
property where the
and amorous – con spend their nights
dancing chic-to-chic under dazzling lights.

Here, against the outrageously decadent background of Beverly Hills with its hop-scotch bedrooms and grand estates, posh restaurants and luxurious hotels is the shocking story of society dame Belle Cooper, and her passionate struggle to become a woman of integrity and independent means.

Not since SCRUPLES has a novel laid bare the lives – and loves – of the totally un-scrupulous super rich.

RODEO DRIVE

Barney Leason

THE SHERIDAN
BOOK COMPANY

This edition published in 1993 by
The Sheridan Book Company

First published in Great Britain 1982
Reprinted 1984 and 1987

Printed and bound in Great Britain by
Cox & Wyman Ltd, Reading, Berkshire

ISBN 1–85501–436–X

Chapter One

The traffic tie-up at the corner of Wilshire Boulevard and Rodeo Drive was worse than usual that Friday afternoon. But then, it was just two hours before the official beginning of the Memorial Day weekend.

Ah, Belle Cooper told herself wryly, a better reason for a traffic jam than flight from the city lay up ahead.

A Cadillac Seville had rear-ended a Bentley aiming to make a left turn into Wilshire, and the two drivers, oblivious of the commotion they were causing, were standing in the middle of the intersection screaming at each other. A policeman, his face in a "slow burn," moved slowly toward them.

Belle whistled to herself and turned on the car radio.

That, she thought, would be about $2,000 for a Bentley right rear fender, probably more. The Seville was no doubt leased—most of them in Beverly Hills were.

One would not have known this, judging by the way the Seville driver, a portly man, red-faced, in a striped sports shirt and red golfing pants, was waving his arms. Mr. Bentley—Belle did not recognize him—fumed nervously, hands shoved in the jacket pockets of his tan safari suit, now and then fidgeting, barking contemptuous responses to the oral onslaught, lifting a hand to adjust the foulard tucked in the collar of his jacket.

The cop prevailed. The two got back into their cars and did as directed: pulled a few yards into the parking lot behind the Gibraltar Bank. The law followed, dragging a notebook out of his back pocket and grinning at his motorized audience.

The traffic in Belle's lane began to crawl across Wilshire into Rodeo and she eased her white Corniche ahead, turning down the radio, which by now had switched from music to an advisory of a second-stage smog alert in the San Bernardino Valley—and it was only the end of May.

Status. She considered the matter of status. The automobile, more important in California, particularly in Beverly Hills, than anywhere else in the country . . . The car and the house, the location of the house, the clothes one wore, even on a lazy afternoon, were supremely important. What one did to make the money to buy the Rolls, to lease the Seville, to make the down payment on the house, which had to be north of Santa Monica Boulevard, preferably north of Sunset Boulevard, to keep the charge accounts liquid was far less important, provided, of course, one's occupation did not somehow make one indictable.

One of the latest good news-bad news jokes popped into her head. Real estate agent to client: "I've got good news for you. They'll sell you the house for two million. The bad news is you've got to put down $2,000."

Status. In the East, they called it "front."

Belle stopped again at the first light on Rodeo—to the left, Giorgio's; to the right, Van Cleef and Arpel's. Giorgio's front door was open and inviting; inside, it was as crowded as a cocktail party. She could see a little group gathered at a bar where a jolly black man in a white mess jacket was serving free white wine, or whatever the heart desired, and more serious customers flipping through the clothes racks. Van Cleef's, being jeweler to the affluent of a dozen countries, was screened at the front for security reasons but it, too, would be relatively crowded, representatives of the rich and mighty weighing precious gold and silver pieces against the rising tide of the heavy metals market.

Belle drummed her fingers on the carved wooden steering wheel, waiting for the light to change.

Her status was simply defined. She was the wife of Martin Cooper, president and chief executive officer of Cooper Advertising Agency—C.A.A.—the largest in the city of Los Angeles and among the most prestigious in the country, the world. In this case, Los Angeles meant greater L.A., including the golden enclave of Beverly Hills and that geographically nebulous place called Hollywood. She was the wife of Martin Cooper, former All-American fullback, now advertising and public relations genius, real estate entrepreneur, notorious man-about-town, some said womanizer, con artist of certified skill.

But . . . she could not legitimately complain. As a newcomer to this lifestyle, she had willingly become part of the system and was now as deeply involved in the "con" as the men in their Bentleys and Sevilles, women in their chocolate-brown Mercedes convertibles, their silver Alfas, their Corniche convertibles. The Cooper house was located well on the "right" side of Sunset, where these days a million dollars would buy you an acre lot, no more. Belle dressed extremely well and entertained expertly, with elegance; her invitations were never turned down. The charge accounts were promptly serviced by Martin's secretary at C.A.A. since so much of what they did was write-off. They were recognized and sought after by the best stores, best restaurants, best hotels. Her daughter, Susan, Martin's stepdaughter, went to tennis camp almost every summer, if she hadn't been sent off to Europe with friends and a chaperone, and Susan drove a peppy little Pinto, a seventeenth-birthday gift.

Martin had bought Belle the white Rolls Royce Corniche a couple of years ago. It was "her," he'd said, the kind of car a woman named Belle Cooper should drive. It was fast and sleek, velvety in look and feel. Like her, he said. But that had been two years ago and things had changed. Among other things, at the time, Martin had been after the Rolls account for the United States.

They had been married eight years. Belle was forty-two now and she knew she was dead-ended in status, front, image. If you got it, flaunt it, they joked out here, "on the coast." But she hated it. It was not her way and she didn't want it anymore, not for herself, and not for Susan.

A red light stopped her again at the corner of Little Santa Monica, and Belle spotted Bernard Markman. Arms swinging loosely, bald head shining, Bernard Markman was strolling down Rodeo, his chin high, his eyes restlessly observing the sidewalk crowd. His corporate law offices were a few blocks to the west, on Roxbury.

He saw her and waved, calling out, "See you in the desert tomorrow . . . Come early, Belle. Sally's taking you to lunch at the Tennis Club."

She nodded, grinning. He waved again and sauntered on.

It would be a good weekend, she thought happily. Sally

was her best friend in the West, older than she was, but down to earth, not fooled or deceived by any of the sham. They were to drive to Palm Springs in the morning. Tonight, they were booked: Martin was giving a little party at the Bistro.

Jesus! Another party. But she was good at that; everybody said Belle Cooper was very good at parties.

She had not needed to marry Martin Cooper, that was the thing, she told herself, as she neared the invisible border between what was north and south of Beverly Hills. She was still amazed that she had. Her friends in New York had thought she was crazy. What! Marry this raucous man and leave New York? Insanity!

Own up, she advised herself. She had married Martin precisely because of the characteristics she now found so unpleasant: his outrageous extroversion, a rough-cut poise that lent him a charisma so potent that at one time there'd even been talk of Martin Cooper, *a* party's choice. Not *the* party's choice, because Martin was such an opportunist he'd have gone either way: if nominated, he'd serve anybody.

By contrast, eastern men had seemed effete to her, Martin virile and strong. Her first husband, Peter Bertram, had been a quiet man, an introvert really. He came from an old family, was a scholar, a graduate of an Ivy League law school. He had entered a room so quietly no one had noticed him. As quietly, he had died, leaving Belle and Susan alone in the East.

Cooper was boisterous, a prankster, with an impetuosity that at one time had been endearing. She had needed someone to lean on and she had accepted Martin Cooper, eventually loved him. But in the crucial eight years of aging, taking him from age forty-four to fifty-two, he had not grown well. The charisma, the magnetism, had made a rough crossing from youthfulness to middle age. The jarring edges of his personality had not smoothed; they had been further abraded by added years. The boisterousness had turned to arrogance, the impetuousness merely to bad manners. It was now completely obvious that Martin Cooper did not give a damn about anyone. He was for Number One—Numero Uno, as they said on the coast—nothing else.

The more she had come to dislike him, the more painful the memory of Peter Bertram had become. They had had a good life. Peter had been a real person, an individual with norms and values. Martin was like the California real estate in which he was heavily invested: the land unstable and the houses with nothing underneath their foundations, planted shallowly in the mud.

The Cooper house was up in the hills, off Angelo Drive, one of the "old Hollywood" showplaces, not because the area was part of Hollywood but because it had once belonged to a famous actor, long dead and very nearly forgotten: Frank Farr. Farr had been Hollywood-handsome, five times married, a star in dozens of early Westerns. He had made it in the days before income tax, had kept five Rolls along with the girls, the horses, a yacht. He'd gone to Europe and back on the luxury ships, played on the Riviera, gambled in Monte Carlo. Finally, it was said, he died of too much drinking, and there were enough wet bars scattered through the house to give that gossip credibility.

And now? Mention the name Frank Farr and the kids' faces went blank. Susan claimed they'd made the man up.

So much for status, for image, for fame. It dried up or rotted in the sun, cracked in the earthquakes, and finally disappeared in debris, like broken pottery and bones in Pompeii. California . . . the coast. Jesus!

Chapter Two

Belle turned her car into the brick drive leading under a canopy of fruit trees and up the hill to the house. A beautiful place, it was built in the Spanish colonial style that was so popular in the twenties. She parked on the apron in front of the house, brick like the drive and trellised with bougainvillea and wisteria in full bloom. The front door was set in a low gallery lined with large clay pots filled with geraniums, which connected the main house with the servants' quarters and the huge garage, ample for the two Rolls—her Corniche and Cooper's Silver Cloud—and her red two-seat Jaguar and his sporty Jensen.

The gardener put down his pruning shears to help her with her packages, an I. Magnin box and dresses in their Neiman-Marcus plastic bags. These they put on a chair at the bottom of a wrought-iron railing that marked the way up tiled steps to the upper floors.

Belle walked down the hallway, past a paneled library, a cheery morning room and butler's pantry, into the kitchen.

Mrs. Atkins, her housekeeper, was sitting at the breakfast table in a bright alcove overlooking the pool, a hundred yards of smooth lawn, and a large guest house whose downstairs doubled as party and projection room.

"Hi, Frances." Belle slid into a chair beside the older woman.

"Would you like a beer, Mrs. Cooper? Coffee?"

Her voice was soft with a hint of Irish lilt. It was also veined with sympathy, almost as though she read Belle's forlorn thoughts, which would not have been surprising. Frances had been around Belle longer than she liked to remember, as a maid in Belle's mother's town house and then with the Bertrams in their first apartment in New York, from the time Susan had been born. Whatever happened in Belle's life, Mrs. Atkins was the first to spot it. She was aware of Belle's unhappiness before Belle felt it.

"Okay, Frances, since you're offering it, a beer. The traffic was miserable."

Mrs. Atkins drew herself out of her chair with a sigh, got a bottle of beer out of the refrigerator, and poured it.

"You're not going to be dining at home tonight."

It was not a question, but a statement of fact. The Coopers hardly ever dined at home. It made no sense to keep a cook. On the rare occasions when it was just two of them eating off trays in the library, Frances prepared the meal. If they were giving a small dinner at home, even for four, Belle was in the habit of calling a caterer. Why not? It was almost always for business purposes, a write-off.

Belle considered telling Frances that, yes, she would be home but that Martin had entertaining to do in town, but . . .

"No," she murmured, "we've got a party."

"Run, run, run."

"An important man from New York," Belle said, winking.

Frances understood her irony. "Always the same . . ."

Still, Belle did not have to defend her social life to Frances Atkins.

"Did Susan call?"

Mrs. Atkins shook her head. "No, but Mrs. Markman called about an hour ago. She wants you to call her back. Rose is ill. She's gone to bed." Rose, the maid. "I think she's got summer flu."

"Summer flu? It isn't even summer yet."

When she'd finished her beer, Belle retrieved the box and dresses and carried them upstairs to her sitting room. She shrugged out of her blouse and skirt, a Valentino she'd bought in Rome the summer before, and hung it on its padded hanger. She stripped out of the lace-edged teddy that she ordered by the dozen and went into the bathroom. She made a face at herself in the mirror, whistling softly. She looked tired and there were circles under her eyes. The fine lines had begun to form. What Sally said must be true: We age in cycles, every seven years. But unlike so many of her friends, Belle had never had anything done to her face, had never really seriously considered such a project. Perhaps, she told herself, the time was approaching.

Sally Markman was sure to have that new plastic surgeon in for drinks in Palm Springs over the weekend. Dr. . . . What was his name? Yes, Hans Unterlinden. He had become quite the rage in certain wealthy circles, like Suki, the status hairdresser, half-French, half-Japanese, and arrogant. Or Claudine, the new makeup artist who could take ten years off your face using no more than her subtle hands.

Maybe she'd have a little chat with Unterlinden. Just maybe it would help her mood. It would nice to be reassured: No, no, Mrs. Cooper, out of the question. I would not think of it.

Considering her age, her face was comparatively unlined: the broad forehead, large gray eyes, luminous, the mane of russet hair brushed back from her face, a sparseness of gray adding highlights. She was aristocratic, not beautiful. She had never been beautiful in the accepted sense: her face was too narrow, her nose too aquiline. But she had known how to make the best of what she'd been given. If anything, realism about herself was her strength. And she understood that looking good—looking sleek, looking expensive—was a profession, too. She would have made a hell of a courtesan, she told herself critically. But that had been her basic failing, too. She was too critical, too honest, and she could not make love to a man she did not love, or at least like exceedingly well.

In the beginning, back in New York, she had liked Martin Cooper exceedingly well and they had made love. Then she had loved him, had convinced herself she needed him, and had agreed to marry him. The decision had been an impetuous one—for once she had not been cautious. She had been caught up in Martin's derring-do. She had to say yes, he had urged, because he was leaving for a European business trip in a week and he wanted her with him. She would give him class, he had argued, grinning and laughing about it. And she *had* added class to his act. He had gotten that international account. She could no longer remember what the account was but she did acknowledge that for once he had not been lying. She did have class, an inbred sophistication, and she had lent it to Martin Cooper.

Now, she was telling herself, the time had probably come to call the loan. She was too good for him; looking back, there had never been a time when she wasn't too good for him, despite her compromises.

Belle slid her hands down and across her body. Her belly was flat, firm, unlined. The breasts were not large and had retained their lift although, realistically, she told herself, turning for a side view, they were beginning to lose a little resiliency. Silicone, perhaps? She grimaced. The silicone or "lift" route was too Hollywood. She was still able to handle a deep-cut dress. A smile lifted the corners of her lips as she thought of all those women who obviously never looked closely in the mirror and didn't have a clue how ludicrous they appeared in V-necked evening dresses, especially from the side. God, no, mustn't start thinking Hollywood. She would exercise those muscles. That woman at Elizabeth Arden was supposed to be a miracle worker in keeping flab at bay. And after she talked to Sally she would have a swim, the best exercise going.

Belle slid into a St. Tropez bikini, wrapped herself in a white terry robe, and went outside to the pool house to call Sally.

"Markman res-i-dence," a voice drawled, deep in southern fry.

"Cut that out, Sally! It's Belle."

"Oh, hiya, kid." The voice became crisp and sharp. "Never know who it might be."

"You called me, madame?"

"Right, I did," Sally said. "What you been doing today?"

"Had my hair done. Went shopping. Lunch outside, at the Bistro Garden."

"Who with?"

"That pain in the neck, Marjery Cannon. It's been overdue and I finally had to say yes."

"Jesus," Sally groaned, "what's new on that front?"

Sally did not think much of Marjery Cannon, nor of husband Gregory.

"Gregory is just so successful you wouldn't believe it," Belle said sardonically. "He's peddling a new issue of tax-free bonds."

"That goddamn fake," Sally said. "She tell you who she's laying lately?"

"Nope, we were being too ladylike."

"Last I heard she was carrying on hot and heavy with J.W. Fortnum, movie mogul."

"Well, whatever—or whoever," Belle sighed. "I had to go to buy a dress for tonight. I needed pepping up so I bought three. Couldn't make up my mind."

"What's tonight?" Sally demanded. "A big deal, huh? Listen, in all your social falderal, don't forget about Palm Springs. Bernard and I are going tonight after dinner."

"I know, I waved to him. You're taking me to lunch tomorrow and don't you forget that." She fiddled with the curly telephone cord. "Cooper has got a big shot in from New York, the head of Cosmos Cosmetics. A little dinner party upstairs at the Bistro, the small room there in the back. Very *intime*. We're trying—you guessed it—to impress him."

Sally chuckled huskily. "Would I be right in thinking this is a hot new prospect for C.A.A.?"

"Right on. Cosmos is getting ready to launch some new kind of fragrance."

"Oh, goodie," Sally said. Then she lapsed into a silence so serious Belle did not try to interrupt it. "Listen, kiddo, I'm going to talk to you more about this in the Springs, but I want you to start thinking about it now. Get this: In exactly six months, we are going to put on the greatest charity event this town has ever seen. That'll be some time in the first week of December. Not very long from now, I know. So we're going to have to work our asses off. But it's something that you and I are going to pull off."

"God, duckie, not another benefit! Sal, don't we have enough already? Too many maybe?"

"We do," Sally agreed, "but this one is special." She paused again, then went on in a low voice, "This one is to raise the money to build the Sally Markman Pavilion at a Southern California women's cancer research center—neither of which now exist!"

Belle felt a finger of apprehension tickle her insides. "What the hell are you talking about, Sal?"

"What I'm talking about is this," Sally responded fiercely. "I've got six months to live, maybe a year, and I'm going to do this thing before I die."

Belle's stomach was tight; she was holding her breath. "You know about my trouble?" Belle nodded silently. "Well, it's over five years now. I began to feel funny, didn't think anything about it until I went to see Tom Glenn this week . . . It's back. He told me straight out, no punches pulled."

Something like a wretched sob burst through Sally's control, crashed into Belle's ear. Belle clutched at the phone, gasping. Tears welled up in her eyes.

"Sally! Jesus! But Glenn's not a specialist. How could he be so sure?"

"I know he's not a specialist. He's an internist, Belle," Sally said impatiently. "But he 's been my doctor for years. We went through the last siege together. He knows me like a book—"

"But still . . ." Belle began to object.

"Never mind," Sally exclaimed. "We went to a specialist, Belle, Tom's close associate. And there's nothing anybody can do. He didn't take long to figure that out. It's inoperable, Belle, goddamn it."

"Sal—"

"Look, Belle," Sally continued powerfully, "I know you're feeling down—"

"Down? I—"

"Belle, I know you're fed up with the whole scene and I don't blame you."

"Sal . . . Never mind about my problems, for God's sake."

"I know your life is not easy with that asshole Cooper. But this has got nothing to do with him—or with Bernard Markman for that matter. And," she emphasized, "I don't want you saying anything to him or anybody else."

"Bernard doesn't know?" Belle asked faintly.

"No, and there's no reason he should. At least not now. My purpose is to get this money-raising show on the road. I'm not going to try to explain to you all the forms of women's cancer. There are plenty of research centers, but Tom Glenn has confirmed to me there isn't a single one that specializes in women's cancer—its various forms and treatment. You do know about the trauma a woman goes through when she has a mastectomy. Well, most of our doctors are men and they are damned callous about the whole thing. How lightly they'll recommend a mastectomy, but when it comes to a man losing his balls to testicular cancer, Christ, they go crazy trying to figure out how to avoid that. One thing we can do with this is try to attract some women cancer doctors who understand what the score is. It's a hellishly complicated business, Belle, and I've got to get the ball rolling . . . while I've got time."

Belle could not stop herself. She began to cry; her voice burred over. But Sally would not allow grief.

"Shut up, goddamn it! I tell you, Belle, I've got to ride it out, and part of the reason I want to do this is to keep myself occupied."

"Blast it," Belle cried, "it's just like you, you miserable . . ."

"Miserable son of a bitch, that's right," Sally agreed, laughing abruptly. "And I want to tell you this: If they think I've been tough on the fund-raising scene before now, they ain't seen nothin' yet."

"Goddamn it!" Belle muttered. "Look, I just don't believe —I can't believe—"

"Believe, Belle!"

"Well," Belle said, more matter-of-factly, "you won't be able to keep it a secret. Everybody's going to understand why . . ."

"No, they won't understand a goddamn thing. I don't want a dollar raised out of some misplaced pity either. A center like this is long overdue and you know we're not going to get anything out of the federal government for it. What they're not going to know is that all I want out of it is a Sally Markman Memorial Pavilion—and they're not to know that until . . . later. You'll see to that when the time comes."

"Oh, no . . . no . . . no," Belle said softly, "I don't believe this."

"I'm telling you: No tears! I won't stand for that. And keep it under your hat."

"Yes, madame . . . Sal." Belle stifled another sob.

"I'll see you tomorrow then. While the two great ones are off playing golf, we'll talk."

Sally said no more. She hung up without a goodbye, as was her habit, leaving Belle hanging in midair. Belle put the phone back on its hook, then covered her eyes with the palms of her hands. This time she cried in earnest, for no one could hear her. Part of her sorrow, she knew, was for herself. In six months, she would be losing the best friend she had. Then, she'd have no one to talk to, no one who really understood her problems, her troubles, and who was tough enough to demand logic and decision from her. Susan was a bare seventeen and already wrapped up in her own life. Belle did have Norman Kaplan, but he was in New York as much as he was here. Norman would be devastated when he heard this. He had been friends with Sally even longer than Belle had. It was Norman who had gotten her together with Sally when Belle had first moved to the coast. After that, nobody.

Belle stretched out on the chaise longue, too depressed now to think about the pool. Her life was coming apart.

Six months. The prognosis was as cold as the pages of the calendar itself. Six months to live, maybe a month or two longer, and Sally would be gone. And Belle still would be here, living her life, such as it was, try as she might. Six months: The term, the sentence, burned her heart.

Chapter Three

"Would you like a glass of champagne, my dear?" Bernard Markman asked Marjery Cannon.

"I think I should, Bernard," she said, her tanned face cracking around the lips with a smile. She pushed back her long, sun-streaked mousy-brown hair. "I'm very very nervous."

"Nonsense," he said, smiling back at her. "What's there to be nervous about?"

"Gosh, Bernard, suppose somebody found out about us?" Her voice was baby-soft and pouty.

Markman knew better. No one was going to find out, with the possible exception of her husband, Gregory. And Gregory was certainly not going to tell anybody. Besides, Markman knew that this was not the first time Marjery Cannon had agreed to a late afternoon of love. She'd been through at least a half dozen of the town's leading citizenry. It would cost him, he knew, and for a second he wondered why he was bothering. Marjery was pretty but not that attractive—God knows, most of the secretaries were better built. Perhaps it was merely that she intrigued him. And part of the attraction was that she'd slept with so many of his friends.

"I've been looking forward to our meeting, Marjery," he said softly.

"Me, too," she replied, inclining her head and peering up at him from under her false lashes.

Obviously, she didn't know how he would make his move. Preliminaries were always tough. He sat quietly, observing the effects of Marjery's last face lift, the one that had finally made her face a stiff mask. Her eyes crinkled worriedly; the surgeon had done work there, too. The wrinkles around her mouth had been smoothed, but nevertheless gave her trouble when she smiled. The mouth, he had been told, remained an important feature in Marjery's amorous repertoire.

If you didn't look too closely, however, didn't spot the marks, perhaps if you were on the other side of the room or across the table at a dimly lit party, Marjery still had the look of a debutante.

"How's Gregory?" he asked. Small talk.

She shrugged and made a face, as best she could. "The same, not doing well. Sometimes I wonder how we'll make it—the house, cars, the entertaining." She sat opposite him, her arms tense on her knees. "You're so different," she said frankly. "I've always thought you such an attractive man."

He chuckled modestly. "Bald . . . and aging, Marjery."

She reached across the space between them and took his left hand in both of hers. "Did a bald man ever lose a girl because he was bald?" she demanded, winningly. "Do you remember dancing with me?"

"Could I forget?"

Markman remembered the party upstairs at Perino's, about a month ago now. Marjery hadn't been put off by the small dance floor and the fact that they were very visible. She had come on strong, thrusting herself against him, her crotch like a grasping hand on his thigh. Then she had begun calling him at the office to ask contrived, inane questions, advice about this or that. Finally, almost annoyed, calling her bluff, he had suggested a quiet meeting where they would not be disturbed. Naturally, Marjery had agreed.

"You're such a marvel of a man, Bernard," she murmured soulfully. "People say you're one of the best attorneys in the country. While Gregory . . ."

"Is what?" he asked quietly, "a flop . . . a con-man?"

Her eyes widened; he had challenged her. Was she going to defend Gregory? She smiled and avoided the question.

"Gregory would be wounded if he knew you thought that of him." She looked down, still playing the ingenue, pressing his hand.

"Well, I don't ever like to be unkind, but why is it Greg can never seem to get himself placed in a reputable firm?"

Now she challenged him. "You could take him into yours. He's not bad, Bernard. He's honest. He's just ineffectual. In a good, big firm, he could get lost. I don't think he would do any damage." She continued to pull his hand, stroking it, absently caressing his fingers. Then, as if on an impulse, she dropped to her knees at his feet and looked up at him plaintively. "Would you kiss me, Bernard? I'm so miserable."

Markman bent his long body and kissed her gently on both cheeks. She twisted her head and kissed him hungrily on the mouth.

"Bernard," she whispered, "I want you."

Well, he thought, she *was* an actress. She had carried him effortlessly across foreplay. It was a charade, but he did not argue.

Marjery reached up, removed the gold-framed glasses from his nose, and placed them carefully on the table. She put her arms around his chest and buried her face in his shirt front. He could feel the warmth of tears through the shirt. Carefully, he slid his hands between their bodies and felt her small, droopy breasts under her blouse, secretly pleased she was not wearing a bra.

"I want to get undressed for you," she said.

She knew damn well, Markman understood, that he could not see her properly without his glasses. She stood up, unbuttoned the blouse, pulled it off her arms, and unzipped her skirt, then stepped out of that and stood before him in sheer panty hose.

Markman took off his suit jacket and threw it on his chair. The gesture, his half-turn, brought her to him again. She pressed against him, loosened his tie, and began unbuttoning his shirt, then unbuckled his belt. She thrust her hands inside his pants and took him in both hands.

"Bernard, I want to do this. You know, I can always tell by the fingers."

She had begun to breathe heavily. She dropped on her knees again. And now, slightly but pleasingly surprised, Markman understood what it was about Marjery that attracted so many of his peers.

Chapter Four

The Bistro sparkled in the night, a cozy refuge, like a Swiss mountain chalet in the middle of architecturally eclectic Beverly Hills.

A parking valet helped Belle out of Martin's long Silver Cloud, and Cooper jumped nimbly from his side.

"Take care of it, pal," he said harshly, "no bumps or grinds."

"No, sir, Mr. Cooper."

Martin took her arm above the elbow, smiling down at her from his six-one height, making Belle feel smaller than her own above-average measurements.

"You look good, Belle," he said, but the compliment like everything else had a business connotation. "Now remember, Sam Leonard is very precious to me. A worldwide campaign is at stake."

He was gripping her too tightly. There would be a bruise there in the morning. But she did not flinch.

"Why? Haven't you got enough already?"

"Why?" he replied irritably. "Why the hell do you think? Because you can't stand still in this business. Stand still and you start sliding backward. You know that, Belle, goddamn it. It was one of the first things I taught you."

His face was square, implacable, as if cut out of stone. His eyes were blue, a little bloodshot, the graying blonde hair short and sculpted close to the skull. He had played football well enough at the University of Southern California to make All-American and he still looked the part of the ex-jock, although slightly gone to pot. The latter he concealed under a double-breasted Brioni pin-stripe suit run up especially for him in Italy and imported by Giorgio's.

Inside the front door of the restaurant, they were greeted by Casper, the maitre d'hotel, who ushered them upstairs, past the big party room, empty that night on account of the holiday, and into the small Victorian dining room.

In more pleasant times, Belle would have thought the decor pleasing. One table, large enough for a comfortable eight, had been set up in the middle of the room. The center piece, a blaze of spring flowers, as Belle had ordered, was surrounded by votive lights planted in crystal swans. Tall informal arrangements on commodes lightened each end of the room, and a bottle of Dom Perignon stood cooling in a frosty silver bucket on a side table. When they had all arrived, one of the waiters would bring caviar with wedges of lemon, thin toast, and a bottle of chilled Russian vodka.

"Drink?" Martin asked her abruptly.

"A glass of the champagne," she said indifferently.

He moved to the table and picked up the Dom and a tall champagne glass. His eyes were hooded, somehow annoyed as he looked at her.

Handing her the champagne, he demanded, "What's the matter, Belle? Come on—wake up. This is a big night. You look like you've lost your best friend, for Christ's sake. You'll have to do better than that."

Belle lifted her head, pulled herself taller, and answered in a cold, haughty voice. "I'll be all right."

"Room looks good," he said. "You always do a good job on that."

"Oh, yes," she said, still chillier, "you can always depend on me to do that properly. Right?"

His eyes blazed at the sarcasm. He turned away and curtly ordered a vodka martini from a waiter who'd just come into the room.

"Listen, Belle . . ." His arm shot out. On the end of it a finger, the finger pointing at her face. "Cool it. Be your . . . charming . . . self."

"Yes, sir," she said sardonically. "I'll dazzle Mr. Leonard."

"Jesus Christ," he spat disgustedly. "Listen, Belle . . ."

He pulled himself together as two people appeared in the doorway. He took a deep breath and stepped toward them.

"Hiya, Charley," he sang out, his voice booming cordially. "And Miss Montonya. I'm happy you could be here tonight, Miss Montonya."

"I wouldn't miss it for the world," the smallish woman declared, her large Latin eyes shining. "Sam Leonard is one of my dearest friends."

"Naturally," Martin exclaimed, as if he hadn't known, "you're the cosmetics queen. Hell, did I know that or forget it?"

She smiled smugly. "I think that's why I was invited, Mr. Cooper."

Martin chuckled and made a motion with his hand. "My wife, Belle . . ."

"We've known each other for years," Miss Montonya said. She took Belle's hand and squeezed it.

Belle was not fond of Lucia Montonya, known on both coasts as "the makeup queen." Lucia was short with a good figure, a round face, although her cheeks were perhaps a little too puffy, her lips too large and smooth. It was said Miss Montonya had had her face and eyes done so often no doctor would touch her again.

"Hello, Charley," Belle said quietly to Lucia's escort.

"Belle! How are you?" Charley Hopper demanded, smiling broadly at her. His eyes, which had been blank during the exchange between Martin and Lucia, perked up. "You're looking well, Belle." He laughed. "I don't see enough of you."

"No fault of mine, Charley."

It was a relief that Charley Hopper would be there. If all else failed, she could talk to him. Charley was always easy, relaxing to be around.

Charley was Martin's partner at C.A.A. Together, they had founded the agency in the early fifties, together had built it into an internationally known and respected P.R. and advertising mini-conglomerate and, at least until now, had always daringly, even scornfully, resisted takeover by the giants, such as Interpublic.

"How have you been, Charley?" she asked.

He shrugged carelessly. He was as tall as Martin but leaner, thinner, his posture not as heavily impressive as Martin's. His face was bony and the dark circles under his eyes were pronounced. He did not look particularly healthy. Martin had remarked several times that Charley had been drinking too much in the last couple of years.

"I'm about as well as you might expect for a fifty-year-old bachelor."

Charley's wife had left him over a year ago. She had taken up with a flashy Las Vegas mogul, played around behind Charley's back for a few months, then applied for a divorce.

Martin was helping Lucia Montonya to champagne, so Belle had time to whisper to Charley, "Some date you've been landed with tonight, Charley."

"Strictly business, Belle."

"I hear she draws blood," Belle murmured.

"Ha, now you tell me."

Charley ducked away to get himself a drink, then to have a quick word with Martin. They were standing together uneasily when the next guests arrived. This had to be Sam Leonard and, with a sinking feeling, Belle recognized the woman Leonard was with. It was that barracuda, Pamela Renfrew.

"Sam!" Martin greeted the man effusively. "Sam Leonard! Hey, I'm glad you made it. Have any trouble finding the place?" Then, casually, too casually, "Hi there, Pamela . . ."

Leonard was short, very nearly a tiny man, with a sallow, waxen face and large amused eyes that had heavy bags underneath them. If it weren't for the eyes, his expression would have been one of canine woefulness.

But it was Pamela that Belle was staring at. She was tall with a classic bosom and light blonde hair swinging at her shoulders. She was blonde through and through, her skin a dead white. But her hands, her features, tended toward coarseness. Belle had never spoken to Pamela Renfrew, but she knew enough to despise her.

"Marty," Leonard said grumpily, "tell me, how I could get lost? I've got a driver and a car, and if the son of a bitch doesn't know his way from the Beverly Hills Hotel to the Bistro by now, then he better hand in his ticket."

Plainly, Leonard considered it an insult that Cooper even suggested that he had walked or come by cab. Martin reddened slightly; he was annoyed again. But he had been dismissed. Leonard moved quickly across the room to take Lucia Montonya by the hand, to kiss her warmly on both cheeks.

"Lucia, darling, how are you? I haven't seen you since . . ."

"The boat, darling," she supplied. "Easter, our Mediterranean adventure. And Sylvia?"

"She's fine," Leonard said. "She loved our time together."

Sylvia, Belle thought, she must be Leonard's wife. It was a lesson in manners that Lucia so smoothly ignored the fact Leonard had shown up with a date, Pamela Renfrew, obviously arranged by Martin Cooper. Ah, modern times, she thought wryly. The boat? Belle had read somewhere and often that Leonard and Cosmos Cosmetics kept a yacht in the Mediterranean. It was apparently the size of a minesweeper and was called the *Cosmopolitan*.

"Have we met?" Leonard asked her. He took Belle's hand.

"I'm Martin Cooper's wife," she said, "Belle."

Leonard quipped, "My commiserations. What's it like being married to a huckster?"

Belle smiled sweetly. Leonard lived up to his reputation. "It has its moments," she said, giving nothing away.

"Ah . . ." His bushy eyebrows arched, as if to say he'd gotten the message. "You know, my ship was once named *La Bella Figura*—it could have been named for you." He threw back his head, studying the effect of his words on her. She smiled again and said nothing. Leonard glared into her eyes. "I hope you've been ordered to be charming to me tonight."

Jesus, she thought, he had hit it right on the nose. "My orders are to charm you right out of the tree, sir." She glanced briefly at Lucia Montonya. "You're to have Lucia on your right and me on your left. Does that please you?"

The tone of her voice was ironic enough to cause another lift of the Leonard eyebrows. "To perfection," he said. He looked around. "What's happened to my date?"

Pamela Renfrew was still at the door, talking to Martin. Leonard hopped across the room again and took Pamela by the arm, drawing her toward Belle and Lucia.

"Do you ladies know this lady?" Leonard demanded slyly. "Pamela Renfrew . . . Belle Cooper . . . Lucia Montonya. Lucia is my prized advisor: what she says about cosmetics goes."

"I'm happy to know you," Pamela said. Her voice was hard, unaccented.

Bitchily, Belle observed her boobs, which were almost bulging out of a tight-fitting red satin dress. From this outstanding start, the plentiful flesh sloped to a smooth satined belly and resounding behind. She was no taller than Belle, but there was too much of her.

"Pamela is in the real-estate business in Beverly Hills, aren't you, my dear?" Leonard asked, feeding her lines but at the same time, Belle judged, mocking her, and not gently. His teeth bared under his upper lip. "Pamela specializes in houses going for a million and up, nothing less. Right, my dear?"

"That's right," Pamela said. "I don't fool around with the cheap stuff, Sam. If you're in the market, say a million."

"Pamela drives a white Seville," Leonard went on, delighted over what he obviously considered one of the great finds. "What's the plate read, my dear? Tell me again."

"Big Pads," Pamela stated, a little miffed by now. "I figured it comes right to the point."

"Didya hear that?" Leonard demanded, growling with laughter. "Big Pads, holy Christ."

Pamela's small blue eyes studied Belle's dress, her hair, then dropped from the slim, pleated Mary McFadden gown to the satin evening slippers. Plainly, Pamela was not very impressed by what she saw. But, Belle told herself grimly, it was completely mutual.

"And who else is coming tonight?" Leonard asked her, suddenly bored with Pamela and her profession. "I see eight places."

"The Robert Stones . . . Bob Stone is president of . . ."

Leonard interrupted her. "God, don't tell me. I know. He's a self-satisfied retailer if ever there was one, always looking for markdowns, cheap crap he can put on sale after Christmas. He should know better than that, shouldn't he, Lucia? Cosmos doesn't cut its own throat to make Stone's balance sheet look better."

Lucia's round chin tensed. "Certainly not, Sam."

Had Martin made a big mistake inviting Stone? "Surely he's an important customer," Belle commented.

Leonard grinned craftily. "Cooper invited him to show *me* that C.A.A.'s got big clout with the local merchants. What Cooper doesn't understand is that you've got to be very careful with these big store groups—*and* we don't actually get along that well. At one time, they used to push Cosmos to the wall. But not now. Now, we dictate to them.

They play *our* game, or screw them." He frowned. "I'm not even sure, Lucia, that the big promotional department stores are the right market at all for our new fragrance."

Authoritatively, Lucia responded, "I'm not sure either, Sam. We've found that any sophisticated new fragrance should be introduced at the exclusive level. That's where the power is, and the money."

"Exactly," Leonard said, turning to Belle. "Are you getting an idea of what this is all about, Belle? We're bringing out a new line aimed at the youthful sophisticates—people like you, Belle. It'll be quite separate from our main line of middle-priced stuff. It'll be for women who want and can afford expensive cosmetic help."

Martin approached briefly to hand Pamela a hefty martini.

"Sam?" he asked.

Leonard shook his head. Then his eyes lit up when the waiter came in with the tray of caviar and vodka in tiny glasses nestled in crushed ice.

"Here's exactly what I want, Cooper," he said.

Martin said evenly, "I'd like you to meet my associate, Charley Hopper."

Sam had spooned caviar on a piece of toast. Now he lifted a vodka. "Do I have to?" he asked sharply.

Charley had taken position next to Belle. She felt him tense. "Not if you don't want to," Charley drawled. He began to turn away.

Leonard's studied rudeness had been called. He glanced at Charley, stuffed the caviar and toast into his mouth, and thrust out his hand.

"Hi there, Charley."

"Good evening to you, Mr. Leonard," Charley answered formally.

They shook hands limply. Belle could read Charley's expression: damn little pip-squeak! Good for Charley, she thought.

Martin relaxed enough to say, "Where in the hell are the Stones?"

They arrived at that moment. Stone was a slender man in a dark suit, white shirt, and nondescript tie. As a personality, he was colorless. His face was thin, his eyes unsmiling and guarded behind highly polished bifocals. Stone was from one of California's first families and had chosen his wife, Paula, with great care. Paula might have been his twin. She had the same dieted features, tightly coiffed iron-gray hair, and a weathered face. She was an athletic woman, very successful on the golf course. Belle knew her to be a good and sincere woman, a woman to be trusted.

"I'm sorry we're late," Stone murmured to no one in particular, taking in those present with a sweep of enigmatic eyes.

Of course, he was not sorry at all. He was a cold and ruthless man. But he was important in Los Angeles and in the California state power structure; and he knew it. He served on several of the governor's advisory commissions and, together, the Stones were patrons of the arts. The sudden thought occurred to Belle, along with it a pang of worry, that the Stones would be important to Sally's project. Paula Stone would certainly be a member of whatever committee she and Sally formed.

Martin was mumbling names. Finally, he said, "I think you two know everybody. And you're not late, not late at all."

"I," Leonard huffed, "was precisely on time. Hello, Bob, how are you?"

Stone's face was bland. "Sam, good evening. I'd like you to meet my wife Paula."

"I can't think why I've never met your wife, Bob," Leonard muttered.

"Fate," Charley murmured.

Leonard was startled. He cast a withering glance in Charley's direction, then carelessly said, "This is Pamela Renfrew . . ."

Belle noted Stone's flat eyes skitter across the bosom. "A pleasure, Pamela."

Ah, she thought, a life sign at last. Belle kissed Paula Stone on the cheek, remembering Stone had once been described to her as an ass-grabber. He'd caught a friend of hers alone in a room and, well . . .

The Stones helped themselves to caviar, and turned down the vodka in favor of champagne. When it was time to sit down, Belle had Charley on her left; next to him, Paula Stone; then Martin; and between Martin and Bob Stone, Pamela Renfrew. This completed the circle.

Dinner started with smoked salmon. Martin told the waiter to bring more Dom Perignon, and looked annoyed again when Pamela asked for another vodka martini. But he composed himself once more, and when the champagne glasses had been filled, he lifted his.

"Cheers, everybody," Martin said smilingly. "And, Sam, it's good to see you again. Doubly good to have you with us tonight in Beverly Hills."

Leonard grinned. "I guess I've been with worse crowds in my life. No, seriously, I'm always glad to see old friends and make new ones."

Very ostentatiously, he put his hand on Belle's and squeezed. At once, he turned to continue a whispered conversation with Lucia. Martin, Belle thought amusedly, looked distinctly perplexed. He was used to a lot of P.R. prattle—bullshit, they called it, B.S. Off balance, he turned to Paula Stone, leaving Pamela to Bob Stone. In a matter of seconds, Pamela had turned the talk to real estate, but Stone listened only perfunctorily, his eyes focused on Pamela's cleavage.

"How's it going, Belle?" Charley asked.

She detected in his voice the same edge of sympathy that had been in Frances Atkins' earlier. "Well, fine," she said defensively. "Nothing new, but all's well." She tried to sound as positive as she could and hoped he would accept that.

"How's your daughter?"

"Oh . . . good. She's off to Princeton in the fall—I hope." She had doubts even about that and searched for something neutral to say. "What're you doing over the weekend, Charley?"

He shrugged listlessly. "Nothing. Think I'll pass out by the pool and do a little heavy reading."

"Still living alone in that bungalow?" she asked him, teasing gently. Charley had moved to a compact little house in the West Hollywood hills off Trousdale after his divorce. It was not in Beverly Hills proper but it bore a Beverly Hills post office address. Even Charley, despite his casualness, observed the rules of social status. "I'm going to have to fix you up with one of my friends, Charley," she added.

The idea did not please him. "No thanks, Belle," he grunted.

"I do have a couple of nice friends, and some of them are single."

"Widowed or divorced? Or sometimes widowed and sometimes divorced?" he muttered sardonically.

"Charley," she said quietly, "I'm not trying to bug you."

He was immediately apologetic. "I know that, Belle. Jesus, I know that. But, you see, I am very tired with that whole melange of Beverly Hills broads. They bore me, if you'll pardon the expression, shitless."

She was shocked. "Charley, you're talking about Belle Cooper!"

She was aware of Martin's quick look. He'd heard her, but not what Charley had said. Martin didn't want any more commotion that night. He was pleased to let Leonard bury his attention in Lucia Montonya, for Leonard to devote his snide comments entirely to Lucia.

"Belle, not you," Charley mumbled. He was apologetic. "Not you. Hell, you've got more class and style in one finger than all those broads have in both hands."

His flattery, which she knew was sincere, swept through her. She agreed with him—now. But how long would it be before she became one of those sun-baked, dumb broads?

In a low voice that no one else could possibly hear, Charley added, "You're beautiful tonight, Belle. You know," he stumbled, "some day I'd like to talk to you. I mean . . . talk."

"Well, sure, I'd love it. Any time, Charley. Just call me," she said, feeling the flow of sympathy reversed.

Belle was happy she'd had the foresight to put Charley on her left, for her own sake, and because, she realized, Charley was not at ease with the rest of the people at the table. Despite the years of enforced jollity in the P.R. business, Charley remained his own person, a pretty private person at that. Charley was the quiet man in the back room at C.A.A. Martin was the hail-fellow-well-met front man of the agency. But then, as a clear broth with crusty cheese sticks followed the salmon, it became time, according to the etiquette book, to change conversation partners. Charley turned to Paula Stone, not an ogre certainly, and Belle wondered what to say to Sam Leonard. The shortcut, she knew from her own experience with such men, would be to ask him something about his favorite topic, Cosmos Cosmetics.

"What do you think you'll call the new line?" she asked.

He considered the question, then confessed, "We don't know yet. That's one of the things I'm hoping to get help on from your clever husband. He claims C.A.A. can come up with a winner—if I give 'em the account. You think they can handle it, Belle?"

She laughed. "You're asking me for an objective opinion?"

"Naturally," he said. "You're an independent woman, aren't you? Or are you tied to Cooper's cart, body and soul?"

God, Belle thought, Leonard never gave you a break. She had been challenged again. Before answering, she glanced across the table. Martin and Pamela were engaged in *sotto voce* conversation. Pamela's bare arms hugged her chest, and she was staring adoringly at Martin.

Coolly, Belle told Leonard, "I'm sure C.A.A. could do a good job."

Leonard chuckled. He had seen her look, felt her anger. Now he astounded her. "Honey, that dame is a whore. Do you know he actually fixed me up with that cow?" He snickered wickedly. "You know how she sells real estate? I hear she throws in an animalistic fuck every time you pass escrow."

Belle held herself in check. She felt like screaming something obscene at them and rushing from the room. Had she had any doubt about it? Naturally Martin and Pamela were good friends, and more. Pamela was his type. She fit him to a "T."

"Pamela Renfrew," Leonard continued, speaking from behind his right hand, his elbow on the table. "Jesus, now there's an unlikely name. She told me she used to be in the movies—Renfrew of the Canadian Mounties." Again he chuckled disparagingly. "I venture to think she's been mounted more than the Lone Ranger's horse. Who was that? Silver? Yeah. Hi-ho, Silver and away. Galump, galump . . . galump."

He began to laugh so boisterously at his own joke that the others stopped talking.

"Hey, Sam," Martin shouted across the table, "what's the joke?"

Leonard chortled. "Something Belle said. Christ, that is *so* funny." Then as suddenly as he had started laughing, he stopped and got back to the question of business. "The name for this line is super-important. If you don't get the name right, you can forget the whole thing. It's got to have class but be suggestive, got to have dignity but indicate a wantonness that goes a long way in selling a scent."

"Name it 'broad,' " Belle suggested, her pique showing.

"Shit no," Leonard said disgustedly, "don't try to be funny."

He stared down at his hands, folded on the edge of the table. They were small, as refined as the rest of him, as the rest of his physical being, that is. In mind, and word, he was as tough as Martin, maybe tougher.

"Sorry," she said. "I shouldn't be flip."

"Forget it, Belle," Leonard said. "Belle . . . Belle . . . Now, you know something, that's not a bad name right there. Hell, it suggests . . ."

She took him up blithely. "What? Dignity but wantonness?"

He grinned. "Sure, I can see it there, right in your eyes. Dignity, but way back there, a sensualness. Wow! Boy oh boy! He seized her hand and pressed it, hard. "Yes, I do see it. Belle . . . Belle . . . Belle. What *would* you say if we named the new fragrance after you?"

"My God, sir," she said taken aback, "the things you say."

"Look," he said coldly, "it'd be a purely business proposition. The image would be just right. Somebody like you —that sort of woman, that approach to the product. It would be classy and could go right on the battlefield against Estee Lauder or a line like Princess Marcella Borghese."

His grip on her hand had not lessened. He wanted an answer. Why not? She could go along with the idea. What did she have to lose? In any case, it was something he'd likely have forgotten by the morning.

"I'd be flattered," Belle said. "If you think that's my image . . . well, great."

"Good," Leonard said. "Don't think I'm not serious, Belle. I may get shot down, but right now that's the best idea I've heard this year." He snorted. "Naturally, my own ideas are always best. Belle, I'm going to take you out of the ivory tower."

"Ivory tower?" she repeated. "You'd be surprised if you knew . . ."

"About him?" Leonard demanded, with such precision he took her breath away again. Speaking too loudly, Leonard said, "Let me give you a little advice: Just water down his Grecian Formula."

Mindful of Martin's look of wonder and concern, Leonard was again convulsed with mocking laughter. He pounded weakly on the dinner table, did everything but point jeeringly at Martin. Belle heard Bob Stone grunt, his signal that he had heard.

"Sam, you son of a gun," Martin said wanly, "you sure are having a lot of fun over there."

"Marty," Leonard sputtered, "you have no idea. Listen, you know, I think I've got the name for our new fragrance, and I don't even have to hire C.A.A. now. You know what it is? Belle! How about that?"

Martin's face darkened. "Belle? I don't like it."

"Why not?" Leonard demanded. "I think it's great. You don't think it's too obvious, do you? What do you think, Lucia?" Lucia merely nodded, smiling vacantly. "What about it, Marty? Would you mind if I named a cosmetic line after your wife?"

Martin, perplexed, shook his head. He didn't know what to say.

"It's not bad," Bob Stone intoned.

"What about you, Charley?" Leonard demanded. "What do you think?"

Slowly, Charley said, "It's a name you could work with. Got a lot of mileage . . ."

"Charley!" Belle protested, laughing, "who are you saying's got a lot of mileage?"

"Pamela?" Leonard was going around the table, doing a survey.

Miss Renfrew tossed her blonde hair. "How would it look on a license plate?"

"Dumb broad," Leonard snarled, then recovered. "It sounds good. Tell me, Belle, would you be willing to work on the promotion?"

She was flustered now. Martin was so angry he could not speak and, beside her, she knew Charley Hopper was wondering what the hell was going on.

"Are you really serious?" she demanded. "I'm not an actress. I don't know anything about promotion. For that matter, I don't really know anything about cosmetics except what I read."

Leonard snorted, "No, merely how to make yourself look beautiful. You did your own makeup tonight, didn't you, and it's perfect. Wouldn't you say so, Lucia?" he demanded, interrupting Miss Montonya's conversation with Stone. "You *are* Belle. It's you!"

It was bewildering. But she was intrigued. Belle? Then it came to her again, the other consideration, not ever very far from the surface: Sally's benefit. Leonard was a rich and powerful man. What if she made a bargain with Leonard? He could use her name, use her, launch the new cosmetics line called Belle. But in return, Cosmos Cosmetics would underwrite the cost of the party—every ticket, every donation made would be clear profit.

Leonard's excitement subsided, but he could not stop talking about his brainstorm.

With the demitasse, Belle managed to interrupt him.

"I'd like to talk about this later. I think I have an idea that will be very attractive to you."

Leonard's eyes smoldered. "Tell me now."

"I can't. Not yet. But I'll be in touch with you."

He fumbled in a vest pocket, then presented her with a card.

"Here," he said. "But wait a minute." He retrieved the card and with a gold pen wrote a number on the back of it. "My private number." He winked elaborately.

Chapter Five

When they were in the Rolls and on the way home, Martin let himself go.

"Of all the goddamn fouled-up nights," he cried, "Jesus, what the hell were you doing to Leonard? He behaved like a maniac. Goddamn it, Belle, you've screwed up the whole fucking thing."

She huddled in her corner, next to the door, staring straight ahead.

"Didn't I do what I was supposed to do? I talked to him.

I charmed him. Isn't that what I'm for?" she demanded bitterly.

"Jesus, you didn't have to go so far. Jesus, Belle, for Christ's sake, what the hell kind of a name is that for a perfume?"

"Not a perfume, a fragrance. I think it's quite a nice name."

The comment only served to infuriate him the more. "Horseshit!"

"Think what you want," Belle said coldly. "I don't care. Sam tells me your friend Pamela Renfrew is a hooker."

"My friend? What the hell do you mean?"

"What I mean is," she said evenly, "that everybody in the room tonight thinks it's obvious you're an exceedingly good friend of Miss Renfrew's."

"Oh, balls," he yelled, punching the seat between them. "She's been around town for years. Everybody knows Pamela. She's no hooker, for God's sake." But he was not so sure of himself now. His voice was hostile. "We do business together."

"I should say you know her all right. That was apparent. The hands . . ."

"Hands? Hands? I'll tell you about hands. That bastard Stone grabbed her hand and put it on his cock under the table. I saw him do it. Christ!" Martin said disgustedly. "What people! What a lousy party."

He was barreling the Rolls down Camden Drive and toward Sunset, going too fast.

"I thought the party went very well," Belle said calmly. "You'll get your account. And I wouldn't be too worried, if I were you, about that Belle business—if it does worry you so much. Sam was just talking, making waves, trying to get at you."

He was somewhat reassured. "Oh yeah, what makes you so sure of that?"

"I've talked to enough of your business prospects to know a little about how they operate."

Cooper nodded irritably. "Well, it's sure true that little fart Leonard is very tricky. He could promise you the moon one day and hit you in the face with a turd the next."

"How graphic," she drawled. "Anyhow, I can't believe Stone did what you said."

"I tell you, I saw him do it. They all appear to think Pamela is some kind of a whore. Well, she's not."

"She looks like one."

Violently, he hit the seat again. "Belle, goddamn it, you listen."

Even-voiced, she charged him, "She is your girlfriend, isn't she?"

"No!" But his very vehemence gave him away. Belle understood him.

They said nothing more. Inside the house, Martin went straight to the bar in the library, mumbling about a beer. Belle left him to climb tiredly upstairs. In her dressing room, she slid out of her party dress—party dress, Jesus! some party—and hung it carefully in the closet.

She had had enough of everything.

It was then that he reappeared, closing the door firmly behind him, eyeing her angrily as she stood before him at her most defenseless, undressed down to her bra and pantyhose.

"Pamela is not my girlfriend," he said sullenly.

"You're a liar."

He walked toward her menacingly. She thought for a second he was going to hit her.

"I am not lying," he insisted, then sneering, he asked her, "And just what was it you promised Leonard?"

"Nothing, and that happens to be the truth."

"A little rendezvous before he leaves town?"

His bulk confronted her: the height, the weight, the jowly, dark face, eyebrows knotted in frustration over the bridge of his nose. Even his short, steely hair seemed ominous as he stared at her, his teeth bared.

She didn't answer, merely stared back at him, waiting, contemptuous.

"Well," he said, "if you did, it'd be in order."

"You wouldn't care," she said in a low voice.

"Shit! You talk about Pamela Renfrew being a hooker. Just what the hell are you, Belle? You're a kept woman. You don't make a nickel and you don't have a nickel. I keep you. And you resent it. I support you and that kid of yours—and she doesn't even respect me enough to take my name."

Ah, Belle told herself shakily, her legs trembling, that was one of the sore points. Susan had refused to change her name from Bertram to Cooper, which would have added another layer of callus to his ego.

"Why should she take your name, and what's the difference anyway?" she asked. "She loved her father. She wants to keep his name."

Stating this fact, she was close to crying. But she'd be damned if she would. She drew her shoulders back and faced him.

"His name?" Martin exclaimed. "She got shit from him. I'm the guy who pays her bills, buys her a car, and she doesn't talk to me."

His voice had risen from grim complaint to loud condemnation.

"Please . . . she'll hear you. She's afraid of you already."

"Good," he shouted. "I don't give a good goddamn if she does hear—or if that old bag Atkins hears, too."

She backed away a couple of steps, steadily watching him. "Martin, I can't talk like this. It's terrible. What do we have in common now? Nothing. At least in the old days, we had fun. Now, you don't have any time. You're away at night . . . on business—or pleasure. You and your . . ."

Growling, he warned her, "Don't say girlfriends, Belle. But let me tell you something straight out: If a guy doesn't get it at home, then he goes out looking for it."

She stared down at the rug between them. "I never turned you away. You left."

"You're an icy, frigid bitch, Belle. You're cold to me." For a moment, he seemed shattered, about to break down. "I know when the gates are closed."

"No," Belle said. "I won't accept this. Martin, you wanted me for what I could give you—the class, you said. That was always rubbish. Sophistication—rubbish! And now you're tired of it. You don't need me anymore for your front, your class, your image. Don't say I haven't helped you with that, done my duty. I've put on your parties, talked to your friends, charmed your clients, like Leonard."

He grinned mockingly, and held up his hand. "Enough, enough, you poor thing. And what have you done for me today?" He couldn't resist that.

"Today, I suffered through Sam Leonard."

"And it didn't seem to bother you too much, Belle. I hope it worked. It better."

Belle felt her eyes tear over. "That is all you care about, isn't it? Face it, Martin, if you thought it'd do you any good, you'd throw me to Sam Leonard. Just like you fixed him up with your girlfriend."

"You goddamn bitch," he stormed. "I'll tell you what. Any time you want to, you can walk out. Take off! Leave! Take yourself and that kid and Atkins with you and go back to New York to your tony friends."

He had said it all now. It was not the first time he'd said it, but each time was the more final, the more definitive ultimatum. He stood, hands planted on his hips, glaring wildly.

She stifled her sobs. "Maybe I will."

"You won't, Belle," he thundered, "and I'll tell you why. You don't have any money, and money is important to you. You wouldn't know what to do without it."

"No," she groaned, "it's not everything. It's nothing."

He was close to her again, his face inches from hers. "You face it, Belle; who's the hooker? At least Pamela makes her own living."

Instinctively, she slapped him.

He was surprised. He put the palm of his hand to his cheek. "You! Why, you bitch. You finally got excited."

He thrust his hand forward and seized her bra, yanking on it so hard the strap broke. He grabbed her in his arms, pinned her hands behind her back, and dropped to his knees, pulling her with him to the floor. Sitting astride her knees, he pulled off his jacket and threw it across the room, then unbuckled his trousers and pulled them down. He did not bother to take off his shirt or his shoes and socks.

"Now, my dear wife," he grunted, "you want a fight, I'll give you a fight."

He forced her pantyhose off her buttocks, ripping them down her legs, and tugged apart her rigid thighs. Belle went limp with fear. She was frightened of him now. Passive beneath him, she felt his hard knot of anger, focused in his crotch. But his anger and her fear had not prepared them. He didn't care. He forced himself, mindless of the pain, inside her. She did not move or cry out. He planted his hands on the floor beside her head and stared down at her, a senseless expression in his eyes. He lifted one hand and pinched her nipples. Belle bit her lips, determined to make no sound.

It did not take him long. His frustration, fury, and incomprehension quickly peaked and the expression of his hate flooded her. Slowly, he subsided and collapsed on top of her with a miserable exclamation.

She lay dead still beneath him. It was, she knew, the end. On that, her mind was clear. She realized that she could have killed him then; a crime of passion would have been committed. But, instantly, she told herself that murder was not her style.

His apology was as forlorn as his face. "Belle . . . I'm sorry . . . I . . ."

"Get off me," she commanded.

Obediently, he moved away from her. "Belle . . ."

"Don't say anything. Just leave me alone."

Martin stood up and found his tangled trousers. Still, she did not move, but lay supine on the needlepoint rug in the same position, the violated being.

He tried to smile, and for just a second looked like a guilt-stricken grubby little boy. But that passed. "Jesus, Belle, you get me so excited. Christ, you're so unobtainable."

She did not respond. Blinking to keep the tears at bay, she stared at him, stony-faced. She was rewarded with another flash of illumination: Sally's deadline was in six months. She would make it her own, her stab at another kind of freedom.

Sam Leonard was at his ease, brandy snifter in his right hand, a cigar in his left, his body buried in a cushioned wicker chair in his bungalow at the Beverly Hills Hotel. He was tasting the forbidden fruits, for his wife forbade him brandy and cigars. Lifting the glass, he sipped appreciatively on the fine Napoleon and took a shallow drag on the Havana. Super. With satisfaction, he noted the traveling Modigliani hung on the wall over the sofa. He always took this painting with him on his trips—the haunting, thin, slightly grotesque figure of a young woman, surrealistically elongated. This was about as close as Modigliani had ever come to Picasso.

"Well," Pamela Renfrew said, interrupting his thoughts, "do you like what you see?"

Leonard grinned wolfishly at her—the other forbidden fruit. On the whole, he thought, a woman's only a woman, but a cigar's a good smoke, and as for Napoleon brandy . . . why, he wondered, had he invited her inside? Why had he given her any brandy? It was too good to waste on inferiors.

Feeling cheated, he'd ordered her to take her clothes off and now she was standing before him in the center of the room, stark naked. She was a big woman, too big for him. Christ, she must be the Abominable Snowman's sister. But the Snowman was a lot more shy than Pamela. She held her brandy snifter at belly level, waiting for his verdict, lifted it in a detour around her tits. He wondered what Howard Hughes would have made of those. They stood out as if supported by invisible cables. Being that his business was what it was—beauty—Leonard judged that Pamela had had an implant or two to keep them peaked like that. Jesus, California was the home of the lift, nip, tuck, and contour, all of which had so little to do with real beauty. Her stomach was quite flat—a little surprising since he'd watched her eating like a horse . . . or cow—and gave way to a pubic region covered by a lush growth of blonde hair. At least the hair was true, he thought, unless she'd taken the trouble to immerse herself entirely in a vat of peroxide. Her thighs and legs were like trees, big feet planted in the carpet.

"Very Rubenesque," Leonard finally murmured.

Pamela licked her lips, savoring the bite of the brandy. Obviously, she did not quite know what to make of him and she regarded him wonderingly. What would he want her to do next?

"There's plenty of meat," she said smugly, patting herself. "But I'm not fat, am I?"

"No," he agreed. "You must exercise."

"I do, every morning. But they say the best exercise is the one you enjoy most."

"Let's see you touch your toes," he said playfully.

Pamela put her glass down on the coffee table, and dropped her upper torso to touch the floor with her fingertips, then the palms of her hands.

"Very well done, darling," he said. "What else do you do?"

She dropped heavily on the floor, feet planted in front of her and raised herself into an arch, hands behind her. This maneuver was a lascivious one, for, pointed straight at him, was the heavy bush which, now incitingly, she twitched at him, making it jerk up and down.

"In the name of God," Leonard muttered to himself, "a man could get lost in there. They'd have to send in a search team." He laughed heartily, causing her to hit the floor with a bump of her rump.

"What's funny?"

"You are, darling." But there was something else on his mind. "Tell me, Pamela, you are Marty's mistress, aren't you?

"I wouldn't say that," she said cautiously.

"Come now."

"Well, it depends what you mean by mistress," Pamela said. "I mean, I do what I want to do and he does what he wants to do."

Leonard nodded wisely. "I have to say I find it a little odd that Marty would fix me up with his girlfriend. Doesn't he care?"

This observation brought a pensive, slightly petulant look to her face. "Well, he had to come to the party with his wife, and he wanted to make it an even eight. So he just asked me if I wanted to go with you, that's all."

"I see."

Irritably, she said, "Well, Marty didn't know that the first thing you'd ask me to do was undress. I don't think he had that in mind."

He chuckled. "It didn't take much coaxing, did it?"

"I wanted to, so I did," she said peevishly. "I don't like wearing clothes anyway."

Leonard laughed raucously. Before speaking again, he drew on the cigar and refreshed his mouth with brandy. "Are you in the process of selling me a house in Beverly Hills, darling?"

Still stretched out on the floor, hands clasped comfortably behind her head, Pamela smiled broadly. "I'd love to sell you a house in Beverly Hills, Sam. We've got some good ones going, too. Do you know about the Frank Feiffer estate? Fifteen acres, pool, French provincial . . ."

"Rooms with a view?" he asked, again laughing. "I must say, this is the most unusual real-estate pitch I've ever experienced . . ."

She grinned toothily, like every toothpaste ad he'd ever seen. "My motto, Sam, is a hump with every dump." She sat up and clasped her arms over her knees, completely oblivious of the fact she was naked, he fully dressed. Her eyes glittered greedily.

"I thought it was a scrow with every escrew," Leonard murmured.

It was getting a little out of hand. Pamela was too hardened a specimen for him to be taking chances. Christ, he sighed to himself, so unlike that Belle Cooper. Belle was intriguing. Belle seemed so terribly vulnerable, yet . . . He wondered where her layer of toughness began. Everyone had it there somewhere beneath the surface.

"Look, Sam . . . "

He held up his hand. "Are you going to take Cooper away from his wife?"

The question didn't surprise her. Why should it? Obviously, if she'd slept with the man, she'd considered it.

"I wouldn't mind," she answered frankly. "He's not happy with her, not happy at all."

"He'd be happy with you?"

"At least I'd give him a good lay when he needed it. Look . . ."

"Christ," he said, feeling distaste for her rising. He could not conceive of Belle Cooper being anything but a sensational lay. He had not been joking when he'd told her over dinner that he could almost see a depth of passion, obviously unexplored, behind her eyes. "Pamela, I should warn you that Mrs. Cooper would be a very tough customer. Tangle with her and she'd take you to pieces, that is, if she wanted to keep Cooper."

Pamela laughed harshly. "I'd like to see the woman that could take me to pieces. I've been to the wars, Sam. I'm a veteran." But she had been put off long enough. She rolled up on her knees and placed her forearms on his knees. Her eyes simulated surrender, but, for his part, Leonard had trouble concealing his sudden disinterest. "Shall we have a little tumble?"

He wondered what Cooper took him for. If the object was to gift him with female flesh, Cooper might have done better than this, given him credit for a little discrimination. This was disgusting, an insult.

"I think my aging bones are too brittle, darling," he murmured faintly.

She shrugged. "Well then . . . They say I give very good head."

"Uh-uh," he grunted, turning her down. He was not such a fool. One slip with a woman like this and she'd never let him forget it. And, Christ, if Sylvia ever found out, she'd kill him. "Not interested, darling. I just sort of wanted to see . . . what the game was." Now he had to say something that would make her go away. He reached down gently to heft her right breast. "I think I'd reduce the size of those tits, you know, get that silicone out of there—if you can at this point."

Pamela went through instant withdrawal. She jerked back and jumped to her feet. She was furious.

"What I mean to say, darling," Leonard went on flippantly, "is that it's been nice seeing you—all of you—but it's getting late."

Chapter Six

"Norman, my love," Sally cried, almost too thankfully Belle thought, sliding into the booth and kissing Kaplan resoundingly on first one, then the other cheek. "It's been months. Where *have* you been?"

Kaplan smiled eagerly, showing prominent, uneven teeth. His eyes, hooded at the corners and lazy, absorbed Sally's face.

"Darling, it has not been months. It's been weeks—too long, I admit. Where have I been?" Kaplan's voice was modestly aggrieved. "In New York, wading through spring slush and going to any number of extremely boring parties."

Belle had booked the table for them in the Polo Lounge at the Beverly Hills Hotel—not inside in the bar area but on the bright terrace. The P.L., as it was often called, was not ordinarily Belle's kind of place. She preferred the more sedate atmosphere of Jimmy's or, farther downtown, of old-fashioned Perino's, both places less devoted to the ritual of seeing and being seen, to blatant huckstering, the unruly show business hype, the constant paging.

"Call for Mr. Flynn . . . Mr. Flynn!" A short, aging bellboy poked his head through the terrace door.

Sally coolly appraised Belle. "Well, recovered from the desert, kiddo? We spent the weekend together, Norman."

"Oh?" He lifted his eyebrows in mock surprise.

"Norman!"

Kaplan patted Sally's arm affectionately. Slouched in the booth, he seemed all head, his small, stocky body hidden beneath the pink tablecloth, stubby hands clasped together as he beamed at them.

"Darling," he said, lisping slightly, "you look marvelous."

"Today I feel marvelous."

Today? Belle thought it impossible that Tom Glenn and the specialist had made a correct diagnosis. Sally could not be ill. She was in a vivacious mood. She was wearing a light blue wool dress, pearls at her neck, and just enough lipstick to call attention to her bright gray eyes, the full head of graying hair. Sally's face and arms were tanned dark brown and muscles, hardened by days of tennis at the beach, shone tautly through the skin.

"Belle and I were in Palm Springs over the weekend," Sally explained, "accompanied by our lovely husbands, of course."

Jesus, Belle thought, how obvious it must have been that she and Martin Cooper were finished. It had taken all Sally's snappish energy to pull Belle out of her deep funk; even then, she hadn't troubled to say more than three words to Martin in as many days.

"And how are the lovely husbands?"

"Just lovely," Sally said.

"And, Belle," Kaplan said, "tell me, how's your Susan?"

"She's fine," Belle replied.

But she was not fine. Naturally enough, Susan had heard their raucous quarrel, the raised voices, that night after the Bistro party, and the next morning, before she and Martin had driven off to Palm Springs, Susan had let her know she'd heard—she had begun talking again of moving out, into an apartment of her own.

At the last minute, Belle had considered calling the Markmans and bowing out of the weekend. But then she'd thought of Sally and dismissed the idea. Cooper, of course, was concerned only with keeping up the pretense of "loving couple" and getting a weekend of Palm Springs handshaking under his belt.

"Susan is a beautiful girl. I love her," Sally exclaimed. "Belle, why not let her come down to the beach to stay with me for a while? She'll be out of school in a few days."

Although Belle hadn't allowed her own problems to surface in Palm Springs, Sally knew she was worried.

"She'd adore it," Belle said. "But do you think . . ."

"What? That I can handle it? Of course. I'm an expert on kids."

Belle smiled. "I'm sure she'd love to come."

Sally hit the table. "Done, then. Where's the man with the drinks? You didn't order anything yet?"

"Got here only a second before you, darling," Kaplan said.

They waved down a waiter. Belle and Sally ordered white wine and Kaplan a dry martini, straight up—"pure New York style," he grinned.

"Well, Norman, come on now," Sally commanded, "what *have* you been doing? We want to hear all."

"Well . . . well . . ." Kaplan mischievously presented his report on parties in the big city, weekends in the country and out on the island. He was a witty raconteur. He could be acid-tongued, but he took more pleasure in the joy of telling than in actual dismemberment of the body social.

"You remember Rita Harlow?" he asked slyly, naming a prominent lady in the New York set, "well, my dears, *quelle scandale*! Husband Peter, it seems, has gone quite berserk over a left-wing radical." Peter Harlow was a New York City politician of a rich, establishment family.

"But is she chic?" Belle asked.

"Ha, ha, my dear, she is very radically chic. She used to go to all the chicly radical parties Leonard Bernstein gave. Now she seems to be doing something with Palestinian refugees."

"That'll do her a lot of good in New York," Sally remarked sourly.

"Her name," Kaplan related delightedly, "is Tina O'Kelly and, personally, I suspect she's a lay-ison between the PLO and the IRA. Anyway . . . anyway, Rita was supposed to be down in Washington, something to do with the antique-ing of the State Department. But, lo and behold, she didn't go. Upon her return to the apartment, she discovered Peter . . . and Tina, late one afternoon . . ."

"About cocktail time, shall we say?" Sally interjected sardonically.

"Yes, yes, darling," Kaplan giggled softly, "making whoopee—au flagranti and all, cheek by jowl to the U.N. building. *Quelle scandale,*" he repeated, "and now Rita won't let him back in the place, even to pick up his suits."

"Not to say that Rita . . ."

"Yes, yes, Belle, not to say that Rita's simon-pure either, no, not by any means. Ha, ha, the stories we know about Rita, good grief."

"The stories *you* know, Norman. I've always sworn you know more dirt than Truman Capote," Sally said, leaning to kiss him on the cheek again. "You're the one should have written *Answered Prayers*. You know more stories than Truman ever will."

Kaplan nodded complacently. There was some truth in the remark. "Darling, my problem is I can't write," he said gently, "only my name on contracts and checks. I, my dears, am nothing but a dilettante. Come the revolution, I'll be first on the guillotine."

"Norman, not so," Belle objected.

"You'll save me then, Belle?" he asked fondly.

"No," she said, "but I will go first."

"Belle, Belle," Kaplan disagreed, "you are not a dilettante. You're a mother, a working wife."

"Working wife? Hardly."

"You work for Martin Cooper," Sally said sharply. "Think of it that way."

Belle nodded. As usual, Sally had made her point. "I could think of it that way, yes."

"Well, do it then," Sally insisted. "Christ knows you're important to his business."

Kaplan looked more bewildered by the exchange than he should have. He was aware of the basics of her problem—and he was a very intuitive man.

"Belle . . . is anything wrong?"

"Wrong?" Sally echoed. "She and that bastard didn't speak to each other the whole goddamn weekend."

"It's not very good," Belle said, "to say the least."

They greeted this admission with dead silence. Belle hated herself for letting her misery show. Wryly, she broke the quiet. "I think I'll ask him for a contract."

"I'd take a contract out on the bastard," Sally said fiercely.

Kaplan chuckled uneasily. "Murder is still illegal, Sally. Speaking of which, one of my tenants here in Beverly Hills has taken to packing a pistol. He shot out the car tires of some poor chap who'd parked in his space by mistake. I'm petrified of asking him to move."

"The tribulations of the landlord class," Belle murmured.

"Yes . . . yes . . . well, ladies, the man is hovering. What are we going to eat?"

"My usual," Sally said. "A McCarthy salad, and I want a hard-boiled egg on the side and some kosher pickles. Wouldn't know I was terminal, would you?"

The shot came out of the blue. Belle flinched. But, no, Kaplan did not know. Without glancing up from the menu, he muttered, "Darling, what you are is terminally insane."

Sally howled with laughter.

Belle pretended she hadn't heard. "I'll have a club sandwich, and I'd like a pickle, too."

"Gawd! What you eat is beyond belief. I," he announced profoundly, "will have the cold poached salmon, just lemon on the side. I refuse to gain back the weight I so painfully lost. Maybe some fresh asparagus. And I think a bottle of champagne. Yes, definitely. I don't have a welcome-back party every day, you know." Not pausing for their answer, he ordered a bottle of Bollinger Brut. "Now then . . ." He settled back comfortably. "What else do you wish to know from me?"

"How's Jackie?" Sally asked.

Obviously, she was referring to the former First Lady. "Oh, she's fine, just fine," Kaplan said disinterestedly.

"And Pat?" Sally persisted. Mrs. Nixon was once again part of the New York scene.

"Delighted to be back home," he said. "But, really, ask me something interesting—like, 'Norman, you rascal, have you bought any new pictures lately?' "

Sally relented. "Norman, have you actually bought some new pictures?"

"Yes, as a matter of fact," he chortled. "I've just bought

two Matisse—I hope they're not forgeries—and I'm having them sent out here for the penthouse."

Kaplan lived, when in Beverly Hills, atop one of his apartment buildings. One room was devoted to his business life: management of his real estate and avid, if semi-retired, attention to the daily meanderings of the stock market.

"I'm becoming vaguely interested in some of the modern abstractionists," he added, "but it's a hell of an unsteady market, at best an unreliable market. The bankers all tell me modern art is a good investment. The problem is," he said thoughtfully, "I don't like it that much. Matisse is about as far as I'll go in that direction."

"Norman, for God's sake," Sally objected. "You don't buy it because you like it but because you can make more money with it than from IBM or T-bills."

"No, no, I can't buy anything I don't like."

"Balls, Norman," Sally exclaimed, "thinking like that, you're never going to be a rich man."

He clucked nasally, taking one of their hands in each of his. "All right, what's the real reason for this luncheon? I can tell when you two have got something on your mind."

Kaplan glanced first at Belle, who shook her head, then at Sally.

"We need advice—and help." Sally stated it bluntly.

"Oh, good God, another fiendish scheme."

"We're putting on a benefit," Sally began.

"Hell, not another one of those . . ."

"Yes, but the biggest bash ever," she said forcefully, "historic, unique. The party is going to be twice as big as anything they've ever thrown here. But we need ideas, Norman, ideas!"

"Ah," he sighed. "It is ever so—come to the idea man when you're in trouble. What, may I ask, is the cause this time?"

Sally paused, then said, "It's for a hospital and research center devoted to women's cancer problems."

"It doesn't exist," Kaplan said, then his eyes widened. "Ah, I see. It doesn't exist *now*, but it will."

"That's it," Sally said. Turning to Belle, she said, "You don't know this yet, but I've bought the land—a whole block over on Pico—about as centrally located as you can get in this globby town. And I've got an architect doing renderings on the building and facilities."

Belle was surprised. "So we are committed."

"Did you ever doubt it?" Sally demanded. "Of course, we're committed. And we've got to raise lots of money from everywhere in the country, and we want a huge attendance at the party of the crème de la crème. The trouble is, Norman, there's no hotel in the town big enough to hold the party, and Christ, we can't go downtown to the Convention Center."

Kaplan nodded. He was not thrilled by what he'd heard and Belle could see he was worried by Sally's presentation. His eyes became wary. He nodded again, clicking his tongue against his teeth.

"Well . . . All right. I see what you've got in mind. You're talking in terms of what? A couple thousand people. More? Well . . ." He snapped his fingers. "It's elementary, my dear Sally. I'm surprised you haven't thought of this yourself. We'll throw a party in the new hotel: the Beverly Splendide. Naturally. The place they're finishing right now down behind the courthouse with all that Arab money. When's the party to be?"

"Early December," Sally said.

"That's merely perfect," Kaplan said smugly. "The Splendide is due to open in January. I know you could get the first party in there in December, but move fast. I'm sure everybody in town will be getting the same idea very soon—if they haven't already."

"Is the ballroom big enough though?"

Kaplan stroked Sally's hand soothingly. "No problem. The ballroom is designed to hold 3,500. It will open out in the back to a garden, pool, tennis courts. With proper management, you could pack 5,000 in. Good God, though, how many people do you want?"

Sally compressed her lips determinedly. "Four thousand . . . or more. Hell, Belle, why didn't you think of that?"

"Just dumb, I guess." The truth was, she thought, that she had been doing her best not to think about it, for thinking of the party only made her think about Sally. "Do you think we could get it, Norman?"

Kaplan held up his hand as the food arrived and commanded silence until the waiter was gone. When they were private again, he said, "Ask your Uncle Normy anything. A secret: You know who is going to be running the Splendide? None other than the great Archibald Finistere. He's leaving the Beverly Camino. This is true. True also: Your Uncle Normy has invested *uno poco,* a little, that is, of the Kaplan riches in the hotel. How the Arabs would have me, I don't know. But a certain prince named David Abdul and Normy are now respectively . . ." He bubbled. ". . . major and minor shareholders. So, I've seen the plans. The Splendide is going to be just that: splendid. But now, just a minute, darling. Haven't you ever heard that exclusive is better than big? What are you planning to charge?"

Sally hesitated. "I thought $1,000 a couple."

Kaplan mused, "That'd bring in two million. Did'ja consider keeping it select, say at 500 couples, and charging $4,000?"

"Still two million," Sally said.

"My point is," Kaplan said, "4,000 people is too big. I don't know how many you'd get. Hell, darling, it would be like going to a football game."

Sally nodded. "Yes," she said, "I just thought biggest-ever might be enough attraction."

"Maybe if you handed out hot dogs. But then you could only charge fifty or a hundred. I'll compromise with you. One thousand couples, that is, 2,000 people. The Splendide ballroom could handle that comfortably. There'd be space enough for dancing, good service. You could call them the Blue Ribbon One Thousand, get them in from all over the country. Charge $2,500 per couple: net, two and a half million, not bad for a beginning effort. My friend Clive David—he's the master party planner in this country—would quail at so many people, but it could be done. Entertainment would have to be tops. You need a draw, big-name attractions . . ."

"'I know . . ." Sally nodded doubtfully.

"Remember," Kaplan pressed, "less and exclusive is better than gargantuan."

"I think he's right," Belle remarked. "Four thousand would be frightening."

Sally smiled. "As usual, the little bastard is right. Normy, when can we go see Archy?"

"Darling," Kaplan promised, "I'll set it up." He studied her face for a moment as she drained what was left in her wine glass. "Sally, I get the feeling this is a project the likes of which you've not done before."

Ah, Belle thought, he was getting to the point. Sally's mouth twisted; her eyes came down from their high. She put her hand over Kaplan's.

"Norman," she said miserably, "I wouldn't try to keep a secret from you. Belle already knows."

His face dropped. The flesh under his chin wobbled and his eyes misted. "You're dying . . ."

"Yes," Sally said.

Kaplan's reaction shook Belle. He thrust his face close to Sally's and hissed, "You are *not*, goddamn it. You are not dying, goddamn it. I won't have it. You are *not* going to leave us here in this fucking world, all alone."

Sally was taken aback by his anger, the strength of it. She drew back. Her face went white under her tan, as if she had dealt him a terrible insult and was now suffering his retaliation. She could not speak. She glanced pleadingly at Belle, but there was nothing Belle could do or say that would help, for she felt about it the same way Kaplan did.

He was infuriated. "I won't have any part of this! I won't acknowledge what you've told me. No, never."

"Goddamn it, Norman," she exclaimed bitterly, "I'm telling you the facts. Shit! Don't be such a baby about it."

Sally grabbed her pocketbook off the leather seat and slid out of the booth. Without another word, she stomped away, leaving him with Belle and the still chilling champagne. Norman covered his face with his hands, not saying anything for a moment. When he put his hands down, his face was withered with anxiety.

"Damn it," he muttered, "I've loved that woman all my life. I *can* do something: I can make her mad. She can't just . . . accept it. She's got to fight. She sounds like it's setting off on a South Seas tour, another little vacationing adventure—la-de-da . . ."

"But . . ." Belle started to say.

"Oh, shit," he said hopelessly. "Oh, goddamn it. Of course I'm going to help, God help us all."

Hesitating, Belle pointed out, "She doesn't want anybody to know . . ."

"And do *you*, pray tell, think I'm going to spread the word?"

"No, no, of course not. We're the only people who know."

"Bernard?" Belle shook her head. Kaplan took her hand and put it to his lips. "Oh, Belle, Sally's been my great friend since the very early days in New York, long before I knew you."

"Norman, you got me together with Sally, when I first came out to this . . . place."

He frowned. "Place? You were happy enough to come to this . . . place . . . eight years ago."

"Yes," she murmured, "that's true. Well . . ."

No, she thought guiltily, now was not the time to get into her problems. Kaplan sat silently, staring at the tablecloth. When he looked up, his eyes were gentle, grieving.

"I'm sorry," he said, "Tell me about it."

She didn't want to, but she did. "I've come to the end. I can't live with him anymore. We quarrel. We can't talk. I don't know, maybe it *is* me. He thinks I'm cold . . ." The words rushed out. She hadn't been so open, not even with Sally.

"Cold?" Kaplan's expression became incredulous. "You cold?" Then he was angry. "The man's an idiot. But . . . what are you going to do?"

She shrugged, miserable that she had reached such a state, miserable to confess it. "I suppose the only thing I can do is divorce him. That's what he wants. He wants me to leave. Of course," she said bitterly, "he's afraid I'll strip him bare and leave him naked in the street. Which would not be my intention."

"Naturally not," Kaplan said, a bit irritably. "You're the type to play angel of mercy and generosity. Christ, Belle, you don't have to be quite so nice."

"You're going to say, 'I told you so.' "

"I am not," he said indignantly. "I wouldn't. And what good would *that* do? What about the girl?"

"Susan?"

"Didja think I meant his girlfriend?" he asked sarcastically.

Belle laughed hollowly. "Susan heard us going at it the other night, fighting . . . and so on . . . I think I will have to send her to Sally."

"Good," he said acidly. "Then do it: put the wheels in motion. Talk to Bernard."

"No, too close to family." What had Kaplan said? "Girlfriend? Why did you mention that? You assume, of course, that he's got a girlfriend, don't you?"

"Yes, certainly I do. That kind of man would have several . . . You know I never liked him. If that's saying, 'I told you so,' then I've said it. I recognized the type as soon as I saw him. But, of course, you had to be swept off your feet. Typical . . ."

"Not typical of me," she disagreed warmly, her face hot. "It was my one lapse."

Slowly, Kaplan nodded. "Yes, I suppose so. Well . . . anyway . . . if you're going to divorce him, do it. Don't fool around. Get it over with. Now, I want to know: what about Susan? Princeton? She will be there in the fall, won't she, and under my wing?"

"I don't know," Belle said doubtfully. "I may have to drop that plan."

"Why?" he demanded angrily. "Because of the goddamn money? Belle, Belle, if it comes to that I'm going to pick up the tab. I adored Peter Bertram. In effect, and maybe you don't know this, I promised him I'd always look after you two. And believe me," he said earnestly, his voice urgent, "it would give me a lot of pleasure—never sent a child of my own through school."

"Norman . . . " Tears came to Belle's eyes. "It's all too much." But there might not be any choice. Martin was right: she didn't have a nickel.

"You may have noticed I have quite a bit of money," Kaplan said.

And she had nothing—her mother's jewelry, a tiny trust fund that counted for nothing these days. She had no claim on the house off Angelo. Martin had bought it before their marriage.

"Norman . . . it wouldn't be right of me," she protested.

"I'll make it a loan at zero interest," Kaplan said. "Even as soft as you are, you should come out of this with something . . ."

"I don't know," she said woefully.

"As I said," he muttered, "you won't have any problem proving your case."

Belle nodded listlessly. The question remained whether she'd have the guts to go through with it.

"Belle, don't worry," Kaplan said. "You're going to be fine."

She smiled. "Yes, I guess so."

They left it at that.

Chapter Seven

Archibald Finistere was combing his perfectly trimmed white Van Dyke beard, proudly bunching his pink lips before the mirror, looking by turns haughty, imperial, benevolent, sagacious. People had often commented that Archy looked as though he could have been one of Napoleon's cavalry officers and, perhaps, he thought, he was in truth descended from one of the dashing heroes of the *Grande Armée.*

Lou, his wife, sometimes said he reminded her of one of those old-school-tie Englishmen who made movie careers playing butlers, accountants, or retired Indian Army colonels.

Whatever, Archy chuckled to himself, he was a fine figure of a man in the full maturity of his years. He'd fathered five children, and was a grandfather three times over, although he did not like to think about that.

This morning, Archy was feeling splendid—yes, that was the word, splendide, as in the new hotel by the same name. He hadn't told Lou about this yet. But she would be pleased when he did spring the news on her. Here, at the Camino, Lou had always been something of a Johnny-come-lately; the established forces had resisted her best efforts to be involved in the everyday affairs of an internationally known hostelry. The entrenched bureaucracy was just too much for her, Archy thought, rather satisfied this was so, for it was not necessarily a bad thing that Lou, now and then, got taken down a peg or two.

He hadn't married Lou, after all, because she'd gone to the Cornell School of Hotel Management but because she was good for his aging old bones. She had revived his sexuality and Archy knew it was good for the health to keep the motor turning over even into the seventh decade of life.

"Jolly good, too," he mumbled aloud, glaring at the mirror, "they think I'm sixty. *Bon et bientot*!"

Lou appeared behind him. She wasn't dressed yet and her full—yes, splendid—breasts lolled out of her loosely tied dressing gown.

"Bumsy," she said, "you're talking *français* to yourself again."

"Raven-haired beauty," Archy proclaimed. "Turtledove. It is my heritage."

Playfully, Lou reached to tweak his beard. "French boy from Port Huron, Michigan, makes good."

"Most people believe I was born in Paris and left there when only a bit of lad," he said sternly.

"And what they don't know won't hurt them, bumsy."

Lou cupped her hand under his distended balls. Archy jumped, but he turned to put his arms around her. *Dieu*, he told himself, she had been good to him again. In the early morning hours, she had commenced flirting with him in bed, waking him from a sound sleep, made sounder by the half bottle of Bordeaux he had consumed before turning in, then worked him up to a growling passion with her full-lipped mouth. It took him time these days, but he had managed to remain sufficiently erect to bring it off, and her, too, he believed. Did Lou simulate? He hadn't been able to figure that out.

"Was it good for you, turtledove?" he asked her tenderly, head reared back to look into her eyes.

She nodded, her eyes round, peeking coquettishly out of smooth, unlined cheeks, not noteworthy when one considered she was only thirty.

"Madame, *pour mois*, it was perfecto," Archy said.

"Archy," she said, "you know, when you get going, you have a great, hard thing."

At her words and the manipulation of her hands, Archy, to his wonderment, felt himself growing stiff again.

"Lou, turtledove," he groaned.

He couldn't make it again. His back hurt and, remembering the condition of his discs, he turned flaccid. A shadow of annoyance crossed her face.

"Off to work, my dear," he said, blustering, "a new day faces us."

"What's for today?" she asked. She always did.

"I'm having lunch with Norman Kaplan. He's bringing Sally Markman and Belle Cooper."

"Am I invited?"

He knew she would ask and then be irritated that she would be left out. It was not good to make Lou angry; for then she was likely to hold out on him and whip him with frozen silence.

"Turtledove," he pleaded, "it's some sort of business thing they want to discuss with me."

"All right, Archy," she said grimly. "Suit yourself. I think I'll go have lunch with the girls, at Ma Maison."

"Your clique," he smiled, pleased to be let off so easily.

"Pat Hyman and Daisy Cox. Yes."

"Hmmm, my dear. Why is it when women go out it's always a threesome, hardly ever four?"

"Easier to gossip with three, bumsy," she said, grinning sourly.

"I don't altogether approve of those two."

"Archibald," Lou said, "they're my friends. And I don't think you should forget that their husbands have money invested in the Camino."

"What? Here?" But, of course, it was so.

Pat Hyman was the wife of one of Hollywood's biggest independent producers, the ex-wife of an eastern politician. One thing about George Hyman, he never had trouble raising money for his pictures. It came, people whispered, from the oddest sources. The other one, that Daisy Cox, was a total witch, Jake Cox's fifth or sixth wife. Goddamn, Archy mused, Jake had beaten him out in the wife-stakes. Daisy had nabbed his friend Jake in a moment of vulnerability and was determined to hang on to Jake at all costs. They'd been married out of a taxicab in Las Vegas one time when Jake was under the weather, drunk that is. God knows, Archy told himself gleefully, how Jake kept on inventing so many electronic gadgets.

"Well, don't be out all afternoon, turtledove," he said hesitantly.

When those three got together, they drank with more abandon than any three men. Once or twice, to Archy's great embarrassment, Lou had come back to the Camino drunk as a skunk, raised hell with the desk people, then a bartender, an elevator operator, and, finally, a defenseless penthouse cleaning woman.

* * *

Archy was sitting with a glass of champagne in the bar when Kaplan arrived with his two ladies.

"Norman!" Archy exclaimed. "Well . . . Sally . . . and Belle."

"Archy, how are you, my boy?" Kaplan asked cordially.

My boy? Archy didn't much like Norman Kaplan. Kaplan was too wise, too bright, his high-pitched voice too grating on the nerves and eardrums. Kaplan could never have belonged to Archy's inner circle of friends and drinking buddies.

Nonetheless, he was effusive. "Sit down! Sit down! Ladies, a little champagne? *Garçon*!" Archy called. *"Champagne pour les dames, Et, Monsieur Kaplan?"*

"*Aussi, s'il vous plait*," Kaplan murmured.

The little bastard, of course he spoke French. Best switch quickly back to English.

"Well," Archy said, beaming as a good host should. "It's a thrill to see you here at the hotel. I know you don't often get away from the Bistro and Ma Maison."

He cast the veiled reprimand jovially, but they would get the message.

"Archy, it's so bloody dark in here," Sally Markman said.

Archy sniggered. "Deliberately, my dear. Elsewise, where would the advertising tycoons take their secretaries?"

Ah, *merde*, he thought, he had made a faux pas. Too late, he had remembered Belle's husband was that thorough-going rascal Martin Cooper. But she only smiled icily. True, Archy thought, she was a frosty one; easy to see why Cooper played around so much.

When the champagne had been poured, Archy lifted his glass. "To you, beautiful people. Haven't you been in New York, Norman?"

"Just got back."

Kaplan sat quietly, smiling pleasantly, squat and almost deformed next to Archy's erect, guardsmanlike posture.

"Do you like this?" Archy asked. "It's a Moet brut, nothing outrageous, but a good wine, don't you think?"

"Very nice indeed," Belle said politely, "but you know, frankly, I like beer better than champagne."

Archy widened his eyes mockingly, chuckled disbelievingly. "My dear, is that possible? You like beer better than champagne?" She nodded. "Well, Belle, we have a hell of a good bottle of Kronenbourg in the house. Let me get you one of those."

"Oh, no, not now. This is fine."

Well, one thing, Archy thought, she was a modest woman, if cold.

"Archy," Kaplan said, firmly putting aside the pleasantries, "we've got something important to discuss with you."

"Fire away, *mes amis*."

"The Splendide," Kaplan said.

Oh, oh! Now was the time for great caution. What had Kaplan heard? "Yes, yes, the new hotel."

"Well, you're going to be moving over there, aren't you?"

Archy feigned astonishment, blinked rapidly. "I am?"

"Sure you are." As Archy hesitated, Kaplan went on, "Look, Archy, I've put money in the place, so I know what's going on."

"My dear man . . ."

"Come on now, Archy," Kaplan pressed him. "We're not going to spread it around town."

Archy began to perspire. He truly did not want people discussing this. The offer of the new job had been a stroke of good fortune: the fact the post was his, the fact his health was still good enough that he could accept. Archy had been getting the idea recently that they were breathing down his neck at the Camino. There had been a casual mention or two of the joys of retirement. But Archy could not retire; he could never leave this business, except feet first. He loved it and the hotel business kept him alive.

He leaned forward to whisper, "All right. But nobody knows yet."

"Our purpose is very simple," Kaplan said, equally confidential. "We want to book with you, right now, the first big party at the Splendide."

"But . . . I don't know . . . if I . . ."

"Yes, you can," Sally said. "Has anybody else asked?"

Archy shook his head. "Not that I know of."

"We want it the first week in December," Sally glared. "First party—guaranteed."

"Madame, the hotel is not opening until January."

"But the ballroom will be finished," Kaplan pushed.

"We won't need the rooms upstairs. Just the ballroom. Archy, you can't turn it down—it's going to be the biggest party ever."

The aggressive little Jew. But Archy smiled grandly. "I'll do whatever I can."

"Better than that, Archy," Sally cut in. "We want it guaranteed!"

"Sally," he protested, "how can I guarantee anything like that, at this point? It's so early."

Kaplan would not get off his back. "Archy, I know the downstairs is going to be finished and it's just begging for a special opening party. If you need any assurances, I'll speak to my friends in New York."

Archy knew Kaplan was not giving him any alternative. He was telling him either-or. And he was smart enough to know that when Kaplan talked about having a little money in the Splendide, he was talking figures of a million dollars and up, which was very heavy influence.

Trying to keep his distance, Archy asked, "What's it for?"

"A brand-new cancer foundation," Belle said quietly.

"Yes, a very worthy cause, if I may say so."

"So we're on?" Kaplan demanded.

"Oh, yes," Archy said reluctantly, "insofar as it's in my power to promise . . . "

"You promise? We've got it?" Sally demanded. "Now, you're not going to turn around and promise it to somebody else?"

"Madame," Archy said pridefully, pulling himself more erect, "if I promise, would I break my promise?"

"No matter who it is, and I don't care," Sally insisted.

Kaplan, thank God, patted her arm to quiet her. "Sally, if Archy says yes, then yes it is."

"Who's going to foot the bill?" Archy asked.

"The Splendide is," Kaplan said crisply. "Don't worry about that part of it."

"How many people?" Archy asked tiredly, feeling cornered.

"About 2,000," Kaplan told him. "And now, Archy, I'll give you the zinger, a proposition you won't be able to refuse. Do you know who are going to be the honorary chairwomen of this event?"

Belle and Sally glanced at Kaplan. Clearly enough to Archy, they didn't know either.

"I'll tell you who," Kaplan continued excitedly, "and I'm going to do my damdest to get them— *all* the former First Ladies, at least the ones well enough to make the trip here."

"Dieu!" Archy was impressed. This would take the affair above the run-of-the-mill charity party level. "All of them?"

"Invitations will go out to all of them. Naturally, they won't *all* come."

"Norman!" Sally exclaimed. "Do you think you can do it?"

Kaplan shrugged modestly. "Like I say, I'm going to try. That'll be our drawing card."

Archy was suddenly very interested in the project. All the First Ladies, good God, the publicity for the Splendide would be enormous. For himself, it would be a feather in his cap the size of an eagle wing.

Respectfully, pulling at his beard, he asked, "Do you have a committee yet?"

"First things first," Sally said. "First, we needed the hotel."

"Madame, as far as I'm concerned, that's nailed down," Archy said. "Let me say . . . uh . . . I would be greatly honored if my name . . ."

"Archy, you're going to be an important member of the committee, naturally," Kaplan said.

"And Lou, my wife . . . umm."

"Archy, she's already on our list for committee member, too."

"'She'll be delighted, I know, to help in any way she can," Archy said.

"Done!" Kaplan cried delightedly, clapping Archy on the shoulder. "Let's drink to it. God, what a blessing you are, Archy. When I see the prince . . ."

"Just mention my name: Archibald Finistere, hotelier extraordinaire."

They lifted their glasses, all smiling. Ah, Archy told himself wickedly, Kaplan knew enough to know Archy's word was worthless unless it was sealed in a champagne toast. He had been mousetrapped, given no choice. But it was a happy choice. This would be Archy's crowning achievement. Never mind about the goddamned charity. Archy couldn't care less about that.

Chapter Eight

Only the beginning of June, it was already moving toward Condition Heatwave underneath the slapdash composition roof of the Ma Maison terrace. This had never been a deterrent to the regular lunchtime crowd.

After a shaky start, Ma Maison had become a favorite of a curious mix of society ladies and the younger generation of Hollywood agents and show-business personalities. The restaurant was a dramatic example of what could be accomplished with the astute use of reverse P.R.—owner/proprietor Patrick Terrail had taken the unusual course of "un-listing" the phone number and with great Gallic "un-humor" turned away the unwashed nobodies who, by word of mouth, had heard Ma Maison was *the* place to visit if ever on a Cook's Tour of greater Los Angeles.

When Lou Finistere arrived that day, Terrail kissed her lovingly on the cheek and pointed out Pat Hyman and Daisy Cox. "But your friends said they hoped you wouldn't join them today," he muttered in her ear. "They're telling very private stories."

After a second of stunned surprise, Lou said, "Oh, Patrick! I wish you wouldn't do that."

Pat was waving at her. Smiling, Lou stepped down to the terrace and crossed to the table.

Pat Hyman was bone-thin, her face eager, somewhat feral under a head of close-cropped dark hair, while Daisy was a blonde creature, smooth-skinned, her body maturing toward slightly plump. Daisy always looked as if she'd just climbed out of bed; her scent was one of recent sex. But she had taken the time to put on her eyelashes, which battered the upper parts of her cheekbones when she blinked.

"Hello, girls," Lou said.

Lou slipped into the third chair at the table while Pat indicated a bottle of wine stuck in a cooler. "We're drinking Patrick's white wine," Pat said. "Will that do you?" Lou considered wine for a moment, then opted for a vodka martini on the rocks. "Well, dear, what have you been doing this morning?" Pat asked.

"Nothing," she said. "Getting Archy underway for another big day of 'hotelling,' as he calls it. He's having lunch with that man from New York, Norman Kaplan, and Sally Markman and Belle Cooper."

Pat drawled, "There's an unlikely combination."

"*Bor*-ing," Daisy Cox said slyly, adding, "except for darling Archy, of course."

Of course, Lou thought to herself. Little did they know. "They're talking over some kind of business."

"Really!" Pat Hyman said. "Probably another of Sally Markman's schemes."

"Kaplan is as rich as Croesus, isn't he?" Lou asked.

She had begun to learn the names of the players since moving here from Chicago but she was still relatively unacquainted with their in-depth biographies.

"Not filthy rich," Pat mused, nervously lighting a thin cigarette, "but rich enough. My other husband—first husband that is—knew him pretty well. He used to be active in politics. And, of course, he's Sally's oldest, dearest friend."

A waiter delivered Lou's martini. "Madame," he said grandly.

When he'd gone away, Daisy said softly, "He's a nice-looking young stud. I wonder where Patrick gets them. Looks like he's got a big one, too," she added flippantly.

Pat gasped with laughter. "Daisy, you are too much."

"No, not enough," Daisy disagreed with great seriousness. "What about you two? Are you getting enough?"

The question was really meant for Lou. Everybody knew Archy was an old fart. But did he deliver?

Pat continued to laugh. She eyed Daisy with amusement. "Did you ever hear of a young actor named Wayne Stravinsky?" Pat asked. They admitted they had not. "Well, just as well, dears. God! I met him at a party the other night. Absolutely gorgeous. Absolutely nothing left to the imagination. Daisy, you'd flip. Tight pants, the whole thing . . ."

"Probably some kind of fag," Daisy sniffed.

"No, no," Pat said slowly. "I don't think so. I'm pretty sure not."

"How do you know, dear?" Daisy said insinuatingly.

"I have my ways. What about you, Miss Clever Pussy? Who have you been doing lately?"

Frankly, Daisy replied, "The poolman. Times are a little thin. But he's not bad. I caught him in the poolhouse a couple of weeks ago. Boy, was he surprised. Now he's learned to like it very much, and our pool is the cleanest in all Bel-Air. God," she said glumly, "do you think I'm oversexed?"

"No, no," Pat Hyman said, "just perfectly normal, Daisy dear."

"I don't know," Daisy said, "sometimes I wonder about myself. Of course, you," she accused Pat, "you can get anybody you want. With George Hyman for a husband, who would dare turn you down? All you've got to do is snap your fingers."

Pat reacted coolly to this observation. She was willing to joke, but only up to a certain point. She changed the direction, if not the subject of the conversation. "Speaking of fucking," she muttered, "there's Jane Farelady over there."

"Jane Farelady, the star fucker?" Daisy squealed, "who's she with? Who's she with?"

"I dunno. Never seen him before, probably some agent," Pat said.

Jane Farelady, the young starlet, fit her name to perfection. She was perhaps the most wholesome-looking young woman Lou had ever seen. Her face, stunningly beautiful, was long and placid, the eyes large, almost introspective, and topped like something delicious on the menu, with a head of thick auburn hair that fell neatly on her shoulders. Jane was wearing a snug red tunic cut in front to show the incipient swell of perfect, unlifted boobs. The rest of the body was long and fluid.

"Christ," Daisy said disgustedly, "I used to look like that when I was dancing, before I married Jake. Jesus, she drips with it."

"But she is a star fucker, isn't she?" Lou remarked hesitantly.

Now that she seemed firmly entrenched in Los Angeles,

she told herself, she could afford to start using the local dialect.

"That's right," Pat said, "she takes them all on. Wouldn't think it to look at her, would you? To think she's been here only a couple of years, a little Catholic schoolgirl, they say. Ha! Now fucks the biggest, only the superstars; she doesn't fool around with supporting actors, whether they're good, better, or best. She must keep a list to check them off after she scores."

Jane Farelady must have been aware of their stares. She shifted the placid body, put her right hand up alongside her cheek, and continued to talk earnestly to her companion.

Lou whispered, "Archy says she's damn near broken up three or four marriages already. But he says she'd never marry anybody here. She wants somebody very rich and very, very important."

"Not an actor then," Pat said.

Daisy interrupted them petulantly. "Shall we order?"

Daisy did not like to be reminded that sexually she might some day be over the hill—or hump, Lou noted maliciously. Their attention to Jane Farelady teed her off.

Pat ordered a simple mushroom salad, rejecting an offer of freshly baked bread. She was so well-dieted that the peaks of her breasts were the breasts themselves, pecking at her blouse. Her waist was small and her legs next door to emaciated. Daisy, on the other hand, was awash with flesh. She was not fat per se. There was merely a lot of everything: full breasts and buttocks, plump arms and a neck voluptuously firm. Lou wondered what these two thought of her.

The heat inside the tentlike structure was increasing. Lou felt perspiration gathering in her armpits, between her legs. God, heat like this, it was enough to make a nun horny.

She ordered sole, boiled new potatoes, and a small green salad. Daisy chose steak and french fries.

"And I want the steak very rare," she told the waiter, "I want it to walk to the table." Then she murmured, "You know, women who like their steak rare are the sexiest, you can always tell. Remember that. And Jake likes them well-padded. No wonder. He's so skinny he'd break bones screwing anybody as slimmed down as you, Pat."

Pat Hyman chuckled huskily but did not respond. Lou

could almost wonder whether Pat had taken Jake on at one time or another. It was not impossible, she thought. This was a very incestuous community, once one had penetrated to a certain level of it.

It was 1:30 now and the tempo of chatter had reached its highest pitch. Every table on the terrace was taken, and inside, where it was dark and a little cooler, seemed equally filled. Patrick's waiters, white-aproned and quick on their feet, danced among the tables, taking orders, politely joking with the patrons. On the other side of the half-wall and plastic roof that supposedly protected the diners from the dust of Melrose Avenue, four Rolls Royces had been backed up against the terrace. Another Terrail gimmick: park all the Rolls ostentatiously in front; Cadillacs and anything as common as Fords went in the back.

Terrail was standing in the doorway of the tacky wooden shack that had become his renowned eatery, a telephone at his ear, its snakelike cord stretching back inside. He surveyed his customers as he talked, with a benevolent scorn.

"Aha! Pat Hyman barked, "there's Martin Cooper, Belle Cooper's husband."

"Who's he with?" Daisy demanded, turning in her seat.

"The real-estate pusher, Pamela Renfrew," Pat sneered. "Jesus, can't he do any better than that?"

"Should he?" Lou asked.

"Christ, he's always screwing somebody. But why her?" Pat said disgustedly. "Probably business screwing. Cooper is all tied up in real estate."

"Good-looking guy," Daisy judged. "But she does look like a pig."

"You've met him, Daisy, for God's sake," Pat said. Cooper and Pamela walked into the dark interior. "Oh, oh, inside."

"Hankypanky?" Lou asked.

"You know it, dear."

"Speaking of hankypanky," Daisy murmured, "where's George? Doing his usual?"

"Naturally," Pat Hyman replied complacently, "having lunch with Morris Mauery at one of their places."

"What do they find to talk about?" Daisy asked.

"Labor problems mostly," Pat replied succinctly.

Lou was aware of Mauery, a very tough corporate attorney who specialized in keeping the studios free of union problems. People said that if Mauery ordered work, then they worked; if he said strike, then they struck. Mauery was apparently a very rich man in his own right and earned enormous fees from the studios and unions alike. His connections across the country were complex and led into some mighty strange corners.

"And your Jake," Pat asked sardonically, "where's he?"

"You think he's out doing hankypanky?" Daisy laughed. "He's at the lab. Where else?"

Jake Cox was a genius—that was the general word around town. He was an electronics innovator, and an inventor whose fortune had been made in the manipulation of silicon chips, the ingredients of the modern communications industry. It was amazing, Lou thought, the uses to which silicon was being put.

Martin Cooper and Pamela Renfrew took a small table in the back corner and Cooper immediately ordered two double gin martinis. Pamela looked exhausted. Weariness showed easily on such pasty white skin as hers, and she had rushed her makeup that morning, he thought critically. The mascara was too heavy and had run in the heat of the day. Her body was overwrought, tense.

"So, what's the problem?" he demanded.

Pouting, she said, "No problem. I just wanted to see you."

"Well . . . so now you see me."

"Jesus, you're in a great mood, aren't you?"

"Yes," he grunted, "really great."

"I haven't seen you since that party of yours."

"Pamela, I've been very busy. I'm trying to put something together for Sam Leonard, the little shit. He's not easy to work with. I think I'll turn the whole goddamn thing over to Charley."

"I don't know why you don't," she said bitterly. "You seem to turn everything over to somebody, including me to Sam Leonard."

Cooper chuckled mirthlessly. "Pamela, do you have any idea what his account is worth? I'll tell you: the ad campaign should run around five million. Ten or fifteen percent of that—well, you figure it out. You're good at mathematics."

"Yeah," she said sarcastically, "the new line: 'Belle.' Shit!"

Cooper turned furiously on her. The one thing he didn't need today was to be hauled over the coals by this dumb broad. "Look, don't remind me of that, Pamela. Anyway, it's dead. He was only being a smartass. But I am still trying to get the account. Don't bug me."

"Yeah," she said again, clasping her big hands tightly on the table. "Does that mean I was supposed to lay for him?"

"Did you, goddamn it?"

"No, but only by the grace of God! I practically ran screaming, naked, into the road to get away from him."

Well . . . He had been hoping for that, expecting nothing else. The trouble was she *hadn't* laid for Leonard. "That son of a bitch," he said more mildly, "of all the rotten little bastards. What did he do?"

"Do?" she cried, outraged. "He tried to get into me. When he came at me, I had to put a bear hug on him. Then he wanted to know, since I'm so faithful to you, why you didn't drop that wife of yours and marry me."

"How's he know about us?" he demanded coldly.

"He merely knew," she said loftily. "He said he could tell by the way you looked at me."

"Bullshit!"

"Well . . . why don't you?"

"Why don't I what?"

Pamela laid one strong hand on his fly, nudging him. "Why don't you dump that cold bitch and marry me?"

Cooper nodded. He felt himself becoming hard, the tingling in his balls. He looked at her full, lipsticked mouth and thought of that great vacant spot between her thighs.

"Maybe I will," he mumbled, "maybe I will. But listen, while we're here, let's talk about that piece of land in the Valley. I think I want to sell it. I need some cash."

Pamela scowled. "Fuck you, Marty. Always business first."

The threesome had finished lunch. Pat Hyman ordered another bottle of the house white wine.

"God," she said, "there's Bertha Moore. Shit! I didn't see her come in. She's with Camilla Young. Her father used to be in the Cabinet." Again, this was for Lou's edification. "And that P.R. idiot, Deidre Francis. Hi!" Pat waved. "Jesus, there's a collection of dreary dames for you."

Bertha Moore was a pinch-faced woman of about fifty-five. Her face was gray despite an earnest effort at tanning, her eyes large and insolent. Camilla Young was in her early thirties and looked stunningly average, almost unkempt beside Bertha, who was implacably coiffed and severe in an unwrinkled linen suit. Deidre Francis was a weepy-faced little imp who looked so helpless one suspected she'd just been beaten by some brutish man or was expecting a beating any minute.

"What are they doing together?" Daisy murmured. "Doesn't Big Bertha know Sheldon Moore is crazy about Camilla?"

Venomously, Pat said, "He can be crazy about anybody he likes. If Bertha ever catches him fooling around, she'll string him up by his nuts. Is Camilla divorced by now?"

"Yes," Daisy said, "that's why she looks all gone to pot. She got the two kids, much the wonder of that with all her boozing."

"Isn't Bertha a lot older than Sheldon?" Lou asked.

They ignored the question to gaze transfixed at a new arrival in the restaurant.

Pat crowed, "And here comes Darling," stretching the words in astute mimicry of McMahon's introduction of Johnny Carson.

"God almighty," Lou sighed.

Darling Higgins had made her entrance. She was very slight, with a tousle of red frizzy hair and a pointed, curious face. Darling was impressively dressed in brown riding boots, tan whipcord pants, and a blue denim shirt. In one hand, she flourished a riding crop, and with the other led a swarthy-complected man, also dressed in equestrian togs. Without waiting to be seated, Darling preempted a just-vacated table near the terrace steps.

"That must be her riding instructor," Pat muttered. "Let's see what Patrick does about that."

"He looks like he's got a big one, too," Daisy giggled, the wine beginning to show.

"Looks more like a faggot to me," Lou interjected daringly.

"Why does Ellsworth Higgins put up with it?" Daisy wondered.

"Because he doesn't give a good shit," Pat Hyman said. " 'Dearest' lives for his friends—boyfriends, that is."

Darling was a mere child, twenty-four or -five at most, her husband, Ellsworth, whom everyone had started calling

Dearest, a few years older. Neither of them did anything, Lou thought piously, and didn't need to. One of their closest friends was a Brazilian playboy, Baby Perez, whom they supplied with girls when he was in town, as well as, it was rumored, endless lines of coke.

"How does Dearest make all that money?" Daisy asked.

Pat snorted. "He doesn't make it. It's been made. They live off the overflow."

"Dearest is a faggot," Lou said.

"No kidding, dear?" Pat said sardonically. Then, as if she had been waiting for the precisely most unexpected moment, she dropped her little hand grenade in Lou's lap. "When are you and Archy moving over to the Splendide, dear?"

"Splendide? The new hotel?"

"Yes, dear. Archy's moving to the Splendide, isn't he?"

"Oh, that," Lou had the wit to dissemble, "just a rumor. I pay no attention to rumors like that. Everybody's got Archy doing something."

"Well," Pat said, "remember where you heard it."

The son of a bitch, Lou told herself furiously, the dirty low-down cocksucker. He hadn't told her anything about it. She'd get even. Morosely, Lou downed some wine and joined them in hazily surveying the thinning crowd. It was 2:30. Martin Cooper's big blonde scuttled out of the restaurant and stomped down the soggy green carpetway toward the cars. In a moment, Cooper himself sauntered into view, a long cigar stuck in his mouth.

Pat waved, calling, "Hi, Martin!"

He waved back, hesitated, then walked down to their table. He bent to kiss Pat on the cheek. "Hi, ladies." He puffed on the cigar.

"Martin, you know these people," Pat said. "Lou Finistere . . . Daisy Cox."

"We have met. Hi, girls."

"Sit down, Martin," Pat said, "and have a glass of wine with us."

He looked around absently, then nodded. "Okay, why not?" He pulled a chair up between Lou and Daisy. Cooper was a big, athletic creature and Lou could feel the masculinity come off him in waves.

Daisy batted her eyelashes rapidly. "At last, a man. Having lunch with the girls is *bor*-ing."

"Martin," Pat said, "who was that gorgeous hunk of woman you were with?"

"Oh, Pamela Renfrew," he said carelessly, "you know her. She's in the real-estate business. We were talking over a property deal." He smiled easily, showing them square, white teeth. If one hadn't known it, one would have concluded anyway that he had been a football player, an athlete of some sort, the way he handled his body, the face—the confidence. Christ, Lou thought, that secretive bastard Archy must have looked like this once, what with his barrel chest and slim legs. But Archy's center of gravity had shifted. Cooper held up his glass. "Well . . . here's to you, girls. Chin-chin."

Lou impulsively said, "You know, your wife is having lunch with my husband." His heavy eyebrows lifted, then dropped. "She and Sally Markman and that Norman Kaplan."

"Oh," he said. "I wonder what they're up to."

Clearly, he could not have cared any less. He flicked a chunk of ash off his cigar and took some wine.

Daisy, tuned like a grand piano, immediately sensed his mood. "Up to no good," she chuckled slyly. "An orgy in the making."

"I doubt that very much," Cooper said coolly. "I don't think orgies are up Mr. Kaplan's alley."

Pat's eyes flickered, like a wolf's shining red beyond the campfire. "I think you're right," she said.

But the news from Lou had nevertheless thrown him off balance and into a suddenly dark mood. Abruptly, he stood up, put down his glass, and stuck the cigar irritably in his mouth.

"Well," he said, "thanks for the wine. I've got to be getting back. Got a three o'clocker. Anybody need a lift?"

Daisy did not miss a beat. "If you're going toward Beverly Hills."

"Sure. Come on, I'll drop you off, Daisy."

Daisy stood up quickly, gathering together her things. "Pat, your lunch, right? My turn next time?"

Pat Hyman's face was frozen with astonishment. "Sure . . . sure . . ."

"Well, we're off then, girls," Cooper said nonchalantly. "See you around."

"Bye, girls," Daisy chirped.

Her eyes opaque, Pat watched as they walked up the steps, down the green carpet, and until Cooper had driven away. "Well," she finally said, "I'll be goddamned. That little cunt! She left her car here."

"Maybe she'll send Jake to pick it up," Lou suggested, chuckling.

God, she was thinking, as much as she might have liked a go at Martin Cooper, she'd never have been able to pull that. How did Daisy get away with it? Didn't Jake have any inkling of how hot her pants were?

Pat Hyman said what she was thinking. "How does she dare, goddamn it? Now, Lou, you and I both know for a fact that inside a half-hour Martin Cooper is going to be screwing her. Jesus, she's like some kind of an animal. And so is he."

The strident accusation sounded a bit ironic coming from Pat, who had as much as admitted that she took her solace from striving young actors.

"I think you're jealous, dear," Lou murmured.

"I am, goddamn it!"

"Shit," Lou said loudly, "so am I."

Lou drove very carefully back to the Camino. She'd had the two martinis and lots of wine. Now, she was hot and tired but no less lividly angry with Archibald Finistere. He had shamed her by putting her in an impossible situation. Should she be the last to know? It was inexcusable of him not to have told her first. Goddamn it, she thought, maybe he'd forgotten she was his wife. Was he so senile?

Storming into the lobby, she demanded, "Where is Mr. Finistere?"

"Oh, Mrs. Finistere," the deskman said, "he's in his office with Mr. Jurgen Ehrlich who's joined the staff, replacing Monsieur Emil, I think."

"Ehrlich! I don't know any Ehrlich!"

"Madame, he arrived only today."

"I see," she fumed, "I'll find him there then."

Lou marched to Archy's office and burst in on them. She lifted her arm, pointing at Archy's heart. "I want to see *you*!"

Archy heisted himself up from behind his desk, thrust out his chest, and grabbed his beard. He knew when trouble was on the way.

"Ah, sweetheart," he said. "I'm glad you're here. I want

you to meet Jurgen Ehrlich. He comes to us from Zurich, where he managed the famous Vierjahrezeiten Hotel."

"Hello," Lou muttered.

Ehrlich, a youngish man with a raw, red face, bowed from the waist, deftly took her hand, and kissed it. "Madame Finistere, a great honor for me," he stuttered, his English strongly accented.

"How do you do?" she replied, still glaring at Archy.

"Jurgen is going to be our new banquet manager, sweetheart."

"How nice," she said sarcastically. "I wasn't aware of your impending arrival, Mr. . . . "

"'Ehrlich, madame."

Lou realized she shouldn't take it out on him. What did he know? Ehrlich seemed like a nice enough man, despite the fact, she thought spitefully, that he was so Germanic, and so ugly, with deep-set, hollow eyes, sallow face, and widely spaced front teeth.

"No," she repeated irritably. "I wasn't aware. But then, I'm not aware of anything that goes on around here."

Archy's beard retreated into his neck. His eyes darted apprehensively. He knew when he was about to be gored. "Sweetheart . . . "

"Mr. Finistere," she said, heavily sarcastic, "I do want to see you, privately, if you please."

She did not give a damn if she made him look foolish in front of his new employee. She waited as Archy brushed Jurgen off, then closed the door and loosed her wrath.

In the end, swearing her to silence—stupid, she knew, since the whole town was aware of the new job—and promising her the moon, Archy managed to calm her, but only because she decided to be calm.

"Turtledove, I was keeping it a surprise for you. I don't know how all these people find things out. Say you love Bumsy."

Stiffly, Lou said, "Bumsy, you can be a big pain in the ass. Don't you ever do that to me again. I won't forget this for a long time. And don't come scratching around tonight for a little piece either."

Chapter Nine

As they were driving home from the Beverly Hills Hotel, Belle reminded Martin that Susan would be graduating from high school at the end of the week.

"I don't suppose you'll want to go," she said quietly.

"Jesus!" He banged his fist on the steering wheel. "You certainly phrase a question in a very negative way."

"Well?"

"Since you ask, no! As a matter of fact, I'm going to be out of town Friday. I've got to go to San Diego, not that you want me there anyway."

"That's not so."

"It is so," he cried. "Not that I even knew she was graduating. She doesn't talk to me anymore, and neither do you. So be it. Goddamn it, so be it."

"Why is she so frightened of you?" Belle asked.

She had begun to think there was more than dislike in Susan's attitude toward Cooper. Susan did not talk to him if she could avoid it. In Cooper's presence, Susan stiffened to tenseness. She tried to keep away from him.

Cooper growled, "I don't know why—if she is frightened. Who can tell?"

"She heard everything that night."

"Too goddamn bad."

Without saying anything else, he whipped the Rolls like a tired horse toward the house in the hills. On a deserted curve, he swore heavily and slammed on the brakes, stopping the car.

He turned toward her and said, "Look, you didn't say a goddamn word tonight. Do you have to be so surly when we go out?"

They'd been at a humdrum reception, then dinner. This one, for what? Had she forgotten already? No, for Lord somebody-or-other from the British Board of Trade. Cooper, his near-miss with the Rolls account not entirely forgotten, had been invited because he was such a long-standing friend of British export.

"I don't think I was surly," Belle said. "There wasn't much to say."

"Jesus," he said disgustedly, then more reasonably continued, "look, I told you I was sorry for what happened that night. I was really pissed off the way you were joking about me with Leonard. I can't put up with that kind of horseshit, Belle. I'm a man. I'm not going to say I'm an important man, but I have some stature."

Coldly, she heard him out. His attempt at apology was framed in such an intimidating manner. Jesus, she was not his slave, she told herself, mustering her courage.

"Because you're a man does that give you the right to push me around and make a fool out of me with Pamela Renfrew—your mistress!"

"Goddamn it," he yelled so loudly his voice boomed against the car windows, "I've told you before, she is not my mistress."

"Whatever. Listen, Martin," she said, "we made a contract. I keep the contract. I help you. I'm your front. Leave it like that. I'll tell you, I don't care anymore. If you want Pamela Renfrew, go ahead . . . and I do what I want."

This stopped him dead. He was still enough of the white Protestant male to be surprised by the reminder that the double standard could work both ways.

Slowly he interpreted. "You mean we go our own ways, is that it?"

"Yes."

"The very modern marriage?"

"Yes, why not? I fulfill my part of the business contract—which is all it ever was—and I get paid: expenses, clothes, household money, school for Susan. I go to the parties, entertain your friends. I think I'm worth an annual salary of twenty or thirty thousand. That's no more than you pay a good private secretary, is it?"

He drew back, rather collapsed in the driver's seat, staring out the front windshield. He drummed his fingers on the steering wheel, and finally turned to stare at her, his eyes hot and wild.

"Bullshit," he snarled, "you get nothing. You know why? Because if you don't like it, you can walk out on me. Sue me!"

"All right," she said. "I will. There are lawyers in this town that'd make you squirm. Marvin Mitchelson, for instance. He'd take you to the cleaners."

He could not know how close she was to screaming. She did not dare look at him. It would not have surprised her at this point if the fullback's hand had flashed between them to punish her.

But when he spoke next, there was something of admiration in his voice. "Son of a bitch," he drawled, "you are a tough broad. I didn't know how tough you are." But everything he said came too late. "I'll think about it," he added. "I really will think about it."

Sally Markman had arranged to go with Belle to Susan's graduation ceremony and, afterward, the three of them had lunch at Jimmy's. Susan, Belle knew, was relieved Cooper had not been there, but she was moody and silent nevertheless. Belle ached; it should have been a very happy day. Sally was annoyed.

"Come on, you two," she ordered, "let's have a few laughs, shall we?"

"Laughs?" Susan repeated.

"Well, you just graduated from school, nitwit," Sally said sharply. "Shouldn't that be enough cause for at least a little merriment? I'm ordering us a bottle of champagne. Jesus, what creeps!"

"That's right," Belle said. "Think of it, you've closed a chapter of your life. You're going down to Sally's, then in the fall you're off to Princeton. You should be happy as a lark."

"Princeton? Who cares about that?" Susan brooded.

Belle faltered. "You've got to take advantage of the chances you have, Susan. You should care! I'm not going to see you waste your life, if that's what you think."

She leaned back in the booth and folded her hands.

"Wasted life?" Susan's chin came up and she stared defiantly at Belle, her eyes sparkling with hurt. Cruelly, she said, "Speaking of wasted lives, what are you doing about yours?"

"Susan!" Sally turned ferociously on the girl. "You twit! How dare you talk to your mother like that?"

Tears came to Susan's eyes. "I'm sorry, I shouldn't have said that."

"You better be sorry," Sally said.

Belle leaned forward, patted Susan's hand. "Never mind. I know what she's saying. Listen, daughter, we all have our battles to fight."

"But are you fighting?" Susan demanded anxiously.

"Yes! Things take a while to work out, blast it!"

"How long?"

Sally muttered, "Susan, I'm going to slap you right in the chops if you don't stop bugging your mother."

"Damn it," Susan replied urgently. "Don't I have a right to know? She's my mother. I don't want her to be miserable."

Belle gripped her hand. "All right, all right, you want to know. Six months—more or less. Is that exact enough for you?"

"What the hell are you talking about?" Sally demanded furiously.

"You know what I'm talking about. I'm leaving him, for Christ's sake!"

Sally's face was drawn. This was not one of her better days and Belle didn't want to subject her to this additional problem. Her eyes were veined with red. The stress was reflected in them. Then she relaxed.

"Good," she said.

"You promise?" Susan pressed. "I want you away from him."

"Yes, Christ, I promise," Belle said wanly. "Now, let me drink some champagne."

Slowly, it was better. And in the end, they were all in a good mood, Belle especially so, relieved that she had publicized her deadline, promised.

"Listen, twit," Sally said as they were parting, "I want you down at the beach bright and early tomorrow."

"Yes, ma'am," Susan said meekly.

"And don't you dare be hung over."

Hours later, Belle was waiting up for Susan, sitting quietly in the living room with a book. Martin arrived first, at about one A.M. The Jensen pulled up with a roar and screeched on the bricks. She hadn't been expecting him. He came into the house, his gait uncertain. He was drunk. Seeing her, Cooper stopped in his tracks, wavering. He stared shrewdly at her, with that sharpness men get on the very edge of incapacity.

"Well, old Mother Hubbard," he slurred, "what's in the cupboard, ole Mother Hubbard? Got any scotch there?"

"Plenty in the bar," Belle said softly.

"Righto!" he exclaimed. "Lemme ask you a question, ole Mother Hubbard, got any bones for the dog?"

"Martin," she said, almost fondly. The booze relieved the pressures, made him seem more like the old Cooper. "I think you're smashed."

"Smashed, am I? Let me tell you, ole Mother Hubbard, there's a long long road between smashed and drunk." He approached her and peered down at her, as if very short-sighted. He placed his hands on the arm of her chair and leered. "How 'bout a little lay, Mother Hubbard?"

It was a direct proposition and Belle did not know how to answer. She could easily have said yes, and it would have been as simple as that: a reconciliation, regardless of how temporary. But no, he would not change. He was merely drunk now and it was only in this condition that his boyish charm ever returned. His private horrors were anesthetized and he needed loving. But she could not love him again. That was over. She remembered her promise.

Her hesitation served as her answer, and his charm fell away like a mask thrown to the side. He grabbed her chin in his right hand and glowered.

"No," he sneered, his breath laden with the stench of his drinks, "I see Mother Hubbard ain't for that. You," he said furiously, "cold cunt! Fuck you!"

He flipped her head against the chair and backed off, breathing hoarsely.

"Yeah, that's it," he gasped. "Living our own lives, huh? Okay. But no money for you and none for Miss Junior Cunt either."

Belle jumped up to face him. "Go to hell!"

Cooper only laughed. "I ought to drop you in your tracks. Lemme ask you—you never told me—what were you doing with Kaplan the other day, you and him and Finistere and that bitch Sally Markman? Is that your new guy? That little dwarf?"

She crossed her arms protectively across her chest. "Go get yourself another drink. You know better than that. Don't act like such a . . . punk."

He stood uncertainly, an arm's length away from her,

not knowing in which direction to go or what more he could say to hurt her. It was frightening moment, and she wondered how she could defend herself. Would he leave her alone, go for a drink, or would he attack?

"You know I hate that little bastard Kaplan," he muttered. He wiped his hand across his forehead. "Why do you keep seeing him?"

"Because he's my friend."

"Shit! He's the one who told you that you were making a big mistake marrying me. I've never forgotten that, Belle."

"Well," she answered, "at the time, I didn't care what he said. Now . . . it seems . . . he was right."

"Son of a bitch!" He whirled and slammed his fist into the paneled wall, then, bellowing with pain, shook it numbly. "I'll tell you what—you can have Kaplan and you can have Sam Leonard, too, that other miserable little goat! I'm sick of the whole goddamn thing, the lot of you. Leonard wants to name his new stink after you, great with me. How 'propriate. I'm giving the goddamn account to Charley. You can deal with him. I've had it."

"I'm not dealing with anybody," she exclaimed. "I haven't heard any more about it. Why does it worry you so?"

"It doesn't worry me, Belle. I don't care. But you'll be hearing from him, don't worry. Shit!" Miserable, leaning against the wall and holding his hand, he groaned, "I'm weary, Belle, very very weary of everything."

His eyes, unfocused, were so vulnerable and forlorn that for a second she was shocked.

"Martin! Jesus, what's wrong with you?"

His expression was blank, as though he had forgotten where he was, who she was. Then, saying no more, he turned into the hall, toward the bar in the library. Next, she heard the clinking of glasses, bottles, ice. Then there was silence. She knew he was sitting at the bar. There was the rasping of a match as he lit a cigarette.

Susan got home from the graduation dance a half-hour later. She was saying good-night to her date. The front door opened softly. Belle put her head back, pretending she'd fallen asleep. Susan tiptoed into the room and put a hand to Belle's cheek. She opened her eyes.

"Sorry," Susan said, "I'm a little late."

Belle put her finger to her lips, drew Susan's head down,

and whispered, "Go upstairs quietly. He's in a terrible mood. Lock your door."

She added the last advice unwillingly, but it had to be said.

Susan nodded. "I always do."

"Oh . . . I see. Tomorrow morning, we'll get you off early for Trancas." When Susan had gone, Belle went down the hall. She saw the glow of a cigarette in the dark.

"Martin . . . "

"Belle, leave me alone, will you?"

"Are you all right?"

Again, there was a brooding silence. Then his voice crackled, "Sure, I'm all right. What the hell do you think? No thanks to you. Leave me alone."

"All right," Belle said, her voice hushed. It was perhaps appropriate that she projected her next statement into the darkness. "I am going to leave you, Martin."

But he was too engrossed in himself to catch the meaning.

"Good," he said.

Chapter Ten

Out of deference to Archy and Lou Finistere, Belle chose the Beverly Camino Hotel for the first luncheon meeting of the inner committee to organize the December ball. There would be a dozen women, more or less, and only two men: Kaplan and Sally's doctor, Tom Glenn.

Belle was waiting for Sally in the lobby when she arrived with Susan, and together they went upstairs to the Acapulco Room, a small dining room that would assure them privacy.

Lou Finistere was already there, fussing around. She was inordinately proud to be part of the inner core and obviously determined to do her best. She was wearing what looked to be a new dress and her heavy brown-red hair was brushed to a luster.

Lou's first question was, "Should we have place cards? I didn't think to ask you."

Sally nodded. "Best have them. Otherwise, they'll be scrambling all over themselves for position."

"Okay, I've got cards right here. I'll just write in the names . . . Sally at one end of the table, Belle at the other. Mrs. Chandler? On Sally's right?"

It was done in a few minutes.

Susan looked around anxiously and said, "Look, I'm not supposed to stay, am I?"

"No, dear," Belle said.

"Good. I'm taking off then. I'll walk around Rodeo Drive for a while, then I'll have a sandwich downstairs. I'll be waiting for you," she said to Sally. "Bye," she told her mother.

Susan flounced away, long and swaying in a calf-length granny dress. She was uncommonly pretty and already well on the way to physical maturity. Susan was not quite as tall as Belle, but her legs seemed impossibly long. Blonde hair, a thick mop of it, hung to the small of her back, gripped at shoulder level by a rubber band. She was perfect, Belle thought.

At her side, Sally murmured, "She's a hell of a girl, kiddo."

"I know. But is she a pain in the neck?"

"No, not at all. She's good to have around. Bernard never gets home 'til late, the bastard. Nothing but work, work, work."

"Why don't you two go away somewhere?"

Sally shook her head. "Can't go away now. Getting treatments three times a week. Susan," she murmured, seeing Belle wondered how much Susan knew, "Susan thinks I've got a bad gastritis—which I do, in a way."

Hesitantly, Belle asked, "How's it going?"

Sally merely shrugged. "How's it going with you?"

"The same," Belle said. "Terrible. Sometimes," she paused and took a deep breath, "I think he's headed for some kind of nervous breakdown."

Sally scowled. "Bullshit! Just don't get wishy-washy

about him. He's past worrying over. It's that phony business of his. It's getting to him. He's beginning to believe all the bullshit."

"But Charley Hopper isn't that way," Belle objected. "Charley Hopper is a different kind of guy."

Lou interrupted their quiet exchange, apologizing, asking if there was anything else to be done. Sally handed her a Tiffany shopping bag. "There's little gifties in here, Lou. Be a doll and put one at each table setting, will you?"

Pat Hyman arrived first, with Sharon Peters. Sharon was a widow who, through the sudden death of a rather elderly husband, had become principal owner of one of the nation's biggest trucking firms. But she seldom visited the firm's Midwest headquarters, preferring to remain far away from industrial strife and in the California sunshine. Sharon was a chunkily built brunette in her mid-thirties. Her face was clever, the eyes widely candid and intelligent.

When Bertha Moore entered the Acapulco Room, Sharon turned deliberately and made for a waiter carrying a tray of wine. Sally had warned Belle about the potential of this personality conflict. At one time, still new to widowhood, Sharon had allowed herself to become attached to Sheldon Moore. But Bertha had discovered them and had quickly put a stop to it.

Bertha looked around the room, smiling maliciously. But to Sally, she was positively respectful. "Sally, it is nice to see you."

They kissed in midair, not touching. The study of kissing patterns would have been an interesting one, Belle suddenly thought: some touched fleetingly on the cheek; some kissed vigorously, daringly, lip to lip; others, such as Sally, didn't care for the physical contact, thus kissed space.

The former Cabinet member's daughter, Camilla Young, was next to arrive, a solitary figure, forlorn. She looked out of place, trying for a schoolgirlish youthfulness but not making it. She was dressed in a pleated white skirt and navy blazer, but somehow looked sloppy. Belle spotted a red stain at the bottom of the skirt. Camilla ordered a gin and tonic and said her hellos in a low voice, then glumly inspected the table to see where she'd be sitting.

Maude Mannon, who had friends all over the country, had flown in from Houston for the luncheon. She was staying at the Camino and had obviously taken her jewelry out of the hotel safe for the occasion. She entered the room with a clatter of baubles. Maude dressed to the hilt day and night. It was said she wore her pearls even in the swimming pool. Her face was highly powdered, the skin drawn tight at the corners of her eyes and mouth. Her money was in oil, pipelines, and ranchland, and had been providing her with the wherewithal for the good life for all of her sixty-odd years.

"Hi, ever-boddy," Maude sang out boldly, for she would never be fazed entering a room. "How's ever-boddy today?"

"Maude!" Sally said warmly, "it's marvelous to have you here."

"Marvelous to be heah, darlin'. What's the occasion?"

"Aha!" Sally cried, "we'll get to that."

Sally was looking better today. Rampant, almost uncontrollable energy had returned to her and she was in a vivacious mood. What Sally had said was true: the project itself was a restorative.

Norman Kaplan arrived in decorous haste. He was wearing a crisp white suit, which de-emphasized his pot belly, and a carnation in his lapel. He beamed a smile for everyone, uttering swift expressions of delight as he went from one woman to the next.

Another out-of-towner, Shiela Brown from San Francisco, was a banker's wife, long-bodied and awkward, flat-chested, but with the saving grace of a face that habitually, at the slightest provocation, broke into unexpected laughter so genuine no one could ever suspect her of putting it on. She was also one of Belle's best friends. They fell into each other's arms.

"Belle, you look swell."

"How're the children, Shiela?"

"They're fine. I suppose you had a graduation, too. What's Susan going to do?"

Kaplan had joined them. He put his left arm around Belle's waist.

"Well," Belle said, "she's going to Princeton in the fall."

She turned her head to kiss Kaplan's cheek—her acceptance of his offer.

"That's right," he said, "I need a new date for the East Coast."

Mrs. Chandler, queen-mother of the *Los Angeles Times*, had still not appeared when Carlotta Westmoreland bustled in. Carlotta, short and dumpy with white hair and a cherubic face, was a mainstay of the city, an old-time Californian, and publisher of the city's other newspaper, the *Los Angeles Record*. They had placed Carlotta on Belle's right, in the spot equivalent to that reserved for Mrs. Chandler, next to Sally.

Tom Glenn was close on Carlotta's heels. Glenn was the favorite local internist, a thin, stooped, harassed-looking man with a thin face and thick white hair. He wore thick glasses through which he peered like an anxious bird. As Kaplan's voice was high-pitched and excitable, Glenn's was so soft it was difficult to hear what he said. By the look of him, one suspected Glenn suffered much, perhaps more than his patients.

As Belle was somberly saying hello to Glenn, a tall, erratically articulated man rushed into the room.

"Excuse me, please," he said to Belle, "I am looking for Mrs. Finistere. Ah, there she is. Excuse me, please," he apologized again. "I am Jurgen Ehrlich, new banquet manager of the Beverly Camino Hotel. I trust everything is perfect."

"Oh, yes . . . yes," Belle said, somewhat startled by the burst of accented English, "Mr. . . ."

"Ehrlich, madame, Jurgen Ehrlich."

He bowed stiffly and hastened across to Lou Finistere, mumbling something in her ear. Lou nodded, then curtly dismissed him. Bowing rapidly again at the various women, Ehrlich humbly exited the room.

Lou edged up to Sally. "A phone call from Mrs. Chandler's office. She's not able to make it today."

"Hell," Sally said, "if it's not something to aid the Music Center, she doesn't want to know."

"Don't worry," Kaplan said, "the paper will be interested."

Overhearing, Carlotta Westmoreland sharply said, "My opposition is not going to be here?"

"It seems she can't make it," Belle said.

"Okay. Good," Carlotta snapped, "we'll take the exclusive—whatever it's all about."

"That, my dear Carlotta, you'll soon find out," Kaplan squealed. "Sally, shall we sit down now?" She nodded, and Kaplan banged his glass with a spoon. "Ladies . . . ladies, please to take your places."

The Acapulco Room had been nicely decorated in a low-key manner. Three baskets of spring flowers sufficed for the long table. Bouquets had been placed along the walls. Lou had put a Laykin et Cie jewelry box at the place settings, as Sally had requested, each tied with a small white ribbon.

"Ladies, ladies," Kaplan called for their attention. He had moved into Mrs. Chandler's spot next to Sally. "Kindly tell the waiter what you'd like to drink. We're offering champagne and a superior white bordeaux . . . or whatever you like."

Martin, Belle remembered, had always said more could be discovered about a personality by a person's drink preferences than by handwriting analysis, and Belle agreed now there was something to the theory. Camilla Young switched from gin and tonic to champagne. Maude Mannon crisply ordered a scotch and water. Sharon Peters stayed with wine, while Tom Glenn, on her left, shook his white head sorrowfully and said he'd have a Perrier. Carlotta Westmoreland, in *Front Page* character, wanted a whiskey straight, no rocks, no water. Belle and Sheila, whom she had placed on her left, ordered champagne; then Belle changed her mind, thinking what-the-hell, and asked for a Kronenbourg beer. Bertha Moore joined Glenn in Perrier, and Pat Hyman continued with white wine, as did Lou Finistere. Sally ordered a double gin martini with a twist, and Kaplan, predictably, took champagne, rolling it lovingly in his mouth.

For the first course there was cold cucumber soup or smoked salmon, and the main course was a multiple choice: roast beef, thinly sliced, or grilled white fish with mustard sauce, or a skimpy diet salad.

When they'd finished with the waiters, Sally lifted her glass.

"Hello to everybody and thanks for coming. This is a woman's affair, but we've called in two men experts for reasons that will soon be apparent. Bon appetit!"

After the first course was served and consumed, a few lit cigarettes, much to Glenn's disapproval, and Sally addressed them again.

"Now," she said, very much in command, "I'd like you all to open the little boxes in front of your plates. Party favors, but with a message."

Belle hadn't any idea what was inside the box but, opening it like the others, she found nestled in a wad of cotton batten a silver, heart-shaped pin upon which had been inscribed "December Group."

"Beautiful, Sally," Carlotta said, "but what does it mean?"

Sally smiled. "It means that you are all charter members of a group that is going to organize the most important benefit since we all helped build Cedars-Sinai Medical Center."

"Which is?" Bertha Moore demanded.

"Which is that *we*," Sally explained, ignoring Bertha's scowl, her natural expression, "are going to build the first medical and research center devoted exclusively to study and treatment of the various forms of *women's* cancer. December means we're going to organize a benefit ball in December—what we actually call it depends on you—to raise the seed money."

Carlotta Westmoreland, to whom they all deferred in the matter of age and judgment, nodded vigorously. Her eyes lit approvingly. She leaned forward to have a nip of her straight bourbon, her cheeks growing appreciably ruddier.

"Yes," she said, "I like it. I like it very much. I can back that, something for the women. The men have had it their way long enough, with their livers and prostates."

Tom Glenn chuckled quietly behind his hand.

"Now, Dr. Glenn," Sally went on, "can it be done, and is it worth doing?"

Glenn nodded soberly. "Of course. The answer is yes on both counts. And it's long overdue."

"Mr. Norman Kaplan?"

"Definitely affirmative," Kaplan exclaimed.

Kaplan then put forward his own plan to make the present first lady and all former first ladies honorary sponsors of the event.

"Maude," Kaplan said, "I'll need your help in Texas. I know you're a friend of the mighty."

"I am," Maude agreed, but a little doubtfully. "I just wonder, Dr. Glenn, I can't believe there's not already a center for these ailments."

"Dr. Glenn, take the floor," Kaplan said.

Glenn nodded. "Sally's right. Specifically, there isn't any one center combining clinical treatment and research in women's cancer per se. I don't want to sound flip about this, but women *are* entirely different from men, at least in the hormone makeup of the body. Yes, Maude, of course there are specialists in all the big hospitals, and there are cancer research centers. But do you have any conception of the magnitude of women's cancer in this country: uterus, cervix, ovary, not to mention breast cancer? Each form is treated differently. We have medical oncologists who specialize in breast cancer, then gynecologic oncologists who work on the gynecological forms. But what we're saying is that the expertise, if you will, in these various fields has never been gathered in one place. The reasoning is that a woman can suffer breast cancer and seemingly recover. But a recurrence, God, as much as thirty or forty years later, can bring it back in other parts of the body, at which point it's no longer breast cancer per se but must be treated as breast cancer because the original virus is of the breast cancer variety. It's a matter demanding ongoing study and treatment, and that's the advantage of having all the cancer disciplines gathered in one place—to track the problem, treat it, or catch it before it's too late. Plus, I would hope we could do considerable work in endocrinology, that is the study of hormone balance as it interacts with the disease. I don't want to talk too long. But I assure you this is something well worth doing, well worth your time and effort."

"I'm sold," Maude said.

"That's what we want to hear," Carlotta barked. "Let's put this thing on the map. We'll be proud to lead the way in Los Angeles. But, Dr. Glenn, I'd like to hear your estimate. How much do you think we'd need to raise?"

Glenn ran his hand through his white hair. "It's not cheap, as you can imagine. The best opinion is that to get a small but effective treatment and research center going would require about sixty million dollars."

"Whew!" Carlotta whistled. "How big would the hospital part be?"

"Not big," Glenn warned. "Probably fewer than 100 beds."

"We're not going to make any sixty million on one party," Bertha Moore said darkly.

"Of course not," Sally snapped. "But we will get the ball rolling. I'm hoping we can raise two and a half on this pop. Then we'll go ahead. We'll go to the national foundations for more. We can get started."

"Sounds like a very long shot," Bertha objected again.

"Please," Kaplan interrupted. "Let's not get discouraged before we even start. We can do it! Think big!"

Pat Hyman, puffing on one of her long cigarettes, observed, "No question about that. I'm convinced, too. Let me ask a petty question: Do you think our First Ladies are going to want honorariums? Some of these women have got agents by now. Some of them wouldn't go to the opening of a can unless they get paid for it."

"No honorariums," Sally decreed.

"Right," Carlotta said. "They even have the nerve to ask and we'll tear 'em apart in the newspaper."

Sharon Peters sighed, "Trouble is, there's not much time between June and December."

"Time!" Bertha Moore snapped, glaring at Sharon. "What's to arrange? You get the First Ladies, we've got the hotel. What the hell else?"

Murmuring, Sharon said, "I'm thinking of all the incidentals. Have you ever worked on one of these things, Mrs. Moore?"

"Yes, it so happens I have!"

Kaplan raised his hand and said soothingly, "Now, ladies, let's not bicker over whether we have time. That's a non-question, because we've decided to do it." Bertha blushed and Sharon retreated sulkily. Kaplan continued, "As to decor, one of the incidentals I have in mind is blackmailing Marcello Zavier, the New York decorator. I know he's had plenty of commissions out here, for instance from you," he pointed at Bertha Moore, "and if he ever wants another, he'll go along with us."

This was thought to be an excellent idea and Bertha agreed she'd join with Kaplan in lowering the boom on Zavier.

"Flowers, and we'll need tons of them," Kaplan went on. "I know you all have your favorite florists, but none of them are going to supply flowers for nothing. They might just do it for cost. I think we've got to recruit somebody to subsidize the flowers and greenery. You've got to remember the Splendide won't have elaborate landscaping in by then."

Lou Finistere listened raptly. Belle suspected this was her introduction to big-party planning. "We could get them to rush in the trees and grass," she suggested.

So far, it had not been hinted at even obliquely that Archy Finistere would be moving to the Splendide, and Kaplan gave no indication now that this was to happen. "Not so easy, my dear," he said, shaking his head. "If you've got an army of men carrying and hauling, no man in his right mind is going to put in flowerbeds to get trampled to death."

Sally grinned. "Would any of the ladies present like to foot the bill for the flowers?"

"Well," said Maude Mannon, "out of my great respect for Dr. Glenn, I'd like to. But I'd have to ask my husband. See, I hope to be married again by December."

Sally guffawed and Pat Hyman drolly suggested, "Why not get Darling Higgins? She likes grass."

Carlotta Westmoreland sputtered ferociously. She was up on the latest terms.

"The menu we'll leave until much later," Kaplan continued. "For this, we can count, I'm sure, on my friends who've invested so heavily in the new hotel. It's to their advantage that this ball take place at the Splendide."

Belle debated whether to tell them about Sam Leonard and her hopes for backing from Cosmos Cosmetics. No, best hold off on that. She didn't know what was going to happen and she'd heard absolutely nothing more from Leonard, or from Charley Hopper here in Los Angeles.

"Party favors, those little doo-dads," Kaplan said, "that's never a huge problem."

"No," Belle said quietly, "I don't think we have to worry about that."

"Entertainment," Pat Hyman murmured, "I think I can help there."

"Yes, yes," Sally said. "Also, Pat, we're going to rely on you to coordinate the whole Hollywood aspect of this. You're Missus Show Biz. The rest of us don't know diddly about it. How much do you think we can count on the big studios—for celebrities, entertainment . . . money? It'd be to their advantage, too—very good P.R."

"Don't worry," Pat said. "I'll take care of that. Just to begin, I'll get in touch with Rolly Starr. You all know him—Mr. Super Agent. Belle, you can help there, too. C.A.A. has got lots of clout."

She nodded, thinking of Cooper. How much could she count on him?

Shiela Brown piped up, "I've got San Francisco in the palm of my hand. I'll bring you . . . how many do you want? How many couples?"

"We'll get to that in a minute," Sally said.

"No, no, I already know what I'm going to do," Shiela

yelped. "I'll bring down an Amtrak-carload the day before, with a band, booze . . ."

Maude Mannon said, "Texas is mine. Like Shiela, just tell me how many you want, what size and what bankroll."

Kaplan nodded, beaming. "And I've got the East Coast."

Severely, Sally said, "Shut up for a minute, Norman. When you say East Coast, how far west does that come? Chicago?"

"Sure, Chicago. Then we'll get some out of Arizona, Colorado . . . Ladies, I tell you, they'll be knocking down the doors for tickets. I plan to give my friend Suzy—in the *New York Daily News*, you know—a preliminary story when I get back to New York. Once she mentions it, *pas de probleme*!"

"Wait a minute, buster," Carlotta said, raising her hand peremptorily. "Since Mrs. C. is not here, the *Record* gets first cracks, *then* Suzy. After all, this does happen to be a West Coast story first."

Kaplan laughed a shrill staccato. "Madame Westmoreland, you are absolutely right. But keep me advised. I want Suzy to have it in New York the very next day after you . . ."

"Done. I'll call you, or Belle will call you."

Camilla Young slowly asked, "What about the Europeans? Should they be in on this?"

"Sure," Kaplan shrugged, "if they want to be. But, one thing, we are not paying freight for that Beautiful People Club in Paris. If they want to come, they buy their own tickets, pay for their hotel rooms and all other expenses." Looking around, Kaplan explained what to him was obviously a basic fact of life. "A lot of times, people who want to boost a big charity pay for these people to come—Duchess and Duke or Prince this-and-that, charity mercenaries, I call them, to add luster and get better press coverage. We won't need anything like that. If we get what we want, *pas de probleme*," he repeated.

"I certainly agree to that," Carlotta said acidly. "We don't need a bunch of freeloaders in our city."

Camilla nodded, chastened. It was not that Kaplan had put her down, he had merely roughed up her suggestion.

Sally spoke again. "I'd like us to give some sort of research award that night. I suggest Dr. Glenn give this his attention. It should be a money award for research achievement in the cancer field, and I think it should be repeated every year." She paused, significantly, then added, "I do hope you all understand you're committing yourself to an annual ball. Tom?"

"Certainly, certainly," Glenn whispered.

God, Belle thought, he looked worse than any of his patients, certainly more sickly and run-down than Sally, whose cheeks were flushed with pleasure and excitement that it was going so well.

"What are we going to call this party?" Bertha Moore asked sourly.

Meekly, Lou Finistere said, "What about Splendide Affaire, with an 'e' on 'affair'?"

Sally nodded, but Pat Hyman drawled, "Sounds like a dirty weekend."

Glenn looked amused. "How much money did you have in mind for the award?" he asked.

"I don't know," Sally replied. "I was hoping for something like ten grand, tax paid."

Maude Mannon said, "Seems about right for a good man."

They all chuckled. Then Sharon Peters posed the question that should have been uppermost in their minds.

"Sally, how many people are we going to have? And what's it going to cost them?"

"Well," Sally said, "that's the question. We've been thinking we'd shoot for 2,000 people. That's 1,000 couples—a tall order. The Blue Ribbon 1,000."

"Wow!" Shiela Brown exclaimed, "you're talking big money just for food at fifty a head—and that's not much these days."

"I know, I know," Sally said impatiently. "But I'm not worried about the price of the food. Norman is taking care of that." Sally stopped and breathed deeply. "The price of tickets. I think that should be at least $2,000 a couple, so that with luck and the right kind of help, we should be able to clear several million dollars. We've got to clear at least a million. Otherwise, it's not worth talking about."

Camilla Young muttered, "Two thousand a couple is not much these days."

"No, that's true," Sally said. "But on the other hand, we don't want to scare them away. I keep thinking of Cedars-Sinai—look how much they've raised over the years. Hell, millions."

Bertha Moore said sensibly, "A million would go just for the land."

"That," Sally said spiritedly, "we don't have to worry about. The land is taken care of, along with plans for the buildings."

"Where'd it come from?" Bertha demanded, her eyes narrowed.

"It was donated," Sally said coolly, "and I can't tell you by whom—but only on condition we go ahead with the rest of the money-raising."

"But who is this generous patron?" Bertha insisted on knowing.

It was Glenn who took it upon himself to answer her. Gently, he said, "The donor is someone who has a special interest in the matter, but who prefers to remain absolutely anonymous."

Bertha wasn't satisfied, but she would get no more information. Sally was determined to keep her secret. The others were impressed, for it gave what was a still vague scheme a legitimacy against which there could be no argument.

"We should charge more," Sharon Peters said. "I agree with Camilla. Why not $5,000 a couple? What the hell, it's a write off."

Kaplan shook his head. "I think that's just too much, too greedy. I can see $2,500. Not five."

"What about testing the water at $2,500?" Maude asked.

Sally slowly agreed, and Carlotta Westmoreland took advantage of the moment of silence to order another whiskey. Then she said, "Ladies . . . and gentlemen, I'm having a little trouble with this. Those kind of prices you're talking put a deal like this out of the reach of all but a few of our readers."

"Carlotta," Kaplan said superciliously, "was it ever not so?"

Sharply, she glanced down the table. "Don't be fatuous, Norman," she chided, bringing Kaplan to a blush. "It's not an easy thing in the presentation. A lot of my minorities get really spooked when they read about the high life of the beautiful people."

"Spooked! A good word," Bertha snorted.

Then she suffered Carlotta's reprimand. "We don't say things like that anymore, Mrs. Moore."

"I'm sorry. I didn't mean . . . I wasn't being serious."

"Never mind," Carlotta cut her off. "Now then, I'm trying to explain something to you, if you'll listen. Obviously this new center is going to benefit the entire community."

"Absolutely," Sally said.

"Well, then, people do understand a lot of money has to be raised for something as ambitious as this—and I can explain that. But you know, there's something I want to impress on you: the have-nots, or those on modest wages, or on the borderline, are never asked to contribute. Don't you think they'd like to?"

Sally slowly nodded. "I would hope so. But how do we go about it?"

Carlotta mused, "I'm thinking of doing something in the paper . . . at least a contribution blank they can fill out, send in, whatever they like. Maybe next year, some kind of a big clambake with entertainment that'd cost a much more modest five bucks a head."

"Carlotta, that would be marvelous," Sally said. "I have to admit I hadn't thought about that aspect of it."

"One other thing, while I've got the floor," Carlotta said. "A black or two on the committee perhaps? A Chicano?"

Sally grinned. "I did think of that."

Murmuring, Kaplan said, "*Dieu*. I wonder, won't your minority groups be, as they say, P.O.'ed that we're eating cake while they're eating hot dogs?"

Carlotta smacked a plump, pink hand on the table, a purely boardroom gesture. "No! What the hell, Norman, most of them would be deadly bored at your party. And you've got to remember something—women's cancer is very prevalent downtown. They just don't know what the hell it is and they get pushed around by the doctors in the free clinics—excuse me, Dr. Glenn . . ." Glenn woefully nodded. "Sometimes I wonder about you people," Carlotta went on bitingly. "It's you who think in terms of the upper and lower classes. They don't. They may be jealous of your money, but they're not jealous of you. All I'm saying is we should put two and two together and get four million or eight million instead of half that amount."

Norman laughed gleefully, blowing a kiss in Carlotta's direction. "My word, we've just been subjected to a class diatribe. Been properly deflated, too."

Carlotta, fortunately, did not take him seriously. "Norman, you are a fatuous ass," she exclaimed, but she was smiling.

"My, my, now I'm a fatuous *ass*," Kaplan said, clutching his bosom in mock despair.

Sally put her right hand on his arm. "Shut up, Norman. Well, now then, it looks like we've bitten off a lot. I hope we can chew it. My head is swimming."

"We can handle it, kiddo," Belle spoke up.

"Yes, yes. The committee has got to be expanded, that's obvious," Sally said hurriedly. "Think of others who would like to help. Also, if you would, begin drawing up lists of people you think should be invited. And—my God, and this is fairly urgent—somebody's got to design the invitations and the program."

"We'll get Marcia King," Belle interrupted her, thinking Sally was suddenly looking tired. "You all know her, the decorating studio on Robertson."

"Marjery Cannon and Daisy Cox," Pat Hyman said, "those two will work . . . And our friend Darling Higgins."

"And a few of the young-marrieds, like Priscilla Murray," Sally added. "We need some slaves for the leg work. I suppose the lot of you are going to be away over the Fourth of July weekend. Then vacations. Let's get the expanded committee together again at the end of July."

Chapter Eleven

Sheldon Moore was parked alongside the hotel, waiting for Bertha, when Camilla Young came out.

The others had lingered to chat. But Camilla had had to get away. It wasn't that the thing had bored her. She was just not up to being a part of it. She'd already determined she'd bow out of the committee.

"Hello, Camilla," he said, poking his head out the window of his car.

"Oh, hello, Sheldon."

"You're looking rather splendid today, Camilla."

"No, I'm not," she replied, tight-lipped. "I look like hell."

"I wouldn't say that," Sheldon said softly.

Sheldon was wearing a tweed jacket, tattersall shirt, and a brown tie. He was a sad-looking man with thinning hair and a large nose.

"How are *you*, Sheldon?"

"Rotten," he said. "How about you?"

"Double rotten. It takes a while, I guess, to get over things."

"What are you doing right now?"

"Going home, what else?"

"Want to drive out to the beach?" he asked, suddenly alert.

She shook her head. He was joking of course. "You're waiting for Bertha!"

"She can take a cab home."

Camilla was surprised. "That's not like you, Sheldon."

"Come on, get in. Let's go. I mean it—before she comes down."

"God," she said, "she'll kill you, Sheldon."

She remembered vaguely what had happened over Sheldon's brief fling with Sharon Peters.

"Well," he said, smiling, "she can't do any worse than that, can she?"

Tom Glenn appeared at the lobby entrance just as Camilla Young and Sheldon Moore drove off in Sheldon's brown Mercedes convertible. They hadn't seen him. He stood silently, considering this remarkable matter, and was still lingering on the steps as Bertha Moore joined him.

"Well," she said grumpily, "that was some lunch, wasn't it, doctor?"

"Very interesting indeed," Glenn replied softly. "I'm always amazed at the energy you women have."

"Sally's the one with the energy," she said admiringly. "Now . . . where is Sheldon? He promised he'd be here to pick me up."

Glenn shook his head miserably. "Probably delayed in the traffic. Always bad along here this time of the day.

Well, I must be going. It was so nice to see you, Bertha."

He shook her hand limply, and as he was turning away to leave, they were interrupted by the tall man who'd come into the dining room at the outset of their meeting.

Bowing, the man spoke politely. "Ah, your luncheon was a success, I hope. My name is Jurgen Ehrlich. I am the new banquet manager at the Beverly Camino Hotel."

Ehrlich kissed Bertha Moore's knuckles and shook Glenn's hand.

"Well, are you enjoying Los Angeles, Herr Ehrlich?" Glenn asked haltingly. "You come from . . ."

"Switzerland, sir," Ehrlich replied promptly. "I was with the Vierjahrezeiten in Zurich. Yes, yes, Los Angeles is a wonderful place . . . Blue skies and the sun. I am so happy indeed to be here. Also to be working with Mr. Finistere."

"Quite a change, isn't it?" Bertha demanded.

"Oh, yes, a very big change."

Ehrlich was as tall as Bertha, and just as cadaverously skinny.

"Good luck to you," Glenn said, and then he did leave for his office.

Pat Hyman could not wait to tell Daisy Cox about the luncheon. She was on her way to her health club for a massage but called the Cox number from downstairs.

Daisy answered the phone in a breathless voice.

"Darling, did I wake you . . . or what?" Pat asked impishly.

"What," Daisy said.

"Well, darling, the luncheon was fabulous. You're going to be on the committee."

"What committee, for pete's sake?" Daisy asked, irritated.

"For a big benefit in December. Sally Markman and Belle Cooper are organizing it. There's another meeting next month and you're going to be invited," Pat told her. "Back to sleepy-byes, darling."

"Thanks, sweetheart," Daisy said. "Bye . . . "

Daisy rolled away from the telephone, laughing. "Your wife is putting on a big charity thing in December," she told Martin Cooper. "But as far as I'm concerned, this is the only charity benefit I'm interested in, right here."

"Daisy," Cooper said, glowing, "you're really a sketch."

Daisy had a figure the likes of which one did not often

see, full and soft, voluptuous but not sloppy, firm but not harshly muscled like Pamela's. The breasts, as she lay beside him on the bed, were round and smooth, topped with rust-colored nipples, the belly rounded and the thighs wiltingly tender.

The phone call had interrupted them and now they resumed. Cooper put his arms around her, his hands on her chubby buttocks. She squirmed against him, and as he ran his fingers between her legs to grasp the lips of her vagina, she began to pant loudly. She moved frantically to grip him with both hands, then, kneeling beside him, she took him in her mouth, her long blonde hair tracing caressingly across his belly and thighs. She brought him close to blowout, then, sensing it, stopped, flopped around so that he was behind her. Smoothly, with one long motion, he slipped inside her, holding her at the waist and rocking. She began to cry out, pounding the mattress with both fists and then coming with a terrific rush of passion. Cooper thrust cruelly, making her yell hoarsely, and then ejaculated himself. Still inside her, he leaned on her back, her breasts in his hands.

"Jesus Christ," she muttered, "is that all?"

"All! Give me a second or two, will you?"

She wriggled away from him, giggling, and pushed him over on his back. From the bedside table, she got a tissue and wiped him off, then went down on him again, chewing his rod, mouthing the bulb of his penis. He stuck his fingers into her sopping muff and found the clitoris, working it roughly until she jerked in another, but more minor, orgasm. Still, this was not enough for her. She tongued and hammered at him until she had renewed his erection and then took him on top of her, whining and urging him on. In seconds, she erupted into another quick flurry of orgasmic activity, then seemed somewhat assuaged. It was not in Cooper's power to come again so soon. Finally, he simply stopped.

"Christ, Daisy, you're beautiful."

"What? Beautiful-beautiful? Or a beautiful fuck?"

"Both," he said. He kissed her full lips, tasting sex, her earlobes, and mouthed the flaccid nipples. It was time for him to leave. "Daisy, I've got to get back to the office. When can I see you again?"

"Any afternoon. I'll cancel a lunch any time you ask," she said. "Martin, would you say I'm sex-mad?"

He didn't know exactly how to reply. "You seem to like it okay."

"A nymphomaniac?"

"No. Why would you say that?"

"Marty," she said, using the abbreviated nickname he disliked so much, "do you like it when I suck you off?"

"I have to tell you it's very pleasurable indeed," Cooper said, grinning. He was getting into his clothes, thinking he'd have a shower at the office later in the afternoon. There was one thing he wanted to clear up. "I wish we could meet somewhere else. I don't much like visiting women in their homes. What about that dame downstairs? Do you trust her so much?"

"Flora? She's mine. She's been with me forever. She wouldn't say a word."

"All right, what about the electronics genius? Doesn't he ever come home early in the afternoon? That could be embarrassing, you know. Very embarrassing."

Daisy smiled at him, licking her lips. "Jake never, never comes home in the afternoon," she said cheerfully. "So what anyway? You could always slide down the bougainvillea, except you might rip up that dingdong of yours." She turned on her side to look at him, her breasts pillowed on her soft arm, one leg thrown over the other. "Marty, did anybody ever tell you you've got the biggest schlang in town?"

Cooper laughed heartily. "Daisy, you're funny. Do you think I do? How would you know, though? Old married lady like you?"

Daisy frowned. "Old married lady, my ass. I know a woman keeps pictures of all the ones she's had. I think you'd win the prize. Let's have a little feel before you go."

He was pulling up his tie. He walked to the side of the bed. Daisy put her hands under his boxer shorts.

"Daisy . . . Daisy," he said, "I do have to go."

"Marty," she said in a low voice, "that was really very good. I hope I didn't sound too impatient."

He was wavering, holding his pants in his hand. "Daisy, we could try for a weekend away sometime. Could you get away to Vegas with me?"

She made a face. "Vegas! Balls! Besides, Jakes wouldn't stand for it."

"I better go."

"It's only three," she urged. "One more time. I don't

have to get up 'til 3:30. The pool man is coming, and there's some work I want him to do."

Cooper stooped to kiss her pouty lips and ran his hand across her breasts to her crotch.

"Marty," she warned him, "Marty . . ."

An hour later, Cooper whipped his Jensen into the parking space at the big advertising building on Sunset and dog-trotted across the garage to the elevator. Christ, he was feeling good, strong, vital. He'd managed another shot into Daisy. Who said the old juices were giving out? She was a hell of a girl, some lay.

Upstairs, there were a half-dozen phone messages for him, and a note from Charley Hopper. "Something to discuss," it read.

He got Charley on the intercom. "What is it, Charley?"

"Sam Leonard called at one. He wants you and Belle to fly over to France with him for the Fourth holiday, spend a couple of days on his boat."

Oh, shit, he thought, that was out of the question. Not now . . .

"A command performance," he said angrily.

"Wait a minute," Hopper said. "I'm coming over."

In a moment, Charley came into Cooper's office and threw his gangly frame into an easy chair at the side of the desk.

"Sam wants to talk to you about the campaign. You'll have to take all the first-draft artwork with you."

"Goddamn it, Charley," he said, very annoyed, "this is your show now. Why don't you go?"

"Don't fancy a ritzy week in Cannes? He asked for you, Mart."

"And Belle," Cooper said darkly. "I suppose he's made up his mind about that?"

"Yeah, he's certain now. He wants to call it 'Belle.' "

"And you couldn't talk him out of it? Jesus!"

"I didn't try very hard," Hopper admitted, his long face grinning.

What was Charley thinking? Charley was quick and very sharp.

"So you think it's a good name for a line of cosmetics, do you, Charley?"

"Yeah, as a matter of fact, I think it's very good the more I think about it."

"Christ," Cooper said disgustedly, "all the little cookies

will be rubbing 'Belle' vanishing cream between their legs to get rid of freckles and God knows what else."

Uneasily, embarrassedly, Charley said, "Don't put it like that, Mart."

Cooper laughed loudly. "Offend your sensibility, Charley? Shit! You go. You like the name, you go! I thought Sam knew you were handling it now."

"He wants Belle there," Hopper said distantly.

"Well, then, goddamn it, *you* take Belle to Cannes, Charley."

Hopper stood up and put his hands on the edge of the desk, his face lowered to look at Cooper.

"Mart, why are you dodging this thing? What's the big deal? It'd be a nice break for you—and I think you need a break. You look like shit."

How, Cooper thought furiously, was that possible when he was feeling so good? He wanted more of Daisy. Hopper stared insistently at him, making him feel uncomfortable. Goddamn it, what right did Charley have to hound him? At the same time, he was thinking how much his relationship with Charley had deteriorated, like everything else.

Face flushed, he finally exclaimed, "Maybe I don't want to take Belle over there, did you ever think of that? Maybe I don't want to take Belle anywhere. Did you ever consider that?"

"I'm beginning to," Charley said slowly. "I'm beginning to see that something's wrong. What the hell is going on, Mart?"

Hopper's voice was sympathetic, Cooper judged, as it should be. Whatever the present strain, they were old friends, cronies, the founders of C.A.A.

Grimly, he said, "I don't want to talk about it, Charley. I'm asking you: will you take Belle to France?"

Reluctantly, Hopper nodded. "If that's what you want. If it makes you comfortable. But you'd better tell me what's happening."

"What's it look like's happening, Charley, for Christ's sake?"

"So you're putting me on the spot, Mart."

"Why?" he cried. "Why should that be so? It's a business trip, for Christ's sake. Are you afraid they're going to be saying that good old Charley Hopper is making out with the partner's wife?"

There, he had said it, and to Hopper it was an insulting

suggestion. Charley's face turned red and his mouth closed to a furious crease.

"That's a lousy thing for you to say," Charley said. "Guys get socked for saying things like that."

Cooper smiled. "Want to take a sock at me, Charley? Go ahead. I'll flatten your ass."

For a second, he thought Charley would swing at him, and Cooper almost hoped he would. It would be a pleasure to vent boiling rage on somebody. But Charley backed off.

"All right," he said evenly, "I'll take Belle to France. I like Belle a lot, Mart, and it'll be a pleasure to travel with her."

Smugly, Cooper said, "That's my boy. Maybe you can talk to her, make her understand that old Martin, old Coop, old asshole, is not such a bad guy after all."

"I'm not going to say a fucking word to her," Charley said. "You solve your own problems, buddy-boy."

He laughed. He was very relieved. The long weekend, the Fourth of July. Daisy Cox. Losing track of his thought, he wondered if they'd ever called her Coxsucker. Then the other plan materialized in his mind, as brilliant as any advertising campaign he had ever conceived. If it came to divorce, he would say Belle had cheated on him aboard the *Cosmopolitan* with none other than . . . his best friend, yes, good old Charley Hopper.

Pat Hyman luxuriated under the powerful hands of Boris the Magnificent, a mustachioed masseur from the old country. Pat lay on her stomach on the hard table as Boris pressed, stroked, squeezed through the towel. Her breath was forced out of her by his efforts. Now he was doing her ass, stimulating the buttocks, pushing her pelvis into the table.

"Uh . . . uh . . . uh," she grunted.

In the back of her mind, Pat was wondering who'd been with Daisy when she'd called. The pool boy? No, more likely that stud, Cooper.

Boris was doing the backs of her thighs, his hands working around her asshole, then slipping between her legs down the line of her pussy.

"Uh . . . uh . . . uh," she moaned, forgetting Daisy and Cooper.

Boris had been there before. He flipped up the towel and she felt his moustache on her legs, then his tongue inside her. She commenced to shake, for Boris was a master. He savored her clit to numb ecstasy and she came, came again, her ass heaving against his face. She closed her eyes, succumbed. From the curl of his lips, she knew Boris was smiling.

Sharon Peters had business that afternoon, something to do with the trucking fleet. The president of Peters Transport had flown in from Cleveland in the morning, with him the chief of their labor relations department. There was always some goddamn thing or other to solve with the Teamsters. Christ, she was thinking, it was *bor*-ing, as Pat Hyman had described something over lunch. Didn't she do enough for the company as it was? They had to bother her with every little incidental? After all, who was it who kept tenuous labor peace? None other than Mrs. Owner herself; and that through her close friendship with Morris Mauery, premier labor attorney. And she paid.

Mauery was a lascivious pig, more than she had bargained for when she had married Oscar Peters. Little had she known then that it would in due course be up to her to perform for Morris Mauery in the interests of labor tranquility. Mauery was so accustomed to using and abusing Las Vegas playthings that he'd forgotten how a normal woman behaved. Sharon never ceased to wonder that Madeleine Mauery didn't seem to realize what was going on. Sometimes Sharon even traveled with the Mauerys; they'd made several trips to Europe together, and Mauery never hesitated to leave his sleeping wife for nocturnal visits to Sharon. But Madeleine was over seventy now and very nearly past it. One thing for sure: she slept like a log.

Morris, Sharon thought, was definitely not Mr. Wonderful. It was not very satisfactory, this life of hers. She'd have liked to shake loose of the whole thing. But who was there willing to buy a trucking firm with nothing but problems: rising fuel prices, ever-stickier government regulations, and labor difficulties every step of the way?

Sharon kept a large penthouse apartment in a high-security building on Wilshire Boulevard between Beverly Hills and Westwood and now, having just returned from the Beverly Camino, she'd changed into a faded old pair of jeans and T-shirt and was wandering around her private terrace, taking the sun, feeling it soak into her body. She bent to pick dead leaves from the potted trees, then lit a cigarette, and sat down for a moment in a deckchair to look at the horizon—rather, segments of horizon, since the latter was too frequently interrupted by other high rises to the east and north.

The closest high rise was on the other side of Wilshire and, as Sharon reclined, her eyes half closed, her mind wandering, she suddenly realized there was a man on another terrace across the way. He seemed to be staring directly at her.

He was tall, bearded, wearing sun glasses and a tennis hat, and, she realized with a shock, the briefest of shorts, more like a jock strap than anything else. Did he know that she could see him?

Yes. She raised her head and he waved nonchalantly. Then he did something very surprising. He took off the cap and glasses, put his hands down on the terrace floor, and, in one quick motion, lifted himself into a handstand. He pranced back and forth along the terrace, then straight at the terrace wall. Sharon gasped; she thought he would go over. No, with another swift motion, he propelled himself back to his feet and stood there, grinning. At least, she thought, he must be grinning.

He waved again and idiotically pounded himself on the chest, like Tarzan. Despite herself, knowing better, she lifted her hand and waved back.

Did she know him? She ran through her mind a catalogue of bearded men, but none fit this description. She sat silently, staring at him, fascinated. He was a tall man, very well built, a head smaller in proportion to the rest of him than it should have been. Was he some kind of nut? Was there any way he could figure out her precise location at the top of her high rise? No, she admitted, a little frightened, that wouldn't be too difficult.

Then he waved again and retreated into the dark of the apartment opposite. Christ, she thought, it would be an innovative way to meet a new man.

For some reason—the physicalness of him probably—he reminded her of Martin Cooper, and she wondered how Cooper was making out these days. Belle had looked beautiful at lunch, and Sharon was aware of a pang of guilt as she remembered her brief dalliance with Belle's husband. Belle was such a patrician woman she would never have indicated in any way that she knew about it. The affair with Cooper had happened by accident and had been so short-lived and totally unsatisfactory that it hadn't warranted any sort of fond memory. After only a couple of meetings, Sharon had called it off. He was . . . what? Too aggressive, too much the male chauvinist. He was like Mauery: he did not treat a woman well. Telling him it was quits, she had warned him to forget it, not to pursue her. And Cooper had known she was in touch with Morris Mauery, a man who could promise him great physical harm.

Sharon had not done too badly, though, come to think of it. She'd been Oscar Peters' secretary for five years before the brooding widower had even noticed her. Once he had, they had been married in two months. Financially, she thought, she had not done too badly.

Then Sheldon Moore, of course, married to that hatchet-faced bitch who had been taunting her at lunch. Sheldon was such a kind and gentle man, so put upon, and Sharon had enjoyed their fleeting relationship. But basically, Sheldon was too weak for her—and, in any case, Bertha had frightened him away. Why was he so petrified of Bertha? The money was his, so it was not as if Bertha could cut him off and throw him out, penniless, into the street. Sheldon's money came from an old meat-packing family and it had been invested wisely and well. Sheldon was very generous with the local charities; he had put tons of money into the museum, into the Music Center and into the ambitious but still not well-organized ballet effort.

There was movement again at the terrace door opposite. The mystery man re-emerged. Now he was wearing a three-piece business suit. He waved once more, then disappeared.

Sharon smiled and, somehow, she was disappointed he was gone.

Then she heard the intercom signal from downstairs. Her men were here. She went back inside and put on fresh lipstick and, by the time she reached the split-level living room, her housekeeper, Mrs. Robinson, was letting them in the front door.

"Hi, fellas," Sharon said, still fascinated by the mystery man.

Maude Mannon had taken an after-lunch drink with Norman Kaplan and Sally, then returned to her room upstairs for a nap. But first she had had to call Charley Hopper.

"Hi, there, Texas," she bellowed, when he came on the phone. "It's your old buddy Maude, here."

"Maude! You're in town. How are you?"

"Very good, Charley, as you know. There's nobody better."

"Ah, Maude." He laughed.

"Charley, why don't you take me out to dinner tonight? I'm leavin' in the mawning."

"Maude, have dinner with me tonight."

"Charley, my boy, come over to the Camino 'bout seven. We'll have a few drinks and then go out."

"I'll be there, Maude," he said.

Gawd, Gawd, Maude told herself, old Charley Hopper. She'd known him since he was a boy, just getting started in Dallas. Such a terrific man now, cool, never uptight about anything. And honest, straight as a die. Maude loved Charley Hopper in a maternal sort of way—and, hell, if he'd been a few years older . . . Maybe he was almost old enough now. She wasn't that much older than him in years, maybe ten, not an unacceptable margin these days—and hell, everybody knew spirit counted for a lot.

Jake Cox's chauffeur got him home at 6:30 on the dot, as always. He never missed, traffic or no traffic. Daisy was waiting for him downstairs in the library, mixing his first drink of the evening, a gin martini in a frosted glass. Jake put his briefcase down on the desk.

"Thank you, my dear," he said gravely, putting the glass to his mouth.

Jake was a stringy man with a thin, furrowed face descending to a minor sort of chin and prominent Adam's apple. He had shaved badly that morning, as he usually did: little patches of gray beard bristled along his jawline. He needed a haircut, and his suit was sloppy, unpressed. He was, Daisy told herself, the very caricature of the mad scientist, interested only in theories and equations, caring nothing about his personal appearance. He showered every morning and sometimes in the evening, but nonetheless always gave off the acrid scent of electronic circuitry.

Jake drank half the martini, sighed, and proceeded to his music stand. He lifted a clarinet and commenced to play from sheet music as dog-eared at the corners as he was.

Pausing a second, he muttered, "A Bach fugue, my dear." Then he solemnly continued blowing into the instrument.

Fugue you, too, Daisy thought to herself. She said nothing, gathering her legs under her in her easy chair and drinking from a huge marguerita glass.

Jake performed for a half-hour, consuming one more of her martinis, then led Daisy into the dining room where Flora sullenly served them a steak, rare for Daisy, well done for Jake, a green salad, and a bottle of red wine, most of which Jake had. When he'd finished and wiped his thin lips, he stood and came to Daisy's end of the table.

"Shall we, my dear?" He took her arm and they went upstairs. "Now what do you have for me tonight, my dear?"

"You'll see," she murmured.

Daisy undressed and put on a frilly pink nightgown while Jake occupied himself in his bathroom. When he joined her in the bedroom, he was wearing a floor-length cotton robe with big blocks of Mandarin characters printed on it.

"Sit down, my dear," he said.

Daisy took her usual place on a long and deep couch covered in flowered satin, and Jake, now armed with a big jolt of brandy in a balloon glass, sat beside her. Putting the brandy down, he picked up an electronic control console and, at his first signal, a movie screen rolled out of the ceiling next to the bed.

"Roll 'em!" Jake exclaimed in his cracked voice.

He pressed another button. Blurred images appeared on the screen, then focused.

"This is better than Betamax," Jake muttered.

God, Daisy groaned to herself as her bed appeared on the screen, then herself nude upon it, legs in a scramble. Seconds later, Martin Cooper entered the screen. He sat down on the edge of the bed, leaned over her to kiss her.

"Martin Cooper," Jake murmured.

"None other. Same as two days ago."

"So it is," Jake said.

Cooper was kissing her, her mouth, then her breasts, running his hands across her stomach and between her legs, making her hips jump. She was fondling him, and she watched again as he grew hard and huge. Seeing the replay of their activity made Daisy gasp with pleasure. Her legs twitched and she squirmed.

"Control, my dear," Jake muttered.

"I'm telling you," Daisy whispered, "I do think he's got the biggest one in town."

"Yes," Jake agreed, "quite possibly so."

Cooper, big and beefy, was beside her, running his face down her belly and into her crotch while she, full-face, lifted his penis and rubbed it against her cheek before putting just the tip of it in her mouth.

"Ah," Jake breathed deeply, "Daisy, you are finally beginning to respect the camera angle."

As Daisy went from foreplay to full-blown passion, Jake's free hand stole across the couch and under her nightgown.

The camera angle was perfect as Cooper entered her from behind, her face precisely at the point of focus of the camera, and it caught her every expression when Cooper brought her to the point of frenzy, then multiple climax. Her mouth yawned open and her eyes darted in fearful abandon.

"My dear," Jake drawled as they went on, "you could have been a great actress."

Irritably, Daisy mumbled, "I wasn't acting, Jake. I forgot about your goddamn camera, you know."

"The better . . . the better."

She noticed that Jake was getting hard. A modicum of erection poked at the folds of his dressing gown. Daisy put her hand on it, as she was supposed to do, feeling the stubby force.

While Cooper was resting, inert on the bed, Cox took a long pull of his brandy, then watchfully returned it to the table. Now was the moment when Daisy bent to revive Cooper, her hair swinging over his pelvis.

She'd known Jake would be annoyed at this point. "Goddamn it. Next time, tie your hair back. What can we see? Nothing."

Then it was better as Daisy flopped on her back to pull Cooper into her. The camera had a perfect back view of Cooper's balls swinging, the flash of his cock entering her.

"Ah," Jake sighed.

And, with the repeat, the "one more time," Jake was even more pleased. At the end, the closing scene, she was lying alone again, waiting for Cooper to leave. At this point, Jake keyed onto the screen his usual, final credit lines: Produced by Jake Cox. Director of Photography: Jake Cox. Starring: Daisy.

"Ah," Jake sighed lengthily. He looked at his watch. "A full hour, my dear, almost as long as a feature film. My congratulations. Hurray!"

His breathing had become agitated. His pressure on her vulva increased and Daisy did the only thing she could to stop him from hurting her. She threw aside his robe and fell on her knees between Jake's legs, taking his stubbiness into her mouth.

He collapsed backward on the couch, panting. "Positively Academy Award-winning caliber, my dear."

Even his personals smelled of chemicals, wiring, sophisticated alloys.

Chapter Twelve

Charley Hopper was in a thoughtful, almost preoccupied mood when he picked Belle up in the morning and contemplative he remained as they boarded the 747 at Los Angeles International Airport. Two seats had been reserved for them in the smoking section up front in first class.

"You're sure you won't mind the cigarettes, Belle?"

"No, not at all, and since you're smoking like a chimney . . . "

"Christ, yeah," he said glumly.

He was carrying a thick portfolio, which Belle knew contained renderings for the Cosmos advertising campaign.

He placed them carefully in the closet at the front of the cabin.

"Window or aisle, Belle?"

"Which do you want?"

"Well . . . aisle, if you don't mind."

"Fine. Come on, Charley, cheer up. You said you wanted to have lunch with me."

"Yeah." He smiled. "I had in mind Nate and Al's. No, not really. I couldn't take Belle to a deli. But they do have good beer."

"Charley," she said lightly, "you know I'm a down-to-earth girl."

She had trouble keeping her excitement at bay. She was feeling wonderful—why exactly, she didn't know. An outsider might have said, "My God, this woman's husband is shipping her off to a business conference with his closest associate. And she's happy about it?" Yes, she was more than happy. She was relieved. She couldn't have handled a long flight, then the days on Leonard's boat, with Martin. She felt vaguely as though she'd been freed from dire bondage, but at the same time protected and secure with Charley.

Belle had dressed for the trip in loose-fitting khaki slacks and a navy turtleneck, and she was carrying over her arm a khaki safari jacket with plenty of pockets for passport, tickets, all the incidentals that go with a long, long flight to foreign territories. Leonard was to meet them at the plane in New York and, from there, they would transfer to the Cosmos company jet for the flight to Paris and Nice.

"Mr. Hopper," a stewardess was saying, "would you and your wife like a drink after takeoff? We'll take your order now."

Charley chuckled. "Mrs. Hopper, what would you like?"

"A Bloody Mary," Belle said. "Mrs. Hopper always has a Bloody Mary after takeoff."

"The same." He paused. "I'm wondering about this expedition, Belle."

"Forget it, Charley. We do make a handsome couple."

"Your half is handsome enough. But look at me."

He was wearing blue jeans and wrinkled white blazer, suede shoes, and a blue and white striped shirt.

"I think you should open the shirt a little," Belle suggested. "Otherwise, you won't look totally California."

Charley shook his head mournfully. "I ain't California. I get no gold chains and medallions."

He lapsed into silence and studiously flipped through the morning paper. Belle sensed something was wrong, that Charley was somehow embarrassed.

"Charley," she said firmly, "did Martin say something to you?"

He shook his head. "No, not really," he said evasively.

But she knew there had been some kind of exchange between them. Quite possibly it had not been a pleasant one.

The plane was in the air, and a few moments later they had their drinks.

"Here's to my traveling çompanion," she said.

He turned toward her. "And here's to you, Belle." He smiled but his long face was still concerned. "You know," he said slowly, "I didn't plan it this way. I don't know why in hell Mart wouldn't come. Leonard asked for him, not me."

Belle's ears popped at the change of altitude. She made a face.

"Charley, I'll do my best not to be a pain in the neck."

"That's not what I'm saying," he muttered. "Mart should have come."

Levelly, she said, "The way he explained it to me was he's got too much work of his own and you're in charge of the Cosmos account. You're doing the work. For that matter, why should I be going?"

"Because," he said, "Leonard is sold on the idea of using your name. You know that."

"No." She shook her head. "I don't know that for a fact. But *if* we're both to be involved, then we should both go." She stopped for a moment, wondering how much she should tell him. But there was no reason she should not be frank and open with Hopper. "Charley, you know as well as I do why he wouldn't come." She looked him straight in the eye. "Because our relationship lately has become very strained."

"Strained?"

"Yes, strained to the point of breaking," she said impatiently. "So . . . so, what can I say? I'll tell you what: I'm happy we're traveling together, and it's a big relief for me to get away. There!"

"Jesus, I'm sorry about that, Belle."

"I'm not," she said stubbornly. "This has been building a long time. Can I tell you something? Yes? I feel marvelous and I'm not at all depressed. Maybe that sounds awful to you. But I did give this thing my best shot, Charley."

"I know you did. I know you did . . . Goddamn it," he said angrily, "Martin Cooper is a very difficult son of a bitch. And dumb! But," he remembered something, "what about Susan?"

"She's okay. She's down at the beach with Sally Markman. And Charley . . . you've got to stop worrying about Martin Cooper. He can take care of himself."

"Yes, I know. I won't think of him again."

"Good," she said. She leaned a few inches to kiss his cheek. He turned his head and their lips met. Belle pulled back, flustered, felt her cheeks light up. "Charley, I meant to kiss you on the cheek."

"A likely story." He grinned.

Belle laughed softly. "I don't care, Charley . . . But I don't want to scare you. Women are very forward these days, aren't they? They're the predators," she teased. "We take the initiative now."

Growling, but pleased, he said, "It won't work with me, baby. Speaking of predators, my old friend Maude Mannon was in town. She was at that lunch of yours. What are you girls organizing now?"

"A big party in December. That was the first meeting of our committee."

"Who else you got?" Charley asked.

Belle chuckled. "All the heavy charity hitters. Maude, Carlotta Westmoreland, our own bouncy newspaper tycoon. Sally, of course. Then, let's see: Pat Hyman, super-thin, super-chic mate of well-known producer George Hyman . . ."

"Mrs. Anorexia . . . I know her," Charley muttered. "Wow."

"Right. Next, Bertha Moore . . ."

"Mrs. Scowl, Frown, and Hiss-Hiss," Charley supplied. "I've never seen her smile and 'nary a cheery word was heard. But, you know, her husband, that guy Sheldon Moore . . . He's nice, albeit rather ineffectual, I think."

"Right again," Belle said. "Lou Finistere you know—Archy's wife."

"Yes. She's from Chicago; they say she used to be a chanteuse in a Mafia supper club."

"She's good-looking, miles younger then Archy, of course."

He nodded, laughing. "Archy is something. You know, he's not really French. It's said he's actually Rumanian. In the thirties, he ran a hotel in Atlantic City, trained at the Waldorf, was an intimate of Charles Ritz, acquired the white beard in Vienna."

"Charley," she said, "you're a wealth of information."

"Archy is terrific. Who else?"

"Well . . . Camilla Young. She's just gotten divorced and is kind of on the skids right now. But she's a good kid. I hope she'll snap out of it. She will. She's sort of a fragile beauty, very vulnerable I would have thought." She shook her head, wondering how Charley would have classified her. "Then we brought in Sharon Peters. I doubt if you know her. She's very Midwest, a straight-shooter, kind of short and square in shape. She was married to Oscar Peters, a big trucking tycoon. Oscar died and Sharon moved out here a couple of years ago. She's loaded, but a pretty good lady. That's about it. Norman Kaplan is our leader; I don't think you know him. He's an old friend of Sally's and I love him."

"I know the name," Charley grunted. "Maude is a friend of his, too. Maude—God, she just got divorced again. She's looking for a man."

"Not *you*, Charley." Maude was too old for Charley, but it wasn't so unbelievable that she might entertain the idea. "Charley, I think you're the young-Hollywood-starlet type."

"Oh, yeah, is that so? No, Belle," he murmured, "Since we're suffering from high-altitude giddiness, I'll tell you straight out: my type is much more along your lines."

"Charley Hopper! You Texas boys take one's breath away."

The flight was an easy one, comfortable, and, after the uneasy preliminaries had been put aside, Belle and Charley relaxed together. They landed at Kennedy at 7:30 in the evening. Sam Leonard was waiting for them with his chauffeur downstairs in the baggage claim area.

"Hello, there, Belle," Leonard said, smiling slyly. "Well, thank God your plane was on time, a rarity these days. Hopper, how are you?"

Charley hadn't made up his mind about Leonard yet. They shook hands a little warily and Belle realized that

Charley was embarrassed for her that Cooper was not there.

"Charley, my name is Sam. At least let's get that straight," Leonard grumped. "So Cooper wouldn't come after all?"

"He thought I should since I'm working on the campaign," Charley said.

Leonard shook his head disparagingly. "That guy is something else. He still doesn't go for the name, does he? Belle?"

"We haven't talked about it," she said, honestly.

"Well, screw him," Leonard said caustically, drawing his small figure up erectly. "I like it and Charley likes it. Okay! Your bags? Howard, grab those bags. Jesus, that all you've got? Sylvia carries ten—you'd think we were staying a month. She's already on the plane, waiting for us. Let's go."

The Cosmos plane was called the *Jetsetter*. It was parked outside the Air Research hangers on the margin of J.F.K., cabin lights bright in the gathering dusk. A short gangway was pulled up to the open door of the plane, a gleaming, antiseptic white, the inscription *Jetsetter* slashed across the cabin door in lipstick red.

"All aboard," Leonard said, clambering spryly out of the back seat of the limousine, holding his hand for Belle.

Inside, Sylvia Leonard, tiny like Sam, was sitting in the front of four rows of seats, leafing through the newest issue of *Harper's Bazaar* magazine. As soon as she saw Leonard, she commenced telling him the color had run on one of his ads.

"Sylvia," Leonard said irritably, "don't tell me. Tell Charley Hopper here. He's the advertising genius. Sylvia, these beautiful people are Belle Cooper and Charley Hopper. People: this hyper-critical woman is my wife, Sylvia. She's a beauty, but boy does she pick at you."

Sylvia paid him no attention. "Sit down by me, Belle." She patted the seat next to her. "We'll let those two talk business—which I'm sure they'll do all the way across the Atlantic. I'm sorry your husband couldn't come, too."

Belle repeated their excuse but Sylvia wasn't interested. Her button eyes bright, she was appreciatively inspecting Belle's traveling outfit.

"The important thing, Belle, is that we're going to France, my favorite country. And you'll love the boat."

Tolerantly, Leonard said, "Sylvia loves France above all else. She can never wait to get out of New York. She's been on the horn all day, hustling me along. Goddamn it, Sylvia, you think all I've got to do all day is talk to you on the telephone."

"No," she said sarcastically, "I think you've got a lot of other things to do—like feel up your secretaries."

"Blast it, Sylvia," Leonard spouted, "is that any way to talk? I'll have you know I was in meetings all day."

"I'll bet you were, you pip-squeak!" she yelped. "Pipe down and fasten your safety belt. Jarvis," she demanded of the flight steward who was busily arranging them in their seats, "when are we taking off?"

"As soon as the bags are on, Mrs. Leonard."

"Tell them to drag it," she ordered.

Leonard leaned across the aisle. "Jesus, Sylvia, shut up for a while, will you? You don't want to leave your clothes behind, do you?"

Vaguely, at some point in the past, Belle had heard stories about the battling Leonards. They staged scenes in the most unlikely places: hotel lobbies, at restaurants, in museums, one or the other apt to storm away, trailing insults and epithets. But she understood at once, seeing them together for the first time, that they actually loved each other very much. Perhaps the fighting was just their way of showing it. In a moment, Sylvia was out of her seat to pat Sam's hand and give him a pouting kiss.

The kiss. She was sorry she wouldn't be sitting next to Charley. That one kiss on the 747 had ignited within her a dark, unexpected emotion, a speculation, wonderment. But they were the guests and she would be sharing the flight with Sylvia.

After another flurry of acrimony over what movie they would, or refused to, watch, the Cosmos jet left runway and New York behind and headed out over the wide Atlantic. Leonard had already opened a bulging brown briefcase and was leafing through sheafs of reports, now and then handing one to Charley or throwing him a comment.

"That's his traveling desk," Sylvia said loudly. "Everything Cosmos owns or does is in there. If we ever went down, so would Cosmos."

Not bothering to turn his head, Leonard snapped, "Sylvia, will you stop that crap? We're not going down. What a thing to say!"

"It's always possible, Sam."

Leonard snarled, "It is not possible if I'm on board the goddamn airplane, Sylvia."

"Indestructible you," she mocked. "The plane would not dare go down."

Jarvis laid dinner things on tables that unfolded from the cabin sides: white tablecloths, silverware, and glasses. Then he served a first course of Beluga caviar and ice-cold Russian vodka.

"Sam went to Moscow once," Sylvia observed. "He never got over it."

For once, Leonard did not disagree. "That's right. Caviar and Stolichnaya have got to be the best first course ever invented."

"We must remember that next time you're in Los Angeles," Belle said.

"But you did serve caviar and vodka that night," he remembered. "It was one of the things I liked about you."

Charley murmured, "Belle is a master party-giver, Sam."

"My one gift to the world."

Leonard shook his head violently. "Not so. I've got an idea for you that's going to make you sit up, Belle. We'll discuss it when we get to the *Cosmopolitan*."

By the time they finished the main course, juicy beef served with a vintage-year Bordeaux, then Camembert with a light red Burgundy, and finally a demitasse of coffee, it was nearing midnight: five A.M. in Europe, and Belle thought she could detect the beginnings of morning light on the eastern horizon.

It was still early morning when they landed at Orly. After customs clearance and re-fueling, the *Jetsetter* took off for Nice. They were there within the hour and quickly into a black limo waiting outside.

In another forty-five minutes, they were at the boat dock in Cannes and then aboard the *Cosmopolitan*. The ship, in its earlier days, had belonged to one of the Greeks. Leonard, and Cosmos, had bought it some ten years before. The *Cosmopolitan* was a 200-foot ocean-going luxury sailing ship, black-hulled with three white masts and white fittings and trim.

"You keep this here on a year-round basis, Sam?" Charley asked.

"Of course," Leonard said proudly, "with a captain,

crew of six, and a chef. It runs these days to about a million a year. Not bad really, when you consider inflation, and also the fact I can rent it out during the film festival for a couple of 100,000. It's cozy for entertaining, Charley," Leonard grinned mischievously. "And don't think you two are not going to be a write-off."

Hopper laughed. He was feeling better about Leonard. "I'd be insulted if we weren't," he said.

The main drawing room, or salon, in front of the wheelhouse was forty feet long, marble-floored and ebony-paneled, furnished with comfortable sofas, easy chairs, and a scattering of glass-topped coffee tables. Low bookcases circled the walls under oblong windows. On the aft wall, Leonard had hung a collection of his favorite Impressionist paintings. At the forward end of the room, a neat mahogany bar filled one corner and a mini-grand piano the other. A doorway led downstairs to the lower cabin deck. The galley was located at the bow of the *Cosmopolitan*, then a dining room spacious enough for a long table and a dozen chairs. Rear of the dining room, there was a billiard room and smoker. Then the cabins.

"The master cabin is all the way in the tail end," Leonard said.

"And that's where I'm going right now for a nap before lunch," Sylvia said.

"Come on," Leonard said, as Sylvia trailed away, "I'll show you your cabins." He winked shrewdly. "I assume it is to be *cabins*."

Wickedly, Belle said, "Well, if you're cramped for space, Sam, we could always double up. Eh, Charley?"

Charley shook his head. "Boy-oh-boy!"

Leonard snorted laughter. "Don't worry. I'll be your witness."

Their cabins were side by side off a carpeted corridor opposite the entrance to the billiard room. They were not large but compactly laid out and decorated in red and black fabrics, the colors of Cosmos' lipstick and the black hull of the *Cosmopolitan*.

"I suggest we all have a little nap," Leonard said. "Keep us fresh for the evening. I thought we'd go out to the casino . . . or, if you want, just wander around. Make yourselves totally at home, and I mean it."

Belle's bags had been unpacked while they'd been on the tour. The bathroom was luxurious, inviting her to a hot soak, then soft bed. She undressed, absorbed in the activity of the busy port, which she could watch through wide portholes. The *Cosmopolitan* swayed easily at its mooring, unflustered by the wake of passing motorboats. Above, she heard the sound of feet and conversation as the crew went about its business.

Belle lay in the tub for a half-hour, washing away the trip for, as smooth as any flight might be, there is always travel residue at the other end. Amazing, she thought, they were already so far away from Los Angeles, Beverly Hills, Hollywood. Lazily, she dreamt of sailing the Mediterranean from Greek isle to island, putting in at tiny ports, swimming over the side, eating black olives and drinking sweet local wine. She saw herself at the tiller, guiding a small sailing ship through the straits and narrows, the azure waters, alone, solitary, aloof, sunburned, body-strong, wind-swept, the mind cleared of all anxieties. Now and then, when the mood or need struck her, she would anchor in hidden coves and command the presence of a lithe, young sailor. Take him, then cast him aside, sail on.

Smiling to herself at the conceit, she shifted in the warm bath and stared down at her body. She was all there, she thought. She put her hands to her breasts, then down her stomach and between her thighs, feeling a response of muscle, and nerve. Disturbingly, she thought again of Charley Hopper, separated from her by a tiled wall.

She jumped out of the tub and toweled herself down fiercely, putting Charley out of her mind. Now, she was too refreshed to think about sleeping. She pulled on a pair of white slacks and, leaving aside her bra, a loose silk blouse which, she realized, had been a packing inspiration—it was red with black figures.

When she climbed back to the main deck, Charley was at the stern, talking to the captain.

"Belle! You didn't sleep either. You met Captain Forbourg?"

Belle shook hands again with the burly man. "I love the ship," she said.

"Ah, madame," Forbourg said, "it is one of the prizes of the sea."

Politely, he left them alone, putting a hand to his braided cap, explaining he had many things to do.

"Well," Charley murmured. "So here we are. Not bad for a little change, is it?" He turned to lean on the railing, staring inland at the harbor. "Not too shabby at all, is it, Belle?"

"I find it marvelous," Belle said gently. "And I like your shorts, Charley."

He had on sandals, tennis shorts, and a white polo shirt. "My yachting costume," he said.

A white-jacketed steward appeared to ask if they'd like something to drink.

"I don't know," Charley said. "What do you say, Belle?"

"Well . . . since we're here to enjoy ourselves, Mr. Hopper, what would you say if I ordered a beer?"

"I'd say, let's make it two."

The waiter asked if they'd prefer French or German.

"But French, of course," Belle decided.

"*Deux bières françaises,*" Charley translated, smiling.

"Charley, you speak the local lingo."

"Enough to order a beer, my dear," he said breezily. "Let's sit down and look at the city."

The other side of the dockside parking lot was a busy commercial plaza of small shops, dusty cafes, and a smattering of disreputable-looking hotels. What would it be like, Belle thought wistfully, still dreaming a little, to check in there anonymously, to hole up in one of those dives for a year or so? To disappear, never to be seen again?

"You're thinking. About what?" he asked.

"Of fading into a side street," she said.

"Why would you want to do that?" he demanded, concerned again.

"Do you think I really want to go back to California?"

"Can't run away, Belle. It can't be done."

She knew he was right—realistically. But unrealistically—why couldn't she run away? It was her life, the only life she'd been given. Was there any justification for using it so badly? Was she going to squander more of her years, never very happy? No, she promised herself, she was going to live again and, to start with, she was going to sweep Cooper out of her mind.

Charley could not have known what she was thinking, but there was no need to tell him.

"Belle, let's go for a walk. We've got time."

They told the steward they'd be back in an hour, in time for lunch, and walked back down the wooden causeway toward the harbor street.

But the subject of fleeing was still on her mind. "Charley, wouldn't it be fun to get a small boat and just sail away?"

"Into the sunset, you mean?" He was amused now.

"Yes, red sails into the sunset and to hell with everything else."

"You'd get bored, Belle."

"No, I don't think so. I'd pick up a little sailor-boy whenever I got lonely."

"Dangerous and reckless talk, madame," Charley drawled.

They paused to look at shop windows, to feast their eyes on the colorful wares in small markets. Belle peered into the entrance of one of the small hotels; it was not nearly as seedy as it had looked from the distance. They circled the harbor on foot. In the distance, the *Cosmopolitan* lay restfully at anchor: their refuge, a floating palace.

Belle was not a stranger to such luxury. Hell, luxury had become a way of life. When she and Cooper traveled, they stayed at the best hotels; they'd been in Cannes many times for the film festival, put up in one of the flashy places along the Croisette, the high-rolling boulevard between the cabana-crowded sand and the hotel terraces. They'd sailed the Hawaiian Islands in a comfortable schooner, up the Nile from Alexandria to Luxor in an Egyptian riverboat, been paddled through the canals of Kashmir. They'd always been superbly fed, well-housed, and well-hosted. But this was somehow different. It was her mood. She was alone, alone with Charley, true, but alone, free to feed her senses without thought of Cooper's demands, his preferences, his clock. Was it as simple as that?

"Charley, let's sit down and have another beer and look at our ship."

They took a corner table in a cafe on the west side of the port and ordered two more beers.

Comfortably, feeling her ease, Belle leaned back in the sunshine and stared at the harbor. Charley slumped in his chair, one white ankle cocked up over his knee. His feet were big and bony. He lit a cigarette and drew on it as if it were the ultimate satisfaction. His brown hair was unruly and his face seemed pallid, almost pasty, alongside the Mediterranean colorations.

"Do you tan, Charley?"

"No, I sunburn fourteen times, then tan. Why? Do I look unhealthy?"

"Just very white-skinned. Nobody would know you're from California."

"Just as well," he said laconically. "They might ask me to go surfing."

Belle chuckled and happily stretched her arms above her head. She felt like flying away. The rich ambiance—water, boats, good food smells, the lively taste of the beer, even the smell of his cigarette—tuned her to the universe, adventure.

"All this," she said. "I don't know, it seems so real."

"And now, please, you're not going to tell me that everything in California is crass and phony and ugly?"

"No, no," she said hastily. "But, Charley, you know something? I think this is maybe the best trip I've ever been on."

"It's just that you love France . . . like Sylvia."

"No, it's true. I've never felt so relaxed. Charley," she said slyly, "do you think it's maybe because I'm with you?"

Charley winked at her over his beer glass. "Sure. I always have that effect on women."

"Do you take many of them away on excursions like this?"

He put down one foot and hoisted the other one over his knee. "Let me think," he muttered thoughtfully. "No . . . seems to me I haven't taken a girl away for an illicit weekend in maybe . . . what? Twenty years?"

"God," Belle exclaimed. "What a square."

"Ma'am," he said sardonically, "old Charley Hopper is as square as they come."

"Also very evasive," Belle said. "But I know what you're thinking."

"And just what am I thinking?" he demanded.

Stolidly, she replied, "That I'm acting like a child, maybe trying to lead you on, but that you'll protect me from myself, keep me out of trouble."

Steadily, he looked into her eyes. "Well, partly I was thinking that, I admit. Partly also that whatever problem you've got will pass."

"Charley, it won't pass. I've made up my mind. I'm not going to throw away the rest of my life. Susan challenged me."

"Susan? What's she got to do with it?"

"She is my daughter," Belle said insistently. "She hates him."

"Oh, Jesus," he said forlornly. He put his right hand to his head, singeing hair with his cigarette. "Belle, I don't want you to be unhappy. You've got to do . . . whatever you've got to do."

"You are my friend, aren't you?"

He nodded, wagging his head without answering.

"Charley, you know what he's like. Goddamn it, Charley, it's as plain as that huge nose on your face that Cooper is carrying on with that tramp Pamela Renfrew. Don't try to deny it."

Again he merely nodded and inclined his head.

"Charley," she pressed him, sorry she was forcing him to the wall. But she wanted answers. "Charley, you're so goddamn loyal to him. I like loyalty, it's admirable, but come on!"

Finally, he muttered a reply. "Belle, I've known him a lot of years. Christ, there was nobody like him. But he has changed. He's not like he used to be, not at all. We can't communicate anymore. I don't know what the hell is wrong with him."

"Sally said he's been ruined by the business. He's gotten so he believes all the B.S."

He smiled bemusedly. "If him, then why not me, too?"

"What Sally said was Charley Hopper is a different sort of man."

"That's good to know," he said uncomfortably.

"Well, you are."

He held up his hand, his sign that they should hold it. "Don't go overboard, Belle. I'm not any different, really. Christ knows, I've had my problems. There must be plenty wrong with me, too."

"Why?" she demanded fiercely, "because your wife ran out on you? Maybe that was her problem, not yours. Wait!" She drew away. "Ah, now you're going to say I'm running out on Cooper—even-steven? You don't think . . ."

Charley grinned at her. "No, no. I'll admit it—you've got a case. But, listen, I don't like talking about myself. I'm a shy man." He reached across the table to lay his hand on hers, just for a second. "You're right about me. I'm terrific and she was just plain stupid."

"But you don't think I'm stupid? Feeling like I do?"

Charley shook his head. "No, you're not stupid. No way."

The lunch table had been laid out under an awning on the fantail of the *Cosmopolitan* and Leonard, in a tight bathing suit, which revealed that with his litheness came a taut, if tiny, potbelly, was sitting there when they returned, reading glasses on his nose and newspapers strewn on the deck beside him.

"Sam, don't you ever stop reading?" Belle demanded.

"Nah," Leonard said self-effacingly, as if caught in the act of something disgusting in the sun of southern France, "there's always catching up to do. Reading: the curse of the job. Christ," he grumbled, "a lot of the people who work for me need a lesson in abbreviated thought and memo-writing."

He launched into a long story about his old friend, the late J. Edgar Hoover and Hoover's requirement that his agents keep memos to a page and a half and with margins wide enough for scrawled corrections and directions.

Belle's attention drifted. She gazed back at the quayside activity for a moment and then at Charley. Charley was paying close attention to Sam, nodding, chuckling at the story. Charley: she wondered how desperately in love Charley had been with that wife of his, whether he had been as badly broken up by her desertion as she thought. Was Charley that rarity, a one-woman man? He sat with his elbows cocked on his bare knees, spectacularly untanned alongside Sam's nut-brown skin. His hair was just going gray; as he pushed it back on his head, she noted a distinct widow's peak. He stroked his forehead, then scratched the side of his nose. The latter was prominent; another few minutes in the womb and he might have come out looking like a hawk. Charley, she thought to herself, why had she ever taken him for granted? He was the physical and mental antithesis of Martin Cooper and, as she considered him now, she realized he was more like Peter Bertram than anybody she'd met since.

Again, she felt the unusual, or long unaroused, surge of . . . what? Desire? Agitation? That same uneasiness she'd experienced downstairs made her draw a deep breath.

Sylvia's arrival on deck served to end Sam's story. Sylvia was dressed in a breezy cotton caftan and she was carrying a multicolored parasol.

"Well, here you all are! Did you have a good nap? Leonard, naturally, only slept five minutes."

"A catnap," Sam said with satisfaction, "that's all I need.

Like Napoleon; he slept in three-hour snatches." He grinned devilishly. "We're pouring chablis. . . . I thought we'd have cold lobster for lunch and a salad."

"Perfect, Sam," Sylvia said.

"For once I've done the right thing."

Sylvia acted shocked. "Sammy! You always do the right thing."

"Oh, yeah? Not when it came to remodelling this tub, I didn't." Sam looked to Belle for his audience. "She hates those marble tiles in the salon."

"Sammy," Sylvia protested coyly, "I hate them because they're not real marble."

"Jesus," Sam groaned, "here we go again. I'm telling you, tiny dummy, it's marble and it cost plenty."

Sylvia accepted a glass of wine from the white-coated waiter. "All right, I'll agree they're marble if you'll apologize for calling me tiny dummy."

"That's the beautiful thing about you, Sylvia," Sam cried, grinning, "you're always open to reason."

Sylvia bent over Sam and kissed him.

"God," he said, "what's that you're wearing?"

" 'Belle'," she said innocently.

"Don't jump the goddamn gun, Sylvia," Sam exclaimed. "That's for later."

Charley smiled at Belle. "Pleasure before business, Sam?" he asked lightly.

"Certainly not going to sniff perfume in the middle of the day," Sam said.

Yes, Belle thought, pleasure before business. She was hungry now. She sipped white wine, cold and sharp, aware it calmed her. Charley was watching her, his eyes very serious. Sitting beside him at the lunch table, she felt his bare arm against hers, hair tickling her skin. She realized if she moved her knee she would touch his leg. Shifting in her seat, it happened. She felt the muscles of his calf. At the contact, a racing sensation leapt up her leg. Then . . . He had slipped his feet out of his sandals. His bare toes pressed the uncovered arch of her foot under the table. God! She almost cried out. Charley glanced at her, chuckling at something Sam had said.

Chapter Thirteen

Drowsy now from the beer before lunch, then the rich lobster and wine, Belle and Charley began to feel the need for some sleep. The Leonards were sitting at the lunchtable, avidly discussing the soaring price of diesel fuel.

Leonard glanced up to say they'd all be leaving for dinner at the casino at ten—one of the crew would awaken everybody at 8:30.

"Sleep well," Belle said when they were downstairs.

"You too, Belle."

He smiled a little sheepishly, obviously not knowing how deeply she had reacted to the touch of his body. For a second, smiling back, she considered yanking him into her cabin. No, that would never do. What happened would happen very naturally, if it happened at all. Breathlessly, she closed the cabin door and leaned against it. God, she thought, it was dismal to think that it might not happen at all. She wanted it to, did she? Yes.

Nodding to herself, Belle took off her clothes, threw them on a chair, and slipped into the soft bed, between silk sheets. Up above, as she drifted off, the hustle-bustle of activity eased off toward siesta. The harbor noises subsided. The Leonards came below; they were still chattering amiably as they went down the passage past her door. Belle willed herself to sink into rest. She dreamt, not a cohesive dream, but rather, a fragmented one, the dreamer skipping through memories of recent time.

In a half-hour, perhaps an hour—she wasn't sure—she opened her eyes. Charley was standing at the side of her bed, a cigarette in his hand. She pulled the sheet up to her chin.

"Charley! You woke me up. I smelled smoke."

"I just walked in this minute," he said. "I heard a noise. Your door was ajar. I couldn't sleep. No, actually I came in to watch you. Do you mind if I watch you while you sleep?"

Belle touched a hand to her hair. "You've been watching me, Charley? That's not fair."

"I couldn't help it." His face was solemn. "Don't worry. I'm a perfect gent. I didn't feel like being alone."

Belle followed his eyes along the outline of her body under the sheet. She felt a warm flush rise from her toes. "It's okay," she murmured, knowing she sounded very languid. "I don't . . . mind . . . Charley." She drew a careful but nervous breath.

He sat down on the bed beside her and she felt a tremor pass through his body.

"Now sleep," he said.

She felt his hand on her forehead and obediently closed her eyes. She wanted to give in, to drift away. Then his lips were lightly on her cheek, against her lips. She kept her eyes tightly closed. The pressure increased; his hand was on her shoulder. She sighed, opened her mouth to his tongue, then put her arms up and around his neck and pulled him down.

It was time. She kissed him, not mistakenly this time, but surely and strongly. Her head swam for a second, dizzily.

"Charley," she whispered, "you're trying to seduce me." She felt his head move. "And you're succeeding."

"Belle," he murmured, "just tell me no and I'll get out."

"No, I don't want you to get out."

She very much wanted him to make love to her, she decided. She had decided that hours before, she realized, on the plane from New York. It was time and she was ready. It was an extension of her mood, her feeling earlier in the day that she was free. Now, she gladly acknowledged the desire creeping up her legs.

His hands were under the sheet, fondling her breasts. He moved the sheet back and his lips were on her nipples, then the undercurve of the breast where it met her ribs.

"Charley," she breathed, "get in bed."

He stood for a second and shucked his blue robe. He was skinny all the way down; his ribs were like welts under his skin. She kicked the sheet to the bottom of the bed and moved to make room for him at her side. He kissed her again, on the mouth, the eyes, ran his lips across her breasts to her belly. His hand moved from her hip to her leg, then gently he smoothed the skin of her inner thigh, put his fingers to her trembling center. Now she felt him vividly, against her, the hard muscles of his belly and the rock of his being. She stroked him, and, responsively, he gasped.

"Yes, Charley. Now . . ."

Fiercely, Belle pulled Charley on top of her and eased the erect length of him inside her. It was a thoughtful, measured entry until, endlessly it seemed, she was filled, occupied, complete. The ship rolled pleasantly with the gesture. Staring down at her, something like puzzlement in his eyes, he reached for her passion, pulled back, then restored the caressing movement. Full of him, she paused, as if to comprehend a spoken word.

"Belle," he murmured, "I've been in love with you a long time."

"Don't talk about love just yet," she sighed. "Just make it."

It had been a long time for her, she remembered, as Charley held her fast, pinned luxuriously to the bed. Cooper had not satisfied her in any deeply moving way for months and, sickened, she recalled the last time he had tried. No, her bridges were burned and damn what people might say now.

She felt the weight of him, the pleasurable crush of his chest on her breasts. Charley proceeded slowly, controlling himself, holding back, rocking slightly, in keeping with the movement of the boat, touching all her most sensitive places. She became aware of a gathering knot of nerve ends as his stroking focused her want and desire. She closed her eyes and concentrated on the marvel of what was happening to her. Charley put his lips to hers again, his mouth open, tongue seeking. She heard herself gasping; the knot was unraveling inside her and she could have screamed with the release. She lifted her legs to bind him to her and tugged, pushed, gaping to gather him inward. She was panting, groaning, and climaxed like that over long seconds of coming and going in waves of abandon. Now, Charley loosed himself and she felt his seed mushroom within her, to the very ends of her. The muscles on the backs of his legs relaxed and he declined within her.

But still she held him there, fast to her body. They did not move or speak.

Finally, he drew a shallow breath. "God, Belle . . ."

"Oh, Charley." She could get out no more. "Charley . . . Charley . . . I wanted that very much indeed."

He lifted himself to her side and she rolled to face him.

"I do love you, Belle," he repeated.

She pondered the words. Her primary perception now was that she had done it, fully and freely, no holds barred. She kissed his mouth, his neck, then his chest where his nipples were small and hard. She kissed his bellybutton and ran her hand down to his loins, where he lay flaccid now and at rest. He was a lot to explore.

"Charley . . . dear . . . I've got a long way to go before I start thinking about love again. It's too early for me. Right now, I think I'm just relishing my freedom."

"You'll come through it," he promised. "Meanwhile . . ."

"Meanwhile, I'm crazy about you," she said drowsily. "Should we sleep a little?"

In his arms, Belle fell asleep almost instantly, and descended the steep spiral toward forgetfulness, then nothingness. She slept dreamlessly now, deeply, as if in a darkened womb, and didn't wake again until there was a sharp knocking at her door and the announcement that it was 8:30.

Dazedly, she remembered what had happened. But Charley was gone. Had she dreamt the whole thing? She hopped out of bed and put on a robe. She opened her door and knocked at Charley's.

"Charley," she called, "what are we wearing?"

From inside, his voice resounded warmly. "Sam says black tie."

He opened his door. He was already dressed in black trousers, a stiff white shirt with studs, and a black bowtie. He smiled and said in a lower voice, "Black tie, Belle. You know that. Did you sleep well?"

She was stricken. Had she really dreamed it? He was behaving as if nothing had happened.

Confused, she nodded. But then she knew it was all right—she had not imagined it, for Charley bent his head to kiss her.

Leonard's limousine was waiting for them at the dock. They eased through the automotive clutter of the Croisette, heading east toward the edge of Cannes, where the casino, like a sparkling ocean liner, lay on a promontory overlooking the sea. The dining room was jammed but the maitre d' guided them to the Leonard table, bowing and mouthing platitudes to Sam as they proceeded.

Leonard was tired and he was complaining of stomach cramps.

"Sylvia, goddamn it, I told you never to let me eat lobster in the middle of the day."

Calmly, Sylvia said, "Dimwit, it was your idea to have lobster."

"Jesus," Leonard grumbled, "poisoned by my own goddamn wife. Charley, you carry any of those white pills with you—you know, the gastritis ones?"

Hopper shook his head. "I never use 'em, Sam."

Leonard looked extremely exasperated. "Charley, you mean to tell me you're in the media business and you don't even have gastritis—let alone a sleeping duodenal?"

"That's right, Sam."

"Then I guess you don't take it very seriously, do you? You don't give a goddamn about the business, huh?"

This was a damning charge, but Hopper was not perturbed. "Sam, my experience is, people who get ulcers are not very effective in their jobs. They're always holding their guts and feeling miserable."

"Talking about me, I suppose."

Sylvia interrupted, "It's a good thing Charley doesn't take you seriously, mein husband."

Not looking at her, Leonard said, "Shut up, Sylvia. Well?"

"You've got a stomach upset, not an ulcer," Hopper said easily. "You're too nasty to get an ulcer."

Leonard's eyebrows shot up as Sylvia delightedly clucked. "Jesus Christ, Belle, I can't believe it, they're all in cahoots against me."

"Not me, Sam," she said. "I can see you're suffering."

"Yeah," he growled, "and screw you two smartasses." He turned his back on them to gaze at Belle. "Belle, you are radiant tonight, absolutely radiant, not like those two slobs. You're sophisticated and elegant, just like my new fragrance, our whole line of 'Belle' products. Where'd you get that dress?"

"It's nothing much," she said. "I bought it in Beverly Hills—at I. Magnin's, I guess."

"Ah . . . They're going to carry the new line. I know they will," Leonard said vigorously, forgetting his belly.

It was a long red dress, again, fortuitously, close to the shade of the Cosmos logo. Two thin straps held the dress at the shoulders and it fell sinuously, to disclose the cleavage of her bosom.

But more than that, she was feeling radiant. She glanced toward Charley. Almost imperceptibly, he winked.

"Don't you think she's perfect, Charley?" Leonard demanded.

Hopper nodded judiciously. "Perfect," he said.

Leonard abruptly pushed his chair back. "Come on, Sylvia, let's dance."

The doll-like Leonards, twins, like figures on top of a Meissen clock, fell into an intricate tango. Sylvia followed Sam gracefully, complacently gazing into his face.

"Belle, you do look radiant," Charley said. "Absolutely and utterly beautiful."

She shook her head. "I'm not beautiful. Maybe I'm stately. But I'm too tall and I'm skinny, like you, with a dearth of chest."

"Aha!" he said. "But underneath the stateliness lurks a different creature, a mad and passionate savage."

"You're my undoing, Mr. Hopper. You'll make me blush."

"You are blushing," Charley said. "Would you like to dance a little?"

"Yes."

Belle moved into his now familiar arms, feeling again the long, muscled body. They moved slowly and after a moment, Belle was aware that Sam Leonard was watching them; Sam murmured something in Sylvia's ear and she nodded. So? This, Belle thought, was not a high school dance; people did hold each other close these days. She felt a sudden pressure against her thigh. When she glanced up, Charley smiled enigmatically.

Back at the table, Sam was barking at Sylvia again. "Goddamn it, clumsy, you stepped on my foot. Jesus! That hurt. Where the hell did you learn to dance anyway?"

"From you, shorty. Is it my fault if your foot was in the wrong place?"

"Sylvia!" Leonard exploded loudly, "my foot was in the right place. You muffed it. And if you don't stop bugging me, my foot is going to be somewhere else—giving you a good swift kick in the ass."

Lividly, Sylvia turned to Belle and Charley. "Did you ever hear the like? A real macho type, isn't he? Listen, you squirt, you're too puny to pull that stuff on me. You kick me and I'll kick you right back, and you know where."

"Jesus," Leonard groaned, "am I ever to be victimized by this pea-brained midget?"

Charley laughed helplessly and Belle joined in. Leonard was furious, glaring at them. Then he relented.

"Sylvia is actually a very good dancer," he said solemnly. "When I rescued her, she was a dancing Camel cigarette on the Major Bowes show—and certainly not a king-sized Pall Mall by any means."

"Good God," Sylvia cried, "don't listen. He's making that up. It's not true. I was a Rockette."

"Yeah," Leonard jeered unmercifully, "the juvenile at the end of the line. They raided Radio City Music Hall once, going to get them for hiring children."

"Don't listen," Sylvia screamed, "don't listen. None of it is true."

They were back on board the *Cosmopolitan* by one in the morning, now, due to the time difference, wide awake. Sam led them into the salon and sat them around a coffee table. He rang for the steward, then told them to wait right there: he had to get something important.

Sylvia asked for a diet drink while Sam was gone. Charley said he'd have a long scotch and soda and Belle ordered another French beer.

Sam was carrying a sailcloth totebag inscribed with the Cosmos logo when he returned. Carefully, he took an array of small red boxes out of the bag and arranged them on the table.

"Now then," he said, "here's what we're doing." Shuffling the boxes, he continued, "Perfume, cologne . . . lipstick . . . face powder. I want you to have a look."

He opened one of the boxes and drew out a small bottle marked "Number One" on sticky tape. Uncorking it, he put a drop of the contents on his left wrist, then shoved the bottle toward Belle.

She applied the scent to her wrist and carefully sniffed. The smell was long and lingering. She decided at once that it was too strong.

Sylvia, then Charley, repeated the ritual, putting noses to wrists.

"Like a wine tasting," Charley remarked.

"Balls," Leonard grunted, "this is serious."

He opened Number Two and they all applied a drop of this on their right wrists.

"Variation on a theme," Sylvia murmured.

It was not difficult for Belle to make a judgment. Olfactory senses may not be as reliable as the tongue and mouth, but Belle was sure she liked Number Two better: it was more subtle, less cloying. Without Leonard's bidding, she passed judgment.

"The second is best. Much more refined."

"Right," Sylvia said. "I think so, too."

"Charley?" Leonard asked.

Hopper shrugged carelessly. "It's hard for me to say, Sam."

"As a man, for Christ's sake," Leonard pressed him impatiently. "Which one would drive you crazy?"

"Well, if you want to know what I think, I think the first one smells too cheap. My guess is the second one would be more in the style you're looking for."

Leonard nodded. "Good. You're all right on. That first crap is put out by one of our competitors. 'Belle' is the second one. Don't you think it fits our image, Charley? It's all there, but it's elusive, hard to pin down. It floats, it swirls, it advances and retreats. It's got a haunting fragrance to it, undefinable." As he endeavored to define the characteristics of "Belle," Leonard's small hands moved in tight, expressive gestures. "And we really do want it to be elusive, aloof, evanescent—like Belle here. It's Belle all over—a little haughty, above us all, a very hard woman to pitch."

Belle smiled doubtfully. "Sam, I'm not really like that at all." She felt like saying, "Ask Charley."

But Leonard turned on her shrewdly. "Aren't you? Maybe you don't know yourself so well then. I'd say you were scarcely the earthy type. There is definitely an elusiveness about you, a certain spiritual quality."

Charley, straight-faced, watched her squirm.

"Hell," she finally said, "I am not elusive. Spiritual? Well . . . I have heard that before. But I still don't believe it."

Leonard clapped his hands, calling her to order. "Doesn't matter what you think you are. It's as we see you—and, for this, you're ideal. It is *you*. I know it's you."

Unthinkingly, Sylvia copied his gesture, clapping her hands. "I think so, too. You are perfect for this, Belle. You're sophisticated. Why, look at you. You could walk through a swamp in that dress and come out the other side ready for a dinner party. I was watching you when you got on the plane yesterday." She was positively enthusiastic in her assessment. "About this business, I admit, it, Sammy is unsurpassed."

Leonard nodded emphatically. "She's right, for once. I am a genius."

"But Mr. Leonard, you wouldn't dare do it if I disagreed," Sylvia said.

"The hell I wouldn't. I don't take orders from you, Sylvia. I run this show."

"And *I'm* the power behind the throne."

"Jesus, birdbrain, don't start now. Leave it go for a minute, will you? This is serious. I'm not prepared to debate with you tonight whether or not you're a ball-breaker."

"Ball-breaker?" Sylvia retorted, "is that what I am then? Listen, short stuff, I pulled you out of the gutter. When I met you, you were nothing—merely the smallest bass fiddle player on the Borscht Belt."

"All right, all right," he shouted. "Enough already, Sylvia. Jesus!" Leonard rubbed his face and fanned himself with one hand. "Belle . . . Belle, this is the basic scent—it's not perfect yet. We're still refining it, honing it down, buffing the rough edges. You can see there are still a few of those."

What could she say in response? Nothing. He was determined. And she was intrigued. She nodded, wanting to hear more.

"Here's the rest of the stuff," Leonard continued, pushing the boxes toward her. "It's the prototype of the complete line. Packaging isn't complete yet, of course. But take it, look it over, try it for size. That basic scent will run right across the line. And our market strategy is that 'Belle' is the most elegant, most sophisticated, most *today* presentation of American-originated cosmetic products ever. *And*," he stressed with an excited grimace, "we're going to have the most elegant, most sophisticated, the *most* woman

I know promoting it: Belle for 'Belle.' There! How do you like them apples?"

She nodded. Now was not the time to be faint-hearted. But she did have reservations. "You know," she said modestly—although with such a buildup how could she feel modest?—"you know, you could get lots of people better known than me. Face it, nobody ever heard of Belle Cooper."

Leonard shook his head violently. "If you'll pardon the expression, bullshit! You listen to me, young lady! When we're through with you, everybody in the goddamn country will know who Belle is. Am I right, Charley?"

Hopper nodded, agreeing with easy aplomb. "Sam, you are right."

"You believe I can handle this?" she asked sternly.

Leonard said, "I know you can. What I'm asking is childishly simple: that you go to work, use your talent. You're meant to be more than a mousy housewife, for God's sake! You have potential—use it. Besides which," he murmured fondly, "you're the only one I've got named Belle. And I'm just nuts about that name."

"Belle," Charley said, "for you, a piece of cake."

Was he mocking her? She glared briefly in his direction.

"Charley's right," Sam said. "The question is: will you do it?"

Belle nodded. "Sure, I'll do it. How could I say no? But I still don't understand exactly what it is I'll have to do."

"Ah, good, good," Leonard said, well satisfied. "What you'll have to do involves a whole packaging and promotional concept. First, we'll want your profile, a silhouette, for the boxes and labels. I want your signature: 'Belle,' Charley's idea." Ah, she thought, Charley's idea; it had gone that far, even before she had said yes. "Charley wants plenty of color for the magazine ads: Belle at work, Belle at play. Thirty-second TV commercials and, eventually, interviews with beauty editors all across the country. Store appearances. The talk shows: we'll make you a woman's spokesman—spokesperson, whatever you like—so we can keep up with all this ERA crap. Don't forget Cosmos has always been associated with the mass merchandising of cosmetics. 'Belle' will be our first attack on the exclusive sophisticated market. We've made a lot of money selling dreck in supermarkets and drugstores. Now we want 'Belle' in the finest boutiques, finest department stores, finest . . .

everything. 'Belle' is something I've always wanted to do."

Leonard jumped up to prance excitedly around the salon.

"Knock 'em dead!" he yelled. "Charley, how far along are you?"

"I've got all the rough artwork," Hopper said. "It's all downstairs. I've brought a proposal for a budget, an outline of all the TV commercial spots. I think I have everything. The only thing I don't know is precisely what's going to be in the line."

"Good," Leonard said. "We'll go over the whole thing in the morning. What we've got to keep in mind is that everything has got to be coordinated—boxes, bottles, jars, cans, the ads, the fashion. The whole thing will flow from one point to the next."

Forearms tense on his knees, Hopper was leaning forward in his chair, listening to Leonard, following his hyperactivity. Finally, he said, "Sam, I had my doubts . . . But I think we're going to work well together."

Leonard's face cracked into a wide grin. He commenced dancing again, waving his arms in self-esteem, hugging himself, slapping himself on the back.

"Sammy," Sylvia said, "you're going to give yourself a seizure."

Leonard roared at her. "Quiet, short stuff. Can't you see this is what makes me tick?" He commenced shouting for the steward, who hurried into the room, alarm on his face. "What's the best bottle of champagne we've got on this tub? Find it and bring it with glasses, pronto! We're celebrating."

His mood was infectious. Belle found herself laughing breathlessly, swept away by the idea itself, her part in it. Leonard grabbed her hand and whipped her to her feet, leading her in a comical waltz.

When the glasses had been filled from a chilled bottle of Roederer Cristal, his mien abruptly became serious.

"Now then, here's to Belle. Belle, you, and 'Belle' the product. I promise it'll be worthy of you and you'll be proud of it. We'll be ready to sail in January. More," Leonard continued, a religious fervor in his voice. "Belle, I'm going to make you a vice president of Cosmos Cosmetics and you'll be in charge of the 'Belle' line. It'll be your thing. And I'm going to pay you plenty. You're worth every penny of it."

She was flabbergasted. She hadn't expected this would be a permanent or full-time occupation; she had been ready for a few appearances, some traveling, some sort of a retainer. Numbly, she lifted her glass to him. Hopper grinned at her, telling her he approved and that he was pleased for her. He wanted her to do this. He loved her.

"And if Martin Cooper doesn't like it," Leonard said spitefully, "then . . . fuck him!"

Leonard was still pouring forth predictions of grand success and promises of fame and fortune when Sylvia dragged him off to bed.

"Tomorrow morning, bright and early, Charley," Sam called over his shoulder from the steps.

"I'll be up at eight," Charley responded. He grinned at Belle and shook his head, still amazed at Sam. He moved to sit beside her on the couch, carefully took her hand, and held it. "Belle . . . Well . . . What do you think about all this?"

"I don't know what to think. I guess I'm in shock."

The significance of what Sam had told them was still penetrating, but evoking within her a developing sense of well-being, satisfaction, anticipation. What was best, she told herself, was that this job, this ambitious project, would free her financially; and she was intelligent enough to know that the challenge and novelty would be good for her spiritually.

"A little shock like this one never hurt anybody," Charley said.

Belle agreed. "It's nice to know somebody thinks you're good for something."

"I never doubted that you were," he said soberly. "Trouble is, I never had a chance to say so."

"Charley," she said, "it's marvelous. The more I think about it, the more marvelous it is. And if what's his name doesn't like it, he can do what Sam said."

"Not up to him now whether he likes it or not," Charley reminded her.

"You're right. Where do I sign?" she exclaimed.

Charley leaned to kiss her. "I'm happy for you, Belle."

"And you think I can handle it?"

"Listen, if it's what you want, you can handle it . . . with one hand. It'll be a hell of a lot of work, Belle—traveling, meeting people, talking, selling—non-stop."

"That's what I do already," she said, for it was true. "I travel, meet people, talk, talk, talk."

Musing, he reminded her, "Cooper will hit the roof."

"You heard what Sam said," Belle said sharply. "But why should he care?"

"What he'll hate is the success of it, that it's going to be done even with his opposition, that we've combined forces against him."

His long face was weary, his eyes concerned.

"What else are you thinking, Charley?"

"Well . . . I'm also thinking, frankly, that this could drag you away from me."

"No, no, Charley. We're always going to be very close—no matter what happens. Charley . . . I wasn't dreaming this afternoon, was I?" He shook his head. "Well, then, Charley, would you mind very much if we went to bed, too?"

"It would be my pleasure," he said. "If you think the Leonards won't mind."

"How could they mind?" she asked, rising from the couch, taking his arm, walking toward the stairs. "They put us together."

Downstairs, Charley closed her cabin door and locked it. "Don't want any strangers bursting in, do we?" Then he put his arms around her waist, pulling her close to him. He kissed her.

"Charley, do you fine me terribly elusive?"

He squeezed her waist. "I did, a little. But methinks you are not so elusive. Mysterious, yes. Aloof, a little. Haughty . . . maybe."

"More naughty than haughty," she sighed. "Mr. Hopper, there are certain things I want to do to you. Would you mind very much if we retired?" Pausing, she added thoughtfully, "Sam already knows . . . about us." Charley agreed. "He's hoping for this," she went on. "He's crazy about you."

"Sam is a wise and perceptive man," Charley said.

They stood for a while, arms around each other, at the windows, watching the harbor lights flickering on the water and, from far off, they could hear the noises of the early-morning Croisette.

Charley slipped down the straps of her red evening dress and helped her out of it. Unabashedly, she stripped the rest of the way, until she was standing naked before him in the center of the cabin.

"Undress, Charley," she said. "I want to see you in all your skinny glory."

Charley took off his jacket, unfastened the studs and cuff links in his evening shirt, and removed it, then his black trousers, finally his underwear.

"I'm going to look funny flashing into my cabin in the morning," he said. "It'd be a lot more convenient if these cabins had connecting doors."

"We'll speak to the captain," she said.

He was so lanky, she thought, his body must have changed little since early maturity. All his muscles were long and firm. He would have been a runner, not a football player. He stood modestly in front of her.

"You're at half-mast," Belle observed. "Here, let me see about that."

Now they merged their naked bodies, standing, then, in bed, warming each other. Delicately, Charley played with her skin, leaving no part of her untouched by hand or lips until, in total relaxation, no nerve untended, they very naturally joined and made long and easy love. Charley drew out whatever tension remained within her and, almost unthinkingly, she achieved the plateau, then climaxed into the still night softly, crying out in a small voice. In the midst of her own surging, she felt the infusion of the quicksilver that joined him to her in every tiny fold and crevice. Breathing gently, they remained locked together, drifting off to sleep.

Chapter Fourteen

"Well," Cooper asked, "is this what you had in mind for the glorious Fourth?"

Sitting on the next bar stool, Pamela Renfrew nudged his shoulder with her bosom. "Perfect," she said, "egg-zactly what I had in mind. I love Las Vegas."

"Well, I don't," he said sullenly. "I think it stinks."

"It sucks," Pamela slurred. "It's sleazy and tacky. But I love it."

It was just like she was, he told himself. Pamela was drinking herself to numbness, polishing off vodkas on the rocks as fast as Cooper could order them.

"The only good thing about this place is upstairs in bed," he said. "I hate all these goddamn slot machines. They're noisy—and look at all those old broads with their paper-cups of nickels, hooked to the machines. Jesus, ugly."

"You like the crap tables, Marty," she reminded him.

"Well, Christ, that's gambling: throwing dice."

Cosily, Pamela pulled at his arm, trying to soothe him. "Marty, what's so bad? It's not often we get a chance to go away together."

"Yeah."

Yeah, he muttered to himself, and she wasn't even first choice. What he'd really wanted for the glorious Fourth was some time with Daisy Cox. But that had been impossible. Jake was taking off work for the holiday. So here, he realized in disappointment, he was with Pamela Renfrew. And to think, at that moment Belle and Charley were in France, wallowing in the luxury of the Sam Leonard yacht. Christ! Maybe he should have gone after all, made it up with Belle, or tried to. Even that might have been better than this, sitting half-drunk and very depressed, in a Las Vegas bar with this cheap broad.

They were sitting on the edge of the gambling pit, dazed by the flashing lights and the unceasing din of the slot machines being fed and sometimes paying off with a thundering rattle of nickels, dimes, quarters, silver dollars.

And it was only three P.M. He was tired and wanted to go upstairs. Pulling strings, and that wasn't easy either on a holiday weekend, he'd arranged a big double room and they'd flown up that morning. Pamela had been playing the machines since their arrival and he, out of boredom, had lost a bundle on the crap table, then more over blackjack. Cooper detested losing; he considered it more than mere bad luck, more like a personal insult paid him by the proprietors of the city.

"Wha'sa time?"

"Three," he said.

"In the afternoon?"

"What the fuck did you think? If it was three in the morning, I wouldn't be sitting here."

He was warm, sweating from the vodka. He was angry, with himself, the world. A sense of outrage, of victimization, boiled inside him. Christ, he had everything; he had nothing. He and Belle were finished: she hadn't been broken up by any means to learn she was going to Europe without him, in the company of good old, lazy Charley Hopper. Christ, that was another thing. Hopper these days had the energy and dedication of a newt. Why, and how, had they ever gone into business together? Hopper didn't care about the business anymore, hadn't since his divorce from that silly wife of his: Fay. Fay had been fey, he thought humorously, and the one thing—ha ha, a deep, dark secret—Charley didn't know, Charley who knew almost all there was to know about his old pal Mart, was that Cooper had had her one afternoon on Charley's desk at C.A.A., even before she'd met her high-rolling new husband. But that was beside the point, he thought darkly. The point was that Charley was indifferent to C.A.A.; he didn't give a damn.

Shit! Charley was such a gentleman. Cooper would not have been the least bit surprised if Charley didn't take advantage of the trip to France to put the arm on Belle. In Charley's shoes, he would have.

Pamela was hurtfully saying, "Marty, I just asked what time it is."

"I told you," he said heavily, "it's three o'clock in the afternoon."

"I'm getting loaded," she said. "Let's go upstairs. I want to be fresh for the show tonight."

"Jesus Christ," he pouted, "Liberace, I can't stand him."

"Marty," Pamela pleaded, "I love him. Did you get a table in front? I want to get to touch his jewelry."

"Yes, Pamela," he said patiently, "I got a table in front. I talked to the boys and slipped them a hundred and got a table in front. And I'm liable to get so drunk, I'll jump on the stage and smash up his piano."

She giggled. "Marty, you wouldn't."

He asked for the check. As he was pulling bills off his money clip, then glancing up, he was startled to see Sharon Peters walking across the lobby toward the elevators, her arm in that of none other than Morris Mauery. Mauery, his head shaved up past his ears to leave something like an Indian warlock on the top, his heavy glasses glinting beneath the deadening neon lights, chanced to turn. Cooper felt the weight of Mauery's eyes—holy shit, he thought, the enforcer.

Then he shrugged carelessly. Why should he feel threatened by Mauery? It was unlikely Sharon had dared tell him about her several screws with Cooper. And, if it came to that, he had enough money to get Mauery hit, just as Mauery had the power to get him hit.

For some reason, perhaps because Cooper had spotted them, Mauery changed direction, pulling Sharon toward them.

"Martin," Sharon said timidly, "what a surprise to see you here."

"Hello, Sharon," he said, then automatically did the introduction. "You know Pamela Renfrew. Sharon Peters . . . Morris Mauery. Hello there, Morris."

"How are you, Marty? Pamela?" Mauery said harshly.

Pamela was too drunk to get across a rough spot. She mumbled a quick hello, then turned to the dregs of her vodka.

"What are you doing up here, Martin?" Sharon asked nervously. "How come you're not in Malibu eating hot dogs?"

Cooper fumbled but recovered nicely. "Pamela and I had to come up on real-estate business."

Pamela ruined that by matter-of-factly stating, "We're up for a dirty weekend, facts be known."

Mauery belched a laugh and Cooper chuckled shakily, "Always kidding. But what are you two up to? How's Madeleine, Morrie?" he asked pointedly.

Unblinkingly, Mauery said, "She's fine." His eyes glittered; he didn't appreciate the shot. "Sharon and I are seeing about a little transportation matter."

"Well . . . " Cooper did not know what else to say. "Hey! It's great seeing you both."

"Take care, Marty," Mauery said.

They resumed their course toward the elevators. "Take care?" What the hell was that supposed to mean? Was it possible that Sharon had told him? The bitch. He wondered for a moment what had gone wrong there. Maybe he hadn't been kinky enough for her. Too bad—she was rich as hell.

He turned angrily on Pamela. "You had to say that?"

"What's it matter?" she said indifferently. "You can see they're up to no good. So we're even. Nobody's going to say anything, if that worries you so much. Your reputation. Jesus! C'mon, let's go upstairs."

"Goddamn it," Cooper snarled, "wait 'til they get in the elevator. Smartass, you didn't have to make that crack. It happens I do have a good reputation."

"Bull," Pamela defied him. "Everybody in L.A. knows you're nothing but a big cocksman."

It didn't displease him to hear it. "I'm preceded by my reputation," he said.

When Mauery and Sharon had been taken away and were in an elevator headed for the twentieth floor, Pamela kissed him hungrily, the flesh of her large frame jumping toward him. She ran her hand down the inside of his leg.

"Your reputation is showing," she mumbled.

God, he thought, did he have the energy, the stamina? He thought again of Daisy. She'd have had no trouble getting it out of him.

"Bad luck, plain bad luck, seeing that son of a bitch here," Morris Mauery said blackly when he and Sharon were in their suite.

"Once he saw us," Sharon shrugged, "you were smart to take the bull by the horns."

Mauery gave no indication he suspected anything of her previous liaison with Cooper.

"Yeah," he nodded. "Yeah, I was smart. Maybe we should have asked them to join us at the show tonight."

"Are you sure you want to go, Morrie?" Sharon asked tiredly.

"To see Liberace? Sure, I'm sure. That guy is fantastic." He walked across the ballroom-sized living room to a bar on the other side and squirted himself a glass of plain soda. "Anything for you, Sharon?"

"A brandy," she said, thinking she'd need it.

Mauery carried her a sizable shot of Remy Martin. He drained his soda, burped comfortably, and put his arms around her.

"You're a doll," he said hoarsely. "C'mon in the bedroom."

Mauery was not one for foreplay. He fiddled with the back of her dress, then slipped his hands inside and around to grab her breasts and pinch the nipples. His hands were powerful.

"Morrie, take it easy."

"Fuck that," he said, "get undressed."

Without another word, he got out of his clothes and stood waiting, like some kind of an Oriental executioner. Sharon slipped out of the dress, then her bra and pantyhose and, hardly giving her time, he came at her again. The hard calluses of his fingers worked at her buttocks, then, unheeding of her protests, he spun her around and pushed her, face down, on the bed. She felt him, hard and wet, and then he was forcing himself into her anus, making her cry out in pain. But she was helpless, there was nothing, nothing, she could do, except think she would like to see him dead. He said it was the price. He grunted like a beast, not caring that he was hurting her, even taking pleasure from it. Mauery was a strange and twisted man. When he came, it was with a curse and then, cursing again, he wrenched away, leaving her, destroyed, on the bed. Aching, and hating him, she heard him fumbling for his clothes.

"You bastard," she gasped. "Morrie, what the hell is it with you?"

"Please," he said, "turn around. You'll be all right."

"No, I don't want to see you."

"Yeah," he sneered, "let me tell you something, Sharon. We need each other. You don't like being cornholed, do you? No. But for me, it's the only pleasure."

A suspicion that was not new to her thrust forward again: Mauery liked little boys and it was true his only pleasure was in getting it off like that, not seeing her face, from behind. She would never have dared suggest it though, even in wildest jest.

She commenced to cry. Tears rolled down her face and she buried them in the bed.

"Sharon," Mauery said, "don't do that. It makes me sad." But she couldn't stop. "Make you remember anything, seeing Cooper?" he sneered.

Oh, God. "No," she said.

"I don't believe you," Mauery said cruelly. "He used to fuck you, didn't he?"

"No, Morrie."

His belt descended on her buttocks. At least, it was not the buckle end. He hit her until she stopped crying and lay stony-faced and silent before him.

It was at the Donohues' glorious Fourth beach party that Camilla Young saw Sheldon Moore again for the first time since their afternoon escapade.

Sheldon, sad-faced under a gay red, white, and blue striped top hat, was standing next to the barbeque, eating a hot dog and sipping a beer out of a can.

"Hi, Sheldon," she said, "how are you today?"

"Camilla! My darling," he said softly.

"Wanta take a ride to the beach, Sheldon?"

"We are at the beach, Camilla."

"Oh, so we are. Wanta take a walk in the sand, Sheldon?"

He looked distressed. "Camilla, are you all right?"

"Right as rain," she said. "Where's Bertha?"

He was pained at the mention of her name. "She couldn't . . . wouldn't come. She's not feeling well."

"Christ! That's a relief." She was not up to exchanging pleasantries with Bertha Moore. "Who's that girl with the Markmans?"

Sheldon turned. "Oh, that's Belle Cooper's daughter. Her name is Susan."

Susan, Camilla noted, was reserved, aloof, like her

mother. Beside Susan's look of health, Sally Markman seemed tired, very haggard and old. Sally was sitting at a table under the shade of an umbrella, Susan next to her. Behind them, standing, hat covering his bald head, Bernard Markman was talking animatedly with Bob Stone, the department store man. Mrs. Stone was sitting on the other side of Sally.

"Where's Belle?" Camilla asked.

"Oh . . . Belle had to go off to Europe. Something to do with that party you're involved in."

"That *they're* involved in, not me."

"Camilla," Sheldon said thoughtfully, "I think you should be involved. You need something to do."

She smiled, shaking her head and remembering the day they'd driven out here, parked, and walked through the sand to sit on a pile of mossy rocks above the Pacific.

"What'd Bertha say that day?" she asked him. "Did she catch a cab?"

"Somebody drove her home," he said, lightly. "She was mad as a hornet."

They had talked a lot that day. Camilla had told him her whole story, how ugly the divorce had been, about the fight over her children, how her now ex-husband had pulled every trick in the book to get them away from her. But she had won, goddamn it, and she wasn't finished with him yet. It had been nice to unload all this on Sheldon and they hadn't even mentioned Bertha.

"Sheldon," Camilla said, "if you had to talk your way out of it, nobody would believe we didn't make it that day on the beach."

"Camilla," he protested weakly.

She put her hand on his sleeve. "Sheldon, it's not such an ugly idea, you know. I think we should."

He didn't say anything to that, He bent and took a can of beer out of a tub of ice. "Here, have a beer. It's good and cold. Have a hot dog. Enjoy yourself, Camilla."

She took the beer and put the metal lip of the can to her lips. Coldness soothed her. "Are you enjoying yourself, Sheldon?" she asked.

"Now I am, after you got here."

"Well," she said disconsolately, "at least I got here first—before her . . ."

The Cannons—Marjery and Gregory—had come into

the patio. Marjery was wearing white slacks and a slinky top unbuttoned to show the mid-chest folds of her pancake boobs. She had tied her lackluster hair back with a yellow ribbon. Gregory, slick, black-haired and sleek, was bespectacled and intent of expression. He quickly found the host, Doug Donohue, and opened what he had been schooled to think was bubbling repartee: something about a game of golf in the morning and a hangover still hanging on. Gregory was truly fatuous, Camilla thought, and a distorted man to boot. He was forever making off-color remarks to women, with not the slightest intention of following through.

"You don't like Marjery?" Sheldon asked, as if astounded that such a person as Camilla could actually dislike anyone.

"She's a barracuda," Camilla replied. "*Jaws Three . . .*"

Marjery made straight for Sally Markman, her mouth gaping with an inane smile that showed pinkish gums. "Sally! It's *so* good to see you." Marjery would have heard by now that she was to be taken on the December committee. Marjery turned to Markman. "Bernard! How are you, love?"

Markman looked absently at her and nodded, his glasses slipping on his vaulted nose. "Oh, hello there, Marjery."

Doug Donohue was president of the Pacific Trading Bank, so many of his financial friends had been invited, none of whom Camilla knew well. Marcia King, her short hair hennaed rusty-red, was stomping around on her walking stick—undoubtedly an affectation, for Marcia played tennis every morning. She was the interior designer they wanted to get to do the invitations and party program. Marcia's husband was a man who lived in a wheelchair, and he had obviously been left home to enjoy the Fourth by himself.

Sitting separately, cliqueishly, the beach people were having their own usual rare and happy time, roaring over their problems: high tides, battered beachfronts, the trial of rebuilding after the last great storm, the high price of everything, their battles with the dictatorial Coastal Commission.

Boring, Camilla thought. "Where's Sharon Peters?" she asked. "She's a pal of the Donohues'."

"I don't know," Sheldon said. "But the Hymans are inside, talking with . . . I don't know . . . all the movie people are sitting in the dark. They like good lighting for the movies, but they always sit in the dark."

"Sheldon," she brought it up again, "I think we should. I'd like to."

His discomfort showed, and miserably he said, "Camilla, we're trapped like rats. Everybody is trapped."

His helplessness angered her. "Don't say that. It's not so. We can escape. Where could we go?"

He shook his head. "That's just it. Where *could* we go? My house out here? There's always somebody there. The house in town? Bertha. Your place? Out of the question. Palm Springs? There's a housekeeper there, too. You see, Camilla, we're trapped. Or," his face grimaced sardonically, "a motel? Would you like that, Camilla? No, I thought not. Nor would I. You see?"

The argument stopped her for a second. "All those places and nowhere to go? It seems impossible."

"That's the trouble. It is very impossible."

She smiled bitterly. "What about the back of your car? I haven't done that since my first year in college."

Now she had genuinely shocked him. "Camilla . . ."

"Well," she said stoutly, "it shows it *is* possible."

More new arrivals were coming into the patio: Daisy and Jake Cox. They looked like movie extras. Jake was wearing an old pair of army fatigues he'd probably bought in one of those surplus shops in Hollywood, an ugly polyester sports shirt; his hair was already stiff from the salt air. Jake stood for an instant, bemused, as if he'd been dropped into Siberia, before Gregory Cannon sighted him and called his name.

Daisy was in a sailor top, navy with white stripes, and brief, brief white shorts, which showed to advantage her tanned legs, the cleavage of her bottom, and the rounded mound of her crotch. Bright red lipstick glistened on her lips. Her hair was pulled back at her ears, held in place by two diamond-studded bobby pins.

Cannon pumped Jake Cox's hand vigorously. "It's a pleasure to see you, sir!"

"He'll be making his investment pitch momentarily," Sheldon murmured. "Jesus, Camilla, these people—where in the world do they come from?"

"You know what they say," she said, "shake the country and all the nuts will slide to California."

Priscilla and Bill Murray sauntered out of the house. Bill was a young and striving banker, part of the Donohue apparatus. It was Priscilla they'd been talking about at lunch the other day as a likely candidate for the committee. She was a beauty—tall, slender, and dark-haired, with luminous white skin. A big sunhat shaded her delicate face.

Bill, looking unhappy, headed straight for the bar. "Hi, Camilla, how are you? Sheldon?"

"Hello, Bill," she said.

They'd attended Beverly Hills High School together and had remained friends, if distant friends, over the intervening years. Now, his marriage was not happy. Word around town was that Bill spent too much time in the singles' bars. But there was not an iota of gossip about Priscilla.

As they watched the thickening melange of people, Daisy Cox drifted toward Sally Markman's table and did everything but genuflect. She bent to kiss Sally's cheek, leaving a red mark across the wrinkles. Sally said something, and motioned behind her at Bernard. Bernard took Daisy's hand and shook it warmly, not letting go. He stared intently at her chest, then, mischievously, at the shorts. Daisy threw him a trifling little smile and there! Camilla noticed Marjery Cannon, still circling the general area, looked anxious.

This small drama was broken up when Doug Donohue bounced out of the house, his arm around a plump, red-cheeked woman: Doris Donohue.

"Hey, everybody!" Donohue shouted, "now here's the star of the show, fresh from the kitchen. Cheers! Applause! Now, we want you to have a good time—eat, drink and be merry. We've got a calliope player coming in an hour or so and then we'll all get to sing 'Yankee Doodle and a Noodle in His Cap . . .' "

"Oh, Jesus," Camilla groaned, "where could we go? Where's the one place on the Fourth of July that's going to be deserted?"

Sheldon, despite his misery, laughed. "The British consulate?"

Pat Hyman emerged from the living room, carrying a glass of white wine, and blinking before the sunshine, her thin face set and her flared nostrils twitching. She saw Daisy Cox talking to Bernard Markman.

Pat butted in without any prelude. "Daisy, sweetheart."

"Hi, Pat. Beautiful day for it."

Markman chuckled. Bill Murray was edging toward Daisy, as his wife took a seat at Sally's shaded table. Coolly, Priscilla watched Murray kiss Daisy's flushed cheek. Daisy looked warily at Murray, as if waiting for him to say something funny or daring. In the meantime, Gregory Cannon had two-stepped Jake Cox into a corner and was speaking excitedly, his face close to Cox's.

"Hell," Camilla said, "I'm going to go sit on the beach."

"I'll saunter down in a minute."

"Jesus, Sheldon, don't take any chances, will you?"

Sheldon's face twisted with hurt. But Camilla, impatiently, did not pause. She crossed the patio, climbed the sea wall, and went down into the burning sand. Holding her beer carefully, she plopped down, cosily by herself, took a cigarette out of her pocketbook, and lit it.

There was a small breeze off the ocean. Up and down the beach, children, clusters of grown-ups, and shaggy dogs went about the things people and dogs do on the Fourth of July. Kites flew overhead, swimmers dashed in and out of the surf, the dogs barked. Here and there, an illegal firecracker exploded. A couple of hundred yards away down the beach, a tall and portly man dressed in full Indian regalia and carrying an American flag was marching back and forth in the sand, hupping, singing, twirling the flag, then again issuing drill instructions. Spaced like decorations across the spread of beach, boys and girls lay together, covered in sand, their eyes closed under the sun, fingertips touching. A solitary jogger, unmindful of the holiday, trotted past, grunting.

The sand swished beside her. But the body that slumped down beside her was not Sheldon's. It was Bill Murray's.

"How you doing, solitary Camilla?" he asked.

"Being solitary," she said, not encouraging him.

Murray was still trim enough, his black hair curly. But the booze showed around his eyes, in the puffiness along his jowls.

"Come on, Camilla, cheer up. Nothing can be that bad."

Murry did not mean to be unfriendly. But she had lost her distance.

"Maybe not if you drink enough," she said.

"Oh, shit, Camilla, don't you say I'm loaded now, okay?"

"Aren't you?"

"Jesus, not yet. It's too early. I've only had a couple. Come on, Camilla, let's have a smile. Want to neck?"

"Sure," she said tersely, wishing he would go away.

But he was not to be put off. "Camilla, what say we have lunch one of these days? We're old friends. You can tell me all about it."

"When did you have in mind?"

"Well, maybe next week," he said, not catching her sarcasm.

"I'll call you," she said curtly.

Sheldon did appear next, evidently, Camilla thought sourly, thinking it would be all right with Bill Murray there as chaperone.

"Wow!" Sheldon said, trying to sound chummy, "what a great day it is."

"A zinger," Murray agreed. Jesus, she could not escape it. Most men were just like her ex-husband. "Wish we had a frisbee or something, Sheldon," Murray groused, "a football, something to throw around. But I don't suppose we'll find anything like that in Doughty Doug's house.

Camilla watched the tiny waves licking at the sand in front of her feet. They came from far away, from China, or Australia, or Alaska, far away from all this. What would it be like to step into the waves, to join those foreign travelers, and leave here with them . . . forever?

Jesus, she pulled back with a soft exclamation. She was thinking of suicide again. The thought, the modus of doing it, had come to her much lately.

Murray took her out of it. He climbed to his feet and set off in a gallop down the beach, running as fast as he could, driving his legs. After a hundred yards of it, he stopped short, lifted his arms, and whooped.

The man with the flag whooped back.

"He's a mess," Camilla said to Sheldon.

"He's driving Priscilla crazy, that's what he's doing."

"Well," Camilla said sensibly, "she should dump him."

He nodded, flicking at the sand with a stiffened bit of gray flotsam. "Sometimes it ain't so easy, Camilla. People hope against hope."

"And screw themselves into eternity," she said harshly, "and for what? Hoping against hope! That's a lot of old b.s., Sheldon."

"I know," he said, then whispered, "I was just thinking.

I'm going to buy a condo. I'm going to buy one in a tall building off Sunset, with a view."

"That'll be nice."

"But you don't understand."

She realized what he was suggesting. "A love nest, Sheldon?"

"I could get one for a couple 100,000, maybe 250. No one would know . . ."

"Not even?" she whispered back, dramatically.

He was deflated again. "For us, Camilla," he said urgently.

For some reason, the idea depressed her even more. "How long would it take, Sheldon? Let's see, a month escrow, then furnishing it, decorating it. I don't know if I can wait that long, Sheldon. Time flies, you know, life goes. Wouldn't it be a lot simpler to check into a hotel?"

"Simpler, maybe," he said stubbornly, "but in the long run not so simple . . . or satisfactory, Camilla."

"Sheldon," she said, softening, "I know. I know what you're thinking."

Marcia King, having parked her cane on the patio, appeared nearby. She was leading Daisy Cox by the hand.

"We're going for a little walk," she announced. "Walking in the samd is good for my leg."

Daisy kicked off her sandals. Her bright red polished toenails poked up in the sand, like exotic shells. The two went to the water's edge, where the sand was firm, and strolled down the beach toward the spot where Bill Murray was running in place, then flinging himself down to do a pushup.

The Donohue patio was full now and the overflow was spreading into the sand.

A small airplane appeared out of the west and came down close to the water to buzz along the beach toward Santa Monica. The pilot waggled his wings.

"He's saying hello," Sheldon observed.

"And goodbye. Hello and goodbye," Camilla added.

Sharon Peters' housekeeper, Mrs. Robinson, was pottering around the penthouse late in the afternoon. Since Sharon would not be there for dinner, Mrs. Robinson was preparing to go out to a movie. The phone rang.

"Yes."

"Could I speak to Mrs. Peters, please?"

"She's not available at the moment," Mrs. Robinson said cautiously. You never said a person was not home; you said they weren't available.

"She's out of town?"

"She's not available."

There was a pause, then the voice said, "I was a . . . friend of her late husband's, Mr. Peters. Could I leave a message?"

"Of course," said Mrs. Robinson efficiently. "What please?"

"My name is Frank Woodley and I'm living in Los Angeles now. I'd like to talk to her." He gave Mrs. Robinson a telephone number.

"I'll give her the message," Mrs. Robinson said.

Cooper was sitting in bed, pillows propped behind him, looking at television. Beside him, Pamela was flat on her back, arms and legs spread-eagled over two-thirds of the king-sized bed, the position in which he had left her. She was staring at the ceiling. She had the blank look of a sated being. Her cheeks were slack after sex, the muscles in her hands twitched. Glancing at her out of the corner of his eye, Cooper thought to himself that she was not beautiful. Her Nordic blondeness was almost masculine. She looked like a Viking warrior, he thought sardonically: Olaf, the Nutcracker. There was nothing about her to remind him of the highly sexed tease, Daisy Cox. She was merely big and rawboned, a farm girl.

"Marty?"

"What?"

"Why don't you dump her? Would you marry me?"

"No."

"What!" She sat up, shocked, for he had never said it quite so bluntly before. He had always maybe-ed.

"I said no," he repeated. "No, I can't dump her. Christ, that'd wreck my business. I'm not in any position to split everything down the middle, and I don't have the cash to pay her off. You have any idea how much that'd take? So, I can't dump her and, therefore, I can't marry you."

Sullenly, she said, "That's it then. I'm not going on like this."

"So don't," he said indifferently. He didn't take his eyes off the TV.

"You don't care?" Her voice was high-pitched, disbelieving.

"I care, yes," he muttered. "But if it's not what you want, then so long, Pams."

Her body trembled, shaking the bed. The bovine face shuddered and tears gushed out of her eyes.

"You . . . Marty. You're a cold, cold man."

"All the better. I won't be all broken up then, will I?"

"Miserable son of a bitch," she yelled. "All you ever wanted me for was to play with, to screw, when you got nothing better to do."

Annoyed at the histrionics, he turned his head and calmly said, "Don't you have a good time?"

"Yes, but . . ."

"But what?" he demanded. "You like screwing, so what's the odds?"

"Bastard!" she yelled, sobbing freely, "don't you ever think a woman might want something more?"

"Such as what?" he said sarcastically. "Marriage, *Pammy*? A little house and kiddies and a fireplace Santa Claus slides down on his ass Christmas Eve? Bullshit, that's not for you, Pamela."

"How do you know?" she howled. "You've never asked me. I happen to come from a big family, and where I come from, those things are . . . sacred."

He chuckled. "Bullshit, Pamela. Don't make me puke."

She slapped him in the face, so unexpectedly and so hard that his head cracked against the headboard.

"You miserable . . ."

Before he could move, she had grabbed his hand and stuck his little finger in her mouth. She was biting. At first, he laughed at her anger, but then her teeth bit through the skin, into the muscle, and were grinding on insubstantial ligaments.

"Jesus Christ!"

Cooper swung his left hand across his body and slammed it against her temple. That stopped her. Her mouth went loose. She was out cold. Cooper painfully removed the damaged finger from her teeth. It dangled, bleeding profusely on the sheet. Weak from shock, Cooper jumped out of bed and went into the bathroom. He turned on cold water and thrust his hand under it, but it only made the wound bleed more. Finally, he wrapped a face towel around the finger and squeezed, willing the bleeding to stop. The finger had gone numb . . . But, at last, the blood ceased pumping through the towel.

He went back into the other room, so furious he didn't know what to do. She was groaning. He dared not let go of the finger, but he managed to deliver a powerful kick to her ass, and punted her right cheek.

"Wake up, you cunt!"

She rolled over. Her right eye was already turning blue. "Goddamn you," she hissed.

"Get your ass out of that bed! Get packed and get the hell out of here, you miserable cunt!"

"Son of a bitch," she muttered, "miserable son of a bitch."

"Moron," he cried, "you damn near bit off my finger, stupid bitch. What the hell's wrong with you anyway? What right do you have to do that?"

"You insulted me, you cocksucker," she screamed. "I wish I'd bitten your cock off. I'd do it now."

"Yeah, you'd do it if you wanted to take a high dive out that goddamn window."

She was on her feet, shakily pulling her overnight bag out of the closet. Still so angry she could hardly function, still staggered by his blow, she threw her clothes into the bag and within minutes had dressed again in the same dress she'd been wearing. She went into the bathroom and slashed lipstick on her face and hastily brushed her hair.

"You gave me a shiner, you mother fucker," she yelled. She picked up her bag and went to the door. "Goodbye, you shit!"

She was gone.

Holding his arm aloft to control the blood, Cooper dialed the hotel operator.

"Get a doctor up here right away." He gave her the room number. "I've smashed my finger and it's hurting like hell."

Bertha Moore drove to the Beverly Camino about five and went into the Polka-Dot Bar for a drink. She'd be damned, she had decided, if she was going to sit home all day waiting for Sheldon. Bertha, in revenge, had backed out of the Donohue party. They'd had a rip-roaring fight in the morning and Sheldon had not been as easily put down as usual. In fact, finally, he'd told her to go to hell. And she was a little concerned. She was not such a fool that she didn't realize that everything, including even men, had a certain point beyond which they would not be pushed without rebelling or breaking. Well, she thought grimly, her face stubbornly set, then let him break. He would break before she would let him loose.

Bertha slid her elongated body up on a barstool and ordered a gin and tonic. She was sitting there brooding when somebody tapped her on the shoulder. Turning, she recognized the new German, the man she'd met the day of the luncheon, the skinny being she'd thought then had looked constipated and probably suffering from hemorrhoids.

"Mrs. Moore?" Ehrlich said eagerly.

"Yes, you remembered my name," she said, impressed. She should not think so scornfully of him.

"Of course. How are you today, Mrs. Moore?"

"Quite well," she said. "I didn't have anything to do, so I decided to drive over here and see what's going on. I preferred not to go to the beach party. I don't care for beach parties. Everything is so sandy."

Her words poured forth and she knew something was wrong with her. What did this Ehrlich person care about beach parties, or whether she'd been invited. She didn't have to explain everything to a comparative stranger.

"Ah," he said sympathetically. "For me, it is a day of duty."

"Well, can I buy you a drink, Mr . . ." She'd leave it for him to pronounce his name again.

"Ehrlich, yes. But no," he said quickly, "it would not do for me to sit with the guests. I will stand here for a moment, if you please."

"Sure," she said. "I guess you still don't know too many people in L.A., do you?"

"Well, I have met a few charming people in just a few weeks," he replied enthusiastically, "such as yourself, for example."

He thought her charming. Bertha was flattered. "But you never get out of the hotel."

Ehrlich smiled desolately. "Not often. My duty is very time-consuming."

"You live right here, don't you?"

"Oh, yes, I have a small suite of two rooms—not with a beautiful view of Beverly Hills, I fear, but for me a sufficiency."

Not a bad deal, Bertha thought. Room for a pittance and food at cut rates.

She allowed herself a rare smile. "Did you bring all your cuckoo clocks with you?"

"Ha, ha, ha." He laughed boisterously, as if this were the most outrageous joke he'd heard since leaving Switzerland. "No, Mrs. Moore, just one which belonged to my grandfather."

"Really? It must be a very old one then."

"Yes, yes, it is very old, but in keeping the time, it is perfection itself. Would you . . . perhaps . . . like to see it sometime?"

"Well, yes, I would," Bertha said, smiling warmly, "I would be very interested in seeing it."

It should not have been an unexpected thing to happen on a hot and hectic beach holiday.

The man had come to play on his calliope. Bill Murray had returned from his exercise, had two more drinks, and was asleep in a deckchair. Gregory Cannon, Markman, and Jake Cox were crouched on the sea wall, where they'd been talking politics. Sally was still holding court at her table. Movie people were inside, gossiping and joking. Marcia King and Daisy Cox were standing shoulder to shoulder on the sandy side of the sea wall, and Camilla, for her and Sheldon's position right behind them, could see that Marcia was holding tightly to Daisy's hand, caressing the backs of her fingers. Daisy did not seem to mind; now and then, she glanced at Marcia and smiled.

They were all trying to pay attention to Doug Donohue, red-faced from the sun and the bourbon he'd been drinking, as he delivered disjointed homilies about the glorious Fourth, its meaning for the present, its hope for the future.

It was just about then that he was stricken.

In mid-thought, Donohue's eyes popped in astonishment, and his lips ballooned with pain. He clutched at his chest and staggered backward, collapsing on top of Bill Murray.

Doris Donohue loosed a shrill scream.

"What the hell . . ." Murray cried, waking up.

"Doug, Doug!" Doris squealed frantically. "Quick . . . everybody . . ."

Sally Markman recovered first and took charge. This, Camilla thought, in the midst of her own frightened thoughts, was not surprising. "Bernard, call Tom Glenn. Call the paramedics."

Markman hurried into the house.

Gregory Cannon huffed, "Come, come, let's carry him inside. Come on, come on."

Sheldon and Camilla, along with Daisy and Marcia, crowded up into the patio.

Donohue's beach friends helped ease the heavy, now erratically panting man into the cool of the living room. George Hyman and his cigar-smoking show-business cronies leaped to their feet.

"Jesus, Doug!" Hyman exclaimed, shocked, as if Donohue had interrupted something intimate or committed a horrible social gaffe.

They placed Donohue on the couch where Hyman had been sitting.

"Quiet, everybody, quiet," Sally ordered. "Get out of the way. Give him room. Let me get at him."

She sat down beside Donohue, loosened his belt, and began massaging his left arm.

Bernard was back quickly. "Everything's on the way," he reported to Sally.

"Take off his shoes," she said.

Donohue opened his eyes and looked around. His eyes were glazed with fright and incomprehension. "Go on, go on," he whispered. "What's this all about? What happened? I'm not drunk. I'll be all right in a minute."

Bill Murray was beside Camilla and Sheldon, just outside the terrace door.

"Christ," he said softly, "that's been coming a while. He lives too hard."

Sheldon left them to go inside. He put his arm around Doris Donohue. Doug's eyes lit on Sheldon, an old friend, and Doris. He tried to smile.

George Hyman took his wife's arm, whispered an explanation to Bernard Markman, and he and Pat slipped away. Susan quietly retreated, passing Camilla on her way to the sea wall. "Tell Sally I've gone, please." For a second, Bill Murray looked as if he might follow her, but he thought better of it.

When the paramedics arrived, they shooed everybody out of the room. One of them quickly gave Donohue an injection. As they watched for a reaction, a blush of color returned to Donohue's cheeks. Then they moved Donohue onto a stretcher and carried him away.

Sally said she would go with Doris in the ambulance. Bernard was to follow in the car.

Doris hesitated.

"Go on," Sheldon said, "I'll take care of everything. I'll lock up."

The party of the glorious Fourth was over. In minutes, the house was empty. In subdued voices, the guests said goodbye and went outside to their cars. The "Beachies" disappeared into the sand to walk home.

"Camilla," Sheldon whispered, "stay with me, please."

Sheldon went into the kitchen to talk to the caterers. He brought back two beers and they sat to wait while the catering crew cleaned up and carried their party equipment outside. Their boss came into the living room.

"Mr. Moore, we sure are sorry about this," he said. "I hope Mr. Donohue is going to be all right. What I've done is leave food in the refrigerator for Mrs. Donohue. She's not going to feel like cooking when she gets back."

"Jack, that's nice," Sheldon said, "very thoughtful. Everything is going to be okay, I know."

"Right. No problem. Well, we'll be on our way then."

Sheldon followed them to the front gate, then came back in, closing the house door. He sat down beside Camilla.

"God," he said, "he was so lively just an hour ago."

She nodded. The first thing she realized was that she and Sheldon were alone. She edged closer to him as he sat there shaking his head, the beer bottle in his hands between his legs.

"Sheldon, you see how fast life can abandon us?"

"But Doug is going to be okay, Camilla."

"I know," she said lovingly, "I always have to hammer home the point, don't I? The point is, Sheldon, that he might have been dead—just like that. There's just not much time, Sheldon."

He understood what she was saying. She kissed him wetly on the cheek and he turned to her, butting his nose into her eye.

"Sheldon, come on, let's go upstairs."

"Yes."

They passed the Donohues' front bedroom and went down the hallway to a guest room on the side of the house.

It was furnished sparsely with a single bed, a chest of drawers, bookcases, and an old TV set.

"This will do nicely," Camilla said.

Standing against him, trembling, she lifted herself to kiss him on the mouth. Then she shook herself and removed her dress and underwear. He was shaking.

"Camilla, you're beautiful."

"No," she disagreed roughly. "I'm not. I'm too fat in the wrong places, and my tits are floppy. That's what you get for having children. I've also got a caesarean scar—right there." She pointed to the middle of her belly.

"I don't care," he said, "you're beautiful."

Shyly, he undressed, turning from her so she couldn't see him, then facing her, his hands modestly draped at his crotch.

Camilla laughed, close to crying. "Move your hands, goddamn it, Sheldon. You're beautiful, too."

By the books, she knew, Sheldon would never have been defined as beautiful. But she loved him. His chest was thin and hairless, he had a little paunch, and his legs were white and crooked. But she loved him.

Chapter Fifteen

On the *Jetsetter* en route to New York, Belle broached to Leonard the idea of a preliminary or preview launch of "Belle" at the December party.

He agreed without hesitation. "It'll be your show, Belle, and it sounds like a brilliant idea. How much do you think it would cost us?"

"I don't know. Our main object is to clear the ticket money. But I feel a little funny about it. If I go to work for Cosmos . . ."

"Not if," he barked, "when."

"Well, my loyalties are going to be divided. I'd want to get as much as possible out of you—or us. But being a Cosmos vice president, I'd want to take it easy."

Leonard nodded. "I appreciate that. Let's just say, don't worry. I've never met this Sally Markman, but I know about her husband. He's very close with a lot of people in Washington. And that's always useful." He thought for a minute, clicking his teeth with his thumb. "You can be sure I'll not let you get away with anything outrageous."

"No, no," she said, "I wouldn't be outrageous about it."

"Let me think some more about it," Leonard said. "I'll let you know before you leave New York. We'd want a guarantee of exclusivity, you know. That means nobody else's products but ours on the table."

Another thought occurred to her while they were in the car driving to the city. Impulsively, Belle told Leonard about Sally's scheme to award an annual research prize.

At this, Leonard's eyes lit up. "Ah, there's something else. What's involved?"

"Sally's talking about $10,000 every year, tax paid."

"Not an untidy sum, even in these days, especially if it's tax paid. Ah . . . huh, well now, there's an interesting idea for you, Sylvia. You understand, I'm sure, what's perking in my mind . . ."

Belle laughed. "I'd hoped it would pique your curiosity."

He kissed her cheek affectionately. "I love you, Belle. You're so goddamn smart. I'll let you know about that, too. If Sylvia and I established a permanent grant—say put in a million of our own money—hell, we could easily pay the thing every year just on the interest, with lots left over for the use of the center. But, I've got to ask, what's the longevity of this project?"

"Sally has already put the money up to buy the land, and she's commissioned plans for the buildings."

Leonard whistled softly. "That's pretty permanent, ain't it? What's the deal? Why?"

Belle thought for a moment, then soberly told them Sally was dying. This was her last grand project.

Grimly, Leonard nodded. "I see. I'm sorry to hear that."

"Why didn't you tell me that, Belle?" Charley asked.

She shrugged. "I just hate to talk about it."

"My God!" Sylvia exclaimed. "What a brave woman. We'll do it, Sam."

* * *

New York was sweltering, and the traffic crawled into the city. Even the sidewalks seemed wet with humidity, and a pall of noise and stink lay over the entire metropolitan area. An inversion. And it would rain heavily during the night. It was a relief to get across the sidewalk and back into the air-conditioning of the Hotel Pierre. Leonard was putting them up in the Cosmos suite for a couple of days. He wanted Charley to spend some time with his art director and advertising people and Belle to be on hand as well to get the feel of the place, Leonard said, to absorb the personality of the staff.

The brief holiday in France had passed all too swiftly, but arriving back in New York that early evening in July, Belle felt she was a new woman. Her spirits had come alive; her outlook had been colored rosy. Her body was fine-tuned, and she felt very confident of herself. She had no doubt in her mind that she was ready for the Comos project.

"We'll see you bright and early tomorrow morning," Leonard said, as they got out of the limousine.

The bellboy got their bags up to the suite, which Leonard maintained year-round for just such out-of-town visitors as they were, and put Charley's bags in one bedroom, hers in the other.

Belle called Norman Kaplan as soon as they were alone.

"Belle! You're here! Marvelous. I want to see you at once."

"I'm with a guy," she told him lightly, winking at Charley.

"You are with a guy?" Kaplan shrieked. "Belle, you're telling me you're with a guy."

"Actually, it's a guy named Charley Hopper. I don't think you've ever met him. He's Martin's partner at C.A.A. and he's working on a new Cosmos cosmetics line—mine! It's going to be called 'Belle.' "

"Yours?" Kaplan exclaimed. "Belle, what have I been missing? Where have I been?"

"Norman, it's all very sudden. You knew I was going to France."

"Yes," he said, "I knew that. Bring this *guy* along, Belle. We'll have some drinks and go out for dinner."

Hanging up, she said, "Well, Mr. Hopper, we're going to have dinner with Norman Kaplan."

He was walking around the living room of the suite, smoking a cigarette.

"You're not tired?" he asked.

"No, not at all. Are you? I feel marvelous, Charley. You have no idea how marvelous I feel. It's because of you, Charley, entirely because of you."

"Shucks, Belle," he drawled, "I didn't do nothin'."

"Yes, you did. You revived me. I've got some news for you: a woman likes nothing better than to be rediscovered as a worthy . . . "

"Don't say it, Belle," Charley exclaimed. "I know what you're going to say. Shucks, Belle, I thought we were just going to sit around, have a little dinner up here, watch television, you know."

"And go to bed again, insatiable sir? Charley, you know, we've been setting records for a week."

"Yeah." He grinned smugly. "But now we're really compromised—in the same suite."

"Mr. Hopper, you can always lock your door, if you're afraid of me."

"There ain't no key, missy," he said. "I must say that Sam Leonard is a lecherous and provoking little bastard. And so is Sylvia. She was going on about you on the plane, trying to get a reaction out of me. They both know what's going on, Belle."

"Well, so be it, Charley," Belle said. "It's not something we can avoid, traveling together like this. People are going to talk."

Soberly, he said, "I'm thinking about you, Belle."

"Charley, I don't care." She put her hands on his shoulders, staring at his long face. "I know I've got to call home, but not today."

"Yes." He studied her eyes. "Belle, what are we going to do about this?"

"Nothing right now, Charley. We don't have to. Let people talk. It's just talk. They don't know what's going on. Charley," she said in a low voice, "I do love you, you know, so far in a very schoolgirlish sort of way. I love sleeping with you. For right now, what's the difference?"

"No big difference—for right now," he said. "But it is something we're going to have to solve."

She dropped her hands and danced away from him, laughing. "And we will. You're a man, Charley, and I think what men have got to understand is that women are not that much different. A woman can hop in the sack with a man she finds attractive without necessarily having to be in love with him. Hell, men do it all the time. They see a woman they find sexy and they do their damndest to get her to bed. And they don't have to love her, God knows. Am I right? Damn it, Charley, aren't I right?"

"Yeah, you're right," he said. "Come here."

Chuckling, she said, "I think I'll try to get you to bed right now, sexy man. We've got a couple of hours. Then we do have to see Kaplan. I love him and so will you. We've got some talking to do about the party."

"Ah, the winter ball. The ball to end all balls."

She kissed the underside of his jaw and he slid his arms around her, caressing her back. She felt his long fingers at her ribs, then across the slick backside of the French jeans she'd bought the day of their excursion to St. Tropez. He cocked his chin down to kiss her forehead, then her mouth as she lifted it to him.

"We do have a couple of hours, Charley," she said.

"Done," he said. "Let us slip out of our travel-weary clothes and rest a nonce."

Still holding her fast, he unbuttoned her blouse and unzipped her jeans.

"Belle," he said, "why is it you've taken to going without a bra?"

"I don't need one," she said. "And I like going without. I like to feel the silk right on my nipples. It turns me on, Charley." She laughed huskily.

"Turns me on, too," he murmured. "What a dame!"

"Come on, Charley, let's dance into the bedroom, shall we?"

"You really want to, huh?" he teased.

"Yes, yes, I do, more than anything in the world right now. Charley, I do love you."

"Puppy love," he muttered.

"Whatever," she said, "come on. I want you inside me again."

Norman Kaplan lived in one of the city's older apartment buildings, in the 60s between First and Second avenues. From the outside, the brick pile looked grimy and pedestrian, but when one passed the doorman, the downstairs opened to long marble-floored corridors and eventually to an antique wood-paneled elevator. Kaplan's duplex started on the fourth floor. An aged butler led them into a vaulted living room with two-story Gothic windows from floor to paneled and gilded ceiling deep in patina. The ceiling had once graced a crumbling cloister in Spain. The walls were covered with rich tapestries and spot-lit portraits, and the dark oaken floor with old Oriental rugs.

Kaplan hustled into the room. "Belle!" he cried, lifting his hands to take her shoulders and kiss her soundly on both cheeks. "And this guy is Charley Hopper. How do you do, Charley. I'm Norman."

They shook hands, Charley smiling loosely.

"It's very nice to meet you, Norman," Charley said. "Belle talks of nobody but you."

"Does she? Does she?" Kaplan bleated. "And, Charley, don't I detect the remnants of a Texas accent, and I know you're a friend of my old friend Maude Mannon. See, Belle, I already know all about this man."

"You must have been on the phone, Norman," she accused him.

Charley was never entirely pleased to be reminded of his accent, be it ever so faint. "I've known Maude for years," he said awkwardly.

"Well, well, sit down," Kaplan said, eyeing Belle, then Charley. "You two have been on a nefarious mission with Sam Leonard." The butler served drinks. "Thank you so much, Thomas," Kaplan said politely.

"It is a pleasure to serve you, master," Thomas said. He winked roguishly at Belle.

Kaplan's voice pealed with laughter. "Thomas! You rascal! Thomas is really my father," he explained.

"Yes, little master," Thomas said, and disappeared.

Then Belle took a few minutes to explain to Kaplan about her new job, the Cosmos project. Kaplan clasped his hands as he listened, then clapped them approvingly.

"My, my, I'm delighted. Leonard *must* be a genius, just as he often claims to be. I think it's an *exceedingly* bright idea to name a fragrance for you—more so to put you to work. And . . . that means you'll be in New York more often. Good, especially since Susan's going to be in Princeton in the fall."

"Yes, that can be definite now."

"Was there ever any question?" Charley asked curiously.

"Well," she said frankly, "I had certain worries about finances."

"No more," Kaplan said, "and you never had to worry anyway."

"Very true," Hopper said, so positively that Kaplan raised an eyebrow.

"Well . . . well." Kaplan hesitated good-naturedly. "So you had a marvelous time in France?"

"Absolutely beautiful," Belle said warmly. Kaplan again looked bemused. He must have seen what was happening between her and Charley.

"I thought we'd go to Cote Basque for dinner. They'll take care of us."

"I'll bet," Belle said. "When Norman calls, they jump."

"Ah, no, not necessarily. Madame Henriette could be a difficult woman."

He was speaking of the brusque French proprietress of the restaurant, now retired, who had ruled help and guests alike with an iron hand.

A half-hour later, they were positioned at the most highly visible banquette near the door. Belle chose this moment to tell Kaplan that there was a very good chance Sam Leonard would help finance the December party if the event were used to introduce the new "Belle" line.

"Why not?" Kaplan said. "That's perfect. We'll need a supply of party favors, and cosmetics are a must. I've never seen the like of it," he muttered to Charley, "the way wealthy women scream and yell and fight over cosmetic samples. But, Belle, the better, if it fits your plans so well."

"Also," she said, "Sam may just set up a funding for our research prize—a Sam and Sylvia Leonard Foundation or something like that."

Kaplan beamed. "Belle, you are an absolute whiz. You've done good work, the two of you. Charley, I gather you're going to handle promotion for 'Belle.' "

"That's right," Charley said. "But any way I can help with your party, just let me know."

"I have no doubt we'll be screaming for all the help we can get," Kaplan said. "Now, I wonder what Carlotta's done about an item in the newspapers. Here's what I've put together for Suzy—the bare bones of it. She can embroider it any way she wants."

He handed Belle a typed piece of paper. In memo form, he had listed the salient details, then the names of the more prominent committee members. Belle scanned the information, then handed it to Charley. He read it quickly, nodding.

"This will please Sam. Gets you in the public eye."

"Exactly," Kaplan smiled. "Leonard is a very shrewd man, and so is Norman Kaplan."

"God! Aren't you ever," Belle said. "Sam is throwing an impromptu little cocktail party for us tomorrow night. I hope you can come, Norman."

"I will, gladly. I've already been invited."

Over dinner, he reported that he'd made his first approaches to the former First Ladies of the East. "I know for a fact we're going to get them. They simply cannot turn this down. Women's power, good heavens! Well, they could turn me down, but they won't. Camilla Young called a couple of days ago. Her mother is at work on the West Coast. Camilla has turned into a real ball of fire, much different suddenly than that draggy little creature at our lunch."

Belle was pleasantly surprised. "I had the impression she was going to pull out of the committee."

"No, not now. I've talked to Sally, too."

A sobering reminder of what this was all about. "How is she?"

Kaplan shook his head. "She didn't sound too tremendous. They were all at a Fourth of July party at the beach—somebody called Donohue. Is that possible? Anyway, halfway through the party, the host, whoever he was, had a heart attack."

"That's Doug Donohue," Charley said. "Jesus, he had a heart attack?"

"Well, he's apparently all right now. Susan was with them. Elsewise, I gather it was a collection of your usual people."

"Where did you celebrate the Fourth, Norman?" Belle asked.

"Oh . . . " He moved his hands restlessly, "I went out to the Hamptons, stayed with Lily Sargent. It was dull." The he brightened. "It occurs to me, Sam wouldn't mind, would he, if I brought my chic friend, the Arab prince, to the party?"

Charley took that question. "I'm sure he'd be delighted. You know, Sam has been thinking about expanding into that part of the world—maybe a factory or two in Egypt or Kuwait, for the export market, of course."

Norman laughed. "I was going to say cosmetics and Islam don't go together too well, do they?" His face was wreathed in a clever smile. "Heavens, it all comes together, doesn't it? There are always wheels within the wheels. This must go down as the latter part of the century of back-scratching: you scratch mine, I scratch yours. So are deals made." He sighed philosophically. "The prince is the man I'm in business with in the new hotel."

Later, as they were having coffee, Kaplan mischievously said, "So, you two, you've been working so hard. What's on now? Going dancing?"

"Oh, no, oh, no," Belle said. "I need some sleep. It's already four A.M. by the captain's clock on the *Cosmopolitan.* I've got to go to work tomorrow."

Kaplan made a sorrowful face. "I must say, that's one hell of an awful name for a boat. But I've heard it's very impressive. I've never had the pleasure . . ."

"It was just beautiful, Norman," Belle said wistfully. "I'm sorry we had to leave."

"Yes," Kaplan said blandly, "I can see that." He turned his solid head toward the room, dodging her eyes, searching for a way to avoid a very obvious deduction. "Ah," he cried as the maitre d' approached, "it was very nice tonight."

"As always, Monsieur Kaplan."

"I'd like you to meet some friends," he said. "Belle Cooper and Charley Hopper—from California."

"How do you do," said the maitre d'. "I see that you are from California."

Belle asked, "How do you know that?"

"The eyes," he said. "You have California eyes."

"Aha," Charley exclaimed. "I knew it. It's not the gold chains."

Without thinking, impulsively, Belle laid her hand on his. "You see, Charley, next thing they *will* ask you to go surfing."

Kaplan laughed faintly. He had noted the gesture. His eyes twitched curiously. He was so inquisitive, yet so reluctant to inquire. But there was no secret Belle wanted, or was able, to keep from him.

"Norman, you sly devil, I know what you're thinking."

"And so do I," Charley said.

"What am I thinking then?" Kaplan demanded archly.

"You're wondering about Charley and me, aren't you?"

"Well . . . yes."

"Business associates," Charley said quickly.

"That's right, Norman," Belle echoed him, "very close business associates."

"All right," Kaplan said easily, chuckling, showing his sharp teeth, "I never said otherwise. I don't know, Belle, when I can remember seeing you look quite so vivacious. This business association—it seems to agree with you. You are looking quite beautiful—ten years younger, I'd say."

Despite her daring mood, she colored. "Oh, thank you, Norman. He's known me practically all my life," she told Charley.

Hopper nodded somberly. "Old friends are the best friends," he said. "Sometimes."

They dropped Kaplan off at his apartment house, then returned to the Pierre. Charley suggested a last drink in the bar and firmly led her inside. They ordered two brandies.

"So," he said, "it does show, this business association of yours."

"Well, it has to, doesn't it?" Speaking softly, she elaborated, "Charley, you know very well when a man and woman sleep together, it has got to show." In full view of the bartender, he of the jaded New York variety, she kissed him, on the cheek, then recklessly on the mouth. "What is it with you, Charley? When we're together, I'm so relaxed. I don't have a care in the world."

"Yeah." He nodded. "Like me. I'm feeling very high."

"I can take on the world now, Charley."

"And you will," he said. "Come on, drink up."

Back in the suite, Belle undressed and removed her makeup and swept her hair back. When she was ready, she went into the living room in her robe. Sitting in his shirt sleeves, Charley was watching the late news.

"What's happening?" she asked.

"The Whirling Dervishes have occupied another American embassy. Christ," he said, yawning widely, "I'm glad I didn't join the foreign service. I might have, if I hadn't met Cooper."

"Are you sorry?"

He shook his head. "No, not at all. We had a lot of fun.

Mart used to be a hell of a guy, Belle. Jesus!" he frowned. "Well, it won't be the first time."

"You mean, first time . . . best friend and best friend's wife?"

"No. I mean first time a close friendship and business partnership have gone sour. The other, too, of course."

"Charley, let me ask you a dumb question," Belle said. "Are you feeling guilty about this?"

"Guilty? I don't know," he confessed, scowling thoughtfully. "I don't think so. Not really. Why should I feel guilty about being in love with you? I'd feel guilty if I thought there was anything left between you and Cooper. But if there was, you wouldn't be here, would you?"

"No." She followed the news announcer for a while. He was on to a local New York story. "Charley, what do you say we get some sleep?"

"Your place or mine?"

"Mine, I think, it's more binding."

In the morning, at Cosmos world headquarters, Leonard introduced them to his top assistants and, for several hours, the group sat around a conference-room table discussing the new product line. Hopper spread out his preliminary artwork and a range of proposals for the initial, or kick-off, promotion. Belle listened carefully as they debated the proposals, amended the artwork, added details, re-wrote—and, in essence, decided the course of her life for the next year.

Leonard sat, uncharacteristically, quietly, here and there supplying an idea or two of his own, and, finally, toward lunchtime, he broke up the meeting.

"Okay," he said with satisfaction, "I think we understand each other. All we lack now are precise dates to go with each stage of the plan. Belle has come up with an excellent idea; to launch the product at this fancy party of hers in Los Angeles in December. It's going to be a party with plenty of pizzazz, people from all over the country, so convenient to key in with geographic promotions. Now, by that time, the packaging will be finished, the logos, the colors—everything. Anyway, it better be, or you'll all be out on your ass. What we'll do for this party is put a sample of everything in the 'Belle' line in a black satin totebag. I want the bag to be good quality satin so they won't heave it out after the party. Instead of the Cosmos logo, we'll have 'Belle' scripted across it in living red." Leonard glanced at her frostily; he was speaking to Belle of the Cosmos apparatus now, not to Belle, his friend.

"Remember," he told her, "by that time, everybody is going to know about this thing. We won't be springing it on them out of the blue. It's not any different from what Lauder does, or Revlon."

She saw what he was getting at. "Don't worry, I won't be embarrassed."

"Listen," Charley reassured her, "all those women will be falling all over themselves—out of envy and admiration."

"And some will say we're using the party," she pointed out.

"Some of them?" Leonard said sharply. "Do you really care?"

Thinking, Belle said, "No. The ones that count will be pleased."

"Okay, so that's settled," Leonard said, smiling. "Now, in the meantime, Lorraine," he addressed this comment to one of the Cosmos public relations people, "We're going to make Belle a lot more visible. For instance, tonight, you can drop it around town that Belle is here for a very special party thrown by me, the one and only Sam Leonard, at the Waldorf Towers. Don't mention the line yet, just that beautiful California socialite Belle Cooper is in town, along with that famous advertising magnate Charley Hopper who's responsible for C.A.A.'s services to Cosmos Cosmetics. Get the picture? Belle, from now on, keep Lorraine advised of all your activities. You take a trip, let her know who you're with, where you're staying. Every party you go to in L.A., tell Lorraine about it so she can plant the information in the columns—anything that comes to your mind. You're going to be in and out of New York all the time now. You better plan on being here in October for the April in Paris Ball. That's about the time we'll let loose the tips that 'Belle' is Belle Cooper. You get the picture?" he asked again.

As he finished summing up his strategy, the phone rang. Leonard snatched it impatiently.

"Yes, Sylvia? Goddamn it, Sylvia, I'm busy. Yes . . . yes . . . Sylvia, I don't give a good goddamn. Tell them we want caviar tonight, and I don't care where they get it, out of what river—the Hudson or the Sacramento. Do it, Sylvia!" He jammed the phone back on the hook. "That was my wife, Sylvia," he grunted, as if they could have no idea who he'd been talking to. "Goddamn Iranians. Don't they know what they're doing to us? Bunch of nuts . . ."

Hopper interrupted Leonard's irritation. "Sam, you've all ignored my budget proposal. What kind of a budget are we talking about?"

Leonard turned on him fiercely, eyebrows nettled. "What's it going to take, Charley?"

"The way we're talking, I'd say about four million just for starters. Add another four to six on top of that for continuity in the first year—at least."

Leonard's little gray head bobbed, but he was not taken aback. "Right, Charley, I figured about that. But we'll want to be a lot more precise. We'll get it back. Goddamn inflation!"

Leonard put his hands on the end of the table and lifted himself from his chair.

"Okay, I'm hungry. Let's go to lunch. Belle, you and Charley . . . Max."

Max was Cosmos's chief of in-house advertising and promotion.

"Lorraine, you better come, too. Let's go to the Grenouille." He pressed an intercom button. "Louise, call the Grenouille and tell them I'm coming. Five of us. Yes, five." He grinned. "With luck, John Fairchild will be there and we'll get our first mention in *Women's Wear Daily*. Keep your eyes peeled, Lorraine."

"*Jawohl*, boss," Lorraine said.

Back at the Cosmos building on Madison, near Fifty-Seventh Street, after a light lunch, then pictures taken by a *WWD* photographer lurking on the sidewalk outside Grenouille, Charley and Belle retreated to the office they'd been given down the hushed corridor from Leonard's own executive suite.

Firmly, Charley said, "Belle, we've got to call Martin."

"Why?"

"Well, to tell him we're here, what's going on."

"What's going on now?"

"I mean with Leonard, the 'Belle' business. Not about us, for Christ's sake."

She hesitated. "Okay, go ahead. I'm going to the john."

When she came back, Charley was finishing his report. "Went very well, Mart. It's sold. We're in. I'm working with the Cosmos guys again this afternoon. Yeah . . . It is 'Belle.' That's decided." She made a silent gesture, telling Charley not to give away too much. "Belle? She's right here," Charley said flatly. "She wants to talk to you." He passed her the phone.

Guardedly, she said, "Hello, Martin."

He asked her how everything had gone, had she had a good time. His voice was gruff over the long distance. "Belle, I've missed you. When did you get in?"

"Late last night."

"Charley said it went fine. It's 'Belle,' is it?" She did not reply. "Well, that's all right with me. What does it involve?"

"Promotions, Martin, pictures, a whole campaign."

"Jesus Christ," he said disgustedly, "that means you're going to be on the road, away from home."

"Yes . . ."

She could see him now, sitting on the corner of his desk, phone in one hand, a cigar in the other, glaring at the hills, the skyline. He would be about to leave for lunch.

"You and Charley had a good time then?" he asked, an edge of anger in his voice.

"A beautiful time," she said calmly. "Sam is a great host."

"Terrific," he said. "When are you coming back?"

"Late tomorrow, or the next day."

She wanted to add, "if ever." But she waited for his next words.

"Why so long, for Christ's sake?"

"Sam is throwing a party tonight. We've got to be there."

"I see," he said slowly. "Susan is coming home from the beach."

"Why? She's all right with Sally, isn't she?"

Cooper grunted and swore. "Goddamn it, she's been down there long enough. I told her to come home."

"Is she home now?" Belle demanded. "Martin, damn it, why can't you leave her where she is? I've got good reasons for her to be there."

"Sure," he grumbled, "to keep her away from me."

"My reasons have nothing to do with you. She's at Sally's because I want her to be there." Belle was furious, but then, as evenly as she could, she said, "She has got to be with Sally. I can't explain it, but she has got to be."

His reply was dead silence, then a question: "What does that mean, Belle?"

"It means just what I said. I don't have to explain it. Susan is my daughter. And as far as we go, Martin, you're not in any position to give orders. You know perfectly well we're in a lot of trouble."

There! She had said it, clearly, forcefully. Let him make the most of it.

"Shit!" he said, "that's nice. Right in front of Charley, eh? Okay, Belle, I've said it before, just take off. I suppose now," he sneered, "it's you and Charley Hopper."

She glanced at Charley. He was sitting with his eyes closed, mouth compressed.

"That's a rotten thing for you to say," she said, shaken.

"Rotten? What do you know from rotten?"

"Is that why you sent us off together? So you could say that?" she asked, suddenly exhausted, drained.

Cooper laughed roughly, mockingly. "I'm only kidding, Belle. And you're wrong about us. Dead wrong. I'm not giving you up. I love you too much."

His words made her feel sick. "I'm sure," she replied faintly. "I've got to hang up now. We're going to a meeting. Goodbye, Martin."

She put down the phone. Charley opened his eyes and looked at her.

"I can see it coming, Belle," he said.

"Let him try," she said grimly. "I'm calling Sally."

Susan answered the phone.

"It's me, honey," Belle said, "your very own mother. I'm in New York. We had a marvelous time. Look, let me talk to Sally."

Susan told her Sally was across the street, playing tennis.

"Listen, Susan," Belle said, "on no account do I want you to leave Sally's . . . yes. I don't care what he said."

Susan slowly said, "I wasn't going to leave anyway."

For the next couple of hours, Charley was off with Max and his advertising team, and Belle kept her date in the art department. She did several dozen specimens of her signature, one of which would be emblazoned on the totebags. Then a photographer shot a half-dozen rolls of black and white and color pictures, the beginnings of the "Belle" press kit.

Sally caught them back at the Pierre before they left for

the Leonards. Belle repeated to her what she'd already told Kaplan about the Cosmos involvement in the benefit.

"Gorgeous," Sally cried. "Belle, you've done us proud."

"I'll know tonight, I hope, about the foundation. Okay, how are you feeling?"

"Not so bad actually," Sally reported cautiously. "I played some tennis today. It's after the therapy when it's bad. Then, the next day, you begin to feel better. The third day, you're on top of the world again. Then, you get put down again. But not too bad, thanks."

"Did Susan tell you I talked to Martin?"

Sally snorted. "Sure, you don't have to worry about that. I didn't have any intention of letting her leave. Fuck that guy. Don't gasp, Susan is downstairs. I wouldn't let her go. You know," Sally said softly, "she's scared out of her wits of him. Did something happen there?"

"What! What do you mean?" Belle exclaimed.

"She won't talk, but I get the feeling Cooper—I don't know—tried something. Belle, I don't know . . ."

Belle drew a long, painful breath. Had she suspected that, too?

"Jesus, I don't know either. God! Don't let her go, Sally, don't let her out of your sight!"

"Belle, don't worry. Don't worry! Everything is cool, Belle."

"Cool?"

"I'm learning the new words, kiddo."

Belle could not put the conversation out of her mind until they arrived at the Leonards. She said nothing to Charley, but she felt her anger crystalizing. If Cooper had ever dared . . . Jesus, she hated him now.

The Leonards' apartment was crowded. Meeting them at the door, Sam was alight with self-satisfaction. He said they'd invited seventy for the cocktail party and many had already arrived. They were standing in clusters inside the deeply beamed drawing room or sitting on couches by the windows high above Fifth Avenue.

"Seventy?" Charley said, impressed, "that's a lot of people to rustle up at the last minute, Sam."

Leonard grunted. "Last minute? What're you talking about? I had Louise invite all these people before we left for Europe."

Belle laughed, again swept away by his dynamism. "You were so sure, Sam?"

"Sure, I was sure."

Norman Kaplan came into the room just after them, with him a dark, slight man dressed in an immaculately tailored, vested business suit.

"Belle, my dear, I'd like you to meet David Abdul. David, Belle Cooper and Charley Hopper. And I do believe this is our host for the evening, Mr. Sam Leonard."

Leonard growled, "What do you mean, 'you believe'? Norman, you know damn well who I am."

Kaplan chuckled wildly, putting up his hands as if to fend off Leonard's annoyance. "Sam . . . Sam, of course."

"How do you do, Mr. Abdul?" Leonard said irately.

"Actually, Sam, it's Prince David Abdul."

"No, no, Norman," the Arab hastened to say, smoothing a closely clipped black moustache. "In New York, I prefer Mr. Abdul. But please call me David."

"I will," Leonard said. "Sylvia . . . where the hell is she? Sylvia, my little love, come over here for a second. Here's Belle and Charley. You know Norman Kaplan, of course, from your social world. And this is Mr. David Abdul. David, my wife, Sylvia."

"Sam, I know who David Abdul is," Sylvia chirped.

"Sylvia, you haven't met him before, have you?"

"No."

"Well," Leonard said sarcastically, "that's why I'm trying to introduce you. My God!"

"How do you do, Mr. Abdul," Sylvia said.

"David," he said softly. He stooped to brush her hand with his moustache.

Leonard's good friend, cosmetic queen Lucia Montonya, was in from the Coast for the party. She glided toward the group, which had now moved from the double doors of the drawing room toward an open space in front of a baronial fireplace. Above the mantelpiece was a life-sized portrait of Sylvia Leonard, obviously done in her younger days.

"Belle," Lucia bubbled, "here we are in New York. Did you enjoy the *Cosmopolitan*?"

"We certainly did," Belle said. "I see why you love it so."

"Lucia," Leonard said, "I want you to meet Mr. David Abdul. David, Lucia Montonya, one of our closest friends."

"Miss Montonya," Abdul said smoothly, kissing her hand.

Lucia smiled winningly. One thing about Lucia, Belle told herself, she had a sure nose for money. She recognized Abdul at once for what he was: a rich Arab. Her cheeks puffed out as if she'd taken a deep breath and was holding it in fascination. She put her smooth hands to her dark hair, fixing Abdul flatteringly with her almond eyes.

"Miss Montonya, you are also in the cosmetics business?"

"I'm a consultant," she purred.

"I see," Abdul said, showing white teeth.

"Belle," Leonard said, "come with me a minute. I want to introduce you to a few people. You, too, Charley. The mayor is here, but he's not staying long . . . A couple of people from the Met and the museum . . . I've got the editor of *Vogue* and *Harper's Bazaar* . . ." Lowering his voice secretively, he warned, "Nothing about 'Belle' now. It's too soon. Just meet them, chat them up, make sure they remember you."

"Sam, how do I do that?" Belle asked. "Spill a drink on them?"

Leonard grinned slyly. "Just act yourself, darling."

By eight o'clock, Belle felt as though she'd shaken hands with everybody in the room twice over. Finally, the guests began to thin out. Kaplan was crouched comfortably beside Sylvia Leonard. He was talking avidly, gesturing with his small hands. Abdul was still talking to Lucia Montonya by the fireplace. Charley and Belle stood with Leonard near the drawing-room doors, where they'd been bidding the guests goodbye.

"Good," Sam was saying, "very good. It went well. You were great, Belle. Precisely what I wanted from this. They won't forget you."

"Pshaw," she said blithely, "I'm very forgettable."

"In that dress?" he responded. "The way you're done up? You've got to be kidding."

"Sam's right," Charley said. "I saw them eyeballing you. The woman from *Vogue* was already sketching you."

"Wait a minute now," Sam said, again speaking confidentially. "Sylvia and I talked over this business about a foundation. And we want to do it. Initially, we'll put the money up for the prize this year. Afterward, if it really looks like a going concern, we'll establish the grant to run to . . . what do they say? Perpetuity? Understand, we just have to make sure of it. Otherwise, the accountants would raise bloody hell."

"Of course," Belle said. "I understand that, but you've got to meet Sally Markman. Then you'd see what kind of a force is behind this."

"I want to meet her very much," Leonard said. "She must be a great woman. And with Kaplan involved, it has got to be pretty solid. He says the party is going to be in that new hotel out there."

"He and Prince Abdul are investors," Belle said.

"Mr. Abdul," Leonard corrected her. "I don't like to hear much about Arab princes."

"I see what's bothering you, though," Belle said worriedly. "You're thinking the center project is fine now, with Sally alive and driving it, but what happens after . . . if Sally . . ."

"Yes," Leonard agreed solemnly, "that would bear thinking about, don't you agree?"

Chapter Sixteen

Pamela Renfrew was elated. She had landed another Arab. The call had come in the early afternoon when she'd been out to lunch. The message was for her to call a David Abdul in New York. She had gotten through to him at 3:30. Her name, Abdul said in a smooth and sibilant voice, had been mentioned to him by Sam Leonard. Ah yes, she thought, that little shit.

"Ah, yes, Mr. Abdul, what can I do for you?"

"I am told you are the very lady to find me a house in Beverly Hills, Miss Renfrew. My business will, you see, be bringing me to the West Coast very often and I need a *pied-à-terre* in your city."

She was hesitant at first. A *pied-à-terre*? Did he mean a condominium? It was scarcely worth her while fooling around with anything so small.

"You had in mind . . . what?"

"A house, Miss Renfrew, with gardens, yes. I must have greenery, yes."

"A pool as well?" she asked, her interest building.

"Oh, yes, I suppose. One must have a pool in California, isn't it so?"

"By all means, yes." She calculated rapidly. She had a couple of biggies on her books. But they ran to the millions.

"Well," she said, playing it cool, "I have several places I could show you. When do you expect to be here?"

"Oh, soon, soon. What would the price ranges be, Miss Renfrew?"

Carefully, she said, "Nothing much for under a million, depending on what you want."

"Miss Renfrew," he sighed, "I wouldn't want to spend much more than two or three . . ."

"Million?"

"Yes, of course."

The figure of her commission on a three-million-dollar deal jumped into her mind as she drove toward home off Benedict Canyon. She'd clear about $90,000; not bad. God, she wished for a second that Sam Leonard were here. She would have kissed him, blown him, whatever he wanted, for he was not such a bad man after all, despite his crude treatment of her that night after the Bistro party. He was, all told, a damn sight better than bastardly Martin Cooper. She was just recovering from her bruise and the other, more mental, wounds he had inflicted on her. What a waste of time that had been. But it was all right now. She would recoup the lost ground.

Pamela made the light on Sunset and turned left in her white Seville. The car seemed to be purring happily, too, despite the weather. The day had been hot and disagreeable, and ahead of her the smog hung electrically in the wilted trees along the boulevard. She got through the next light, too, and passed the pink palace, the Beverly Hills Hotel, on her right. Even the hotel looked tired, worn out.

It was still light when she rolled through her front gate.

Clicking the automatic garage-door control, she guided the car inside and pressed again to close the doors behind her.

The two men grabbed her as she walked into the kitchen. Their faces were obscenely squashed in stockings. They jumped her and knocked her down on the tiled floor. One of them slapped her with an open palm, cracking her head back.

"A big blonde slut," he muttered. "Get up, cunt!"

Dazed and terrified, Pamela couldn't move. The man yanked her to her feet.

"What do you want?" she stuttered.

"What do you think?" he snarled. "Money. Your jewelry. Where is it?"

She knew better than to try to talk them out of it. "Here," she said. She began to pull the rings off her fingers, to undo her necklace.

"Not that," the man said, hefting the necklace. "That's shit. Where do you keep the good stuff?"

"Upstairs," she mumbled.

They were big, taller than she, and heavy. They were both dressed in shiny black trousers. The one doing the talking was wearing a blue nylon windbreaker; the other, a tan cardigan.

"Go on! Lead us to it," the man in the windbreaker ordered. "You watch her, dude," he said to his companion.

"Dude" poked her in the chest, then grabbed at one of her breasts. She pushed the hand away and he slapped her another stunning blow. She commenced to cry. Dude pulled a knife out of his pants pocket and flicked it open. It was a switchblade. He waved it at her cheek.

"Walk, cunt!" Dude said.

Weakly, supporting herself against the walls, Pamela went from the kitchen into the front entry hall and pulled herself up the staircase to the second floor. She led them into her bedroom.

"Okay. Where is it? Get it out," the man in the windbreaker said.

He seemed to be the leader, the older of the two.

Whining, still crying, Pamela crossed to the bookcase beside her bed and, as they watched her warily, the knife still at her back, she pulled books on the floor. Behind the books was her secret compartment.

"There," she muttered.

Dude fell to his knees and began dumping jewelry on the floor.

"All right, Dude," the other said. "Watch her. I'll look at the shit." Dude stood up and the man in the windbreaker knelt to sort out her jewelry. "We'll take this one. This one is paste shit. Okay on this one. I suppose you don't carry insurance on this stuff, do you? I can see why. It's not worth shit." Finally, when he had chosen what he deemed worthy, he stuffed it in his pants pocket. "You blonde asshole," he snarled, "is that all?" Speechless, she nodded. "What's in the purse, Dude?"

"Couple of hundred and credit cards, that's all."

"Jesus Christ, not even worth our while. What do you rich cunts do with your money anyway? Spend it all on clothes?"

Pamela moaned, "I—I don't have much. I work."

He slapped her again, knocking her over on the bed. Her eyes flushed with tears; she felt the bruises rising on her face.

"Smartass cunt!" the man in the windbreaker said.

Pamela cowered on the bed, tried to pull back as he reached for her. He grabbed her by the hair and hit her again. The son of a bitch, she was thinking, the son of a bitch. If only there had been some way, gladly, she would have killed both of them. The older man smacked her again, this time with his fist against her jaw. She felt a bone crack as she nearly lost consciousness.

She heard a voice say, "Get some water, Dude."

Then she heard her clothes ripping; her body tossed with his violence. Now it was coming, she thought hysterically. In several brutal motions, he had stripped her and was whipping her naked body with his gloved hand—the breasts, the legs, the belly. Cold water splashed in her face and she opened her eyes to see him pulling down his pants. In a second, a penis flashed out, ugly and big.

"Go to it, cunt," he gasped, "and right now."

She knew better than to argue. He had grabbed her hair again, knotted it around his fist, and pulled her face forward. She felt it against her lips, forcing her mouth open.

The man grunted and gasped. Pamela stifled sickness and tried to ignore the animal stench. His hold on her hair slackened. She worked him, bringing her hands up to his balls to knead them, pulling the fire out of him. In seconds, he came, filling her mouth.

"Swallow it," he commanded.

He stepped back as she did what he said. She sat on the edge of the bed, her face stiff, frozen with terror. Would they go now?

"You're next, Dude," the older one said. "How you want it?"

"A fuck," Dude said.

Pamela slowly eased herself backwards on the bed. She felt she was in better control now. As coolly as she could, she said, "I don't go for rape. Come on."

The man with the knife, obviously the younger of the two, twitched with nervousness.

"Go on, Dude, go on! We ain't got all day."

Dude dropped his pants and clambered toward her on the bed. It was so incongruous, his face grotesque in the stocking mask, his body revealed, scrawny and white, an undersized cock striving for erection. He was almost embarrassed, but paying no mind, recklessly now, Pamela pulled him down, grabbed him, and pushed him inside her. Her eyes wide open, she glanced at the man in the windbreaker. He was fascinated. Behind the stocking, his eyes were two light globs, pupils beating. Dude was having trouble. He flailed at her. But he couldn't come.

The older man suddenly grew impatient. "That's enough," he ordered. "Come on, get up." His stocking mask creased in a grimace. "We hit it lucky. This cunt actually likes it."

Pamela didn't move as Dude climbed off her and quickly yanked up his pants.

"Tie her up, Dude."

Dude went to her bureau, pulled it open, and threw clothes out on the floor, searching for something he could use. Finally, he tied her feet to the bottom of the bed with brassieres, then her hands to the top of the brass bedstead with knotted pantyhose. When he had finished, the two of them stood there, stockinged faces contemplating her defenselessness, as if wondering what else they could do to her. The younger one was playing with his knife again, and giggling. Jesus, she thought, after all this, was he going to cut her?

"I could carve her up a little," he suggested, hopefully.

"Shit," the older man in the windbreaker said, "want to play Indian? Whyn't you scalp her?"

"Do you think?"

"For Christ's sake!"

Dude knelt over her and, for a moment, teased the hair at her vagina opening with the point of the knife. Pamela held back a scream. A loud noise would only inflame them.

"Dude," the older one said soothingly. "C'mon, that's enough." He pushed the younger man back and approached the bed. He slapped Pamela again, firmly on the cheek. "So long, cunt. You see what I'm saving you from? Try to remember us with fond memories, won't you? Whatever it is, you probably had this coming. Try to remember that." He backhanded her again, viciously, and Pamela blacked out.

Sharon Peters had received the message that Frank Woodley had called while she was in Las Vegas with Morris Mauery, but she'd paid it no heed. A friend of the late Mr. Peters? So what? Who needed that?

Woodley called again that afternoon. It was a polite and neutral-enough communication. He knew it might be an imposition, but Mr. Peters had once done him a great service, so could he come and see her? In the end, Sharon agreed and invited him for a drink. Hell, she had nothing better to do and she was feeling so depressed, so alone. She'd blown the Fourth of July so thoroughly with Mauery. For what? Business, labor peace. So they'd seen Liberace and she'd suffered Morrie's attention.

The intercom rang at seven and Sharon answered it herself, since Mrs. Robinson had gone off to the movies again.

"Mrs. Peters, a Mr. Woodley is downstairs for you."

"Okay, he can come up."

When the door buzzer sounded, Sharon was almost inclined not to answer it. She felt so down. But she was glad she did. The face was familiar and then she remembered. It was the man with the beard who'd been doing the athletic handstands on the terrace across the way. She pretended she didn't recognize him.

"Come in," she said. She ushered him inside and down the steps into the seating area of the living room. "A drink? What can I get for you?"

"What are you having?" he asked. His voice was mellow, modulated.

"I'm having a scotch," Sharon said.

"Then I'll have the same, please."

She made the drink and brought it to him, then sat down opposite.

"Well . . ." She lifted her glass.

This Frank Woodley, who was he? He was too young, about her age, to have been a bosom buddy of her late husband.

"You're wondering about me," he said frankly. "I'll tell you. Oscar Peters helped me out when I was in school. I was a football player. He kept me on kind of a scholarship. Then I played professional ball for a while. I thought I'd just say hello. I've seen you around."

He didn't seem big enough to have played any kind of football. He was only about six feet and he couldn't have weighed more than 180 or 190 pounds.

"You're an old football player?"

"Yes, I was a quarterback, just a shrimp these days, of course," he replied, smiling lightly through the beard that covered his lower face. "And now I'm a stuntman."

"In the movies?"

"Sure. That's easier than being a quarterback and getting your arms pulled off."

He sat back and crossed one long leg over his knee. He was very presentable, Sharon told herself, in a crisp light cotton suit, blue shirt, and striped tie.

"Well, I'm pleased to meet you," Sharon said.

"I wondered . . . could I take you to dinner? Do you have any plans?"

She was about to say yes, she did, that she was being picked up in a half-hour, then thought better of it. She said she wasn't doing anything.

"Dinner?" he repeated.

"Well," Sharon said hesitantly, "let's think about it."

"All right," he said agreeably. "I like your place."

"Where do you live?" she asked, surely a leading question.

"Not far from here, as a matter of fact." He smiled. "But you're probably wondering why I really called you."

"You mean, aside from football and Oscar . . . Yes."

Woodley said, "The truth is, I've always found you to be a tremendously interesting woman. I've always wondered how a woman can take over a big trucking company and manage it."

She chuckled. "I don't really. I have very little to do with it."

"You know," he said, "I worked there sometimes in the summer, driving locally. I used to get up to the front office from time to time . . ."

"Well, I was there, too, you know. I don't remember you at all."

"Yeah, well, I guess I made a pass at you at least a couple of times. You snubbed me." He grinned. "But that's all right. Then I started seeing you around town in Los Angeles. So I decided to call."

"I snubbed you? I don't remember that," she said. "You're making me feel bad."

But she didn't feel bad at all. She laughed and composed herself in her chair and crossed her legs. Woodley began talking about the trucking business, as he remembered it, going on so exhaustively that in the end she raised her hand and stopped him.

"Please, enough of trucking. I can't take it. What about another drink?"

When she returned, Woodley was appraising her without shyness.

"You're just as pretty now as you were then," he said.

"Oh, my," Sharon said. "I don't know how that can be."

"Oscar wanted me to work for him when I got out of school. I don't know, maybe I should have. I went off and played football instead. Then, one fine day, I got sacked behind the line of scrimmage and that was the end of that. And so here I am," he finished airily, "a failed football player and an aging stuntman."

When they were into their third scotch and water, Sharon was sitting next to Woodley on the couch and now was remembering the man on the terrace.

"I don't believe I ever snubbed you, Frank," she murmured. "But tell me, don't you have a terrace on your apartment?"

"Yep."

"You son of a gun, you're the guy who was waving at me, weren't you? And doing handstands?"

"Yeah, that was me." He grinned. "I was trying to get your attention." He lowered his beard into his shirt front. "I was kind of drunk that afternoon."

"But, my God, you could have fallen off."

"I know. Christ," he said, "I was behaving like an idiot."

"You scared me."

"Hell," he laughed, "I guess I'm slightly crazy now from

jumping off bridges and roofs. But no reason to be frightened of me. I'm harmless."

"I wouldn't want to think you're entirely harmless," Sharon said thoughtfully.

By way of reply, Woodley got on his hands and knees on the floor, then jacked himself up on his hands to walk across the carpet. Lightly, then, he did a back flip and landed on the balls of his feet. Loose change rattled out on the floor beside him.

"That's my work," he exclaimed.

"My God, you're an acrobat," Sharon said.

"Nope! Just a stuntman. Nothing special. We have to stay in very good shape." He plopped down beside her again.

"Fabulous," Sharon said. She was thinking of the sleek, muscled body she'd seen on the terrace. "I am impressed."

"It's nothing," he said modestly. "Say, shouldn't we be thinking about dinner?"

"Nope," she said, adopting his clipped expression, "I'm going to make hamburgers. I don't feel like getting dressed."

She was thinking she felt a lot more like getting undressed. She was quite shaken by his agility, the virility of his body, and she remembered how he'd looked, even from the distance, in his brief covering.

"In that case," Woodley said. "what about me making you another drink?"

"Okay," she said weakly.

Then she thought about Morris Mauery. One would not feel petrified of Mauery with a man like this around—and a former colleague. He might even be useful to her. Woodley knew about the trucking industry; he would be acquainted with her union problems. He would know what her management was talking about, might even be able to take her side against them.

He strode across the room to the bar and expertly mixed two more drinks. He handed Sharon hers with a flourish. Even the drink he'd made tasted better than hers, she thought meekly.

"Would you like to get back to the old trucking business?"

He laughed again, that hearty, full-bodied laugh. It made her feel good, sent a shiver down her spine.

"I'm out of touch with all my old rough-neck chums," he said carelessly.

"It's the goddamn unions I'm thinking of," she said.

"Oh . . . that. You got union trouble? They can be handled if you've got the right guy talking to them—at least that's as I remember it:"

"Frank," she said, chiding him, "it doesn't pay to be too modest."

"Ha! We do agree on that. I'm not a modest man, Sharon."

Impulsively, or as if impulsively, he dropped his hand lightly on her shoulder. The touch, the bare touch, set Sharon off. She turned and collapsed into his chest, surprising him, no doubt. But she wasn't the timid girl now that she'd been in Ohio. And there an old saying: If something looks good, then take a chance on it. Pausing only to put her drink on the table, she kissed him. He circled her back tentatively with his hands and took her chunky breasts.

"Frank, I'm glad you came over," she sighed.

"Don't rush yourself, Sharon," he said.

Christ! The absurd thought struck her. She'd kill herself if he turned out to be a fag.

She turned to the side and he ran his hand up under her dress, along her thighs, and touched her gently. She put her hand between his legs, grasping the bulge that had been so remarkable on the terrace. Frantically, she twisted, fearing she would burst from want. The length of him pressed against her leg.

"Come on," she muttered thickly, "let's go to the bedroom. I can't think why I let you get away in Ohio."

He was better than she had dreamed. He was totally masculine, but not rough, much more tender and graceful and caring than she imagined possible.

She was small beside him. Undressed and in her bare feet, she came barely to his shoulder.

"I'm a midget compared to you."

"A little doll," Frank said.

He sat on the edge of the bed and placed her on his knees, facing him, kissing her mouth and her breasts, then sat her on him. He glided far inside her, still kissing her neck and playing with her nipples and belly, the round buttocks. Sharon lustfully ground down on him, swaying and seeking—God!—her head back, breathing with need until, groaning, she climaxed and cried out. But he waited, then lifted her bodily and put her on her back on the bed, still thrusting deeply, easily, pressing but pulling her upward. In the end, his orgasm hurtled into her and he emitted a long sweet sigh.

Sharon was in a stupor. She was amazed at herself but numb; she was astounded at her luck. She had arrived, she knew. She had finally had a climax.

Lou and Archibald Finistere had been at Chasen's for dinner. Archy's philosophy was to spread his dinner trade around town. It did not do to spend all one's time at the hotel, as marvelous as the food and service at the Beverly Camino could be. Not could be, *was*! And this due to his years of diligence, discipline, cajoling, and dictatorial demand.

"Lou," he said, searching his beard for stray crumbs, "drive by the Splendide, please, and let's have a look at how we're getting on."

Lou drove up Beverly Boulevard and circled the acres of land fronting Santa Monica Boulevard. A high wire fence had been erected around the construction site and, behind that, spread in an enormous flattened horseshoe configuration, lay the raw eight stories of the Splendide. The upper floors and roof were lit haphazardly by spotlights, and the ground was a blaze of security lighting, which silhouetted eery night shapes of dump trucks, cranes, pickups, heaps of sand, gravel, bricks, and mortar blocks. A long trailer that was construction headquarters and architect's office was hauled up at one end of the hotel. Inside, as Lou stopped, a watchdog barked and wailed.

The outer shell of the Splendide was finished now. Walls of windows were in place and the balconies facing west had been painted a sandy-desert color. The wooden trims at doors and below the cornice of the building were a dark green, which had been chosen as the complementary color. Archy knew they had reached the stage of installing the air-conditioning equipment, electricity, and plumbing. Elevators were being built into the interior and tons of furniture had already arrived. It was stored now in the huge basement garage.

Archy sat very still, staring out the car window. Any new building was impressive, be it ever so crudely designed. But a new hotel! There was something absolutely magical about a new hotel, a place that, in a few short months, would be greeting and catering to the needs of a myraid of travelers from every land, a place that would become a warm and cheery refuge for thousands, eventually millions, of people.

"Do you know, Lou," he remarked softly, "when they put in the electrical and plumbing, they start from the top and work down? Why? To their embarrassment, they often find if they work from the ground up, the rats are chased upstairs and then they're very hard to get rid of."

"Archy," she protested, "that's an ugly thought."

"But a reality, turtledove," he said, thoughtfully stroking his beard, "it happened recently in a new hotel in London."

"Oh, London," she dismissed his thought, "London is full of rats."

"Aha," he said, "there are just as many rats in Beverly Hills. Maybe more. Haven't you heard? They populate the ivy, live at the top of the pretty palm trees."

"In Beverly Hills? I find that hard to believe."

Archy mused, "The ugly reality, turtledove. Behind the facade, always some sort of ugly reality."

Lou shivered. But the matter was not something that really concerned Archy. There would be no rats in the Beverly Splendide, at least of the rodent variety. What he was thinking, sadly, yet with pleasure, was that the Splendide would be his last great endeavor, possibly his crowning achievement.

"The question is: will it be ready in time for the party?" she asked.

"Have no fear, turtledove." He patted her hand. "They're finishing the basic work. Then they'll paint inside. Finally come the drapes and carpeting. The kitchens are being installed now. The downstairs and the ballroom will be ready in plenty of time."

"Pool?"

The pool was to be in the back, Olympic-sized or bigger, the tennis courts laid out on either side of that.

"The cement is curing now," Archy said. "Then they'll tile it. It'll be done before the rains."

"God!" Lou exclaimed anxiously. "Rain! Suppose it rains that night."

Archy chuckled. "Turtledove, it will not rain. I personally guarantee it. If Archy says no rain for his turtledove, it will not rain. The carpeting for the lobby is all down in the garage—a deep, dark green like the trims. The lobby will all be finished in a light stained oak. Do you know how much oak costs these days?"

"A pile."

"Yes. But the Splendide is going to be the most magnificent hotel on the West Coast, turtledove," Archy said proudly, then excitedly. "Beautiful . . . splendid . . . splendide."

"It *could* rain though," she objected. "What a bad time for a party. It's too close to Christmas anyway. Sally should have waited 'til spring. It'd be a lot safer."

"But then, if you waited, you'd miss your chance to inaugurate the hotel with such a splendid affair."

"Ah, we think alike, Archy," Lou said lovingly, warming his heart, "And that's what I wanted to call the ball: a Splendide Affaire—with an 'e' on the end of both words."

Archy laughed affectionately. "Beautiful, turtledove. You thought of that?"

"Of course," she huffed. "I do have an idea once in a while, you know. When are we moving over here?"

"Toward the middle of November. Isn't that exciting? Think of it: Archibald Finistere, president and general manager of the Beverly Splendide."

"Yes, but what about Lou Finistere?"

"You, my lovely, are going to have your own office and a secretary. You're going to be in charge of social liaison."

"Darling Archy!" He'd known this would please her. "That's super."

"Are you happy with me now, turtledove? You're going to have a real hand in running this hotel. You're going to be very important to the Beverly Splendide."

Lou slid across the seat to kiss him on the cheek and pat his face.

"The only thing, Archy, it's going to be such backbreaking work for you. I don't want you to work too hard."

"No, no," he said brusquely, "I can handle it. No problem. Besides, I'll have young Jurgen Ehrlich with me. He's a workaholic."

"Jurgen?" Her face clouded. "He's leaving the Camino, too?"

"Of course. I brought him over from Switzerland with that expressly planned. The powers that be, in New York, agreed it was an excellent idea. He's to be my assistant manager, turtledove, don't you see? He's an experienced hotelier. He'll be invaluable."

"Do they know that yet at the Camino?"

Archy shook his head. There were some things it was better for them not to know.

"They're aware I'm leaving as of October 31," he said, "and that's all they know. It broke their heart, but *c'est la guerre*, turtledove."

"So, you've burned your bridges behind you, Archy," she observed.

Doubtfully, he agreed. That thought had occurred to him, but he'd had no option. "One has to give notice, turtledove. It's a matter of ethics."

"But suppose something goes wrong?"

"Nothing is going to go wrong," he exclaimed.

"But suppose it does?"

"It's not," he said stubbornly. "I am held in very high esteem in New York. Don't forget, I have a following. Besides, I signed a contract. I'm not that much of an old fool. And Norman Kaplan has turned into a bosom friend. Lou, I am *not* concerned. Please, don't you be either. It worries me when you worry, turtledove."

Reassured but not ready to give in, Lou grumbled, "I didn't even get a hand in the decorating. I have some ideas along that line, too, Archy."

"Oh, oh," Archy said, raising his hand, "sorry, my dear, but that was all arranged before we came on the scene. Valerian Rybar, you know, the designer, did the total decor."

"That'll cost them a bundle," she commented sourly.

"Turtledove, they've got a bundle—in fact, bundles."

Martin Cooper was sitting by himself in the house in the back by the pool. He was running *Hell's Damsels*, one of the newest of the more politely formulated exploitation movies. He thought it a big bore in general, but he had been told to catch one Jane Farelady, the bright new starlet who was so certain to be "very big" in Hollywood within the next five years, according to her agent, Mort Schultz. Mort had sent him a print and a projectionist and Cooper had promised to call him after they'd run it through.

Jane was not bashful about showing skin, that was one

sure thing that could be said about her. She was a tall girl with a look of tempestuous but teasing innocence and she *could* act, although, he thought, the vehicle scarcely called for much of that. Jane was a deep-bosomed young thing with impossibly long legs, a tight waist, and a delicious, dimpled belly.

The phone rang and he told the projectionist to hold it.

"Mr. Cooper?"

"Yeah."

"This is Sergeant Dickson of the Beverly Hills police. I believe you're a friend of a woman named Pamela Renfrew."

"Yeah, that's right . . . in a way."

"She's been taken to the hospital. Two guys jumped her when she came home tonight."

"My God! Is she okay?"

"Yes, she's okay. But they roughed her up pretty good. She's in sedation now, but she told us to call you."

That made him pause. Why should she have them call him after their dramatic, to say the least, rupture? Cooper, remembering all too well, lifted his right hand and stared at his bandaged little finger. It had finally come to the amputation of the last joint, finishing the work Pamela had started.

"What did they do to her?"

"Beat her up, robbed her," the policeman said. "Tied her on the bed. She managed to get loose."

"Christ! Is she okay?"

"Yes, she's okay. I have to tell you, they raped her."

Cooper took a deep breath, gulped. "Christ, the bastards!"

"Exactly. It's not pleasant, Mr. Cooper. She's at St. John's in Santa Monica."

"Is there anything I can do?"

"Not tonight. It looks like a routine breaking and entry, robbery, rape deal. We get a lot of that nowadays, you know."

"Jesus, do I know? All you've got to do is read the newspapers. Did they get much?"

"Some jewelry, a little cash."

"Christ," he groaned, "the poor broad."

The sergeant paused, then said, "I thought you should know tonight."

"Yeah, thanks."

Cooper turned back to bare-chested Jane Farelady. Poor, poor Pamela. Well, she could handle it, he thought grimly. She was tough, a real tough bitch. Ah, an idea occurred to him. He had the projectionist stop the machine again, consulted his address book, and found the home number for his florist, Vince Crocket of Crock of Flowers.

"Vince? Martin Cooper. Sorry to bother you at home. A rush job. Vince, first thing tomorrow morning, make up a couple dozen red roses and send 'em to Pamela Renfrew. You know Pamela. Well, her address for the next couple of days is St. John's in Santa Monica. Put a note with it: 'Red Roses for a Black and Blue Lady.' Sigh it, 'Love, Marty.' Got it? Yeah, yeah, couple of hoods roughed her up tonight. Yeah . . . rotten, Vince. Okay? So long."

The message was an inspiration. It amused him and should cheer up Pamela.

Now he gave his undivided attention to *Hell's Damsels*, the saga of a platoon of lady Marines, a not very adept rip-off of "M.A.S.H." They hadn't made a uniform yet that could contain Jane Farelady's knockers though. She spent more time in the shower than on the playing fields of Camp Pendleton, and naturally, in what passed for a climax, fell for a hard-bitten drill sergeant. Maybe by the name of Dickson, he snickered to himself.

When the credits had run out and the projectionist had put everything back together and gone home, Cooper called Mort Schultz.

"Mort," he said, "she's sensational. What a broad!"

"You think your outfit could do something for her, Marty?"

"Mort, I think we could promote the hell out of her. Yeah, we could take her on. She's got the look of a young Andress. But does Rolly Starr know about this?"

"No reason he should," Schultz said. "He doesn't own her. He only produced the picture. Could you talk to her about it, Marty?"

"Sure."

"Give her a call. Tell her I'm all for it, Marty." Schultz gave him Jane's phone number. "You'll like her, Marty. She's a hell of a girl. Bright as can be."

"I'll call her right now," he said.

"Yeah, she might be home. Give it a try, Marty."

* * *

Cooper was ready to leave for Jane Farelady's place in a few minutes.

But just as he got to the front door, he heard a car drive up. In a moment Belle unlocked the door and came inside, the driver behind her with her bags.

"Good night, Mrs. Cooper," he said.

"Belle, you're back," Cooper said. She was startled to see him standing there watching. "I wasn't expecting you."

"Hi," she said calmly. "I told you we'd probably be back tonight."

"Where's Charley? Why didn't he come inside?"

"He's gone on home. We're both tired out. It's been a very hectic ten days."

"I'll bet it has." He looked at his watch. "I've got a few minutes. I've got to go see Mort Schultz. Tell me all about it."

In full command, quietly, he led her into the living room.

"Would you like something to drink?"

"Not just now," Belle said distantly.

She did look tired, but he felt her inner excitement. She definitely had something to tell him and he wondered what it was. He eased himself into a chair opposite her and thought, but only briefly, of forgetting about Jane Farelady for tonight.

"Well, Belle?"

"Well," she said, smiling warily, "I've got a new job. I should say: a job. Sam Leonard is making me a vice president of Cosmos. I'm going to be in charge of the new line."

This was the news? Cooper was disgusted, then immediately angry.

"My, my," he said idly, not looking at her, trying his best to remain calm. "Belle's 'Belle.' "

"That's right."

"Does that make you happy?"

"It makes me feel good, yes."

"Like you've really accomplished something, I suppose."

"Yes, in a way," she said hesitantly.

She was watching him carefully, her eyes guarded. He knew there was more.

"So, you'll be busy as hell, promoting, traveling, talking to the press, TV, all of that. When do you start?"

"The idea is to introduce 'Belle' at our party in December, then to break the big campaign right after the first of the year."

"Your party?" he repeated. "Oh, yes, I've been hearing about that around town. But you never mentioned it to me."

"I didn't think it was something that would particularly interest you," she responded.

"Belle, I'm interested in everything you do. But December? What an odd time. That's when I was planning our trip to Brazil. You know I've got business down there to attend to. I thought you knew that, Belle. Do forgive me if I'm wrong," he said heavily, "but I'd expected you'd be going with me."

"This is Sally Markman's party. I'm helping her organize it, Martin."

He shook his head firmly, still smiling as best he could. "No, Belle, I'm really terribly sorry, but you're going to have to come with me. I'm counting on you—and all your friends in Brazil are dying to see you."

Her look freezing him, she said, "I didn't know anything about a trip to Brazil. I'm sorry. I can't go. It's not just a matter of the party either. I'm committed to Sam Leonard."

His control collapsed. "Did it ever occur to you that Sam Leonard is using you? He wants the name. He'll throw you out on your ass when he's finished with you!"

Her face turned white, but she did not bend or bow. "I don't think so," she said. "I'll be getting a contract to sign."

"I see," he grunted. "Very nice. I suppose you're committed to Charley Hopper, too, by now."

She flushed bright red. "Charley is working on the campaign. You do remember that?"

"Yes, Belle, I remember that. But he's working on the campaign if I say he's working on the campaign."

"There's no point . . ." She started to say something, then her eyes flicked to his bandaged hand. She had finally noticed it. "What happened to your hand?"

"Nothing, Belle. It's nothing at all. Pay it no mind," he said sardonically. "I caught my finger in a car door. Seems my pinkie finger will be a little shorter on that hand. Be pretty, won't it?"

Speaking in a low voice, she said, "Worse things can happen. But it must have hurt like hell."

He shrugged. He did not give a damn now. It would be a scar to carry: home from the wars.

Fixing her with a stare, he said, "I'm sorry about the party. I count on you being with me in Brazil."

"And I've told you, I can't go."

"Well," he said, getting to his feet, "you just think about it, will you? Yes, think about it." Heading for the door, he turned. "Your daughter is still out at Trancas. We decided she enjoys the sand so much she should stay out there and stuff it up her ass."

Belle's color changed again. She inhaled sharply. "Very nice," she whispered.

"Yes, it is, isn't it? Why don't you go out there with her? Then you could be close to your dear friend and your darling daughter. That might be useful for your party planning. But I suppose you won't leave here, will you? Been getting some legal advice most probably. Don't just walk out. It'll damage your chances in court. Possession is nine-tenths of the law and all that horseshit!"

He put his hand on the door, trying to lean nonchalantly. But he was breathing hard and shaking with irritation, anger. He came back to stand by her chair, to glare down at her.

"Well," he grated, "if you stay here, then you goddamn well are coming with me to Rio de Janeiro. You're going to do what I say. And I'm not at all sure that I want you to take your job with that bastard Sam Leonard, that ugly little goat. When he was out here, he tried to fuck Pamela. And he probably has in mind to fuck you, too."

Belle jumped to her feet, pushing him aside. Her eyes were wild now.

"And what did you try to do with my daughter, you son of a bitch?" she screamed.

Had he not been so startled, he probably would have hit her. He stepped out of her way.

"What are you saying," he bellowed, "that I tried to make out with that little . . . cockteaser?" He sneered as venomously as he could. "I wouldn't touch that with a ten-foot pole. Jesus Christ, jail bait. Are you insane, for Christ's sake?"

Her voice was quivering with fury. "If I ever find out . . . If I ever find out from her. If I do . . . I'll make you sorry you were ever born."

Cooper laughed shakily. "You won't find out anything,

because nothing happened. I pushed her off me. I ran away."

"And you're a goddamned liar," Belle told him.

She walked out of the room. He heard her marching up the stairs, then the sound of her door slamming.

Cooper smiled wanly, then pulled himself up, remembering he had a date. It was useless, he told himself as he left the house and walked to the garage to get out his Jensen. Whatever he did or said, they would never believe him.

Chapter Seventeen

The item about Pamela Renfrew's misadventure did not make the morning papers, the new policy being to downplay or not report at all on acts of violence against the citizenry, for fear of provoking more of the same. But within a few hours, everybody in Beverly Hills, or at least a good share of Pamela's wide circle of business acquaintances, had heard of her misfortune. During the morning, local hardware stores could report a new wave of inquiries about the very latest in alarm systems, and stocks of Alsatian police dogs were quickly run down.

Belle heard of the incident in an unusual manner. Late in the morning, as she was preparing to drive to Trancas, there was a phone call. Belle did not recognize the fuzzy voice.

"Wanta talk to Cooper."

"I'm sorry, he's not here," Belle said. As far as she knew he hadn't been there all night. During the sleepless night she had been aware of every creak of the floor in the silent house. "Who is this?"

"Pamela Renfrew," the voice slurred.

"Oh . . . I didn't recognize your voice."

" 'Cause my jaw is wired," Pamela said. "I got burgled and beat up last night. Called to thank . . . your husband . . . for the flowers. Tell him for me, if you will," she said with an effort, "he's a dirty motherfucker."

"Oh." Belle almost laughed. If she'd thought of it, she might have used the phrase the night before. "I'm sorry. I hope you're all right."

"All right now."

"I'll—uh—pass along the message."

"Yeah, do that."

Belle slowly hung up. Good God! Well . . . It seemed Cooper's close relationship with Pamela Renfrew was at an end. As much as she despised the woman, she felt sorry for her. Surely, it was the worst ordeal, a violation of body, home. Then, thinking of Charley, she felt that at this point she should not even bother to despise Pamela. Pamela was a shady lady, no doubt, a tough and opportunistic creature. But Belle pitied her for Martin Cooper, among other things. And she didn't believe what he had said about Pamela and Sam Leonard. That was just not in Sam's character.

She knew she should pick up the phone right then and there and call a lawyer. It was something that would have to be done. But the thought of it intimidated her. It was ugly, a miserable thing to have to do. She would talk about it with Charley first.

She called Mrs. Westmoreland and made a date to visit the old lady late that afternoon. First, she had to see Sally, and Susan.

They were sitting outside in the sand under a big umbrella when she arrived at Trancas, on the beach, ten minutes past Malibu. Sally was holding the morning paper in her hands; Susan's head was bent over a book.

"Well, hi!" she exclaimed, coming up behind them. "Here I am! Home! What have you two been doing?"

They looked up, startled, like a pair of conspirators.

"Just hanging around, pussycat," Sally said.

Belle stopped to kiss her, then Susan. "Just got back last night."

"Tell us all," Sally said. "We've been waiting for you."

Belle told them excitedly about the Cosmos job and her conversations with Leonard about the party.

"You're going to sell cosmetics, Mother?" Susan demanded, with enough disbelief to set her back on her heels.

"And what's wrong with that, young lady?" Sally asked acidly. "It's a very big business and your ma is going to be an important lady."

"Gawd," Susan muttered, then asked, "How's Charley?"

Belle smiled. "He's fine, I guess. I haven't seen him since last night. He's busy working on the 'Belle' account, you know."

"We know. We know that," Sally said.

Neutrally, Belle remarked, "You're both looking well." Sally's head was wound tightly with a turban and she was wearing a long, matching cotton caftan. "You look like Carmen Miranda in that outfit."

"You got it, kiddo."

Blithely, Sally jumped up and hopped around in the sand for a moment, mockingly humming a tango. She flopped down again.

"But you didn't really tell us, how's Charley?" Susan insisted.

Belle said, "I just told you. Charley's fine."

"We find ourselves suddenly liking Charley very much around here," Sally said amusedly.

"Well, so do I. But I don't know what's gotten into the two of you."

They looked at each other and commenced to laugh.

Stiffly, Belle said, "A pair of nuts. I've come here to talk serious business. I've got to go downtown and see Carlotta about getting some news items in the papers. What, for instance, are we going to call our party?"

"Got any bright ideas?" Sally asked indifferently. "I don't go much for Lou Finistere's suggestion."

"Splendide Affaire? Nor do I. We might not want to go back there next year."

"Yes," Sally said, "we do have to consider that."

Next year? Next year? Belle had forgotten. Sally didn't expect to be around this time next year. Jesus! How could she have forgotten that? She felt the strain of suppressed tears behind her eyes.

"I've been thinking," Belle said, forging ahead, "what about Winter Ball? We don't have a winter ball in L.A., do we?"

Sally shook her head. "Don't think so. Winter Ball? Well, that's not bad. It could be *Bal d'Hiver*, if we wanted to French-ify it. I don't know. For right now, why don't we just refer to it as Big Party, generically. Then we can change it later if we think of something better."

"All right," Belle said. "I don't have any strong feelings about it either. So . . . I can go see Mrs. Westmoreland."

Sally slumped in her chair after her brief exertion, her head back and face pallid. She glanced at Belle once; her eyes were troubled inside, worried, and Belle realized beads of perspiration had popped out on her forehead. Then she shivered too visibly to hide it.

But impatiently, she shook herself and leaned forward. "You know, it seems like we've got our First Ladies pretty well lined up. That part . . . has been amazingly easy."

"Yes, Norman told me."

"We may get as many as five of them. Not bad, really. Rather a triumph. Why didn't we think of this a couple of years ago?" Sally asked.

Susan observed, wisely, "Everything has its time, doesn't it?"

"Speaking of time," Belle said quickly, "you've been here quite some time now. Maybe it's time you started thinking about saying goodbye."

"No!" Sally exclaimed. "She stays here. She can't go home now, can she, Belle?"

Resigned to the facts, Belle shook her head.

"And I'm enjoying it here," Susan said. "Am I in the way, Sally?"

"No, no way. So then?" Sally challenged Belle. "It's good that she's getting a good rest. Princeton is not going to be any easy bag."

Belle nodded. They were right: there was no possibility that Susan could go back to the house the way things were now.

"Has Norman thought about setting up some kind of a committee in New York?" Sally asked, abruptly changing the subject.

"No, not yet. He's waiting to see what happens after word gets around. Then he may need help. If there are, say, 200 people coming from New York, a hundred couples."

Sally shook her head. "Be realistic. More like twenty or thirty couples," she said pessimistically.

"Uh, uh," Bell disagreed. "More . . . Anyway, there'll be plane reservations to make, coordinating on hotel accommodations, but Norman is a whiz, and in New York, he does have a secretary."

"Yes," Sally said tiredly. "But what we've got to think of now is arranging our next meeting. Where do you think we should hold it?"

"Why not upstairs at the Bistro? It's a lot more cheerful than that dreary room in the Camino."

"Cheerful, yes," Sally muttered.

Her mind was drifting, Belle thought. She was thinking of other things. But that was not surprising.

Brightly, she speculated, "Suppose we do get fifty couples out of New York, another ten or fifteen from Washington, forty out of Texas, then a Florida contingent. How many do you think we'll get from L.A.—or how many should we accept from L.A. and environs?"

She was demanding Sally's attention, dragging her mind away from herself.

Sally straightened alertly. "They can pull eight or nine hundred couples for almost any benefit here. Los Angeles is no problem. Hell, we could easily have a thousand just from this area, if you throw in Palm Springs, Santa Barbara, La Jolla, and all that down south."

"At $2,500 a couple . . . Not bad," Belle mused. "Maybe we should have gone for biggest instead of best and exclusive."

"No." Sally shook her head. "Norman's right. It's better to have them beating on the doors trying to get in than to open it to a flood. We've got to think in terms of next year. If we make it exclusive and spectacular this year, we won't have any trouble next year."

Belle grinned, appreciating the spurt of pep and decisiveness. "We wouldn't ever have any trouble with you running the show, Sal."

"I don't know about that," Sally said. "I don't know how much help I'm going to be this time. What about our next meeting? Let's shoot for the first week in August. I'll be feeling better that week."

"You're predicting it?"

"I *can* predict how I'm going to feel. Ask Susan." Sally lifted herself out of her chair, more slowly this time than she had before. "Come upstairs with me. I've got some paper work, lists and stuff, to show you. Go swimming, Susan, run on the beach. You're getting fat lying around like this with a couple of old ladies."

"I am not getting fat."

Susan knew when to disappear. She got up and walked toward the water. Just in the last few weeks, Belle thought, she had matured; and she wouldn't be eighteen until November. Susan's legs were strong, well muscled, and her bottom, in its bikini, wagged gently. Her femaleness was blossoming.

"She looks like a Californian," Belle murmured.

Sally chuckled. "She's got the figure all right."

"Any boys on the horizon down here?"

"The usual quota, sniffing around," Sally said amusedly, "but she's aloof, I've noticed. She doesn't encourage it. Thank God, she's not one of those little beach flirts, of which we've got plenty."

Carefully, Belle said, "I wonder about her, though. You know what they say: still waters . . ."

"Bullshit," Sally said sharply. "If you're wondering if she's still a virgin, probably not. Very few of them are these days. I'd say she's had her experience but, she's not in any great rush to repeat it."

Belle whistled: "The things that soothe a mother's heart."

"Well, Christ, you may as well be realistic about it," Sally said. "Come on upstairs. Jesus, feel the sun."

"It's a very hot day, Sal," Belle said, reassuring her that, no, she wasn't perspiring for no good reason.

"But you don't understand. Hot as it is, I'm shivering cold."

Damn, Belle told herself, that was it, wasn't it? One of the symptoms of this thing? Weakly, she said, "That's what happens to people who sit in the sun too long. It's called heat exhaustion."

"Yeah, and your mother's a paperhanger," Sally jeered wearily. "Never mind, so what about Susan anyway?"

"She *isn't* a flirt, is she?" Belle asked anxiously. "The reason . . . I'm concerned. Well, Martin and I had a hell of a fight last night. And he—he claimed she's flirted with him. The son of a bitch said she was a . . . cockteaser . . . that he had to chase her away."

Sally grimaced angrily. "Bullshit! I don't believe it. I believe he made some kind of a dirty pass at her . . . and she rebuffed *him*."

"Oh, God," Belle muttered. "Do you really think so? Jesus, that's so nasty, Sally."

"Of course it is," Sally frowned. "But it wouldn't be the first time something like that has happened. The miserable prick!" She grabbed Belle's hand. "Look, don't worry about it. It's over. And she's not going back there. C'mon upstairs with me, for God's sake."

Belle followed her disconsolately through the house, more depressed now than angry. In the big front bedroom, Sally sat her down on a long chaise in front of the windows looking out over the sea.

"I'll be right back," she said. When Sally returned, she had removed her turban and in place of it was wearing a wild blondish-gray wig. "What do you think of this, kiddo?" she demanded fiercely.

"It's a wig."

"Well, it sure as hell is. What I'm asking is how it looks."

"You're serious?" Belle could not help smiling.

"Of course! What the hell did you think, Belle? Don't you understand what's happened? I'm dropping hair like mad from those goddamn treatments. Jesus Christ! How does it look, Belle?"

She faltered, then weakly said, "It looks fine. It suits you."

This was true. The wig drew attention to Sally's tanned face, to her eyes, now more vital. It made her look stronger.

"Can I get away with it?"

"You can get away with anything."

"Thanks a lot, kiddo." Sally sat down beside her on the chaise. "Well, it's either this or looking like a goddamn corpse."

"Don't say things like that!"

"Skip it," Sally snapped. "Tell me now. So you had a big fight? A knock-down, drag-outer?"

"Well, not a knock-down but surely a drag-outer," Belle said.

"We here begin to believe you're having an affair with Charley Hopper."

Belle looked away, toward the beach. Susan was strolling back and forth in the surf up to her knees, kicking at the water.

"We?" she repeated. "Why in the world would *we* think that? Just because Charley and I were off on a business trip together doesn't necessarily mean we're having an affair."

"Whatever you're doing, it agrees with you," Sally said.

Glumly, Belle nodded. "Yes, I guess . . . But right now, I don't know what the hell to do." She sighed. "Life is a very complicated affair."

"It doesn't have to be. Does the bastard want a divorce?"

"No, he wants me to walk out on him. He's afraid I'll skin him."

"And you should," Sally said vigorously. "But don't do anything rash until you've talked to an attorney. I'll tell you—go to Tom Sanders. He's good and he's bright and he's not a hustler. He'll give you good advice."

Belle nodded, still watching Susan. The girl had dashed into the waves. She dove headfirst and came up like a mermaid, water streaming from her, blonde hair plastered to her head. She ran back up on the beach, energy bursting from her.

"I'm afraid he'll use this trip of mine and Charley's against me," Belle said.

"So?" Sally demanded harshly. "Does he have any proof something happened between you? No? Then screw him."

"You seem to assume something did happen, Sally. So will everybody else. He won't need proof. He'll just say it. He'll make it very dirty. He's capable of that."

"Jesus," Sally said disgustedly, "men!" Again, she took Belle's hand. "But what about you and Charley?"

She shook her head. "I don't know. I'm not sure. He's marvelous, but do I want it? Or need it? You know, this job with Leonard—it's a godsend. I think I can handle it—and there's plenty of money. He mentioned a figure—so much I can't believe it, plus a share in the profits."

Sally nodded, making a satisfied humming sound. "You're worth it, kiddo, whatever it is."

"I like to think so. Sometimes I'm not so sure. He—Cooper—said last night Sam would just use the name, then throw me out."

"Balls, what's he know? I wouldn't worry about that. You'll come through just fine."

Belle nodded. Her situation, when she considered it objectively, was not at all hopeless.

"But you, Sally . . . Are you feeling all right?"

"Not good. But never mind about that. I'd just as soon not talk about it. Let's go downstairs and have a Bloody Mary. Then we'll have some lunch."

"Don't forget I have to drive all the way downtown. Don't try to get me loaded, please."

When they were in the kitchen mixing the drinks, Belle remembered her call that morning from Pamela Renfrew.

"Martin's friend, that real-estate hooker Pamela Renfrew, got beat up last night," she reported. Despite herself, she smiled. "She called this morning. I couldn't recognize her voice. She wanted to thank him for the flowers, to tell him he was a no-good . . . motherfucker . . ."

"Jesus," Sally said dryly, "well, she's sure right about that. What was that all about, do you think?"

"I haven't a clue. Such language—it rolls right off your back."

"Honeychild, I've heard all the words and then some," Sally snorted. "I didn't tell you—Doug Donohue had a heart attack on the Fourth."

"Norman told us. But he's all right?"

"He's going to need a couple of bypasses. They gave him one of those angiograms. Christ, those things are worse than the operation, from what Tom Glenn says."

"But Tom won't operate?"

"No, Tom doesn't do that kind of thing." Sally sniffed. "For which he's very thankful. Tom hates the sight of blood."

"Speaking of which, dear," Belle mentioned, "have you ever seen any other specialists? Norman was asking about that."

Sally shook her head. "No . . ."

"Wouldn't it be wise?"

"I thought about it and decided not to." They sat down in the living room with the drinks and Sally draped a shawl around her shoulders. "Tom knows what he's doing. We went to see the one guy. You know, Tom has taken care of me forever."

"But still, wouldn't it be an idea? I mean, hell, you never know."

Sally frowned fiercely for a second. "Now, Belle, don't start giving me medical advice."

"You give me enough marital advice," Belle said sharply.

"That's true," Sally smiled, "but I'm an expert on marital affairs and you don't know anything about medicine."

"Expert on marital affairs," Belle scoffed. "Bah! What

do you know about all that? Married to the same man for a thousand years . . ."

"Oh, yeah? You think I don't know about Bernard Markman? That old goat. Christ, he screws around like a pirate. Didn't you know that, Belle?"

"No!" And she was shocked to hear Sally say it, shocked also that she took it so calmly, if indeed it were true. "You never said anything . . ."

"Bernard," Sally said placidly, "has fucked more women in this town than you can shake a stick at. At first, I minded like hell. But, you know, he loves me. I learned."

"You never asked him about it?"

"I did once, only once," Sally said simply. "But I love him. I never gave him any children. He's all I've got."

"You're saying—what about me then?" Belle demanded, confused. "Am I suppose to disregard Cooper's . . ."

"Shit, no! There's no comparison," Sally said so promptly she might have been prepared for the question, and possibly was. "Bernard is not a bad man. He has that . . . failing. A natural-enough one, I guess. But Cooper, he's a bastard and he's cruel along with it. There's a big difference."

"So Bernard knows that you know?"

Sally threw back her head and laughed. "No, that's the fun of it. He might suspect that I have suspicions. But the bottom line is he thinks I'm a naive little thing. Hell, I can tell by the way Bernard says hello whether he's had them or not."

The *Los Angeles Record's* editorial offices and printing plant were located in the steaming flatlands of downtown Los Angeles, a few blocks from the sterile block of building that was the Convention Center, in a thirty-ish building of Mexican and Moorish architectural invention.

Its pastel-colored exterior was faded from sun and seasonal rain, garish scrolls, and murals below the red-tiled roof almost crumbling away from long exposure to the elements.

Belle was directed through a maze of offices, cubbyholes, and large open areas filled with desks, typewriters, and people, to reach Mrs. Carlotta Westmoreland's room on the top floor. The old lady was sitting behind a cluttered desk, typewriter on a table at her side, one foot in a stout shoe on the desk.

She did not get up. "Hello, Belle," she said, pink face genial, and waved Belle into a chair opposite her.

One knew there was no place in the world Carlotta Westmoreland would prefer to be than right here.

Belle took the information Kaplan had given her out of her pocketbook and passed it across the desk.

Carlotta scanned it quickly and nodded. "That'll do. I'm going to embellish it a lot, of course. Now, we're going to say this is the first of what will be an annual event and calling it what?"

"For now, just Big Party," Belle said. "We can change it later if we stumble on a real winner for a name. There's a little additional information, but I don't know if we can use it yet. Sam Leonard—he owns Cosmos Cosmetics—is going to be giving us a sizable piece of help."

Carlotta was appraising her thoughtfully. "How do you manage to stay so cool and look so fresh in this blasted weather, Belle?"

"It doesn't bother me."

"Nothing does, does it, Belle?"

She flushed. " What do you mean?"

"I mean you always look like you carry your own air conditioner with you. Never know you drove down here from . . ."

"Trancas. I went out to see Sally."

Shrewdly, Carlotta said, "She's not well, is she?"

There was no point in denying it. "No."

"My suspicion is that she's afflicted with the very thing we're raising money to beat," Carlotta said.

"It shows?" Belle asked helplessly. "Nobody knows. Nobody should know."

"It's Sally who bought the land, isn't it?"

"Yes, but she doesn't want anybody to know that either."

"God," Carlotta said, her ruddy face twisted sympathetically, "she's quite a woman, isn't she? God knows why I've been spared so long. You know, I've never been sick in my life." She shook her head. "All right then, we work all the harder. So this Sam Leonard is giving us money? Why? And we can't talk about it yet?"

"That's right. You see," Belle said, "I've gotten involved with Leonard in a new line of cosmetics. It's going to be called—you won't believe this—'Belle.' If we can launch it at the party, Cosmos is going to chip in a big gift of money."

"Why, Belle, that's marvelous," Carlotta said. "Congratulations, and why not accept the kind offer? So, you're no longer a woman of leisure?"

"Nope. I'm going to be a career woman now, I guess," Belle said.

"That's good," Carlotta said. "You'll find it a lot more saitsfying."

"Also, I should tell you," Belle went on. "Leonard is considering creating a foundation to fund the annual prize money."

"But we can't mention that either." Carlotta's eyes sparkled. "Sounds to me like you've got this Sam Leonard right in your pocket."

"Oh, no . . . no. He's very much the businessman. He wouldn't do anything if it didn't make sense from the business point of view."

"Well, whatever," Carlotta said vigorously. "We'll do it like this: It's reported a well-known East Coast philanthropist has become very interested in our project and is considering a yearly subsidy for . . . Well, we won't be calling it that yet. But, eventually, I fear, a Sally Markman Memorial Award for excellence in the field of . . . blah . . . blah . . . blah . . . whatever it is."

"Yes, I'm afraid you're right," Belle said.

"Well," Carlotta said fatalistically, "you know, Belle, we mere mortals don't have the power to cure, or reverse, the course of death and disease. All we can do, really, is make sure the living remember the dead. Anyway," she said briskly, "we'll make it the lead item on our social page and I'll run a box on the front page to call attention. I'll see the *Times* gets on this, too." She reached into her desk and pulled out a thin panatela cigar, which she stuck in her chubby lips and lit. She spun a trickle of smoke toward the ceiling. "Hope you don't mind if I smoke. I have this little affectation down here. It impresses my male-chauvinist editors, a cigar once in a while. Now, tell me, Belle, how's life otherwise?"

When Belle got downstairs, she found a public pay phone and made two calls, the first to Mrs. Atkins to say she'd probably be getting home late, and the other to Charley Hopper on his private line.

"Hi! Got a date tonight, Charley?"

"With you," he said softly. "Would you like to come up the canyon and visit a hermit?"

"Yes."

"What time?"

"Right now. I'm downtown. Allowing for traffic, I'll get there around six."

"All right. I'll leave here in about a half hour. I'll beat you there."

Belle guided her Rolls back to the Santa Monica Freeway and drove west. She exited at La Cienega and headed north toward the hills. Easing the car through rush-hour traffic, she thought about what Carlotta had reported on the Pamela Renfrew case. The curious thing was that everybody seemed to know of Pamela's close association with Martin Cooper in the buying and selling of property in the San Fernando Valley and elsewhere. According to the *Record's* police reporter, Carlotta said, the Beverly Hills police were paying more than usual attention to Miss Renfrew's mishap.

Charley's Mercedes was already pulled up in front of the garage of his hillside house when she got there. He was waiting inside for her.

"Long time," he said, kissing her gently.

"Too long," she murmured, "almost twenty-four hours." Then she got straight to the point. "Charley, you heard what happened to Pamela Renfrew? She was beaten up last night. Do you think Martin had anything to do with it?"

Charley dropped his eyes, a stricken look on his face, as if astonished and embarrassed she could harbor such a horrible suspicion.

"Belle! No, no. That's impossible. Just impossible. Who says he did?"

"Nobody. But there's something funny about it, Charley."

She was thinking again about the police, what Carlotta had said.

"No, no," he repeated anxiously. "That's just ridiculous. Crazy. Why would he do a thing like that?"

Belle moved her shoulders in puzzlement. "I don't know. You're right. Just because I—" She broke off her thought; what she had meant to say was that she should not translate her own bad feelings about Martin to such an exaggerated hypothesis. "Everybody does know about all their real estate deals together."

"So what?" he said brusquely, annoyed. "I don't know anything about that side of Mart's life." He left her standing there and walked toward the kitchen. "I've got an ice-cold beer for you," he muttered.

Charley's little house was burrowed into the hillside, with three rooms and a terrace facing a small pool. Belle went outside. Charley was still troubled when he joined her. But he smiled.

"Here's your beer, in a champagne glass, Miss Belle," he said, cuddling his own bourbon and water.

They sat down in a double wicker lounge chair, and Charley put his arm around her.

"Belle," he said softly, "I've got to stick up for him a little. He is my old buddy—whatever has happened between you two. I know he's been rotten, and cruel, but Mart wouldn't get mixed up in a thing like that."

"No," she said, "you're right. I hope you're right."

"Come on, Belle." Charley grinned. "Sweet Pamela probably got roughed up by a rival in pursuit of a real estate killing. Now, I'm going to tell you all about your schedule for September and October."

Chapter Eighteen

Belle posted Susan outside the unfinished Splendide to point the way across catwalks and between the piles of building materials, pieces of machinery, and assorted debris to a plywood-sided hole that would be the front entrance when the Hotel Beverly Splendide was open for business.

The yawning void of the ballroom was on the other side of the unfinished lobby, down several short flights of cement stairs. In the middle of the ballroom, or what would be the Grand Ballroom, a long trestle table had been laid out and covered with white damask. Chairs and benches were drawn up along it and at each end.

Belle and Norman Kaplan were inside standing next to a large cardboard box of hardhats inscribed "Hotel Beverly Splendide"—one for each member of the December Group as they arrived. The hats were Kaplan's gimmick, and they were also necessary for insurance purposes.

It was Lou Finistere's idea to hold their August meeting in the echoing cavity of the ballroom, for in this way, the women would be afforded a rare, advance look at the hotel and, it was hoped, also absorb some of the enthusiasm that went hand-in-hand with the realization of a magnificent plan.

Milton Williams was catering the luncheon party. Each guest would be supplied a picnic basket containing foie gras and slices of roast chicken and roast beef. At the proper moment, Milton's men would serve a freshly mixed salad, hot bread, then cheese.

The December Group was twenty-four strong now, double its original size, and more men had been added: Archy Finistere would be there, along with Marcello Zavier, Kaplan's decorator, and Pat Hyman's agent friend, Rolly Starr.

Kaplan was in an uproarious mood, his hardhat perched precariously on his large head. He peered jovially around the cavernous room, pointing out to Belle the network of steel scaffolding supporting wooden walkways for the painters near the ceiling. The plaster work had all been finished and along the walls lay unopened crates of lighting fixtures to go up when the painting was completed. There were to be six crystal chandeliers, each worth $100,000, Kaplan told Belle. The hardwood floors had yet to be laid.

"God, Norman, it's huge," she said.

"It's going to be the biggest ballroom in town," he said. "But nonetheless, we're going to have to pack them in."

Initial response to the publicity in the *Los Angeles Record*, then the *L.A. Times* and in the *New York Daily News*, then the *New York Times*, had been very positive. And Kaplan had seen to it that the items were either picked up verbatim or rewritten in other cities across the country.

"People are going for it," he reported gleefully. "Going for it in a big way. My partners are very pleased. By the way, Archy will be bringing David Abdul with him. David came out with Marcello and me."

"Have you talked to Sally since you got in?" she asked awkwardly.

"No. How is she, Belle?"

Belle shook her head. "Not so good. She needs a lift."

"This will give her a big lift today. And speaking of Mrs. Superstar," Kaplan said in a loud whisper, which glanced off the bare walls, "here she comes now." Sally was striding purposefully toward them. "God!" Kaplan screeched, "she's wearing a fright wig."

"You little bastard," Sally exclaimed, "I'm so happy to see you. Explain this to him, Belle, will you?" She was feeling so obviously well she was not put out by his remark. Sally's eyes were curious as she looked around. "God, Norman, will they ever finish it?"

"My dear," he drawled, "this room is already in its last stages. This room will be accessorized and carpeted, easily, by the middle of October. We get exactly two and a half hours in here, no more."

Belle carefully placed a yellow hardhat on top of Sally's fake curls.

"Keep this on your bean at all times, Mrs. Markman," she said. "Kaplan's orders."

The Finisteres, with David Abdul and Marcello Zavier in tow, arrived next. Archy was chattering excitedly, his chest puffed out like a bird showing its nest. He took Abdul by the arm and pulled him about the room, gesticulating, and in a moment they disappeared through an opening to the left of the long, deep stage.

"He's taking my associate back to the kitchens," Kaplan murmured. "Archy is beside himself with this place, isn't he, Lou? It was your brightest idea ever to hold our meeting here."

Marcello Zavier had halted to gaze, speechless. Rousing himself, he approached Kaplan. "Norman, my friend, such a challenge. I would almost prefer to leave the decor to my friend Valerian. After all, he designed the hotel."

"Marcello," Kaplan reprimanded him nasally, "don't be

a silly goose. You're here because you're a master of decor. What do you see for us?"

Zavier squatted on his heels and began sighting at sections of the empty space through little windows he made with his fingers.

"It will be very beautiful," he muttered, "very daring, very Mediterranean, yes? You will need much greenery, but all must have a sight of the stage. Thus, table decor must be subtle and low so it will not impede the vision. The party is for December, then? Close to the Christmas season. Thus, trees, decorously placed, and much silver on the ceiling. I must think."

"Marcello," Kaplan said, "please think."

As they watched Marcello sizing up the room, Pat Hyman came in with the almost incredibly tall Rolly Starr, agent to the famous. At the summit of his extended frame, a pudgy, baby face seemed inappropriate.

"Rolly," Pat said eagerly, "I want you to meet Belle Cooper."

"Why good God, we know each other," Starr exclaimed huskily. "Of course. Hello, Belle, how's Marty?"

She nodded. "Just fine."

"Haven't seen him in ages."

"And, Rolly, this is Sally Markman."

"Mrs. Markman, of course, we've met, too, here and there," Starr said. "You're the wonderful lady with all the bright ideas."

"Hi, Rolly," Sally said.

"And Norman Kaplan . . . Rolly Starr."

"Hello," Kaplan said carefully, taking a close look at Starr, who was wearing a three-piece business suit that hung loosely across his stomach.

"Mr. Kaplan, very nice to meet you," Starr mumbled. "Well, here we are at the new Splendide. This promises to be a very, very exciting place, doesn't it?"

He stared into the far corners of the ballroom, then lifted a gold-rimmed monocle, which hung on a black ribbon around his neck, and placed it in the folds under his right eye for a close-up look at Kaplan.

"We're happy you could come," Belle said.

Starr played nervously with the monocle, then dropped it, commencing to bite his fingers.

"What about a drink?" Kaplan asked. "Milton's boys are serving champagne for starters."

The Milton Williams operation had been set up behind screens well removed from the table. Waiters were circulating with champagne and trays of glasses.

"Yes, yes," Starr said, "let's get a buzz on." He glanced up at the ceiling, weighing his hardhat in his hands. "I hope we don't get a bucket of paint on our head," he remarked, laughing breathlessly.

They stood, holding champagne, waiting for the others to arrive.

Bertha Moore looked more pleased with herself and her surroundings than was her usual wont. It seemed to Belle that she had even gained a little weight—fat people were jolly, weren't they? Bertha's face loosed to a smile when she spotted Sally Markman.

Camilla Young came in by herself, kissed Belle and Sally lightly on the cheek, and said a very careful hello to Bertha. The next to arrive were Daisy Cox and Marcia King. Both were dressed in light cotton prints and were wearing straw boaters, Marcia's with a red ribbon and Daisy's a blue ribbon tied around the crown.

"Hello, sweetie," Daisy said to Pat Hyman. "You know Marcia . . ."

"Sweetie yourself," Pat scolded. "I haven't heard from you in days. What the hell have you been doing? Let me introduce you. This tall young man is Rolly Starr . . . Daisy Cox, Marcia King. Are you two supposed to be twin sisters or something?"

"We thought it'd be cute," Daisy said.

"Ladies," Rolly announced himself gallantly, bending his long body to them.

"Norman Kaplan," Pat continued.

"Good afternoon," Kaplan said severely, "Daisy . . . Marcia . . ."

It was clear that Kaplan felt uncomfortable with Rolly Starr, Belle thought, possibly because physically they were so dissimilar—Kaplan very short and round beside Starr's height. And Starr, despite Kaplan's effusiveness, was the more expressive. He gasped and chuckled, keeping up a running patter of comment. He could not stand still and was forever fixing the monocle to his eye, then dropping it to rub his hands and gesture.

He was said to be a brilliant young man. He had started as a mail clerk in one of Hollywood's talent agencies and after only a few years, taking along his immoderately loyal clients, he had opened his own business. With a combination of wile and daring, he'd expanded and was now in the process of moving into the production of motion pictures, his roster of stars, actors, directors and writers becoming his work force.

Kaplan mentioned then that he'd heard Starr was forming a new production company.

"My dear man," Rolly sighed, right eye owlish behind the monocle, "we already have. Our first picture is out. It's called *Hell's Damsels*."

"I'm afraid I haven't seen it," Kaplan said.

"Please don't," Starr cried. "It's trash. You wouldn't care for it. Pure, unadulterated trash, my dear sir."

Coolly, Kaplan said, "In that case, I won't."

"But," Starr said, turning to Belle, "Jane Farelady, the star, is magnificent. In fact, C.A.A. is thinking about taking over her promotion, Belle. Did Marty tell you?"

"No, he didn't."

"Marty and I might be making a package deal for three of Jane's flicks," Starr reported. "Production and promotion. Marty thinks he can get 20th Century-Fox to take on the distribution. I guess, Belle, Marty is pretty tight-lipped about business. Not like me. I talk and talk, talk too much if the truth be known."

Belle nodded, not trying to say anything to this. What Starr said, however, did not surprise her. Cooper had been considering for several years the proper way of getting into the movie business. And, she agreed with Starr: Starr very possibly talked much more than he should.

Marjery Cannon made a rushing entrance. She was wearing a scooped-neck Halston, which showed her tanned and bony chest, and a floppy summer hat. She headed straight for Sally, put her hands familiarly on Sally's shoulders, and kissed her on both cheeks. She didn't appear to notice that Sally's body went rigid at her touch.

"How are you, Sally?"

"First rate, Marjery," Sally said. "Get your hardhat."

"Here you go, Marjery," Belle said.

Marjery was so thick-skinned she didn't realize they were all doubtful of her. She was such a horrendous phony. Marjery paused for effect. She looked around. She knew Pat Hyman, of course, Daisy Cox . . .

"I'm Norman Kaplan," Kaplan announced.

"Marjery Cannon," she replied, moving closer to him as

he took her hand. "You're the Norman Kaplan from New York?"

"Yes."

"The financial wizard. Of course," she exclaimed warmly.

She would not let go of his hand until she caught sight of Archy and David Abdul, returning from the kitchens.

"Marjery," Kaplan said, "I'd like you to meet David Abdul, also from New York. Archy, of course, you know."

Abdul took Marjery's hand and bent over it deliberately, as if analyzing the freckles on her knuckles. She turned away from Kaplan and gave her full attention to the Arab.

"Mr. Abdul, you're new to our city, aren't you?"

"Ah, yes, ah, yes," Abdul hissed.

"Please, now tell me exactly what you do."

"David is in investments," Kaplan said, moving to be part of the group again.

"What!" Marjery gasped, "no oil?"

Abdul chuckled moistly. "Oh yes, oil. But one does nothing with oil. It merely flows. Investment is more interesting."

Marjery's eyes seemed to clatter into focus as she became even more raptly attentive.

"David is the moving force behind the Beverly Splendide," Kaplan explained.

"Really? Really!" Marjery said. "Oh, I am impressed. I am really very impressed. I think this is going to be the most magnificent hotel, Mr. Abdul."

"David," he corrected her gently. "All my friends in Los Angeles must call me David. We hope it will be magnificent. We plan that it will. We are responsible for the building. Mr. Finistere here will do the rest."

Filled with pride, Archy expanded his chest at Abdul's words. "We are going to have the most magnificent hostelry on the West Coast."

"Archy," Marjery complained coyly, "I didn't know you were leaving the Camino."

"Ah, dear lady, that has been a very confidential matter," Archy said.

"And," Abdul asked, "who do I see? A lady in riding breeches and boots."

They turned, following his eyes. Darling Higgins had just made her entrance. Her cheeks were flushed, eyes bright.

"Darling Higgins," Marjery said indifferently, "she goes riding every morning."

Then Priscilla Murray came in, followed by Paula Stone. All said their hellos. Carlotta Westmoreland came down the steps into the ballroom. She was dressed in a light wool suit and an old-fashioned garden hat. She made straight for Belle but brushed aside the offer of a hardhat.

"Hello, Belle, how goes it?" she asked.

Their talk downtown had made more familiar a long but vague acquaintance.

"Mr. Norman Kaplan," Carlotta said, in place of a hello.

"The fatuous ass," Kaplan said playfully. "Do you know Rolly Starr?"

"Do *I* know Rolly Starr?" she snapped, "well, I should. We accept his porno advertising. What's that disgusting new sex movie of yours, Mr. Starr?"

Starr doubled over with laughter. He seized Carlotta's hand and kissed it, then nervously tried to attach the monocle to his face.

"Mrs. Westmoreland, it is a movie of extreme Americanism, about lady Marines," he said fervently.

"And sex."

"But have you seen it, Mrs. Westmoreland? Have you seen it?"

"Certainly not," she said, her pink cheeks charged with indignation. Rolly took her hand and stared fondly at her. "It would give me great pleasure to screen it for you. Just tell me when."

She relented enough to give him a stern smile. "Perhaps I will. But is it safe in that house of yours? One hears it's a den of evil."

"Mrs. Westmoreland," he protested excitedly, "how could that be? I live not three blocks from you. My house is in Hancock Park."

"You live in Hancock Park?" Carlotta demanded, taken aback.

"All we media people live in that area of town now, dear lady. You and Mrs. Chandler and me. It's the *only* respectable part of town these days."

He was referring to a residential area midway between downtown Los Angeles and Beverly Hills, possibly the first suburb of the city, that had been built in the twenties and thirties.

"When you come over, Mrs. Westmoreland," Starr said, cackling with laughter, "we'll put away the coke."

"I could possibly have some grass though?" she muttered.

"Grass you can have," Rolly said.

Tom Glenn was the last to arrive. They were all sitting around the long trestle table when he came in. He hurried toward Sally.

"So sorry I'm late. I couldn't get away."

Sally had saved him a place on her left. She'd put Rolly Starr on her right, next to him, Belle, and across from Belle, Pat Hyman.

When Glenn had been seated and served his usual Perrier, Sally said, "Well, Rolly, I expect Pat Hyman has explained to you what this is all about."

Starr nodded, picking at the salad Milton's people had put in wooden bowls at each of their places.

"We'd like you to help recruit some of Hollywood's finest and biggest names for our December party. Would you be willing?"

"Naturally," Starr purred. "Absolutely. Pat's told me all about it. And," he stressed, "I already have a plan—an unbeatable, unchallengeable strategy. We'll get each of the First Ladies to pick out their favorite entertainer: Sinatra or whoever, a dancer, an operatic star. Then, with that endorsement, we approach the performer. If Mrs. Ford says she would like Whoever to sing for her at the party, are they going to turn her down? No way." He grinned smugly. "And people wonder how I made my fortune. As to run-of-the-mill Hollywood types, Pat and I between us can round up everybody in town."

"A couple of dozen altogether? Is that asking too much?"

Rolly shook his head, chubby cheeks wobbling. He adjusted his monocle for a better view of the salad.

"I don't know why I wear this thing," he muttered, then brightly added, "a pure affectation, of course. No, Sally, no problem, if we get started on it right away. You start out with people like Greg Peck, Kirk Douglas . . . Sammy Davis Jr., he can't turn anything down if he's in town. Milton Berle . . . John Wayne would be there like a shot if he were alive. Are you going to charge your celebrities for tickets?"

"A good question," Pat Hyman said.

Belle murmured, "I think they should contribute like everyone else."

"And so do I," Starr said. "And so they will. No freebies, right?"

"Not if we can help it," Sally said. "Except the First Ladies. For them, I suppose we'll have to pay transportation and hotel."

Starr pursed his lips, his eyes shrewd. "I don't know why they should always get a free ride."

"Well, I don't know," Sally said. "They have to do so much charity stuff, they'd go broke if they always had to pay their own way."

"I guess so," Starr admitted.

At the other end of the table, Kaplan was assuming his now-accepted post of chairman. He clinked his glass for attention.

"Who *is* that little man?" Rolly whispered to Belle.

"And old friend," she said, "and a dear man. You're going to like him."

Kaplan was on his feet. "Ladies and gentlemen, once again I'm appointing myself chairman of the meeting. We must hasten along. We must be out of here no later than 3:30. So, a couple of business matters. Marcia King is with us today and she has, as we'd hoped, agreed to design our invitation and the party program. The invitations will be finished and printed by the middle of September. Am I correct in that, Marcia?"

Marcia bobbed her short-cropped head. "Daisy is going to help me with all the details," she said.

"Our show business committee," Kaplan went on, smiling broadly, "is already in session at the other end of the table: Mr. Starr, Pat Hyman, and Belle Cooper. Now then . . ." Kaplan paused, pulling pieces of paper from his jacket pocket. "Our first publicity effort, thanks to Mrs. Westmoreland and my own brilliant self, and to our friends in New York and elsewhere around the country, has begun to pay off handsomely. I've been getting telephone calls from all my chums and I'm sure you all have, too."

Sally nodded. "All day long over the last couple of days, Norman."

"Well, friends," Kaplan continued, "I hope you'll all start keeping lists. Apropos of that, I think that today we must name our committee to deal with just that—the invitation lists. I suggest Sharon Peters, Camilla Young, and Lou Finistere. You agree, girls? Good! Applause, everybody. All right, enough applause. By the way, it was Mrs. Finistere's idea to meet here today. Congratulations, Lou! All right. What we want are lists from each and every one of you of potential invitees, a horrible word but it serves. Next, I'm taking it upon myself to appoint a worker in each of the cities that show an interest. This will, normally, be somebody I know and trust. So far those cities are Washington, Atlanta, Palm Beach, Dallas, San Francisco, Boston, plus, of course, New York . . . and, my word, I've got it scribbled here that we've already heard from some women in Canada."

More applause greeted this information.

"Hurray for Norman," Maude Mannon yelled, clapping.

"Please, please," he beamed, "no exaggerated adulation, please. Now then: the invitations have got to be mailed out no later than the first week in October. In many cases, they'll just formalize acceptances we already have. Now, Mrs. Westmoreland, Carlotta, I'd like to drop another item on you: the exact date of the party, so people can put it on their calendars. I propose December the second. That's a Saturday and it doesn't seem like there's going to be any great conflict in L.A. that night. We've checked the master social calendar downtown. Now, among other things, we have to decide today what we are actually going to call this event. Lou Finistere has suggested Splendide Affaire, and that would be appropriate since the party will be the first in the new hotel. Belle Cooper thinks Winter Ball or, if you prefer the French, Archy, Bal d'Hiver. Sally has been toying with the idea of christening it simply Big-Party, the two words run together. Do I hear any other bright ideas? The chair will entertain bright ideas."

Bertha Moore raised her hand. "I propose Ball of the Angels, after Los Angeles, City of the Angels, don't you see?"

"Ball of the Angels," Kaplan repeated, "or possibly Angels' Ball . . ."

"No," Bertha said scornfully, "that's corny, Norman. Ball of the Angels."

"Angels," Rolly Starr piped up, "a very show-business connotation."

"So?" Bertha demanded.

Kaplan sang out, "Do I hear any more bright ideas?

Think about it, and while you're thinking, I'd like to introduce the man behind this fabulous new hotel. No, no, not yet, Archy. First, I want you all to meet Mr. David Abdul."

The two dozen applauded politely. Marjery Cannon put her elbows on the edge of the table and stared at Abdul as he rose from his chair.

"Ladies and gentlemen," Abdul said, "a great pleasure for me to be here with you. I congratulate you on your noble endeavor."

Abruptly, he sat down.

Kaplan, grinning, said, "And now Mr. Archibald Finistere, the man who's going to make the Splendide tick."

Archy clambered nimbly to his feet, thrust his head back, and smiled, tugging modestly on his beard.

"Well, my dear friends. Norman, thank you for the kind introduction. And I'd like to second what our friend David here has said. This is a noble effort—matching this noble hotel. I ask you to look around you. In a few months' time, this barnlike room will be decorated and finished and it'll be filled with our friends from all over the country, perhaps all over the world. I will paint a word picture for you. The chandeliers will be in place and sparkling, flags flying, tables elegantly decorated. You will hear the hum of activity, laughter, music, a few speeches—I hope."

As if to underline Archy's words, construction noises outside the ballroom started up. It was the end of the lunchbreak, Belle realized. No wonder it had been so quiet. Now came the sounds of jackhammers, strained truck motors, drills, and hammering. Archy lifted his voice.

"Your cause will be launched; our hotel—the Splendide—will receive its baptism of fire. A wonderful moment. For a hotelier, such as Archy Finistere, a supreme moment."

"Thank you, Archy," Kaplan interrupted him. "We must move along."

Archy looked confused for a moment, then waved, and sat down again.

"Zounds!" Kaplan cried, "they did warn us. A few more things," he exclaimed loudly. "As soon as the offices are finished upstairs, Archy has promised the use of one on the mezzanine floor. We'll have a phone in with a number and, if need be, David will provide us with a secretary—gratis, I should stress. That will be our communications center."

"Entertainment?" Rolly Starr called out.

"That, my dear sir, is your department," Kaplan yelled. "You are hereby named chairman of the entertainment committee."

Rolly nodded complacently. "How long a show?"

"Sally?" Kaplan asked.

Her voice was too soft to be heard at the other end of the table. "Dinner at nine," she told Starr, "at which point the master of ceremonies does a brief introduction. A few more words between soup and main course. Dinner out of the way by ten. Then, say," she said, "entertainment starts at 10:30. Would that be too late?" Sally whispered. "No, I don't think so either, if we wrap it up by midnight. An hour and a half is long enough for anybody. Then dancing."

Starr, in his high-pitched voice, relayed the information down the table. "An hour and a half of entertainment, finished by midnight, then dancing."

"This is not a late town, Norman," Sally said.

"I beg your pardon."

Starr called, "Sally said this is not a late town."

Cupping his hands for a megaphone, Kaplan said, "Don't I know it. Such a boring city."

There was laughter and people began to get up.

"Sally," Starr said, "I'm going to try for Sinatra. I know that's who you'll want. God! Nobody will even come to a benefit anymore unless Sinatra performs. Dancer . . . soprano . . . comedian. Sounds like Santa Claus's reindeer."

"All right," Sally murmured. "But one important thing. I think we should present our award early, maybe between dinner and the start of the entertainment. Otherwise, people won't pay attention."

"I'll figure that out," Starr promised.

Maude was bawling at Archy. "You're going to need an army of valet parkers, Mr. Finistere."

"No problem, my lady," Archy said jovially.

This was Bertha Moore's excuse to ask acidly, "I suppose by December you will have your work force assembled?"

"We're opening in January, dear lady," Archy said haughtily, leaning across the table toward her, "so by December we had better have our personnel in place."

"I mean waiters and all that."

"Well, of course," Archy said impatiently.

Quietly, at Archy's side, Abdul said, "It is not a consideration, Mrs. Moore."

Exasperatedly, Kaplan yelled, "Ladies, ladies, not just yet. I want a small committee to help with the decor." He was reading from a note Belle had given him. "May I suggest Mrs. Stone, Mrs. Moore, and Mrs. Higgins."

The three nodded and stopped for a moment in their flight from the noise. Darling fluffed her red hair with one hand.

"Ladies, ladies," Kaplan exclaimed. "I haven't even adjourned the meeting. We haven't voted yet on the name for our fine affair. Oh well." He threw his hands up in despair. "Undisciplined lot. I'll decide the name myself then."

Chapter Nineteen

Marjery Cannon was furious when she drove away from the Splendide. She'd been invited into the group, then had been given nothing to do. They treated her distantly, as if she were some sort of idiot. Why? Especially Sally: was it possible Sally had an inkling about her and Bernard? No, that was impossible. They had been entirely circumspect. No, she advised herself grimly, this just happened not to be her natural and proper group. This bunch, they were not *old* Los Angeles. They weren't of her sort. They were all nouveaus, starting with Sally Markman, who, by rights, belonged to the Cedars-Sinai bunch. Belle Cooper and Kaplan, both nothing more than transplanted easterners, Kaplan not even a transplanted one. And good God, Rolly Starr, for all his height, an inflated Humpty Dumpty. Maude Mannon, a raucous Texan with all that oil money.

Carlotta Westmoreland was really the only old Californian. One of her forebears had been cannibalized during the winter crossing of the Donner Pass.

Well, she'd play along, Marjery decided. She had no choice and she would make something of the affair.

Marjery drove into the Camino parking lot just as Lou Finistere pulled up with Archy and David Abdul. Now, she thought, there was *real* oil money. Abdul slid sinuously from the back seat of Archy's Seville and went around the car to help Lou.

Marjery put on a surprised little smile when she got out of her Pinto.

"Hi there. Fancy meeting you here," Marjery chirped.

"I didn't know you were staying here," Archy said. "Or just making use of our parking lot?"

"Archy! I've got some shopping to do. Well, David, did you enjoy our little meeting?"

"Assuredly," he said smoothly.

Archy plucked Lou's sleeve. "Come along, sweetheart, back to work."

When they'd said goodbye and disappeared, Marjery asked Abdul, "Do you like California?"

"Very much," he said. "So much so, I'm buying a house here, did you know? A real-estate lady is coming to pick me up at any moment."

Ah, hell, Marjery thought, an opportunity lost. If not for that, he might have invited her for coffee.

"How exciting," she said. "Then we'll be seeing a lot of you."

"I hope so," he said. "So many beautiful ladies here."

"Oh, David," she replied, letting herself seem flustered. "And so few fascinating men."

"Ah . . ." His voice crawled like caressing fingers down her back.

Marjery thought she could easily fall in love again—and she did love to fall in love. But her attack was thwarted when a white Seville came into the driveway. A tall blonde jumped out and looked around. God, Marjery groaned, Pamela Renfrew, that shark.

"David, I think this is your real-estate lady," Marjery said.

"Ah, yes, blonde and in a white car. Miss Renfrew?"

"The same," Marjery said.

"Well then, goodbye, Marjery. It *is* Marjery, is it not?

Well . . . What is it you people say in California? Have a nice day? Marjery, please, have a nice day," Abdul said softly, his wily smile cutting her like a scimitar. Wasn't that the curved Arabian sword?

Goddamn it, Marjery muttered to herself, suddenly alone again and deeply depressed. She watched Abdul hop in Pamela Renfrew's car and Pamela whip the Seville out of the parking lot and away.

Have a nice day? She smiled to herself. Well, she would try to make it a nice day. She pulled herself together and walked through the Camino to Wilshire Boulevard, then in the direction of Rodeo Drive four blocks to the east.

Marjery had an hour to kill before she was to meet Bernard. She stopped at Giorgio's for a few minutes to poke around the racks and accepted a glass of white wine at the bar. Marjery ran a charge here, much to Gregory's long-standing horror, and at the moment was unfortunately somewhat behind with her payments. They would never say anything; that wasn't done. But she realized, again depressed, that the salesladies were not pulling at her sleeves to get her into the changing room. Disgruntled with her lot, Marjery left half the wine and continued up the street. She passed Hermes, where she had never set foot, then Gucci's, which was within her reach but still very expensive, and went as far as Fred's, the French jeweler. She had a quick look at the windows, then crossed to the east side of the street, still hot under the sun. She wandered up to Bijan, one of the most expensive of the men's shops. It amused her to consider a little gift for Gregory; then she thought more seriously of investing in something for Bernard, perhaps a tie. She decided against that, too; tactically, it might be a serious mistake.

Having put out of her head thought of spending money, she turned back, strolling more comfortably, amazed again at all the new stores that had opened. It was incredible that any of them could make enough even to pay the enormous Rodeo rents. Fred's and Van Cleef, well they would do all right in this economy, the price of gold and silver and precious rocks being what they were.

At the end of the street, where Rodeo Drive met Wilshire Boulevard, the Beverly Wilshire Hotel loomed gray and elegant, awnings over the ground-floor windows. She crossed to reach the Brown Derby corner of the intersection, then again to the Bonwit Teller side. Now she was walking westward, in the direction of the Camino. Bernard kept his little *pied-à-terre* off to the left, in the first block south of Wilshire.

He was having a glass of vodka and milk when she arrived.

"Oh, Bernard," she cried softly, voice quivering, "I hope your stomach isn't bothering you again."

"Yes, Marjery," he said. "It is, a little."

He had taken off his jacket and was leaning back in a wing chair, his tanned head against the leather. But his face was pale and worried. She knelt on the floor beside him and took his hand in hers.

"Poor Bernard." She rubbed his hand against her cheek.

"Yes, poor Bernard," he repeated.

"Well," she said softly, "I was at the group's luncheon today."

"And?"

"It was at the Splendide. They treated me like dirt," she said, close to tears.

"Why would they do that?" he asked absently.

"I don't know. I really don't know. They did, that's all. I didn't even get a job to do on any of the committees. I don't think they really want me. Sally . . . was so cold."

He pulled his hand away and looked angrily at her. "She's sick," he said.

Marjery pulled herself up and sat on the footstool by the chair.

"What do you mean she's sick? She looked fine."

Markman shook his head miserably. "No, she's not feeling well."

"What's wrong with her?"

"I'm not sure. She hasn't said anything. But I know."

Christ, Marjery thought to herself, fascinating news. How sick was Sally? What did he mean?

"What can I do, Bernard?" she asked mournfully.

"Nothing." Speaking with an effort, he said, "Look, Marjery, I'm not going to be seeing you anymore. You're a wonderful woman but I'm saying finis. I can't handle it now."

Marjery collapsed into herself, her head on her hands on her knees, and began to cry. She sobbed convulsively, her shoulders shaking.

She moaned, "Just like that?"

"I'm afraid so."

"But you may need me more than ever now," she protested, wailing.

Damnation, she was thinking, if this were so, if Sally were badly ill, now was not the time to be thrown over by Bernard Markman. Given a solid opportunity, finally, she would have cast Gregory to the winds, with scarcely a second thought.

"I wanted to get you a present, something, as a memory," Markman was saying softly, "but then I thought I'd let you choose it yourself."

God! And she had considered buying him a gift, however briefly. If she had, then perhaps . . .

Bernard stood up, leaving her huddled on the stool, and found his checkbook in his jacket.

"Here," he said, scribbling, then tearing a check loose. "I want you to have this. I've searched the firm for a spot for Greg. But there just doesn't seem to be anything to suit his unique talents."

Talents, she thought bitterly, what talents? Markman pressed the check in her hand. She decided not to take it. She waved him away, whimpering.

"What will I do? I don't know what I'll do without you."

"Marjery," he said, "you'll survive. Here, take it. I want you to have it, sincerely. It's the least I can do for you."

She peeked. It was for $5,000.

"No! No!" she persisted.

"Yes."

She nodded miserably. "How do you figure out the sum, Bernard?" she asked bitterly. "Do you start a clock going, like the lawyers? Or is it piecework? So much per fuck? Time and a half for a blow job?"

Markman seemed to reel away from her.

Marjery folded the check and put it carefully in her purse.

Morris Mauery and George Hyman were still sitting with brandy and cigars in their corner spot at three P.M.

Mauery had a disturbing habit of sliding into long periods of silence between spurts of conversation, and their lunch had been interrupted two or three times by phone calls. Now he sat brooding, glaring at the end of his cigar, the waiters, practically anything that moved. Morrie appeared to be in an even more black and nasty mood than usual.

"You were saying?" he asked.

"That all the girls are over at the new Splendide today having lunch. You know about Sally Markman's December party?"

"I've heard," Mauery growled. "Why there? Goddamn Arab hotel."

"Kaplan dreamt up the idea," Hyman said. "He's got money in the place, and he's Sally Markman's closest friend."

Mauery nodded ominously. "We'll see about that. They haven't contacted me yet. I hope they're not going to have any labor problems."

Mauery glanced frostily at him, his stony face breaking almost audibly into a frightening grin.

"Surely they will talk to you, Morrie," Hyman said uncomfortably.

He knew what would happen. If Mauery decided to make trouble, Pat would insist that he, George, try to talk him out of it.

"I don't like fucking Arabs," Mauery said, "and neither should you, George."

"They're not my favorite people," Hyman agreed.

"Well, then."

"Oh, shit, Pat is involved. You know, Morrie, they're going to collect all the ex-First Ladies for the party. It *will* be quite an event for the city."

Mauery shrugged. "So what? Who gives a fuck for all the First Ladies? I don't, and neither should you, George. They never did anything for you, except bring you trouble."

The reference was to Hyman's short-lived indictment for income tax evasion. His pal, Morrie, had pulled him out of that one. Mauery was a valuable friend, Christ, and there was no way of exaggerating how much help Mauery had given him over the years: for movie financing, in bulldozing the actors and producers, demolishing labor problems. The list of favors was unending. Mauery was the man to cut through impassable ranges of everything from petty annoyance to catastrophic obstacle. He managed it with a phone call, a half day's work.

"Sharon is involved, too," he reminded Mauery.

"I know she's involved," Mauery said sullenly. "She's also got herself involved with a guy named Frank Woodley. Goddamn it, a stuntman. The son of a bitch is obviously after her money."

Hyman understood. This was what was bothering Morrie. A thing as simple as that. Hyman rubbed his rubbery tanned face and stroked his eyes. He always needed a nap after one of these lunches.

"How are you going to handle it, Morrie?"

Mauery glared at him opaquely. "There are ways. But I am very pissed off. She ought to know better than that."

Cooper was stroking her back. He ran his fingers across ivory skin so electric with stored lust that voltage seemed to jar his hand, across the side of her rib cage, and softly kneaded her buttocks. He ran the tender nub of his abbreviated little finger through the cleavage of her ass and pressed the bud of her anus. Her body started, then the perfectly controlled cheeks grabbed the finger and she laughed whisperingly. He moved his hand down her gentle thigh to the knee, over rounded calves to narrow ankle, foot, tiny toes. He bent over her to kiss her on the ass, next the taut flesh at the back of the knees where a blue vein throbbed, to run his tongue over the Achilles' tendon. He kissed her instep and, knowing he was a smitten fool and not able to resist, the toes. He actually put her toes in his mouth and sucked them one by one.

Jane Farelady purred like a temporarily tolerant tigress, for she was no little pussycat. She loved it as he worshipped her. Such a body, Cooper thought, and so young, so firm. He had forgotten youth; it was even more responsive, alive, vital, than the insatiable Daisy Cox. Sexually, Jane was amoral, unthinking, a tigress indeed. She absorbed sex like food, as a natural everyday need. But he had the sense to know that, like the tigress, she could easily devour him, then spit out his bones.

She flipped over and drew him down on her, kissing him hungrily on the mouth. Her breasts, stiff and full, bulged under his arms.

"Marty," she said, her wide and innocent eyes gleaming, "you have learned how to make it with me."

Then the eyes went blank. She arched her pelvis expertly, seizing him between her thighs, grasping him and pulling him, throbbing, inside her.

"Jane," he muttered, "you're wonderful. No hands."

Growling and grunting, she said, "I know I'm wonderful, and you know I'm wonderful, but who else knows?"

"Pretty soon, they'll all know."

She nodded and said nothing more. She closed the childlike eyes, biting her lips in concentration. At once, her movements became more agitated, then violent. She heaved under him and climaxed quickly with a lengthy shudder, moaning and drawing him. He came again. Christ, it was a miracle.

Afterwards, he petted and stroked her. Balls, he warned himself grimly, he was falling for her. He was damn near in love with her. He knew that was a huge mistake. She was young and he could not control her. She was completely wild, wanton. Cooper liked them wanton, but there had to be a point at which he could manage wantonness. The first night he'd gone there, after talking to Mort, she'd just come home and was high on something or other, not simply grass, he calculated. They had talked disjointedly for a minute and then she had thrown off her clothes to show him her body, what it was he'd be selling. He had bought it, lock, stock, and barrel.

"What about tonight?" he asked when she finally opened her eyes and stared at him.

She shook her head. "No, I've got a business appointment."

"Who with?"

"Somebody." She would never tell him. "I've got my secrets, Marty."

"I'd rather you be with me," he said. But he was not going to beg for it. "We're going to have to go away maybe . . . When the campaign begins, you're going to have to do a lot of barnstorming."

"You don't intend to send me out with one of your assistants, I hope."

"I'll try to be with you."

"You better. I know you and Rolly are working something out. You two fuckers are not going to exploit my ass," she warned.

"Naturally not. You're getting a piece of it."

Coldly, she nodded. "And you're getting plenty of pieces, Marty. When am I going on the Carson show?"

"As soon as I can get it arranged. That's not an easy one, you know. Not on the strength of one lousy movie. I'll need a better peg than that." He stooped again, this time to gather her left nipple in his mouth. "For instance, I have a mental picture of you as a lady archaeologist. We've got a property along those lines. Ever study anything like archaeology?"

"Shit, no."

"Well, if you were a lady archaeologist and playing one in a movie, now that'd be a hell of a peg."

"I could study it," she said seriously. "I could say I've been on digs."

"What do you know about digs?"

She sat up indignantly. "A lot. I did go to college, you know. I'm not stupid. I know as much about digs as you know about rutting."

"Ha!" he said, trying to soothe her. "In fact, you're very smart. What we've got to do is take advantage of that. Jane, don't worry. I'm working on it."

"You better be, Marty. I'm counting on you."

Cooper frowned, feeling heated with annoyance. If she weren't such a marvel of a lay, he told himself, he might have socked her one and said goodbye. But he was not stupid either: he knew sex was part of his payment, probably all the payment he'd ever see from her. But the pending deal with Rolly Starr was worth more.

Ignoring him, Jane climbed out of bed and went to look at herself more closely in the mirrored wall. She was goddamned long and lithe, still aroused, that he felt almost ready for session number three. He wondered if she'd had plastic surgery done on the tits. Most likely, that gangly monster Starr had paid for it to get her in proper shape for his awful movie, and no doubt, with the connivance of Mort Schultz. Aching, he assumed Mort was also paid in kind. But Christ, he was ready to tolerate almost anything if he could have her.

Jane swung her long brown hair arrogantly.

"You're beautiful, Jane," he muttered from the bed. "A knockout."

"I know that," she said, not turning. "I know that, you know that, but . . ."

Pamela swung her white car into the newly built Preston property, high in the Trousdale hills. Percy Preston had bought the land a year or so before, then put the house on it. Preston had furnished the house with good, not priceless, antiques and pictures with just such a customer as David Abdul in mind.

She parked in a paved courtyard. The house was Italianate, Tuscan in mood, stucco walls a dusty rose, the roof red tile brought up from Mexico. Pamela unlocked a wrought-iron gate to an entry court, then a ten-foot door. Inside the house, a short hallway led into a bright and airy living room whose sliding doors opened to a covered terrace and a pool. At the far side of the property, Preston had planted olive trees and through these a hazy view of the city spread before them.

"Very beautiful," Abdul murmured.

"It's smoggy today," she said, for there was no reason to ignore it. "You see, the pool floats right into the house. That glass wall slides up. There's a Jacuzzi and dressing room in that wing."

The bedrooms, three of them, were on the left, decorated blithely, in keeping with the rest of the house, with pastel shades of fabric and beds with canopied tops. The baths, one for each bedroom, had been tiled with richly veined Carrara marble.

The dining room lay efficiently off a master chef's kitchen in the other wing.

"This house is really a masterpiece, Mr. Abdul," she enthused.

"I see that," he agreed softly. "It is the most beautiful we have seen today. But, please, call me David, for we are doing business. Business should be done between friends. How much is this house, Pamela?"

"A shade under three million dollars," she said.

"I will buy it," Abdul said, without another question. "Give me a paper to sign, Pamela."

"Let's sit down." Carefully, she took the sacred buyer's offer from her pocketbook and laid it on the coffee table in the living room. Abdul signed his name.

"I should also have a certified check for $100,000 or so, just to show you're in earnest, you see."

"You will have that tomorrow morning," he said.

"I congratulate you," she said. "It is a very good buy and a year from now it'll probably be worth a million more."

Abdul flicked his hand, as if scaring away a fly. "I will never buy a house again except from such a beautiful blonde lady as you, Pamela."

"Oh, my," she said, delighted at the deal and with him. "Is a thirty-day escrow all right with you?"

"The sooner the better."

"I'll see if I can't speed it up."

"Please do." Handing her the pen, his fingers touched hers. They were slender but very strong. The contact caused her almost to gasp. Seeing her surprise, he laid his hand on the back of hers and squeezed. "So now, this is my house," he added.

"I think probably so."

"I will not bargain. They ask three million. I offer three million. Therefore, it is done."

Uncertainly, she nodded. "Yes, it's as good as done, I'd say."

"Are you a married woman, Pamela?"

She shook her head. "No, I've never been married."

He seemed amazed. "No man has ever asked you to be his wife?"

She laughed. "Oh, I've been asked. But it never worked out."

And she had also done the asking. She had asked Cooper and he had turned her down, pleading financial risk. And then she had bitten him. And then she had been beaten up and raped. Well, it had been rape and non-rape, all mixed up. She had not seen Cooper since Las Vegas. But she'd received the flowers and the un-funny note. And between nightmares, it had seemed to her there was some unthinkable connection between what had happened in Las Vegas and then to her in her own house, perhaps an ironic repayment to her by the dark forces for what she had done to him. But in the end, she did not like to think about it and she had dismissed it from her mind. All she knew now was that she hated Cooper and that somehow she would get back at him for the Las Vegas humiliation.

Abdul interrupted her thoughts. "I hope you will watch my house for me when I'm not in Los Angeles. I travel a great deal."

"But, my God, you'll put a housekeeper in here, won't you? It should never be left alone in times like these."

"If securely locked?"

"That's still asking for trouble," Pamela said. "I could tell you a story."

"Yes, yes, please."

Reluctantly, for she did not like to dwell on the horror

of it, she told him she'd been attacked and robbed one night recently. She didn't get into the rape aspect of it. She didn't want to frighten away a buyer by being plain stupid.

"No!" he cried, his face glowering with rage.

"Yes, two men. They beat me up. I'm just getting over it. I had to have a wire put in my jaw."

She touched the spot carefully. Fortunately, all but the deepest bruises had disappeared from her body, but sometimes she ached where the man had whipped her with the belt.

Abdul's face twisted. "So terrible! In my country, such men should be executed immediately." He jumped up and began to pace the floor in agitation.

Wryly, she said, "But not in California. Even if they caught them, they'd be out of jail in two or three months."

"It is not possible! Such a poor and darling lady!" Abdul shook his head and smiled disbelievingly. "Such is the philosophical difference between societies. In my country, with one witness, the trial would be over in fifteen minutes and they would be dead within twenty-four hours."

"Well, David, I have to say I like your form of justice. When it happens to you, you become a lot less forgiving."

He sat down beside her again and took both her hands in his own. He bent his head to kiss her wrists. She thought he was going to sob with sympathy. A physical thrill ran through her and then a rolling surge of desire, the first she'd experienced since that night, for the aftermath of the attack had been distinctly unromantic: first, they'd given her a pregnancy test, even though she'd insisted she was on the pill, and then they had tested her for the vile diseases, transmittable equally whether the act be rape or pure love.

"But you were not hurt too badly," Abdul murmured.

Gently, ever so gently, he placed his hand on her breast, then his lips to the spot where the cleft of her breasts began at the top of her blouse. Breathlessly, Pamela retreated a little but he put a restraining hand on her and slowly unbuttoned her blouse. When it was loose, he removed it from her arms and then unsnapped her bra and slid it from her shoulders.

"Beautiful," he murmured, his voice washing her senses, "such astoundingly beautiful breasts."

Pamela's head fell backward against the pillows. He was hypnotizing her. His voice, so low and sweet, lulled her, transported her to passion.

David's body was brown and firm and unrelenting. She was much bigger than he was, but she felt small, miniscule, as he filled her. Pamela thought she had never experienced anything quite like this; he adored her body—the body which transcended all religions—and bringing each component of it to individual delight, then pulling all together with his slipping, sliding, bulging, throbbing vitality and finally easing her to an ecstasy she hoped would never end.

By five o'clock that day, Sharon Peters and Frank Woodley were in her Lincoln and on the road to Palm Springs for a weekend of solitude. Sharon was delighted to get out of Los Angeles, even though they were headed toward the boiling desert. Her house, abutting the fairway at Thunderbird, was air-conditioned from front door to terrace and it was just a short sprint to the pool.

Frank whistled as he drove, as though he didn't have a care in the world. Having finished his movie, he had shaved the beard and his face was still unfamiliarly smooth and pink. He drove rapidly, not recklessly, handling the car like a toy, his eyes on the road and for her, smiling as he hummed and whistled.

"Now, you're going to give up falling off bridges and saloon roofs," Sharon said, putting her head on his shoulder.

"Got to earn my bread," he said.

"You're going to work with me," Sharon said.

"Are you really serious about that?"

"Yes, I'm very serious. I need a good advisor. All those guys are taking me to the cleaners."

They cleared the Santa Monica Freeway and were now into the San Bernardino straightaway. Heavily metropolitan Los Angeles County began to thin out and, after the Santa Anita Racetrack turnoff, traffic was less congested. In another half-hour, they were on the verge of the desert.

"We're not going to do anything when we get there," Sharon said, "just lay around. We're out of season now in Palm Springs."

"Suits me," Frank said happily. "All I want to do is lay around, with you."

Sharon stared at the side of his face. It was thin, its expressions volatile, controlled by his big, dark eyes. The chin was small, almost pointed, jaw prominent. He was a lovely man, she thought, so lovely.

"Would you mind explaining something to me?" Sharon asked. "Tell me how this happened? I want to know."

"You mean you and me? The two of us?"

"Yes. It couldn't be entirely accidental. Did you really work for Oscar Peters?"

He nodded, switching his eyes off the road for a second to look at her.

"Yeah," he said, "I really did, one summer, and it's true he helped me out so I could play football. But the part about seeing you there? No, I was kidding. To tell you the truth . . ." He paused and glanced up at the rear-view mirror. ". . . I never saw you until you came to L.A. I was married at the time. I told you that. She was working in a big production job at Columbia and we used to go around to premieres and so on. I'd see you across the room and I found out who you were. Then the next thing I found out was that you lived across the way. I got to watching you, thinking there's this beautiful little lady living all alone. And since we did both have a connection with Peters . . . Well, here I am."

"But I don't know what you're getting at, what *we're* getting at."

Woodley hummed loudly, showing his teeth. "Well, I hope you realize by now that I'm in love with you."

Sharon sat back. "Jesus, just like that? You take my breath away."

"Think I'm after your money? Is that what you're thinking? Balls, I don't give a damn about money," he exclaimed. "How about getting married? I'll tell you what, Sharon, get your lawyer to draw up one of those prenuptial agreements: what's yours is yours, nothing to do with me. I'll sign it. You pay me to work for you. Prove I'm on the up and up. What do you say?"

Sharon looked at the ribbon of road ahead of them. It was jumping in the heat. "I'm speechless," she said.

"Well, I do love you," Frank shouted. He rolled down the window and shouted it again into the desert.

Sharon began to cry. She could not help it. She snuffled and reached into the glove compartment for a tissue. He was grinning at her.

"What a proposal," she said.

"Well?"

She gave herself time to think. She had her answer in thirty seconds.

"Okay."

"Good," he said, patting her knee. "That's a very good girl. But I'm telling you I want that agreement to sign. All the sons of bitches in town are going to be saying I'm after your dough when I'm not. All I'm after is your sweet ass."

"All right," she nodded. "They'd probably make me get it signed anyway."

"Good," he repeated absently, again eyeing the rear-view mirror. "By the way, I think somebody is following us."

There was a green Ford about a half mile down the freeway behind them.

"Jesus, who would follow us?" She could think of only one possibility. Mauery had put a man on her.

"Well, well," Frank said cheerfully, "I think we'll just have to pull off and buy some gas."

Marking the last settlement before the long curve south toward Palm Springs, a tall and vulgar gas station stanchion poked out of the flat horizon. Woodley pulled the Lincoln into the exit.

"Yeah, he's still there. What do you know? What *do* you know?"

On the side road, he slowed down, bringing the Ford closer in behind them, then suddenly spun the Lincoln and skidded into a complete turn.

"I do stunt driving too," he muttered.

He bore down on the Ford, causing Sharon to gasp. At the last second, Frank veered to the right and stopped. The Ford was already over, almost into the ditch at the side of the road. Frank whipped open his door and trotted to the other car.

Sharon could hear his breezy voice.

"Hey, you okay, pal?"

The driver of the Ford began to shout.

"Hey, pal, let me help you out," Frank said, his voice solicitous.

He pulled open the door and took the man by the arm.

"Hey, pal, you been on my tail all the way from Los Angeles. What's the deal?"

The other man began to holler. "What the hell are you talking about, you crazy son of a bitch? You damn near run into me."

"Don't I recognize you, pal?"

"I never seen you before," the man yelled, not nearly as angry now. "You better leave me alone."

"Who you work for, you asshole? I know when somebody's following me."

"I don't work for nobody."

Sharon began to shake. As Woodley confronted him, the man's hand began to edge toward his hip. Frank must have noticed too, for he grabbed him abruptly by the lapels of his coat, whirled him around, and pushed him over the hood of the car. Frank felt in the rear pockets and came up with a pistol. Sharon cried out; it had to be one of Mauery's paid hoods.

"Well, pal," Frank drawled heavily, "carrying a little piece, are we?"

Sharon heard the driver of the Ford snarl. "We know you, Woodley, you asshole. The message is get out of town."

"Oh, yeah?"

Casually, as if in slow motion, Frank turned the man, put one finger under his chin, and belted him. The man sagged into his arms. Frank dragged him a few feet and pushed him back into the driver's seat. Then he took out a handkerchief, wiped the pistol, and threw it across the ditch into the bushes. He strolled back to the Lincoln as unconcerned as though he had stopped the car to take a leak.

"Jesus," he murmured, "I didn't know I had any enemies."

Sharon was still deeply alarmed. "But how do you know he was following us?"

"What?" He laughed. "He pulled out behind us when we left your place and he's tailed us through two freeway systems, almost all the way to Palm Springs. And you're doubting that he was following us? Please . . ." More quietly, he added, "It's Mauery, isn't it?"

"Mauery?" she repeated fearfully.

"Listen, I know all about that bastard. You can't be anywhere near the picture business without hearing about Mauery. And I happen to know you've been involved with him."

"How do you know that?"

"I just know. I know all there is to know about you, Sharon."

"Well, goddamn it," she moaned, "you see! We can't go on like this. He'll have something terrible done to you."

"What?" Frank laughed again. "Like today? Bull! Besides, my business is taking chances."

Darling Higgins had noticed the close, touching friendship of Daisy Cox and Marcia King during the luncheon and, afterward, walking back through the dust to the cars, she attached herself to them.

"Well, what's for the rest of the afternoon, girls?"

Marcia looked at her skeptically. "Well, Darling, we're going back to the store for a drink. Want to join us?"

When they'd parked at the rear of Marcia's design studios, she led them into the showroom and upstairs to her private offices. Marcia locked the door and opened a liquor cabinet.

"What'll it be, girls?"

Daisy wanted a gin martini and Darling thought she'd have the same. Marcia poured their drinks and, for herself, took a Russian vodka straight.

"Here's to you, fellas," Marcia said.

"Were you satisfied with the lunch?" Darling asked.

Marcia nodded briskly. "Sure. I get to design the invitation—very good publicity for King Enterprises. I'll need help. Daisy, you are going to help me, aren't you?"

"Of course," Daisy said.

"Come sit by me, Daisy," Marcia said, again looking doubtfully at Darling.

Daisy slid over to perch by Marcia on a brown leather and chrome couch. Blatantly, Marcia began to stroke her back, making Daisy wriggle, then kissed Daisy's cheek.

"Darling?"

Mrs. Higgins's skin was tingling. She moved off the matching couch and placed herself on the other side of Daisy.

"I know what they want from me," Darling said, referring again to the meeting. "They want me and Ellsworth to pay for all the flowers."

"Will you do it?" Daisy asked softly.

"Sure, why not? I like Sally, and Belle is a hell of a lady. I'd do anything for them."

Marcia laughed roughly. "They're exceedingly straight, Darling."

"That doesn't matter."

Darling placed her hand on Daisy's thigh and kissed her as Marcia had. Marcia nodded approvingly.

"You fellas want a joint? Loosen us up a little."

Not waiting for a response, she returned to the liquor cabinet and took a joint out of a drawer. She lit it with precision and carried it to them. Daisy had a long drag on the marijuana cigarette and handed it to Darling.

"Don't forget we've got to drive home, girls," Darling said. She inhaled a small bit of the perfumed smoke.

"I love your red hair, Darling," Daisy sighed lingeringly.

"I love yours, blondie," Darling said.

"And I like your riding pants, Darling," Marcia chimed in.

Looking coyly at each other, Marcia and Darling slowly undressed Daisy, then fell upon her as she squirmed on the couch, her eyes closed, mouth open and panting.

"Such luscious boobies," Darling whispered.

Daisy put an arm around each of them and drew them to her in matronly embrace, stroking their bodies and kissing them. Darling allowed Marcia to unbutton her denim riding shirt and unhook her bra, and then, working across Daisy's inert body, she pulled away Marcia's dress and kissed her tiny breasts, biting the nipples teasingly. Grunting ferociously, Marcia slid out of the dress. The three of them rolled off the couch into the thick wool shag rug. Daisy and Marcia pulled off her riding boots, then the jodhpurs, and they savaged her body with their mouths. They formed a rough triangle.

"This is for you, Daisy," Marcia giggled, "a daisy chain."

"I love it," Daisy squealed. "Now, all change, like musical chairs."

Darling moved her head from the sweetness of Daisy to the somewhat bitter taste of Marcia. Not surprising, she thought. Dreamily, for the grass had a telling effect, she remembered a gigantic orgy she and Ellsworth had attended down in Rio. It had gone on for three days, allowing time for sleep, drinks, and drugs.

When she got home, having left Marcia and Daisy in excited dalliance, it was nearly five and the house was a mess. She and Ellsworth could not keep help. People who came to work for them couldn't stand the heat and were so soon gone that all the rooms were in a constant state of disorder.

Ellsworth was just getting out of bed. He was with his new tootsie, an Italian waiter he'd picked up downtown. Ellsworth, and Joe, as they called him, strolled into the living room just after she arrived, dressed in tight jeans, both of them bare-chested.

"Hi, Darling!" Ellsworth sang out, crossing to kiss her. "How'd it go?"

"Fine," she said. "Hello, Joe. Ellsworth, we're going to pay for all the flowers for the December party. Exciting?"

"Sounds it, sweetie."

Christ, Darling thought, Ellsworth was so handsome. His eyes were as clear as the sky on a good day, his skin smooth and unlined yet by the demands of his passion. She often thought he must look like Dorian Grey before the evil transformation. Theirs was certainly a marriage of convenience, she noted dispiritedly, but Ellsworth was the most marvelous companion, a handsome escort. And he was rich as hell.

"We were thinking about a swim, sweetie. Want to join us?"

"Okay."

Ellsworth and Joe walked out on the terrace to the edge of a pool completely hidden from the outside world by carefully arranged foliage. They stripped off the jeans, slapping each other on the ass, and childishly goosing and pulling at each other's dongs. In a wrestling posture, they fell over in the pool. Darling got undressed again, dropping her boots and clothes on the living room floor, and walked out to join them.

"Such a body," Ellsworth whooped. "Ain't she a honey, Joe?"

Darling dove in, merging with them underwater, and then the three of them danced together on the bottom of the pool. Darling grabbed their dongs and yanked. Ellsworth slipped around behind her, hard as a rock, and Joe, shedding whatever inhibition he might have felt, seized her from the front.

"Come on, come on," Ellsworth shrieked, "let's do it!"

They clambered out of the water and there, at poolside, Daisy made her second threesome of the afternoon. God, she thought lazily, playing with the two boys, life could be so wonderful . . . also wonderfully disgusting.

* * *

"And what do you have for me tonight, my dear?" Jake Cox asked Daisy when they were upstairs.

Daisy was a little concerned that Jake might not be quite as proud of her this time. "You'll see," she said timidly.

Daisy put on her sexiest short black nightgown. It came just to the southern round of her buttock and barely covered her in front when she was standing up. Seated, black lace tickled her thighs. Daisy felt luxuriously sated from the afternoon, as if she'd been stroked and massaged by a battery of experts. Jake would never see a movie of that. Well . . . he might. It depended on his reaction to her and Marcia that morning, before they'd gone off for the luncheon.

Brandy snifter in his left hand, Jake made his entrance, dressed again in his mandarin dressing gown. He sat down and impatiently flicked the controls that lowered the screen and started the film.

Focusing, the camera swept in to her sitting on the edge of the bed, her back arched and her breasts thrust forward. Smiling girlishly, she spread her legs for the camera, revealing the bush of blonde hair and the rust-hued portals of her candy box.

A second figure entered the camera's field of vision, a slight and slim, even bony, figure, a stripling of a body, which flung itself down between her legs. A small head, perfectly styled at the neck, pressed into Daisy's groin and a look of surprised pleasure spread across her face.

"Uuh," Jake grunted. "My dear, this is new. I don't recognize this person."

"Yeah," she said, feeling the warmth of memory cross her loins.

"Schoolboys now, Daisy?" Jake asked, perplexed.

"No."

After a few moments of film, a record of intense activity reflected in the troubled yet gratified look on Daisy's face, the boyish figure rose and half-turned to reveal Marcia King, her eyes shining almost fiendishly. She pulled Daisy backward on the bed, then fell on her again, scrambling fingers digging into Daisy's buttocks, tongue moving quickly over Daisy's thighs and in and out of Daisy's trembling orifice. The configuration of bodies, Daisy realized, had presented her with the close-up presence of Marcia's own tiny bud, a shimmering hairless cleft pushing demandingly at her face.

It proved to be too much for Jake. He gasped. He was gaping at the screen and uttering strange, burbling noises.

"Marcia King!" he whimpered finally.

"Yeah," Daisy said.

"Good God, the Heavenly Father!"

He stopped the film and sat there, breathing shallowly. He lifted his brandy glass and drained it. His face was white and he was shaking.

"Well," Daisy muttered, trying to be cheerful about it, "I can see this is not going to be critic's choice."

It was, in that case, just as well Jake had stopped it where he had. For what came later would have disappointed him the more: Marcia had strapped a dildo on her ass and screwed Daisy with that, all the while flexing her non-existent breasts and yelling. It had not been unpleasant; nor had it been the first time Daisy had experienced the simulation of male erection.

Jake threw his glass across the room. It hit the screen and fell and broke on the floor.

"Goddamn it!" he exclaimed hoarsely, "I won't have that, Daisy. Lesbianism is disgusting."

Daisy remained calm. "I didn't know, Jake. I didn't think you'd mind. It does make for something new, you have to admit."

"Never mind what you thought," he said, still struggling for control, his sallow face red and embarrassed, stringy hair sticking wildly out from his head. "I hated it. I won't have it, Daisy. Never, never again. Promise me."

"Sure, I promise," she said carelessly.

"I mean it. If ever again . . ."

"What?"

"I'll cast you out, Daisy, I'll cast you out in the cold."

"Oh, balls, Jake, you wouldn't do that."

To soothe him, she stretched her hand toward him and put it on his robe. But in his revulsion, he had all but disappeared, folded back into himself.

"It'll take me days to recover from this," Jake complained in a strangled voice. "Men, Daisy, men."

"All right, all right," she cried impatiently. "Men. How about that Bernard Markman? He called this morning."

He nodded miserably. "Anything but hags like that.

Hags! She's a hag. She's not even pretty, Daisy, goddamn it!"

Well, Daisy thought sullenly, he could think as he liked. But she admired Marcia King and she would see Marcia again, whether or not their moments were transcribed on film for posterity. Marcia was a very splendid partner and they were both on the committee for the December party. So they would be seeing a lot of each other.

Belle had seen Susan off with Sally, then gone over to Norman Kaplan's place for tea. She reached Charley's house at 5:30. He wasn't going to be home yet, but she had her own key now and had gotten in the habit of going up there in the late afternoon to be by herself, unreachable. Charley's house was a place where she could think and try to sort out her life.

Humming, relishing the quiet, she walked through the quiet dining room and into the kitchen for a beer, then out on the terrace by the pool to sit in the comfortable wicker nest she and Charley shared in the evenings.

A brown squirrel with the bushiest tail Belle had ever seen was rummaging around in the thick underbrush on the steep hillside. If there were ever to be another bad earthquake, she mused, Charley's hill would be right down in the pool, across the terrace and into the living room. And it was not out of the question. It seemed to her that by now everything had happened to her that California had to offer, except a seven-point shaker on the Richter scale.

For now, however, water gurgled companionably through the pool's filter system and a big white plastic goose bobbed on the miniscule swell. It was a hot day, even now, toward dusk.

What was she going to do? Susan would be leaving for New York in a couple of weeks. Norman wanted Susan to stay with him until the day came to travel down to Princeton for registration. And if Belle couldn't be there, Norman was going to take her in his car and see that she was properly enrolled and settled in her dormitory.

That left Martin Cooper. Norman counseled caution, but how long could she carry on the game? The clash in their personal lives had now overlapped into their public front. Rolly Starr, for instance, had invited the Coopers that very afternoon to attend a big party he was giving at his mini-estate. Belle smiled to herself: Rolly was calling it his "Decline and Fall" extravaganza to celebrate, he had told her, the decadence of the West. How right he was.

But she knew she would not be going with Cooper, even if there was an emergent business relationship between Rolly and her husband. She simply wouldn't go. They'd tried it two or three times since her return from Europe and New York, she doing her duty, putting on the pretense. But it had not been even vaguely acceptable; rather unbearable, the silent drive to restaurant or hotel, the equally silent trip back home, perhaps a little less so if he'd had a few drinks. But even then, speaking in short bursts of words, he talked past her, around her. Their communications link had been completely severed. And, at home, Belle would go immediately upstairs, lock her door and go to bed, while Cooper paced aimlessly around, thumping furniture and cursing. He made no effort now, no attempt. Thank God.

Belle stretched her legs in front of her and considered taking a quick swim. But she was feeling too lazy. She finished the beer and went back to the kitchen for another.

Yes, they were completely estranged. When she thought of sex, making love, coupling, she thought of Charley, his body enveloping her, lovingly joining hers, the two of them by now a practiced team, complete unto themselves. It seemed like years since she and Cooper had made love, so long that the memory of their best times had shredded, turned to dust. He held no attraction for her and it was incredible to her that once she had found him so fulfilling, rough, yes, but exciting and stimulating.

Belle got up to walk around the pool in what remained of the sunshine in the narrow canyon. The prime question she had to answer was whether she wanted to try again with Cooper. She sensed he might have wished to reconcile if there had been an easy, face-saving way, perhaps if she took the initiative. He was so clearly unhappy. Belle wondered what had gone wrong between him and Pamela Renfrew. He seemed to have entered some precarious phase of life. He'd accused Charley of being indifferent toward the business, but lately it appeared Cooper had grown bored and cynical about it, too. He was like a boat cast adrift. Was this her doing, her fault? Was she prepared now to offer him solace? She had sworn to do so at their marriage. She remembered Susan, only ten then, standing forlornly at the side, watching with big eyes, worried that she was being deserted. Jesus, they had been so happy, so excited. Champagne had flowed, friends kissed, hugged, danced and sang, and then she and Cooper had gone off to Europe for honeymoon and business trip combined. Now, all in ashes. And Susan. She thought of that, wondered again anxiously what had happened between Susan and Cooper. No, there could be no going back now.

She could not go back, offer herself again at the altar of his ego. Susan would never forgive her if she did. And if she did, nevertheless, even if she were prepared to forsake Susan, what then? His self-confidence recharged, once again his arrogant and pushing self, would he behave any differently? No, he'd find another Pamela Renfrew. He was such a stock figure that only within marriage and by flaunting his unfaithfulness could he feel any sense of accomplishment.

Was she ready to give him this again, the safe harbor from which his buccaneering ship could sail, then return for refuge in time of storm?

Belle put down her beer bottle and dialed the operator.

"I'd like the number of a Thomas Sanders," she said. "He's an attorney in Beverly Hills."

Chapter Twenty

Rolly Starr's property was an increasingly valuable acre of land on a quiet cul-de-sac near Wilshire Boulevard. The entrance was walled and, in the rear, the land sloped down to a long pool with a lighted gazebo at one end and then to an open view of the manicured Wilshire Country Club. The house itself had been built some time during the early twenties by a movie producer. Thus, it was half-timbered in the California version of English Tudor style with a wood-shingled roof and looked, indeed, as though it might, if that were possible, have been planted in the West Coast clay during the days of Henry the Eighth. Rolly had bought at the right time and after he'd struck it rich since then, the house and grounds had been transformed into what many people called a pleasure palace. Had it been put back on the market, the house and land would have netted Rolly a good profit, especially since he claimed to have discovered that John Barrymore had slept here once, and not alone.

Belle and Charley left the car with an attendant on the street, walked down a drive lighted at the sides by votive candles planted in sand in brown paper sacks to reach first the pool area, bounded by trees, rose beds and shrubbery, and then brick steps, which led up a small hill to the house and beyond that a more recently added two-story studio whose doors had been flung open and from which pealed raucous rock music.

"Here! Here!" Starr was yelling at them. "Here I am, your host."

Rolly looked gigantic, like a genie out of a bottle. He was wearing a gold-embroidered caftan and a turban on his head.

He seized Belle around the waist and lifted her to plant a soppy kiss on her cheek. His lips were rough, Belle realized, like sandpaper.

"How do I look, Belle? Ain't I beautiful in my imported Algerian tent? Belle, my beauty, how are you?"

"Rolly, do you know Charley Hopper? You must . . ."

"Why? Why should I? Were we mailboys together? No," Starr cried boisterously, now hugging Charley with his long arms, "he's too old. This man is old enough to be your father, Belle. What are you doing with such an aged, worn-out man?"

"Hello, Rolly," Charley said quietly. "You look stunning."

"Charley! Charley! You damn rascal—where is your Oriental finery? Blast, I might have known he wouldn't risk it. Of course, we know each other. Charley is a prince. Prince Charley . . ."

"The pretender," Charley murmured.

"Pretender to what?" Rolly exclaimed, so loudly Belle wondered what he was on. "To the hand of the fair maiden? Belle? Belle? What are you up to that you're not telling Rolly about?"

Maddeningly, he gripped her waist again and squeezed, as if to press the truth out of her.

"Martin had to go out of town. And Charley thought it would be an interesting experience for him to come with me."

"Ha! Ha!" Rolly screamed. "Ha! again. Don't try to fool Rolly, Belle. Well, go on then. Go inside and get a drink or whatever. Grass finds its own level—it's down in the basement disco. Staunton!" he cried, bringing a young man instantly to his elbow. "Staunton, go in there and tell those men to play louder. I want more noise. What's a party without noise? Louder, do you hear . . . ?"

"*Si*, master," Staunton said obediently.

"Oh, you whore!" Rolly whooped. He stooped to kiss Staunton on top of the head. "Belle, take this deadbeat inside. My guests are arriving at break-neck pace."

They moved through the crowd, already dense on the bricked terrace outside the studio room.

Charley murmured, "I've always liked Rolly, admired him, I guess, despite everything. He's got a lot of balls, although you might not think so."

"I think he's very funny," Belle said. "But if it wasn't a matter of keeping him sweet for the December party, we wouldn't be here."

Rolly had all the beautiful young men and women there, the night people, inhabitants of the world of disco, the outrageous Sunset bars, the expensive restaurants—movie bit-part players, the hairdressers, public relations hustlers, con men and cheaters—all dressed in outfits either so tight Belle wondered how they could move or so loose—caftans, baggy white slacks, Indian tops—they seemed to float in the candle-lit darkness. The girls were lipsticked bright red, their lips oozing with color; some sported wild Afro permanents, others wore their hair slicked smoothly to their heads, or intricately braided in corn rows.

His caftan billowing, Rolly was rushing from one group to the next, whooping anew at each arrival. He was the acknowledged sultan.

They took wine from the bar and examined a table of shrimp, crab, lobster, oysters, clams.

"Want anything?" Charley asked her.

"A little of the chili."

"From Chasen's, mad me," the waiter said.

"Oh, Chasen's is catering? Then definitely a little bit of the chili."

It was typical of Rolly—his present stature in the community and his pretensions—that his feast would come from Chasen's restaurant, an establishment or "old Hollywood" place.

"I don't see anybody I know," Charley mumbled.

"Nor do I," Belle said, "except there's Darling Higgins and her husband."

The Higgins were standing idly, drinks in their hands, silently observing the scene. Darling was encased in a form-fitting silver sheath, specks of silver dust glittering in her red hair, and Ellsworth was impeccable in a black caftan threaded with silver.

"Christ, now there's a couple of ruined beings if ever I saw a couple of ruined beings," Charley observed.

"They are, but Darling has a good heart."

"Which way do they bounce?"

"Every which way apparently. But they seem to enjoy it so," Belle murmured.

"I'm keeping my back to the wall with all these characters roaming around. If the lights go out, run for your life. It's every man for himself."

"Charley," Belle chided him lightly, "you could meet the person of your dreams."

"That is very unlikely. Let's have a look inside."

Belle nodded and silently kissed Darling on the cheek as they entered the lofty studio. All furniture had been removed to make space for low brass Moroccan tables and piles of big pillows. Candles glowed on the tables, in niches in the walls, and, already, people had staked their claims on the floor, snuggling close, smoking, drinking wine from big carafes, and talking mouth to ear or mouth to mouth below the din of the music. At one end of the studio, a door led to stairs and a basement disco built into the grade of the land. Here, Rolly had been inspired—the room was entirely mirrored and the disco lighting leaped and danced crazy migraine rhythm into nerve-shattering reflections. Several couples were writhing to the music, their bodies not touching, but eroticism meeting in the void between them.

"Horrible," Charley muttered in her ear. "This is Hell—at least Purgatory."

One of Rolly's special friends, whom Belle recognized as a pop-record producer, danced by himself, grinning idiotically, his eyes rolling. A glass in his right hand slopped wine, or whatever, on the floor as he jigged, singing incomprehendingly to himself.

In an excavated alcove stuffed with pillows, another couple was touching, and then some. Their bodies tangled. They were grabbing and kissing, giggling strenuously.

"It's a good thing Mrs. Westmoreland didn't come tonight," Belle yelled above the noise. "Rolly's invited her for a special screening of his first picture, *Hell's Damsels*. Carlotta says it's a 'sexploitation' movie."

"We've heard talk of its star," Charley bellowed.

"Yes, it seems Mr. Cooper has got something to do with her," Belle said flatly.

"Not the first time C.A.A. has promoted a sex goddess, Belle," he reminded her.

Back upstairs, the studio was filling up. Rolly shooed people inside. Everyone was ordered to find a cushion and sit down.

"Be good children," Rolly screamed, "and you will be entertained."

Belle and Charley found a spot against the wall under the big windows from which there was a clear view of the lighted garden and below that the stretch of pool. When everyone was in a semblance of order, turbaned waiters appeared with large brass pitchers and heavy towels. They held their hands out to be washed, as this particular eating custom required, then dried on the towels. More waiters brought large wooden bowls of mixed salads, spicy stews, and rounds of crusty bread, which were the eating implements of a Moroccan feast. One scooped meat, rice, and sticky sauce with pieces of bread and used bare hands for the salad. Full wine carafes were placed on the crowded low tables.

Belle and Charley were joined by the Higgins and two strangers. No bother was paid to introductions at Rolly's parties.

"Belle," Darling whispered, "I thought I knew everybody. But who are all these people? Why were we invited?"

"Because we're on the committee with Rolly. We're token . . ."

Darling giggled. Rolly began shouting again, standing in

the middle of the room, and waving his arms for attention.

"Children! Children of decadence! What are the three most important things in life? Power? Money? Sex? Yes, yes, repeat after me: power, money, sex!"

The room rocked as they screamed the words back at him. Charley muttered that Rolly really didn't believe that, not at all.

"Wrong!" Rolly screeched, whirling his yards of caftan like a sail. "What's more important is Madame Lola Hassan, straight to us from the Casbah!"

Riotous, high-pitched, emotion-laden Arab music boomed out of loudspeakers, and a hippy young woman covered with a spangled veil, heavy, boned bra, and a shimmering dancing skirt, swaying sinuously, slid out of the doorway and into the center of the room. Barefoot, she lifted her arms and twisted, moving her hips at first slowly then more recklessly as the tempo of harem sounds increased. The full flesh of her belly pulsed with the music and perfect muscle control.

Shrill voices wailed from the corners: "Hey! Hey! That-a-way! Shake it, baby, but don't break it."

"Simpson, you whore! Shut up!" Rolly screamed.

Madame Hassan was moved to even more violent exertion, and perspiration began to slick her body. Her contortions had set to chattering and ringing the rattles and bells on her wrists and ankles. Toward the end of her act, she whipped away her veil, shook her breasts, and advanced on Rolly. She captured him with the veil, throwing it around his neck, and pulled him out on the floor. Rolly, gasping and laughing, tried to emulate her bumps and grinds, but he rolled awkwardly, then in ill temper pulled away from her and sat down.

"Eat, eat, goddamn it!" he roared, and as Madame Hassan wound down, they picked at the food, wiping their hands on the towels laid across their laps.

"Interesting," Darling Higgins said.

"She has a hell of a body, doesn't she?" Ellsworth asked.

"Good food," Charley said. He was scooping stew avidly.

Rolly began yelling again. "Jane Farelady! Jane Farelady, where are you?"

Belle saw a slim fair arm waving from the other side of the room.

"Over here, Rolly, over here."

"Jane," Rolly cried, "are you going to do a belly dance for us?"

"I can't," responded her strong, young voice.

"A strip then," Rolly roared. "Do us a strip. Jane's going to do a strip."

"I am not, Rolly! I won't!"

Rolly wheezed and choked with laughter and allowed himself to fall backward, kicking bare legs out of the bottom of his golden caftan.

Someone yelled, "Rolly is exhibiting himself. Dirty old man!"

Rolly sat up, slumping. "Never, you whores! I wouldn't show you anything. Jane," he exclaimed, "you've got to! Jane, everybody, Jane is the naked angel in that marvelous new movie, *Hell's Damsels*. Have you all seen it? Well, you better see it. Otherwise, you're going to get crossed off Rolly's party list."

Jane Farelady jumped up and led to the center of the floor a tall young man in a checkered burnoose and long, wrinkled black caftan. Jane began to dance slowly, heaving her chest and grinding her pelvis at no one in particular. She was wearing a transparent blouse unbuttoned and knotted at the waist and a pair of sheer harem pants. Arms extended over her head like Madame Hassan, her eyes closed, she swayed, her breasts rolling in and out of the part in the blouse.

"Beautiful," Darling muttered.

"And so is he," said her husband.

Behind his hand, Charley muttered, "So, that's what Mart is working with: sex goddess, eighth edition."

"She's a whole lot sexier than Madame Hassan," Belle said.

"Madame Hassan is an artist," Charley said. "This is a sex goddess."

Dinner was over now, or ignored. Other couples took to the crowded dance floor. Wine gushed from the carafes. Jane Farelady slipped in front of a mesmerized Rolly Starr and thrust her breasts in his face, whispering in his ear. Waiters delivered crusty, oozing, sweet pastry to the tables.

At ten, Belle was agreeing with Charley that the time had come to slip away. The room was descending toward orgy. Dancers were crammed together on the floor. Hands were everywhere. Pieces of clothing were being removed and discarded and here and there amid piles of cushions intense and unembarrassed activities had begun.

"We better get out of here before they raid the joint," Charley murmured. "Jesus! There's Vernon Pilger. What the hell is he doing here? He's a serious screenwriter."

"What the hell are *we* doing here?" Belle demanded.

"We congregate for Rolly. Pilger probably wants to write for Rolly."

Just as they were getting up to leave, they were interrupted by more shrill words from Rolly.

"Children! Children of decadence!" he bawled. "Now, what, you may ask, do we have in store for you? I tell: Jane Farelady has graciously agreed to do a live sex act. Is that something?"

Jane had ceased dancing. She was breathing hoarsely, her eyes glaring vacantly in the dim light. She was as high as a kite, Belle realized. On what, it was impossible to say.

"Jane and her young man are going to perform on the far side of the pool—in the gazebo," Rolly shrilled. "But none of you can get close. Only as far as the outside terrace. No closer. Come on, one and all, you children of the decline and fall . . ."

People streamed outside to the brick terrace behind Rolly, Jane, and her caftaned young man.

"Christ, can you believe it?" Charley grumbled. "We can't get out now."

"You want to see, Charley," Belle accused him.

They took a spot to the rear of the crowd. Jane and the man walked calmly down the steps and across the garden to the end of the pool. Casually, Jane stripped off her blouse and stepped out of her harem pants. She was wearing nothing underneath. She pirouetted gracefully, showing her long body, then dove into the pool. The young man pulled the caftan over his head. Underneath, he was naked, too. He went in after Jane, then swam with her to the other end of the pool, where the latticed gazebo shone under spotlights. Inside, there was a mattressed divan.

Skin glistening, Jane and the young man emerged from the water and Jane waved at her audience. Then, laughing mockingly, she led the young man into the gazebo and untied the cords that held the canvas sun curtains to the side. They fell, obscuring the divan.

The audience was furious. "Rolly," people protested. "It's not fair. We can't see."

Rolly burst with laughter. He was pleased with himself. "I never promised you'd be able to see. Shut up, you whores, and listen!"

There was instant quiet except for sounds of giggling and laughing at the far end of the pool. Jane's voice, groaning and sighing, then gasping, echoed across the garden, was followed by silence, the sound of brisk movement, finally a chilling scream.

"Jesus, Jane really gets her rocks off," someone said. Laughter. Then, again, quiet. They waited, but there was no more movement or sound from the gazebo. After what seemed too long a time, the audience began to stir impatiently. A few trickled back inside to the cushions and more private moments.

"What the hell!" Rolly exclaimed disgustedly.

Belle felt fear rising within her—the development of horror. The others felt it, too. Bodies stiffened as they stared down the pool.

The curtain shook as the gazebo entrance opened. A shock pierced through Rolly's friends as the young man staggered out alone, his arms shot upward, his face contorted. They all saw it at once, as if magnified. The young man was holding aloft a long knife. The blade was thick and dripping blood.

The young man began to scream. He threw back his head and yowled at the sky.

"Mother of God," Rolly whimpered. "What's . . ."

All stood transfixed. Belle sagged against Charley. Something terrible, something unbelievable, had happened.

Rolly spun around, his face white, his eyes confused, his fat lips trembling. "Whores! You're all whores!" he stuttered. "Look what you've caused. Charley! Charley, where are you? For Christ's sake, what should we do?"

Charley's voice crackled electrically in Belle's ear. "It looks like you better call the police, Rolly," he said.

"Staunton! Staunton! You heard. Call the police," Rolly screamed.

"Everybody get inside," Charley said, "nobody leave. Don't let anybody leave, Rolly."

"Nobody leave," Rolly repeated wildly. "Everybody inside!"

"Rolly," Charley said. "I'd advise them to get rid of their stuff—pills, grass, whatever."

"Everybody flush the stuff," Rolly ordered, more calmly, for this was the sensible thing to do. "Flush everything. You heard, you whores! Everybody back in the house."

"Go on, Belle," Charley told her. "Go inside. Rolly, do you know who that kid is?"

"No, no!" Rolly moaned. "But what's he done to her, for Christ's sake? That knife—it's bloody. I don't know who the fuck he is—one of the studs she picks up. Picked up. Christ almighty!" Rolly shrieked. "My star!"

Charley asked, "What the hell were you giving them, Rolly?"

"Nothing, goddamn you, Charley, nothing!"

The young man had slumped to the tiles at the edge of the pool. He sat numbly, staring at the knife.

"Rolly, we've got to keep him here 'til the cops come," Charley said. "Belle, please . . . go inside. We've got to get that knife away from him, Rolly, before he does something foolish."

"How are we going to do that, for Christ's sake?" Rolly whined.

"We'll talk to him," Charley said.

"Charley." She didn't want him down there.

"Belle, goddamn it, go inside."

She did as she was told. Through the big windows, she and the others watched Charley and Rolly go down the steps, then edge slowly along the pool. Moving carefully, Charley reached the young man and they could see he was talking to him. Jesus, Charley was crazy. Charley put one hand gently on the young man's bare shoulder, still talking softly. His lips moved but there was no way they could hear him and, she realized idiotically, the pounding beat of disco music still echoed from underneath the studio.

Rolly slipped up to the gazebo, spread the curtain, looked inside, then stumbled back and began retching in the shrubbery. Neither Charley nor the young man turned.

Chapter Twenty-One

Ten days later, Belle was sitting in Sam Leonard's office in New York, a weighty document in front of her on his desk.

"Don't sign now, Belle," Leonard advised. "I want you to take it to your lawyer and have him look it over. I want you to be sure in your own mind that you're satisfied. Maybe Kaplan could get his man to look at it."

"That's not necessary, Sam," she protested. "I trust you."

"Got nothing to do with trust," he said, waving aside her objection. "Now then, where do you want to go for lunch?"

Belle had come into New York with Susan. They were staying with Kaplan, and today, while she was busy at Cosmos, Norman and Susan were on a tour of the museums. Belle's daughter would be going down to Princeton in a week or so.

"Say," Leonard said, "tell me about this juicy murder out in Hollywood land. You were at that party, weren't you?" He grinned. "That's something Lorraine needn't push in the columns."

"God, it was awful," Belle said.

"No," he yelped, "beautiful, beautiful—a *crime passionel* of the old school."

"Not so *passionel*. They were both drugged to their eyeballs. In fact, they're not even sure he did it. Another theory is that somebody snuck in there and was just lying, waiting, for somebody, anybody. It would be easy enough. The place is right on the golf course. The young kid can't remember a thing."

"This girl," Leonard mused, "Jane Farelady—she's a cult figure already, on the strength of one lousy picture and getting murdered."

Belle remembered the grisly night all too well: the hush that had fallen over Rolly's house, then the police, the medics. Charley had gotten the knife away from him but, when the police were questioning him, the young man had tried to break free and run. Finally, overpowered, he had been draped in blankets and led away. A list had been made of everybody at the party, their names checked off as they left, while a dozen men in uniforms searched the area.

"I see you've been reading the papers," Belle said sadly.

"Yes. But where did the knife come from? If he swam across the pool without a stitch, where did he get the knife? And I read that one of Rolly's chums got arrested for possession of coke."

Belle shook her head. "Rolly warned them all to flush the coke and grass down the toilet before the police got there."

"Jesus," Leonard said sarcastically, "you people really *live* out there on the Coast. Well, what about Orsini's for lunch?"

The phone rang as they were leaving. "Yes," Leonard growled. He winked at Belle. "Sylvia, what a surprise. Yes, Belle is right here. She's fine, untarnished by scandal and homicide. We're going to Orsini's and you can join us if you like. Okay? Goodbye."

Belle asked after Sylvia's health and Leonard said she was in tip-top shape. "Always bitching about something or other. But I guess that means she's well."

Over lunch, Leonard was full of his strategy for "Belle." The first ads, he had decided, would begin running in the December issues of *Vogue* and *Harper's Bazaar*, as well as in local monthly and weekly magazines across the country.

"We may as well get that mileage out of the party," he said. "But what about Rolly Starr? How's he bearing up?"

"Rolly allowed himself to be all broken up for approximately twenty-four hours. Then he remembered the old home truth: any publicity is better than no publicity—just make sure you spell my name right."

"Jesus Christ," Leonard groaned, "show business." Then, ironically, he added, "Not much different from the cosmetics business actually."

Belle fingered the stem of her martini glass. "It was one

of the most terrifying things I've ever seen—maybe *the* most. But I guess things always have their funny sides, such as the fact Rolly now sees his house going down in the history books. Before, it was a place where Barrymore shacked up one night. Now, it's also the place where Jane Farelady met her ghastly end."

"That'll increase the market value of the dump," Leonard said cynically. "They'll start pointing it out from the tour buses."

"Jim Bacon—you know him, he writes show-business stuff—has already got a report that a red rose is mysteriously appearing at her grave every day."

"Jesus," Leonard said, "like Valentino. Well, never mind. So is legend born. Anyway, how you getting along with that husband of yours?"

Belle eased past the question, but later, when they were drinking their coffee, she told him frankly that she was about to ask for a legal separation. It had gone too far. She was at the end.

Leonard nodded sympathetically and put a hand on her arm. "Don't feel bad about it, Belle. Not the first time it's happened. And it certainly won't be the last. The time comes to cut your losses." He grinned at her, his nostrils twitching. "If I weren't so tied up, I'd make a play for you myself. You're a beautiful woman, Belle. You deserve the best."

"You're the best, Sam," she said.

He chuckled sharply. "Is that a proposition?"

"Sure," she joked.

"Be careful. I might take you seriously. Which brings me to the next question: how's Charley?"

"He's lovely."

"Are you going to marry Charley, Belle?"

The question was not meant to embarrass her. Truthfully, she told Leonard, she did not know. She was reluctant to commit herself. Having achieved a certain freedom, she might not be as eager to relinquish it.

"Well, Belle," he said sagely, "in this day and age, it's not necessary to marry the guy. The two of you could have a hell of a partnership without getting married. And some people think marriage can really screw up a good thing."

"You'd never say that to Sylvia."

Fondly, he said, "No, I wouldn't. And we've been lucky.

You may think we fight all the time like cats and dogs. That's just a front."

"I know," she said.

Anyway, she thought, it was academic at this point whether she and Charley married or not. They'd be together much of the time. After she'd seen Susan safely into school, she was to rendezvous with Charley in Boston to begin their picture-taking travels.

"Charley's going to have you on twenty-five or thirty locations over the next couple of months," Leonard reminded her. "The plan is to saturate the media during the first year. It's going to cost a lot of money—figure traveling expenses alone. Christ! You and him and camera crews. But he's got the right idea."

"Belle gets around," she murmured.

"Yeah, that's right and you go on the payroll starting right now," Sam said. "You're going to be working your fanny off. But I really like the idea of the locations, none of that stuff faked in a studio. And, of course," he went on, thinking aloud, "Charley is going to be with you the whole time. What the hell is going to happen to C.A.A.?"

She shrugged. "It'll go on. But Charley is talking about selling out his share. Things are not great right now between him and Martin."

Leonard snorted. "I shouldn't think so. Never mind. Life goes on. Speaking of which, Sylvia is arranging another party, a week from today. This time, we're really going to lay it on thick. Kaplan promised he'd bring Jackie. We're inviting some of those ballet guys, baseball players, the D.A., two senators, and other assorted bullshitters. Actually, I'm also thinking about commissioning one of our good contemporary artists to do your portrait. A portrait can be a very classy gimmick and in certain presentations a lot more effective than a photo. And I guess Charley has told you about the TV commercials? You're going to have to talk, too, Belle. But that soft voice of yours—it'll be perfect."

"Wow! The cost . . ." She was impressed.

He shrugged solemnly. "We got to bite that bullet, Belle. If you do it, do it right, I always say. We'll have a photographer at the party next week. And now's about the time we're going to start dropping items that Cosmos is getting into a new line of cosmetics. Reports say," he mimicked the words, making a face, "that Cosmos Cosmetics is readying a blockbuster line to be named 'Belle.' Could that be the same Belle Cooper who's being seen around town so often with that little darling Sam Leonard? Question mark, question mark. Get the picture, Belle?"

Sally Markman came into town later in the week. Kaplan sent his car out to pick her up at Kennedy and they were all waiting for her at the apartment when she arrived.

"Surprise! Surprise!" Susan yelled.

Sally looked wonderful. She was deeply tanned from the summer in the Pacific sun. Her eyes were clear and she moved surely, with her old energy. Again, Belle had to think the doctors were all wrong.

"My darlings," Sally said emotionally, "how marvelous. How I've missed you all!" She threw her arms around Susan. "How are you, pussycat?"

"Better now," Susan said, with such deep feeling that Belle gasped mournfully within herself.

His round face earnest, Norman said, "My dear Sally. It's grand to have you here."

"But do you have room for me?"

"My dear, as you know, this place is gigantic," he exclaimed. "And I always feel a lot less guilty when we're at 100 percent occupancy."

"Norman," Sally said, "you know I've always loved you. Is this my chance, finally, to share your bed?"

"Madame!" he exclaimed, baring his jagged teeth, "gladly, but that awful husband of yours, I think, stands between us. How is he?"

"Very, very well," she said happily. "And you know what? He's decided to slow down. Glory be, he's even begun getting home at reasonable hours."

Kaplan said approvingly, "Very wise of him. Next, he should do what I did some years ago—retire."

"You're not retired, little man. You work hard, very hard."

Kaplan shook his head. "Not so. I work hard only when I get roped into one of your benefits. Normally, I leave myself plenty of time for contemplation of the eternal verities."

"And your French translations," Belle murmured.

"Yes. I'm considering publishing my translations of the

French poets. Your Gallic hotelier, Archy Finistere, has asked for them particularly."

"Yes," Sally said sardonically, "Archy and his French background."

Kaplan laughed breathlessly. "Don't tell him I said so. But enough of that. Tonight, I thought we'll go to the Four Seasons. I've booked a table in by the bar. Livelier and for some reason the food tastes better there."

Before they left the apartment, Belle had a moment alone with Sally. "You, my darling, look absolutely ravishing. To what do we owe this transformation?"

Sally looked pained. "Was I so bad before?"

"I thought you were very down," Belle said, speaking honestly.

"I was. I was. But you know, in the last week or so everything seems fine. Knock on wood, Belle." Belle put her knuckles to her head. "Knock on wood. I think I can beat this goddamn thing. And I have to tell you. Bernard—I don't know what's happened."

"Isn't that marvelous? Marvelous!" Belle cried. "And while I get the chance, I want to thank you again for having Susan all summer. It was a Godsend."

Sally shrugged. "What's the bad word from himself?"

"No word. We're through."

"Good," Sally said. "He's not worth saving. Save yourself! You know there's a book about the virtue of selfishness."

"Yes, I think Cooper needs help. But how? Besides, I'm part of the Cosmos thing now. I'm on the payroll."

Sally fingered a strand of milky pearls she was wearing with a light wool Valentino dress.

"Congratulations," she said. "Well done! I say no more, except there are certain things that are out of our power. Don't fight it."

The next morning, Belle and Sally taxied to Cosmos.

The time had come for Sally to meet Sam Leonard.

They went to Belle's office first. Although she'd spent only a few hours there so far, it already had the ambience of a place of activity and decision-making. Proofs of Belle's studio pictures were strewn on the desk, along with memos. Cartons of dummy "Belle" packaging littered the sofa, and on the wall facing her desk Belle had just hung a colorful Matisse lithograph: Kaplan's gift and the first art in her new office.

"Christ, Belle," Sally commented, "the way this looks, you're going to be spending a lot of time in New York. Tell me have you thought about moving back here?"

Belle nodded. She had been thinking about it. What was there now for her in California? Sally, of course. But besides Sally, only Charley Hopper, and that was something she had to think about very seriously.

When Leonard was free, Belle led Sally down the carpeted corridor. Sam was waiting for them at his office door.

"My dear lady, at last I get a chance to meet you!"

"And I am very impressed to meet you, sir," Sally replied.

"Stunning lady," Leonard exclaimed. "I'm Sam and you're Sally. Am I right?" He held her hand, his world-weary eyes searching her face. "Now sit down and let's talk."

"I want to tell you all about our party."

"And I want to hear all about it."

In the month since the last meeting at the Splendide, a complete guest list had been assembled, Sally reported, and with contributions still to come from some major cities, over 1,000 names had been collected.

"That is," Sally said, "1,000 couples, the bulk of them at this point, naturally, from California. We'll have another 500 easily by the time we mail the invitations. We've already done a lot of the work on the telephone. The first 1,000 acceptances become the Blue Ribbon One Thousand. The others—rejected. But, we're going to cheat a little: we'd like 250 or 300 out-of-towners so we don't tilt to the Coast."

Leonard nodded sagely, watching her over his clasped hands. "Smart," he said, one of his favorite words. "Keep it exclusive but on a nationwide basis. Very smart. What about hotel rooms?"

"I've put Marjery Cannon to work on that." Sally made a patient face at Belle. "You don't know her, Sam. She was so burnt up we didn't give her a job. She's reserving rooms. We're keeping the option of canceling in November. By mid-November, we'll have a better handle on it."

"You maybe could get all of them in the new Splendide," Leonard suggested.

Sally agreed. "But we're not sure the rooms will be ready by then. If they are, we can cancel what we've blocked out."

Leonard said, "Wouldn't it be almost better to have it fifty-fifty L.A. and the rest of the country?"

"I don't know," Sally confessed. "This *is* a benefit to support a Southern California institution, remember."

"Yes, but it is to serve the whole country, I take it."

"True," she said. "We've got to see how it develops in the next month or so."

"Whatever happens," Leonard surmised, "it is going to be a goddamn exclusive affair."

He grinned. "I like to be associated with the best. But, as you see, I'm also a little crass about it. You're certainly aware now of Belle's job with us, so what I'd like to do when you get a better idea of the strongest cities supporting you is to gear our advertising to those cities. It sounds commercial as hell, but it'll really be very painless," he assured her.

"Which," Sally said, not missing her opportunity, "brings me to the matter of our annual award." She fastened big eyes on his face. "Belle tells me you and Mrs. Leonard are going to finance that."

Leonard nodded. "What we decided, and our accountants were tough about this, is to provide the money for this year, and later, when you're really solid, turn it into a perpetual trust."

Sally smiled. "There's no way these people are going to be able to get out of it . . . later. It'll be a fait accompli. We'll break ground for the first building in the complex as soon as the rainy season is over next year."

"Yes, so Belle told me. Well, that's longevity," he said, admiringly.

"Don't worry about longevity. I'm determined to make this thing sail."

"Good, good," Leonard said. "I understand that our new friend David Abdul is picking up the tab for most of the basic costs. What other expenses do you foresee? It would be sweet if you could really clear all the ticket money. What I'm thinking is that Cosmos, as a legit quid-pro-quo, could pick up quite a bit, maybe for the orchestra and incidentals. Christ, girls, ain't I generous with Cosmos' money? But it would be fair. I don't think there would be any tax arguments about that."

"Shall I kiss you now, or later?" Sally said warmly. "Belle said you were the best. Now I know it, too."

"Is that so?" Leonard, for once, was flustered. "I am flattered. But don't forget I can also be a tough and unpleasant son of a bitch if need be."

Sally smiled. "I never doubted it."

"Now, tell me, who is it you'll be proposing for the first Leonard Award?"

"We have a committee-of-one working on it: Dr. Tom Glenn. He's my doctor and one of the best internists in the country. Whoever he proposes will be just right."

"An American though?" Leonard asked. "I should think we'd want the man or woman to be an American, wouldn't we?"

Sally nodded thoughtfully. "That's something we haven't considered. But yes, since you bring it up, I would think so—at least for the first year. I agree with that. And Belle has got to because you're her boss."

Chapter Twenty-Two

Cooper didn't get together with Charley Hopper until the morning of the day Charley was to leave for Boston to meet Belle. There would be a picture-taking session at the Ritz-Carleton Hotel, then on a wind-swept and autumnal beach in Cape Cod, or a fishing village in Maine.

"Maybe both," Charley said.

Cooper was scarcely listening. He knew what was going on—and Charley knew that he knew. During the last few weeks in the offices on Sunset, the two had been avoiding each other, conversing only briefly, and only when necessary, on the intercom.

"Sounds good, Charley," he said nonchalantly. "Hard work, but you'll enjoy it."

"Yeah," Charley said, "it'll be nice to see the East Coast in the full bloom of fall."

"Come on, Charley, what you'll enjoy is being with Belle."

"Yeah, I will," Hopper admitted innocently.

"You're working practically full-time on the Cosmos account now, aren't you?"

"It's a biggie, Mart."

"Uh-huh," he said absently, wondering how to phrase his next remark. Casually, that was the way. "Well, Charley, just pass on to Belle the message that it's not going to be easy—maybe a little messy. I think I've got the goods on you two—over in France, up at your house."

Charley, he thought, was stunned. "What the hell are you talking about?"

Cooper smiled. "I had a little man watching your house. I know she's been up there any number of times. Little quickie, I suppose. I've got everything but the pictures to prove it."

Hopper jumped to his feet. "You son of a bitch," he exclaimed, his slimmed-down California accent dropping away to East Texas. "You did a thing like that?"

Still smiling, Cooper said, "All's fair, cowboy."

Hopper stared at him, not believing it, then believing it. "You're out of your mind, Mart," he said softly. "Let me tell you something: the only thing going on with Belle and me is she's miserable with you and needs somebody to talk to. Believe it or not."

"And I don't," he exclaimed, feeling anger overcome his attempt at composure. "I'm sending a guy to get a deposition from Leonard. God knows what happened over on that boat."

"Shit," Hopper growled disgustedly. "What an evil-minded fucker you are. Remember, it was your idea for the two of us to go over there. Shit, you've got a lot of room to talk. You've been cutting a swath through this town for years."

"Bullshit," Cooper said. "Not so. I've been a faithful husband."

Again, Hopper was surprised. "You're crazy, Mart. You want me to start reciting the names?"

Cooper scowled contemptuously. There was no way they

could prove any of it. If you were careful, no one could ever know. But if you made one or two little slips, as they had, it was enough to hang you.

"Don't bother telling me it's not so, Charley. Are you in love with her?

"Of course," Hopper said scornfully.

"Good, then it's easy. You sell me your half of C.A.A., Belle bows out, and we're in the clear."

Hopper was glaring at him, his body trembling. "We'll get to all that when the time comes, my friend," Hopper said coldly.

"And you can take your goddamn Cosmos account with you!"

"We'll get to that, too," Hopper muttered. "But I'll tell you what I'm going to do. This should interest somebody like you very much. Before I leave this afternoon, I'm telling my own accountant to get in here and go over the books. How's that grab you, baby?"

The suggestion was insulting. Cooper rounded his desk and faced Charley at close range. He poked Charley in the chest with his finger.

"Do it, Charley, that's exactly what you should do. What he'll find out is that most of the bread comes in here, I bring in. Not you! It's been that way for years now, Charley. You've run out of steam. You ain't worth your freight anymore."

He had miscalculated. Before he could move, Charley unfolded a short right to his stomach. He thought he would go over. Gasping, he pulled back to regroup, but it was too late. A left floated toward his chin and then another of Charley's fast balls to the side of his neck. Cooper felt himself fading backward. He fell heavily on the couch.

"C'mon, Mr. Football Hero," Charley taunted him. "On your feet. You've been asking for this."

His throat muscles were so numb he could hardly speak.

"I'll get you for this, Charley," he gasped. But despite himself, he had to chuckle. "I forgot about your lightning right, Charley. Want me to apologize? Fuck you!"

"We're through, Mart," Charley said, almost sadly.

"Yes," he said, "we are—and about time, too."

When Hopper had gone, Cooper pulled himself up and staggered to his desk. He let himself down in his chair and put his face in his hands. Already, he could feel a lump forming on his chin, the taut, sore muscles jerking in his neck. Hating himself, salty tears began running down his fingers into his mouth. Jesus, he thought, it *was* all over. Hopper despised him and he was finished with Belle. He was at the end of the line. Jane Farelady was dead, and what was left of his youth had gone with her. The bitch, what a fool he had been. The very day she'd died, he had come down with a case of the clap. Jane had been a carrier, a carrier of the clap and of plague and deceit. Beautiful, a beautiful girl she had been, but ruined and a liar. And now she was dead.

His tears dried up. Cooper turned his chair to stare down into Sunset—the hustle, the traffic—and beyond that, the hills rising toward their crest, sprinkled with houses, pools, and accomplished people. Cooper sensed the city limits tightening around him. There was no place for him to go. With Belle, and only a few months before, his life had been ordered, perhaps not too well disciplined but at least under control. Now, his life, his world, was fragmented, scattered in disarray, and he lacked a master plan for reassembly. Where would he date the beginning of collapse? The night he had so imprudently had Pamela come to the Leonard party at the Bistro?

He reached for his phone and dialed. She answered on the first ring.

"Ah, Miss Renfrew. It's your old buddy Cooper here."

Her voice was icy cold. "Hello . . ."

"How are you? It's been a while, Pamela."

"Not nearly long enough, Marty."

"Pamela, I'm sorry about everything. I thought I'd let you know. I'm leaving my wife. We could . . ."

This time she did not hesitate. "Big deal. We could . . . nothing. Forget it, Marty."

"What do you mean, forget it? Isn't that what you wanted?"

"Not anymore, Marty. Being roughed up by those two guys turned me around. I did a lot of thinking."

This comment caused him to pause. "What's that got to do with us?" He held up his foreshortened little finger and stared at it.

"Sometimes I wonder what it's got to do with us. Keep away from me, Marty. I'm frying other fish right now."

"Goddamn it, Pam," he said hotly. "That's not going to get you anywhere. I'm ready to make you a sensible proposition."

"Too late, buster," she said roughly. "Do you own any oil wells?"

"No, goddamn it, you know I don't. Talk sense."

She was snickering. "I am talking very good sense. Just lay off me, Marty. I don't want you around. I'll tell you why: Marty, you disgust me. How's that?"

"Pam . . . Jesus Christ," he whispered. "How can you say a thing like that? My God . . ."

He looked at the finger again and contemplated the nub of it without its crown of fingernail, sewn across like a cocktail sausage.

"So long, mother . . ." she grumped. "In case you didn't know, that's a half-word."

Slowly, Cooper put the phone down. He had to take another piss but resisted the impulse. It hurt like hell. He was a dumb shit. Why hadn't he gone to a doctor? Catching clap was not the most shameful thing that could happen to a man. But he'd hung on to it, guarded it jealously. Cooper chuckled to himself. It was his memory of Jane and it might last as long as he did . . . Memories, memories of long ago, he moaned, as finally and painfully he urinated piss and pus. Christ, it burned like fury. But it *was* his memory of Jane Farelady, she of the splendid body, pulsing membranes, throbbing heart, and no soul. Fair Jane, the Farelady. A souvenir of times past.

Sheldon sat in a cushioned chair staring out thick plate-glass windows overlooking the City of the Angels. Almost vacantly, he responded to Camilla. She was in the kitchen making ham and cheese sandwiches. She'd slipped a bottle of Dom Perignon into the freezing compartment of the refrigerator to cool. The kitchen was small, compact, but all the appliances were there, cleverly built in, the floor tiled and gleaming. Sheldon had had them put in marble flooring all the way from the entry to the windows to achieve an illusion of vast, templelike space, and then furnish the apartment entirely in light safari-style wicker, ornamental Chinese lamps and lanterns, bamboo screens and tables. It was modest, but it was a home.

Sandwiches finished, Camilla took the champagne out and carried the snack into the living room. She sat down beside him on the couch and gave him the bottle to open. Sheldon turned to smile guilelessly.

"Not a bad sort of place, is it?"

"No, it's lovely," Camilla said. "I'm crazy about it." Teasingly, she asked, "Do you get a lot of girls up here, Sheldon?"

"Me? Sure. All the time."

"Don't run yourself down, Sheldon. You do very well."

"Thanks to you." He filled their glasses.

"Well, here's to us," she said. "Any regrets?"

He shook his head and leaned to kiss her. Such spontaneity was so unlike him. Sheldon was emerging from his shell—he had begun expressing himself with a quick physical frankness. He was no longer apprehensive of contact.

"Here's to us," Camilla repeated softly, "and baby makes three."

He did not get it at once. He nodded absently, then his eyes popped in astonishment.

"Are you telling me . . ."

"Yes, I'm pregnant. I'm surprised you haven't noticed anything."

In the last month, it seemed to her, her belly had become fuller, her breasts deeper. She was more amorous, tender, and needing.

"You're not joking?"

"Would I joke about a thing like that—with you?"

Sheldon put down his glass and took her in his arms. He kissed her very carefully.

Sharon and Frank were staying with Maude Mannon in her big brick house in the Houston suburbs when they decided, with her blessing, that this was the perfect place to be married. They would not be subject to Los Angeles publicity, and there was no way Morris Mauery could be aware of what they were doing.

"Darlins'," Maude said, "there's nothin' I like better than weddings. God knows, I've had enough of them myself. I'll get my friend the judge to perform the ceremony."

It was crisp fall in Texas. The oaks and maples over Maude's parklike front lawn were shedding their leaves, and the rains which came intermittently had cleaned the skies.

Maude and Sharon had been talking about the December Ball—that was the reason for the trip. Maude had been working hard on her particular First Lady and now, through political acquaintances, was trying to corral the governor.

"Sharon, we should form another committee, a governors' committee. Why shouldn't all the western governors come to the party? Your California man has almost got to come, and why not Arizona and Nevada and Texas? Surely, between us all we've got the muscle to get them there."

"It's yours," Sharon said. "You're in charge of the governors."

Frank was outside jogging. They watched him run past in his warm-up suit, heading around the block, then passing the front of the house again. He ran lightly, effortlessly. He was as ethereal in his movements as a ballet dancer.

"Sharon, that's some man," Maude said admiringly.

"He is, that's true."

Sharon felt almost light-headed about her relationship. Woodley was a little wild; he was apt to do impulsive things. He loved to drink but handled it well. And, as far as she could judge—her judgment admittedly colored—he was sincere. He'd signed the agreement her lawyers had drawn up and had put his name to the paper without even reading it. She'd admonished him afterward that he should read legal documents before signing, but now it was too late. He was her slave.

"We'll have the ceremony in the lib'ry," Maude said. "I just wish we could make it double."

They'd met Maude's new boyfriend, a wryly humored man who had little to say but treated Maude like a precious piece of jade, much like an item from her collection in the Biedermaier cabinet in one corner of the lushly furnished living room.

But it was too soon, Maude said. "He's nice and cuddly in bed. But I don't know yet if he really, truly loves me for myself."

"You can afford to wait," Sharon pointed out.

Maude shook a long, bony finger, showing off her rings in the hard morning light.

"Can't evah afford to wait too long, Sharon."

Pat Hyman lay tensely on the massage table as the Magnificent Boris worked over her back. God, he was taking the breath out of her. She grunted as he proceeded.

"Madame Hyman," Boris said, "you are losing too much weight."

"I know, Boris," she sighed. "I'm thin as a rail. A skeleton."

Morris Maurey had told her the same thing the night before. He'd been over to the house to see George about some business deal or other. George had been called to the studio—an emergency in a night-shooting program—leaving Pat alone with Mauery. Mauery had watched her silently for a moment, his eyes blank, and then had told her bluntly that he wanted to screw her.

She had been frightened but in a way surprised it had never happened before. Instantly, she wondered if George had hurried away deliberately, using the studio as an excuse. Had he promised her to Mauery? Whatever, she was not at liberty to refuse. It would have been curtains for George.

Mauery was not a loving partner. He closed the living-room door and made her undress, then rammed himself into her ass. Christ, it had been degrading and ugly and she ached still, remembering his obscenity. But so what? It was only a body, she told herself grimly, a mere piece of human debris; as it would be another lever to be applied to Mauery, the source of all that was good. But . . . she hoped he would not come back often.

Boris was pummeling her buttocks, smoothing the creases where ass rounded to meet thigh. He smacked her so roughly that she began to ache again. She waited for Boris to move the towel aside, then felt his mustache, prickly and wet with his own perspiration. She groaned deeply. Actually, she needed nothing more than this. She didn't even want to meet Boris head-on. Peculiar, he had never asked her to roll over. She wondered how he would have been as a lover in a proper bed. With such a luxuriant mustache, he should have been well hung. His tongue rasped against her, penetrated her outer shell, lit like a bird on the nub of her clitoris. She gasped. Then she did something she had never done before. Her left hand drifted from under her cheek and down the table to her waist, feeling his body, the belt buckle, then the bulge of his manhood. He was throbbing and hard. He jerked in surprise and began to pant. Her gesture made him delve more violently into her body and she came with a flutter of hip muscles. Then there was a slick of moisture in her hand. Christ, he had popped right in his jeans.

When she'd recovered enough to speak, she said, "Boris, we must try this some time in a more leisurely manner."

"I lock up at six. We'd have the place to ourselves."

Pat was startled. He was so agreeable. This was her chance, an antidote to Mauery. But did she have the guts? It could be a happy arrangement. The massage ran her fifty dollars a week. Idly, she speculated how much he would charge her for the real thing.

"You'll come?" Boris demanded.

"Today?"

"Why not?" He was staring at her heatedly when she rolled over, the towel wrapped tightly around her body.

She chuckled nervously. "Well, today . . . I don't know."

"Madame Hyman," he said smoothly, "you will find I give a very good fuck. I guarantee satisfaction."

"Or money back?" she asked sardonically.

He nodded. Christ, he would charge her for it. How much? Another fifty a week? Well, she would think about it. She thought fast. It would be a hell of a lot cheaper than buying cocaine.

Archy Finistere was still trembling a full half-hour after the phone call from Morris Mauery.

Was it possible they could consider Archibald Finistere a traitor for going to work for the Arabs? There had never, never been any sort of labor trouble at the Beverly Camino. Had there been payoffs along the line, all arranged by the corporation, things that he was not aware of? The way Mauery put it, somebody at the Splendide organization should have considered that. It was not in Archy's province to assure labor peace. *Merde! Dieu!* A catastrophe if a labor boycott were thrown at them! It would shut down the hotel. Not only that, but what if there were to be a boycott by all the Jewish organizations in town, a loss of revenue from the charity parties in the Grand Ballroom, the receptions, the business meetings? *Merde! Dieu!* he repeated to himself. Yes, it would be a veritable catastrophe.

It was in Mauery's power to ruin them. He had not openly uttered the threat, aside from calling Archy a turncoat. Mauery was too smart to lay it on the line and over the phone. But, it had been made very obvious that somehow, somewhere, a means had to be found to turn Mauery off.

Archy had reminded Mauery of the importance of the opening benefit: the December Ball. But Maurey had merely chuckled coldly, his voice alone enough to throw the fear of God into you.

"I know all about that, Archy, and I don't give a shit. What I'm telling you and telling you straight is that when the bigshots go ahead with a project like this, they better consider the little people, too."

"Yes, Morrie, yes, yes. I can't imagine why . . . After all," he had laughed humbly, "I am a simple hotelier."

Again Mauery had clucked, ice clattering on his voice. "Bullshit, Archy, you're a big phony."

And now what was Archy going to do? He did the first thing that suggested itself to him. He put in a phone call to Norman Kaplan.

Kaplan was matter-of-fact about it, unimpressed. "I see," he said. "How very interesting . . . Hmmm . . . We'll have to investigate that, Archy. I wouldn't worry about it if I were you."

Feeling much relieved, and what a comfort it was to pass the buck, Archy went upstairs for his afternoon nap.

David Abdul was what they called a pseudo-vegetarian and when he and Pamela were together her sustenance tended to be almost exclusively chicken and rice, and for variety, rice and chicken. She despised both, having eaten enough chicken on the farm to last her a lifetime. But she was ready to forego much for the sake of their relationship. David was talking now about her giving up real estate to make his comfort and well-being her full-time career.

"You see, my dear," he sighed in that soft and persuasive voice of his, "I have to fly to London next week. Come with me. We're staying at the Dorchester."

"Wasn't that just bought by a bunch of Arab investors?"

"A couple of years ago, yes. Will you come?"

"I could take a few days off," she said cautiously.

"It would please me so much, Pamela. I would miss your body if I had to go alone. You see, Pamela, I need a woman's body at all times, day and night, and I would not like to need a lady in London, another in New York and God knows where. With you, I would be satisfied."

As he should be, she thought fiercely, for she treated

him like the prince he was. No act of adoration was too extreme, too intimate. But when she did it for him, it did not seem she was cheapening herself, rather, almost, that she was serving a holy purpose. She remembered the tales of the desert, perfumed and passionate love-making in Bedouin tents while sand rustled in the wind outside, and she dreamt of the fierce tribesmen smelling of raw sex and camel shit and their uncircumsized cocks so long they made tracks of their own through the wilderness.

Pamela knew David was already married. He had freely admitted to at least one wife. But he was allowed by his religion and his state to have more than one wife.

David smelled clean, but even after a bath there was an exciting scent to his body, a muskiness that must come from generations of family glutted from hot sun and spicy Arab food. Pamela devoured him as she licked his belly and fastened her lips to his penis, now limp and tender. She pulled the skin away and tongued the bulb and his body came alive, as if she had plugged an electric cord in his ass. Softly, he hissed words of love.

"Yes," Pamela murmured, "I'll come with you to London."

Cooper had never asked her to go anywhere but Vegas, and Cooper was a rotten and smelly pig compared to this man. She began to understand why people of the East found Caucasians so disgusting: they stank of the things they ate and drank and the way they lived.

David put his hands around her breasts and squeezed them together around his cock. It was hard again, his juices ran, and in a moment he climaxed, his ejaculation spurting against her body. God, he was phenomenal. Compared to David, Cooper was a turd.

"Will you take me to the Splendide party in December?" she asked.

It was a loaded question. What she really wanted to know was whether David was prepared to be seen with her in public.

"Naturally," he whispered.

Marjery Cannon had brought her bills along Rodeo Drive up to date and now she could hold her head high on shopping expeditions.

But that wasn't to say she was not still feeling quite desolate and forsaken. Bernard Markman would not answer her phone calls. There was no one else on the horizon. Gregory was his usual, irritating self. He floundered through life, paying out more for his office and staff than he was taking in, and constantly grumbling about his unappreciated professional talents and unrequited social graces.

Fortunately, Marjery had been brought into the middle of the December Ball organizing effort and thus remained squarely in the social mainstream, even though making hotel reservations was scarcely the most glamorous of jobs. But she was pitching in; they'd never be able to say she wasn't working hard.

There was nothing Marjery wanted at Bonwit's. She took the down escalator and left the store, walking west toward the Camino. Gregory's office was up there in one of the ritziest of the new glass office buildings. Jesus, an office on Wilshire Boulevard, it cost like hell. But Gregory insisted this was where he had to be. Your address, he said, was half the battle. She might drop in and see how her darling husband was doing. Chances were he wasn't busy. No, it would be too boring listening to him, hearing out his feeble jokes and his remarks about the neighbors, the funny things that went on in the building opposite.

Marjery ran into Tom Glenn at the front entrance of the Camino. He was shuffling out of the lobby, black bag heavy in his hand, and his expression, as usual, preoccupied, funereal, his prematurely white hair tousled.

"Tom," Marjery said, relieved to see somebody she knew, starved to talk to someone. He squinted, as if he were trying to see her properly, then took her hand and shook it limply. "What brings you down here today, Tom?"

"Oh," he said in his wispy voice, "I was visiting Madeleine Mauery."

The Mauerys kept an apartment on the penthouse floor of the Camino. "How is Madeleine these days?" Marjery asked, warmly sympathetic.

He made an undecided gesture. "Well, she's fine." God forbid he would ever talk openly about anything so confidential as a patient. There was no way she would have been able to dig out of him what was wrong with Sally. "Frail but fine," he added.

"That's good," Marjery said, smiling so hard she could feel her facial muscles pulling. "I've just been over to see

Greg and I thought I'd stop in here and have a cup of coffee. Do you have a few minutes?"

He smiled shyly. "Well, that'd be nice."

They went inside to the Juarez Room, a glorified coffee shop, and Marjery sat down at a window table while Glenn phoned his office. This was a good spot for people-watching, perhaps the best in town, since Wilshire and the nearby side streets were practically the only places in town where people actually did walk.

Glenn returned hastily and grabbed his bag. His face was more pallid than usual.

"Marjery," he told her, "I've got to go back upstairs. She collapsed a couple of minutes after I left, and Mauery is in a hell of a state. Would you mind coming along with me?"

A white-faced maid was sobbing when she let them in, and Mauery was pacing the floor, his features twisted, eyes glinting ferociously.

"Goddamn it, Glenn, you were just here. She's in the bedroom."

Mauery ignored Marjery and she stood shocked into silence as Glenn disappeared. Mauery crossed the living room and, back turned, his fingers in knots, stared out the window. The maid continued to weep.

Mauery turned on her. "You! Get the hell out of here with that goddamn crying." Then he noticed Marjery. "Who're you?"

In her smallest voice, Marjery said, "Marjery Cannon. You've met . . ."

"Shit! I know. Yes."

"I was with Tom downstairs. Is there anything . . ."

"Yes, make me a drink. A scotch and water."

Marjery found the bar and poured a hefty shot of scotch into a glass, adding water from the tap. She carried it to him at the window.

Mauery took it, glaring at her. "Sure, I know you. You're the wife of that asshole, Greg Cannon."

She did not reply. Mauery might be right about Greg but she was not about to agree with him at such short notice.

Glenn emerged from the bedroom. He crossed silently to Mauery and put a pale hand on his shoulder. Mauery impatiently shook it off.

"Morris," Glenn said very softly, "I'm afraid she's gone."

Mauery drained his glass and handed it to Marjery.

"Dead you mean?" he demanded harshly. "Say what you mean, doctor. Goddamn it." He was staring at Glenn, his eyes flat, metallic behind his glasses. "How can she be dead? You were up here no more than twenty minutes ago. She was okay then. You son of a bitch, Glenn, did you give her something?"

Glenn's mouth opened but no words came out. He stepped backward and sat down. He removed his glasses and rubbed his eyes.

"I—" he stammered. "Morris, please, it's the shock, but don't say things like that. I was very very fond of Madeleine."

"That's just it," Mauery insisted. "Fond enough of her to . . ."

"No!" Glenn shouted, jumping up. "I will not have it. What you're suggesting is very bad, very evil."

That stopped Mauery for a second. "Glenn . . ."

Glenn interrupted, holding up his hand. "Don't say another word. You, sir, are the son of a bitch. You knew she had a bad heart. You! With your non-stop brow-beating and berating. Disgusting!"

Mauery retreated a step. Eyes no less malevolent, he growled, "If she's dead, then get her out of here. See that the body is taken away, doctor."

Glenn said nothing more for the moment. He nodded icily and went to the telephone. He called his office and told his secretary to make the arrangements. When he finished that, he turned again to Mauery.

"There will be an autopsy," he said.

Mauery considered this, then slowly shook his head. "I don't think I'd want that. Let the dead rest."

"Marjery, you heard what he said," Glenn said. "Now, goodbye, Mr. Mauery. The handmaidens of death will all be here shortly."

"You . . . won't stay?" Mauery said, his tone now almost apologetic.

"No, there's nothing more I can do. I prefer to leave."

"All right then, leave," Mauery sneered. "Handmaidens of death, my ass! I would like to know, just for the record, what you did for her when you were here before?"

Levelly, Glenn said, "I gave her a vitamin injection . . . Marjery."

"I want her to stay here with me," Mauery said, pointing at Marjery.

She could not argue. She shrugged helplessly. It was the humanitarian thing to do, to comfort the survivor.

"Very well," Glenn said. He picked up his bag and left the apartment.

Mauery took the empty glass back from Marjery and went to the bar. Over his shoulder, he asked, "Something for you . . . Marjery?"

"A small scotch," she replied.

Men were often pleased, she had noted, when a woman took the same drink as they did. She was watching his shoulders. They were humped and knotted with tension. Mauery was a muscular man. Closely trimmed hair curled on the back of his head.

He surprised her. He was chuckling to himself when he came back. "Do you think your esteemed husband would like to handle a malpractice suit for me? Or is he too busy with his tax-free bonds?"

"Oh . . . I . . . well . . ."

"Yes or no?" Brusquely, he handed her the drink. "Yes or no?"

"Well, I'm sure if it were . . . warranted, Greg would be happy to talk to you about it."

"Yeah, I'm sure he would," Mauery said maliciously. He sat down where Glenn had momentarily perched. He leaned back and yawned. "Well . . . so Madeleine is dead. Christ, she lingered forever. So the old broad is croaked."

Marjery didn't know what to say. The way he put it was unbelievably callous. "I'm sorry," she said.

Mauery waved his hand negligently. "Don't be. She wasn't happy. She's been sick for months, years, it seems like. When the time comes, it's time to go." He performed a small gesture with his big hands, like birds' wings flying into the sunset.

"Well," Marjery said, "I suppose . . ."

"Never mind," he insisted, standing up. "Come with me. I want to show you something."

She followed him from the living room, fearing he was going to take her into the bedroom to view the body. But he continued down a hallway to another room at the end, a study of sorts, furnished with bookcases, a couch, desk, and easy chairs. The walls were covered with pictures. He pointed at them.

"Madeleine in her heyday. I'll get rid of these."

"She was so beautiful," Marjery said.

"Yeah," he said flatly, "and now she's dead as a doornail." He looked at Marjery, smiling. "Get undressed," he said.

"What? I . . ." Marjery was genuinely shocked. She might have entertained certain ambitions, but so soon? "Now?"

"Yes, get undressed—now."

Mauery slammed the door and stood with a hand on his hip, the other holding his drink. His eyes were so insistent she knew better than to refuse. Christ, she thought, the man was in a trauma. Could she help? Tentatively, she moved close to him and touched his face. He was still smiling. He let her hand remain where it was but moved to feel her breasts, then to run his fingers down her stomach to her crotch. Marjery knew what to do. She closed her eyes and sighed lingeringly. She began to unbutton her blouse, wondering nervously what would happen next. She unzipped her skirt and stepped out of it. Before she could get any further, Mauery pulled down her pantyhose with such force they tore.

"I've always heard you were a big cockteaser," he said. "Now we'll see. Turn around and put your hands on the desk."

She saw he had undone his pants. She turned. Roughly, he shoved himself against her, forced her over, and took her from behind, pushing into her despite her cry of pain—and surprise. He held her waist tightly, pulling her back.

"Tiny tits," he snarled. "You should've had them done along with that face of yours."

Marjery felt tears of hurt and fright, humiliation, run down *that* face. But she was not to be undone by anything as weak as insults. She moaned and pushed against him, lifting herself on tiptoes.

"Harder," she demanded.

"Okay, okay."

Grunting ferociously, he bore into her. She took one hand off the desk to reach between them, grabbed his testicles, and pulled. Then, she gave herself orgasm, simulating a climax with such vigor she knew he would be impressed. Aroused by the sham, he came off with a guttural snort. He continued to twist against her, drawing off every last shred of sensation. When he had finished, he quickly withdrew and patted her once on the buttock.

"Better than I expected," he said. "In fact, pretty good indeed."

Now she could safely help herself to a little bitterness. "Nice that you enjoyed it. I suppose I'm supposed to dress now and beat it."

"Well, you have to go home, don't you?"

"Yes."

Stolidly, Mauery contemplated her. "There's no need for you to be so insulted. You could have turned me down."

"What! How?"

"You don't think I'd force you to if you didn't want to, do you?"

She dodged a direct answer. "I've always liked powerful men," she said.

"And now you've found one." He laughed mirthlessly. "I can imagine living with that asshole Greg must get on your nerves. Isn't that so?"

She nodded. Of course, it was so.

"All right, Marjery," he said. "I'll see you tomorrow at the same time. You can help me plan the funeral."

"That's not particularly nice," she chided. She had come far enough to throw him off balance. "What makes you think I'll come?"

"You'll come because I'm asking you to come," he said.

Marjery knew she would. There was no question of it. She was not such a fool. A strategy began to develop in her mind. She was capable of taking him over. He was powerful, yes, but even the most powerful of men could be moved if a woman was strong and clever enough. She though of Cleopatra and Mark Antony.

The doorbell rang as she slipped back into her blouse, skirt, and shoes.

"Well," she said, "back to Pacific Palisades."

"Just hang around in here until they've gone," Mauery said.

He adjusted his clothes and checked his tie in the mirror. Then he did something she would have doubted he had available in his repertoire of facial expressions. He winked at her and went into the hall.

* * *

Marcia King left Daisy's house after lunch, which the two had taken in the poolhouse, out of range, Daisy hoped, of Jake's camera. It had been delicious: first a swim in the altogether, a few kisses, and Marcia's embrace.

"If we could do it, I'd marry you, Daisy," Marcia said happily. "I'd get a divorce and you'd get one and then we'd fly away and get married and live happily ever after. Wouldn't that be sensational?"

"Gays do get married nowadays," Daisy advised her coolly.

Marcia frowned. "I don't consider myself gay, Daisy."

But Daisy was hard-headed about such things. She'd been around and was satisfied enough with herself that she didn't need to dodge behind semantic niceties.

"Well, what are you then?" she demanded. "You're gay and I'm bi."

"You still insist you're bisexual?" Marcia said reprovingly. "It's clear enough to me you go one way."

"No," Daisy said, "I definitely do like men, too."

"And dogs and cats and doorknobs, too, no doubt."

"Oh, no, just men and women."

"Well, I say I'm not gay. I just happen to like women," Marcia said.

"Honey, that's what they call gay."

"I don't like the word," Marcia said crossly."

"I don't like the word," Marcia said crossly.

She kissed Marcia on the mouth, ran her tongue around Marcia's lips, and shoved her breasts into Marcia's face. Marcia gasped and mumbled words Daisy couldn't decipher. Then Daisy walked her out to her car. She pinched Marcia's thin bottom.

Martin Cooper came over about four. This was good, and Daisy was happy he had called, for she hadn't done much footage for Jake lately. The lush, Bill Murray, had finally mustered up enough courage to make an afternoon date, but he'd been so petrified and guilt-stricken he hadn't been much good, even though she'd done her best to pull him out of it. Jake had rated that performance as not fit for Academy consideration. Bernard Markman had never called back. In desperation, for she did not want to worry Jake, Daisy had taken the poolman upstairs one afternoon, describing him to Jake as a ear, nose, and throat specialist, and that had helped. But she had to be careful; Jake didn't like her fooling around with the servant class. Thus, Cooper would be a welcome diversion, for herself, and, she hoped, for Jake. It had been a while now since she'd had Cooper, and his equipment was nothing to be sneezed at.

But, damn it, he was in a curious mood. He had been drinking to start with, and that was not especially good. As Daisy patiently listened to his ranting, she stretched her blonde length on the bed and invitingly slithered about on the silk sheets, spreading her legs and closing them, pinching the muscles of her belly. Cooper sullenly took off his clothes and hopped up beside her on the bed. He fell down to kiss her, paw her breasts and thighs, then excitedly, as if satisfying some driving frustration, buried his face in her candybox and went after her as ferociously as if he'd been searching for the caramel. She was afraid he would bruise her. This would not please Marcia.

Daisy was in for a surprise, and the surprise came when she soothingly took him into her hand and had a close-up look at his plunger. She recoiled. She was experienced and she knew at first sight that there was something seriously wrong with him. His whatsis was reddened, and a filthy-looking slime oozed out of him.

Daisy emitted a thin scream. She pulled herself away from him and leaped out of bed. She began pulling on her jeans.

"What the hell's wrong?" Cooper exclaimed hoarsely.

Daisy kept calm, remembering the camera was running. "I think you better see a doctor."

"What the hell do you mean? You bitch! What are you saying?"

"That you're sick, goddamn it, Marty. And you must know it. Of all the rotten things. Do you think I'm so stupid you could come over here and give me that?"

"Daisy, Daisy," he said in a low voice. "What does it matter? I need you."

"You must be out of your mind."

"Don't say that," he yelped. "I'm leaving my wife. I thought you and I—What the hell! You don't need Cox."

She was astounded. Cooper worried her now. He was in an unbalanced state, and she realized that, for her own good, she had to soothe him, then get him out of the house.

"Marty, I'm in love with my husband," she said calmly.

"What! You've got to be kidding."

"You're divorcing Belle?" She felt like calling him a dumb shit.

"Yes, she's been cheating on me."

"I see," Daisy said doubtfully.

"With my best friend. It makes me crazy when I think about it."

"Who? Hopper?"

"Of course Hopper. I've got the goods on them. She's not going to take everything away from me, I tell you," he said hotly. "Then I thought, you and me, Daisy."

Daisy stood across the room from him, her arms folded over her bare chest.

"Martin, don't you know you've got a disease?"

"What? That? Nothing. It's a prostate thing, an irritation."

"Oh, I see," she said again. "Well, I don't think you should irritate it anymore. You look tired, Marty. I think you need some rest."

"Let me rest here," he suggested hopefully.

"No, no, Jake will be coming home . . ."

"What! Ahead of schedule?" he sneered. "Remember, he doesn't come home 'til 6:30."

"I know, but you might fall asleep and me not be able to get you up. Look . . . I think you'd better go."

"Throwing me out?"

"No, not throwing you out. Asking you to leave. Marty, take care of yourself. Then give me a call."

"Well . . ."

Undecided, he remained sitting in the center of the bed. Christ, she thought, this would take some explaining. If only she had access to those films. What the hell was she going to tell Jake? Probably, she decided, the truth would be best. If he were in his right mind, Jake would approve and thank her for it.

"All right," Cooper finally said vaguely, "if that's what you want. But later, what about us?"

Daisy hesitated. "We'll see, Marty . . ."

After the clarinet recital and dinner, she and Jake came upstairs to what had become center stage. He asked her if there was anything new—or was he going to have to see another re-run?

"Daisy, pretty soon you've got to find a new leading man. I don't know what's holding you back."

"Maybe I'm not as hump-crazy as you think," she said irritably. "There is something new . . . but you're probably not going to like it."

"Why?" Jake demanded suspiciously. "Not another woman, I trust."

After he had seen the promising beginning, then the aborted end of the latest Cooper saga, Jake was more mystified than put out.

"What was that all about, my dear? Why did you stop?"

"I stopped," she explained stiffly, "because I saw that if I went on, I was going to catch something from him."

Jake's mouth fell open. This was difficult for him to understand.

"What are you talking about? Like what? Poison ivy?"

"Jesus," Daisy exploded, "no. It looked to me like he's carrying around a case of clap."

"Good God," Jake exclaimed. "The son of a bitch. That *is* awful. It's hard to believe. I thought our friends were . . ."

Daisy was getting very tired of this. How could they all be so fatuous? Where did they think the real world stopped?

"What, Jake?" she exclaimed. "You thought all your friends were pure and healthy and delightful. Jesus, don't be so naivé."

"Here, in Beverly Hills?" He still couldn't believe it.

"Jake, you don't think they catch clap in Beverly Hills? Hell, they've got everything in Beverly Hills. People die here, they get drunk, they screw a lot, and once in a while, though not often, they get pregnant. They take drugs, they steal. They've got money and influence. And now and then, they go crazy, and every once in a while, one of the leading lights isn't careful and he catches the clap, or worse."

Jake was watching her, fascinated, breathing shallowly. "And it almost happened to you?"

"Damn near. If the lights had been out, who knows?"

"We can't have the lights out if we're filming," Jake said, idiotically.

Daisy groaned. Thinking about it, wouldn't she be better off with Marcia? When the time came, she was in a position now to pull out on Jake. She'd get a good settlement. She knew too much about his strange habits.

"Don't be an ass, Jake," she said. "I did the right thing, didn't I?"

"I don't know," he said petulantly. "You say you saw it. I couldn't see it on the film. You might have gotten him a little closer."

"Jesus H. Jumping Christ, Jake," Daisy hollered, feeling close to her own breaking point. "What the hell did you want? For me to give him a short-arm inspection for your viewing? Hey, Jake, I can never figure out what it is you want. Do you get your kicks from watching people screwing, or is it really the men you're looking at?"

Jake's face became long and flustered. "I forbid you to talk to me like that."

"Forbid, my ass!" she screamed. "You forbid me nothing. I just wonder what my real function is around here. I think sometimes I'm a figment of your imagination. Jake, why in the hell don't you just go to one of those sex shops and buy the movies? They'd be a hell of a lot more professional."

Jake was insulted. He reached for her hand to pull her down beside him, but she backed away.

"My dear," he said. "Mine are every bit as professional, even better. And I like the idea of doing my own. Buying them wouldn't be the same thing, would it? Like buying a whore for the night."

Daisy was in a dead fury now. It was quaint to live the good life, but to be so misused? Jake wouldn't have cared either way if she'd screwed Cooper and picked up the stuff. That was inhuman.

"I think all of you are sick, sick, sick," she said angrily. "Some in the body, some in the head."

"Now, now," Jake muttered, "don't get all het up, Daisy. Nothing is the end of the world. Yes, on examination, you did the right thing with Cooper. The nerve of the man! Doesn't he know anything about communicable diseases?"

Daisy was deflated. She gave up any attempt of getting sense out of him. She sat down at the other end of the couch and related to Jake what Cooper had said about leaving Belle and that Belle had been fooling around with Charley Hopper.

"Hmmm," Jake mused, "Hopper would have been a good one if you ever could've gotten him. Well, never mind, dear. Look at the cheerful side. So this piggish man thinks he has evidence against them, does he?" He chuckled to himself. "Good heavens, I might just send them one of my films. That would take the wind out of Cooper's sails, wouldn't it?"

"What!" Daisy was furious again. "With me on there with him?"

"Well," Jake said reasonably, "you wouldn't care, would you? I wouldn't. Chances are no one would ever see it, aside from a couple of lawyers. And it would be a good way of paying Cooper back for his . . . insensitivity. Such a crass and thoughtless man. I never liked him much with you anyway. Too much the bull, he was. You've done considerably better. I think even Bill Murray was better and he was no great shakes . . ."

"Yes," Daisy said bitterly, "he was hung like a dormouse."

"That's what I thought, too, my dear."

In a patient voice, Daisy said, "Jake, you can go fuck yourself."

Unruffled, Jake said, "Daisy, I forbid you to talk to me like that. Now, I want you to consider me. Surely, with your abilities and your . . . plentiful . . . endowments, you should be able to bring someone more worthy than Martin Cooper into your web."

Morris Mauery had sent the maid packing. Madeleine's corpse had been carted away to the mortuary, and Marjery Cannon was on her way home to Pacific Palisades. Relishing the emptiness of the apartment, the stench of medicine already dissipating, he made himself a long drink and sat down to watch the evening news. It would be too early yet for an item on Madeleine but perhaps . . .

The phone rang and it was Chicago. As powerful as Mauery was on the West Coast, there were others in the country more powerful. The import of the call was succinct: the Hotel Beverly Splendide was to open on schedule and Mauery was to see to it there were no untidy problems.

Ah, he told himself, smiling, the phone call to Finistere had done its magic.

But no, he realized next, it was not exactly like that. It was not that he was to call off any problems that might have occurred. It was that he was not to dream up any problems. He was not to cause trouble.

"This you understand, Morrie?" the Chicago voice said.

"Perfectly," he replied.

He felt a knot in the pit of his stomach, sweat at his armpits and between his legs, mixing with the lingering woman's smell of Marjery Cannon.

Mauery did not bother to mention that his wife had just died.

He went into the bathroom and threw up all the scotch.

Bertha Moore was finally getting to see Jurgen Ehrlich's cuckoo clock. It was truly old, hard-carved in the Swiss forests by Jurgen's own grandfather. A little door in the eave housed a tiny, russet-colored bird, which popped out annoyingly to sound the hour; and the clock ticked loudly, leaving one in no doubt that time was flying.

Jurgen's shanks were thin and white and his rib cage so pronounced, he could have modeled for anatomy students. But he was excellent and untiring, like a lanky rabbit, when it came to what Bertha preferred to call fornication.

He was on top of her in his narrow bed and they were fornicating, these two bags of bones rattling oddly, she thought, skinny legs entwined.

"Mein schatz," he was whispering. "Now, you are mine. Mine . . ."

"You think so," she muttered.

"Jawohl, mein schatz." His breathing became stertorous. "*Schatz* . . . *Schatz*! I am approaching . . . my experience . . ."

"Me, too, me, too," she cried urgently. "Jurgen!"

His thing inside her felt like a leg itself, knotted with muscle, with a foot on the end of it kicking at her pelvis and her spine. He climaxed with a cry, murmuring German gibberish, and Bertha heaved as something like a knee jolted her panic button. She had a shattering orgasm.

Now was the hour. She knew, because the goddamn ugly bird shot out of its house at the top of the clock and began to cuck-ooo, cuck-ooo, cuck-ooo . . .

Chapter Twenty-Three

They did New England in the early autumn—Boston, Cape Cod, Peterborough in New Hampshire, then skipped up to Montreal. Returning to New York, Charley arranged picture sessions at the Tavern on the Green in Central Park, another atop the World Trade Center in lower Manhattan, interiors in the Palm Court at the Plaza Hotel. Then he gave Belle a few days off so she could visit Susan in Princeton. And they set out again.

Washington had to be on the agenda; they covered the capital in three days. Belle did her first TV commercial spot with the Lincoln Memorial behind her, a subtle mix of cosmetics and American history. Next, they went to Charleston, South Carolina, for more history, and caught the remnants of sunshine and summer in Florida—Palm Beach and Key West. From the southeastern peninsula, they swung across to Atlanta, then south to the sticky autumn of New Orleans for color photography and a commercial in the French Quarter. Houston, Texas, and Maude Mannon were next on the itinerary.

They got into Houston late, delayed by rain storms across eastern Texas. But by midnight, they were sitting before a warm fire in the library of Maude's big brick house. Maude said she had something to tell them, but they had to promise to keep it quiet.

"Sharon Peters and her fella, Frank Woodley, were here no more than a week or so ago. They were secretly marr'ed on the premises," Maude said in a hushed voice.

Belle smiled. This was precisely the sort of event that would delight Maude. Maude in love with love, and despite her own half-dozen or so marriages, there was nothing that titillated her more than another wedding ceremony. A secret wedding was a supremely delectable event.

"Why secret?" Belle asked.

"Because the girl is deathly afraid of that awful man—I only met him once—Morris Mauery."

"Mauery? I never knew Sharon had any sort of relationship with him."

Maude waggled her head knowledgeably. "Sharon told me . . . confidentially . . . Mistuh Mauery thinks of himself as her . . . protector."

Charley sighed. "Jesus, don't you know about Mauery, Belle? He's bad, bad news."

"I think," Maude said slyly, "that Frank Woodley is man enough to handle Morris Mauery."

When it was time for bed, they found they were being put up in what Maude mischievously referred to as the "Sharon and Frank Woodley wing" of the big brick house. They stayed there during two days of shooting.

After Dallas and San Antonio, Texas, the latter for a layout at the Alamo, they went on to Santa Fe. It was far too late for the opera season, but Charley rigged up a sprinkling of audience and faked it. From there, they went on to Navajo country and the Grand Canyon.

It was mid-October when Belle and Charley landed in Missoula, Montana. They had a full four days to themselves before they returned briefly to Los Angeles and then East for the April in Paris Ball in New York.

Charley pointed the car northeast toward the Joseph Ranch, an hour's drive into the mountains.

"At last," Charley said, "a breather. You're pooped and so am I."

"Well," Belle said, "it had to be done and may as well do it right, as Sam says."

He laughed. "Already spouting the company line. Belle, the crew thinks you're terrific, a great trouper. And so do I. Now, they're coming out here for only one day. The rest of the time we can relax."

There had been little news from Los Angeles. Charley was in contact with his secretary at C.A.A. but not with Cooper. Things seemed to be all right, although, from what Charley could glean from his secretary, Cooper was not much on the premises these days. "Thank God," Charley said grimly, "for a faithful staff of people." Belle's housekeeper, Mrs. Atkins, was not much more informative when it came to Cooper. He was in and out, more out than in, said Mrs. Atkins.

"I'm worried about him," Charley was saying in the car. Belle knew about their fight, of course. Charley had described his rupture with Cooper when he'd arrived in Boston. "As much as I dislike him now, I'm worried."

So was she, in a peculiar way, even though Cooper was very nearly out of her life. The separation was legal and a divorce was in the works. Belle had had one cryptic phone conversation with her lawyer, who'd told her, without elaboration, that a sensational piece of information had come their way: she had nothing more to fear from Mr. Martin Cooper; in fact, she had the wherewithal now to take him, as they said, "to the cleaners." The truth was, however, that Belle did not really want anything from him, except freedom. The house, scene of high tension and unpleasantness, that was his; the cars, of no importance to her; the business—Charley already owned his share of that. Real estate? The same rule applied. He could hand it over to Pamela Renfrew for all Belle cared. The only question that interested her now was when it could be final. It should be all over by the end of the year.

Belle leaned back in the seat of their rented Chevy and nodded toward sleep. She was exhausted but, at the same time, she was very satisfied. They had done good work, and traveling with Charley was as painless as circumstances allowed. He arranged everything to the last detail: anything that might have gone wrong, he anticipated. And he loved her. He comforted her at night and reassured her in the daytime. For all practical purposes they were living together now. Initially, she had had her doubts, as she'd told Sam Leonard, but then she had slipped naturally into a full-blooded relationship with Charley. It was just as natural from his side. They did not think twice about it. The question of marriage had not come up again since one brief moment in New Orleans.

"Belle," Charley had said that night, "the main thing is you want to be free of any entanglements. The fact of marriage is not that important to me. If I'm with you, it doesn't matter at all. And we can always get married. People do it all the time."

Charley turned off the main road into a two-lane macadam highway leading into the forest and toward the hills.

The road led past several backwoods settlements, clumps of disheveled trailers parked under trees and, in a few more minutes, they were on a bumpy dirt track, crossing a swollen river and then winding along a precipitous bluff. The road, rutted and pot-holed, leveled out. They had reached true wilderness. A mile of twisted, hilly terrain brought them to the first lake, gray and cold and glistening in the pale sun. A half mile away, at the far end of the lake, a tall and unbroken stretch of pine climbed a steep hillside. At lake's edge, many of the trees had been cut and lay with their topmost branches in the water.

"You see," Charley said, pointing, "the beaver. They've got a city over there. They work at night, mark the trees, then hack them down with those sharp teeth."

"Sounds like Beverly Hills," Belle murmured.

He laughed. "Anyway, they drop them with precision, like a lumberjack, skin them, and add them to the dam. They drive Paul Joseph crazy."

Belle felt herself slowly reviving. Charley's enthusiasm at being here was catching.

They climbed to a second, smaller lake and now, through a break in the trees, she could see a wooden house, its protective varnish shining in the sun, and then, as they drove closer, a chimney from which emerged a feather of smoke.

"Joseph did a lot of work on this place," Charley said. "It used to be a hunting lodge. They added the big porch and all those windows."

Charley honked and a man came out the back door, Joseph's caretaker. They unpacked the trunk of the car and carried everything inside. A small fire crackled in the fireplace.

"Mr. Joseph said to get everything ready for you, Mr. Hopper . . . food in the icebox. There's a fly rod over there in the corner, and the fishing's pretty good right now. A shotgun in the corner. We've had a bear around here at night—a renegade. If he comes hammering at the door, one shot out the window will scare him off."

The interior of the house had been laid out in rustic luxury. The living room was furnished with local antiques, Indian rugs, and comfortable couches. The western wall of windows afforded a spectacular view of the creek scrambling through rocks from the highest lake, then a mile-long meadow and beyond that dense forest that surged northward over rising hills toward a low gap in the distant mountains. The fireplace opened to both the living room and a low-ceilinged bedroom. Off the bedroom, there was a large tiled bath with full tub, shower, and sauna, a bathing conglomerate that could have been transplanted from Beverly Hills.

"So," Charley said, looking around, "what do you think?"

"It's perfect," Belle said. "Particularly marvelous there's nobody here. Just us . . . and Pete."

"Pete lives back down the road."

"Oh, good, Charley."

She put her arms around him. His face was tired, too, but already his eyes were brighter and, as they held each other, she felt the strength rise through him and into her. The fire was warm and a flush of desire found its way from there into her bones.

Charley felt it, too. He grinned. "Now's our chance. However," he said solemnly, "I have another suggestion. Why don't you climb in the bathtub, then have a little nap? You see, I want to go fishing."

She leaned back from him, holding to his arms. "Well, of all the rats! You mean you'd rather go fishing?"

"Not in the normal course of human affairs. But, hell, we've got to have some trout for tonight. I'd feel guilty. I'd hate myself. I haven't been fishing in months. They're waiting for me."

She realized he needed this, needed to tramp and fish the sparkling day, to stand by himself by the lake swearing at some trout.

"I'll take a bath," she said. "And I'll have a nap."

"Hell, Belle, you know, you're a good sport."

Charley opened one of his suitcases, threw clothes on the floor, and finally found what he wanted: a pair of corduroy pants, a heavier pair of socks. In a closet next to the kitchen, he rummaged for rubber boots and an old shirt and sweater and even found an Irish fishing hat. In a moment, he was dressed and outside on the porch examining the fly rod and a fishing bag full of lures.

"Okay," he announced, drawling, "well, little lady, here goes Charley."

"Doesn't take much to make you happy," Belle observed. "You really are nothin' but a little old country boy, Charley. You can't wait to get going, can you?"

"Right. Give us a little kiss, little lady."

He tramped back down the road toward the big lake. He was whistling as he disappeared into the trees. Belle hugged herself, pressing her breasts. God, she thought, he was perfect, wasn't he? They were perfect. She was very lucky and she knew then that they would be together a long time.

It was nice to have a little time all to herself. Belle had a look at the kitchen. Food? The freezers were stuffed with it. Meat and fish—yes, frozen trout—and at least a year's supply of canned goods. If it began snowing and went on forever, they had plenty here. She found what she wanted in the refrigerator: a beer. She opened it and, whistling herself, went back to the bedroom. She straightened out his mess of clothes, then opened her own suitcases and took out a pair of blue jeans and a turtleneck sweater. She turned on the bath water, adjusted the temperature, and then undressed. Despite the strenuousness of the trip, she thought she'd gained a pound or two. The tension and hard work made one eat more. But her body was supple, fluid, all the better for Charley.

She was sleeping lightly when he returned. His face was cold, his nose even colder. Drowsily, she put her arms around his neck and kissed him.

"I was tired," she murmured, "you were right."

"Would you believe I caught six little beauties, fat and saucy and juicy? Threw the little ones back. They all have names."

"Don't tell me, Charley. I wouldn't be able to eat them." She pulled at his shoulders. "Come to bed for a minute . . . an hour, 'til it's dark."

"Bed? I've got to clean my fish," Charley cried, mockly indignant. "Stay there. I'll be right back."

"With fish smell all over your hands."

He grinned and nipped at her neck. "I'll take a shower."

He went outside again, banging the front door. Belle got up and put a fresh log on the lowering fire. She stood there naked for a moment, the glow of the fireplace warming her legs. Through the window, in the gathering dusk, she watched him squat by the creek. When he had finished, he straightened and came toward the house, carrying a pail. Belle quickly returned to bed.

"Okay," he called. "All done. Where are you?"

"Waiting."

Charley pulled off his clothes. "One second," he said. Water rushed in the shower and she could hear him whistling and humming. In a moment, he was back, his skin shining in the firelight. "Clean as a whistle," he murmured. He slid in beside her, the line of his body following hers down the length of the bed.

"The hunter is home from the hill," she said.

"No, fisherman home from the . . . what?"

"Flood . . . flow?" She was still only half awake. "Fiord . . ."

He chuckled, his mouth buried in her shoulder, then against the undercurve of her breast. "Belle, you'll never make it in advertising. It's fisherman home with his catch."

"Yes, Charley," she whispered.

He was warm and smelled fresh, of the mountain air and exercise. He had been so easily cleansed of the world and its cares. He held her against him and they exchanged musky warmth. She was ready, never so ready as now, muscles and nerves soothed by her own long bath and the sleep.

"Charley, now," she said.

The length of him penetrated, unending it seemed, and slowly, as if savoring her morsel by morsel, he moved and stirred against her, finally bringing her to a quiet, aching climax. In her relaxed state of body and mind, it went on and on until he joined her in a numbing ejaculation. He went to sleep at once.

Just as quickly, he awoke a half hour later. She had been holding him, her thoughts in a clutter, half asleep, half conscious of the sound of the stream outside, of the mountain noises.

"Belle, my God," he muttered. "We've got to get up. I'm hungry as hell. Get ready for Maude, Sharon, Daisy, Pamela, and . . ."

"Stop! What do we need?"

"Hell, you know, Belle. A big frying pan and some oil or butter or something. You're the cook. I just catch 'em. I hope you're not going to tell me you don't know how to cook, Belle. If you do, it's all off."

"I know how to cook, mister, don't worry about that."

They dressed and went into the kitchen. Charley found two bottles of white Moselle in the refrigerator, and when Belle had fried the fish, they sat down at the table in front of the fireplace and ate and drank the wine until they could eat and drink no more.

"Jesus!" Charley exclaimed. "You *can* cook. That's the best meal I've ever had in my entire life."

He belched thunderously and patted his stomach.

"We're pigs," Belle said.

"Yes, but nice ones."

Charley removed the dirty plates from the table, refilled their wine glasses, and they moved three feet to the couch in front of the dancing fireplace. Charley put his arm around her and they slumped.

"Do you think we'll see the renegade tonight?" Belle asked.

"Who?"

"Who were you thinking of? I mean the renegade bear."

"Not only bears are renegades," Charley observed soberly.

"What were you thinking of?"

"Nothing," he said, yawning elaborately.

The phone sounded three long peals.

"Christ," Charley groaned. "That's ours. I better answer it. Otherwise, they'll send out a search party."

Groaning again, he pulled himself out of the deep couch and stumbled across the room to the telephone on the kitchen wall.

"Yeah?" he mumbled. Then, as she listened, he came suddenly alert. "Yes, Alice, it's me." That was his secretary. "Yes . . . No! My God! Are they sure?"

Belle sat up. His voice said it was bad and shocking news; at least that it was important news.

"All right, all right, Alice," he grunted. "All right, Alice, goddamn it! Just try to keep cool, will you? There's nothing you can do. Yes, of course I'll come back. Naturally! Goddamn it, what do you think? We'll get out of here early tomorrow, try to be in L.A. in the afternoon. Look . . . Listen, for Christ's sake. I'll call you from the airport. I'll want a car to meet us. Yes . . . Okay . . . Yes. Goodnight, Alice—and don't worry."

He hung up, muttering to himself and swearing disbelievingly. He had a bottle of scotch in his hand when he returned and two glasses. He sat down next to her and poured two shots. Then he looked directly into her eyes, handing her the glass.

"Martin Cooper is dead."

She was holding the glass pressed tightly in her hands. She had sensed it was something like that. Her heart began to pound and the force of the words seemed to push her back into the couch.

Rigidly, she said, "Tell me what happened, all of it."

Charley did not touch her. His face was sorrowful, his voice uneven.

"He was on the road from Santa Barbara this afternoon, on that nasty stretch. The car swerved and he ran head-on into a tanker truck. They don't know any more than that. The car burned."

"Dead? Just like that? Cooper is dead?"

"Yes. Instantly, apparently."

"But it was an accident?"

Charley paused, shaking his head. "Yes. It was on the straightaway. There's no explanation why a car would pull a stunt like that."

"He went to sleep. He was drunk," she said.

"No, he'd only had two drinks according to the people he was with in Santa Barbara, and that was at lunchtime. It happened at four o'clock."

"He wasn't drunk."

"No, it seems not. Belle, they can't figure out what happened."

Tears, not especially for Cooper, but for the horror and surprise streamed down her face.

"It was deliberate then," she said, her face cold.

"Belle," Charley said slowly, "I doubt if they'll ever know."

"Jesus . . ." She wept for a moment. "The renegade," she said softly. "He was the renegade, Charley. That's what you were thinking about a few minutes ago, isn't it? Nobody will ever know . . . about Cooper either. Nobody ever did. That was his problem. Nobody knew, and he never told anybody. You had an intuition, Charley," she said. "I know it!"

She sounded as though she were making an accusation and Charley withdrew slightly, his face without expression, except the eyes.

"Belle . . . Belle, maybe I did," he admitted. "We were very close at one time."

"Jesus," she whispered, "such a lost soul. I wonder where he is now."

"Belle, drink some whiskey."

She stared at the glass. She did not want to talk about it anymore. She shivered and her body was shaking.

"Belle," Charley said, searching for words, "there was never anything you could do for him. He went past it. He was a victim."

"Victim?" She laughed bitterly. "Of what?"

Charley shrugged sadly. "The business, the city, the people. Mart had very high ambitions, you know. Maybe he compromised too much—that can kill, too."

"Not like you," she said grimly, then regretted saying it, for Charley was a different sort of soul. "I'm sorry . . ."

"You're right," he said. "Not like me! I never took it that seriously."

She knew this was so. Cooper had always been too hyper, too thrilled and thrilling. It was the part of him that had attracted her in the first place. But the manic side of his nature had equaled, then absorbed, his more reasoned and critical aspects. And, with that, he'd been ruined: the money, the power, the influence, the women throwing themselves at the fullback's body, the hype, the falling in love with his own image, coming to adore that being other people had come to accept, and expect, as his natural self.

"God knows what would make him do a thing like that," she said. "Oh, Charley, they can't blame me for that."

Now she wanted him to touch her. He took her in his arms.

"You're not to blame, Belle. And remember, they don't really know what happened. Most likely, the car malfunctioned somehow."

"No." She shook her head against his shoulder. "Cooper was a tragic figure. I think he was born that way."

"How so, Belle?" he asked gently.

"Shakespearean—the man destroyed by his own failings. It has nothing to do with outside forces acting on him."

"Well," Charley said doubtfully, "that may be so."

Chapter Twenty-Four

A case was closed. At least Detective Sgt. Vernon Wilson had closed it to his satisfaction. They would never know exactly what happened, he wrote in his report, but the pieces of the puzzle appeared to fit, if one allowed much for circumstance and intuition.

They had tracked Jane Farelady from San Francisco to Hollywood and Los Angeles. She had been an unsavory piece of goods, to put it mildly. From her agent, Mort Schultz, they learned that Martin Cooper of C.A.A. had taken on the job of building her to stardom, with a piece of the action in a three-picture deal his inducement. Piece of the action? How much had she seen of Cooper? Impossible to say, Mort maintained, for Jane had seen so many men, had dated, at one time or another, an impressive roster of Hollywood names, those able to get away from their wives for an hour or two or, preferably, for a long weekend at the desert or the beach. So, there were many who might have been considered suspect. But yet . . . Did Mort think Cooper had ever slept with Jane Farelady? Mort would have been astounded to learn that he had not.

And where had Cooper been the night of the murder? Impossible to say. But he wouldn't need an alibi now.

A young man was released from the psychiatric unit at the L.A. County-USC Medical Facility. Under hypnosis, he still couldn't recall what had happened that night, but he said he did remember a figure, the ghostly image of a large and powerful man, wielding a flashing knife. Sgt. Wilson had shown the young man pictures of Cooper, even of Mort Schultz, though Schultz would never know this.

But the young man remembered no face, only the tall and burly figure.

It might have been anyone. But when Martin Cooper died in fiery misadventure, as they customarily described it in the newspapers, in what had definitely been a freak accident on the Santa Barbara road, Wilson, intuitive beyond his station, made the quantum jump from hypothesis to certainty in his own mind that Cooper was—or bad been—their man.

The young man was released from custody, much sobered and very very grateful to Detective Sgt. Vernon Wilson. He was a fortunate young man for many reasons. For one, he had never had time to consummate his date with Jane or she the opportunity to pass along to him the gonorrhea the autopsy revealed to be running rampant through her beautiful body, now slashed from ear to ear.

But when his report came back downstairs, it was stamped "Case Unsolved"—tricks of the trade, the way the cookie crumbles and the ball bounces. So be it. But Wilson was still so intrigued that he gave himself an hour to attend a memorial service at the Presbyterian Church in Beverly Hills for Martin Cooper, founder and chief of C.A.A.

The widow was there, Belle Cooper, dressed elegantly in black with a black veil, and at her side Cooper's partner, Charley Hopper. There must have been 100 people or more in the church—heads of agencies rival to C.A.A., the mayor of Beverly Hills, local attorneys, a few state politicians, Southern California socialites, hotel magnates, and the proprietors of half the expensive boutiques along Rodeo Drive; in addition to all these people, there were those Sgt. Wilson would recognize even better: managers of local saloons, one prominent bookie, a handful of classy hookers, handsome actors and beautiful actresses, directors and producers. An impressive group, a proper turnout to say goodbye to such a respected pillar of the community.

What had happened to Jane Farelady and to Martin Cooper no one would ever know for sure, except that both were left dead.

After it was over, Belle and Charley drove to the beach to see Sally Markman and Bernard.

When they were on Sunset and headed for the ocean, Belle removed her black veil and threw it on the seat between them.

"Well, that's over," she said.

Charley nodded. He hadn't been saying much this morning. Belle did not mention it, but it seemed possible Charley was more affected by Cooper's death than she was. She had made her peace within herself. Whatever Martin had done, he had done to himself. They had been strangers at the end. For all practical purposes, and this was the only way she could look at it, Cooper, this final, ultimate Martin Cooper, had been a different man, not the man she had married. A stranger. She might spare grief for the old Cooper, but not for this one who had crashed and burned.

"It's not all over," Charley muttered. "Now comes the legal stuff."

"No will."

"No, there's no will. The bastard. He thought he'd never die."

But there was love and affection in Charley's voice. He, too, was thinking of the old Cooper.

"What's that mean?" Belle asked.

"It means in the end we'll probably wind up closing the agency. The government has already arrived. There'll be heavy taxes on everything. I'll qualify that. You'll be paying heavy taxes. I'll get half of what's toted up to be the net worth of the business. In the meantime, I don't know. What you're supposed to do is go on like nothing's happened. Christ, I couldn't even sell my half now, if I wanted to."

"Awkward all the way around," Belle summed up. "The house?"

"Same thing, unless it was community property."

"It wasn't. But I don't care about that. I'd sell it anyway," she said.

"Bank accounts?" She shook her head. "I have no idea how much cash he had laying around," Charley said. "You'll probably get an allowance from the estate while it's being settled."

Belle laughed. "I always got an allowance anyway, and not a very big one. I don't know what he's got in the bank either, or where."

"They'll find it all. Don't worry."

Sally had not come into town for the memorial and no reason she should have, Belle thought. She had not been at all fond of Cooper.

But when they reached the Markman place at the beach,

Belle realized there was more to it than that. Physically, Sally could not have made the trip. Belle was stricken far past her supposed bereavement to see her dearest friend. Bernard Markman took them through the house to the sunny terrace above the water. Sally was in a wheelchair, her head covered in a woolly cap. She was so weak her eyes seemed the only remaining vestige of life, and these, thank God, were still bright, almost too bright, and glittering.

Markman was a man in pain. Obviously, he was in pain. He watched Sally constantly, registering her every movement, the expression on her face as she frailly greeted Belle and Charley.

"About time you got here. I've been waiting. You've been away for months." Sally paused and drew breath. "If you want me to say something about Cooper, I will. I'm sorry. It was a hell of a way to go." She stopped speaking again.

Belle took the opportunity to break in. "It's better we don't talk about it. I want you to tell me all about the party. I'm a little out of touch."

"Jesus!" Sally snorted. "You are out of touch. They're hitting us from every side. Do you know what that goddamn bitch Marjery Cannon has done? She's canceled all the hotel bookings."

"For what? Why? We need those," Belle cried.

Bernard supplied the answer. "I can tell you exactly why. Mrs. Cannon"—he pronounced the name as though he were identifying rotten fish—"Mrs. Cannon has taken up with Morris Mauery and Mauery is dead against the party and the Splendide. He's using her. He's calling down the revenge of Jehovah on all those consorting with the Arabs."

Sally weakly stopped him. "But have no fear, Lou Finistere has stepped into the breach. Using Archy's clout, she's reinstated most of the reservations. We'll be looking good. And Archy says we may have enough rooms available at the Splendide for all the out-of-towners."

"That's a relief."

"More good news, more upsetting news," Sally continued, so excitedly Markman put a hand on her arm to calm her. "Norman has got Mrs. You-Know-Who lined up to come, plus the present incumbent First Lady, and it's a possibility the president will come with her. Maud has got a firm yes from her lady, and she's also bringing the governor of Texas along. The other two ambulatory First Ladies are firm 'probablys.' There's one thing they can't turn down—and that's a cancer benefit . . ."

The mention of the dread word caused Markman to wince. He blinked rapidly in the sunshine.

"So," Belle said cheerfully, "we should have five of them altogether. That's not bad at all."

"Not bad?" Charley echoed. "Hell, that's terrific."

"You're thinking from the point of view of Cosmos," Sally said.

"Sure," he agreed, "and yours . . ."

"Well . . ." Sally hesitated. "We'll have three or four governors. That means the senators have got to fall into line."

"Whew!" Belle whistled. "Like a political convention."

"Yeah." Sally smiled. "Almost. But, Belle, we're coming into the crucial time now. You've got to be here." She glanced at Charley. "Cosmos or no Cosmos."

Charley laughed. "Take it easy on me. I'm not the heavy. All Belle's got on her schedule now is that dismal ball in New York. That's a must. Whatever else Cosmos demands of us, we can do here. Right now," he said complacently, cocking an ankle up on his knee, "we've got twenty-five or thirty advertising pages shot and ready to be laid out, along with TV commercials enough to get us into next March. Sally, my beautiful lady, Belle has been working her buns off since last she saw you."

Sally's face broke into a smile. "I'm not surprised to hear it. I told her she had the buns available to work off. Let me, however, continue with good news-bad news time." She pulled herself up in the chair and inhaled deeply, relishing the beach air. "Item one, Norman's little pal, Marcello Zavier, hasn't been any help at all. He's afraid Valerian Ribar will be mad at him if he fusses around the decor. No big problem. Harry Finley and Fred Gibbons were going to do most of it anyway. Darling Higgins has agreed to foot the bill. It'll cost her a fortune."

"Money," Belle sniffed. "She and Ellsworth have got it wrapped in aluminum foil and stored in the freezer."

"Item two," Sally continued. "Believe it or not, Daisy Cox and Marcia King have eloped. Fortunately, the invitation is done and already mailed. We sent more than 2,000, can you believe it?"

Belle was flabbergasted. "Daisy and Marcia have eloped? Isn't that a little unusual?"

Dryly, Charley said, "Not according to modern usage. I didn't know they were divorced and free."

"That's apparently in the works," Bernard chuckled. "Seems Daisy tired of Jake's mental cruelty and Marcia wearied of . . ."

"Her invalid husband?" Sally glanced mockingly at him.

"Sally . . ."

"Can it, Bernie, baby," Sally said. "No if's, and's, or but's. You can see I've slid downhill, Belle. Why beat around the bush?"

"Please, dear," Markman pleaded. He turned to Belle. "You're seeing her on a bad day. Ordinarily, she's spry and chipper as a bird. We're beating this thing, blast it!"

He was so agitated when he made the brave statement that it was clear he'd given up all but the most meager hope.

"Quiet, husband," Sally said fondly. "I continue. Item three: We do not have Marcia available, therefore, to do the program for the nights of nights. You've got to arrange that somehow, Belle. I figure the artwork can pretty much follow what Marcia designed for the invitation. Have you seen it?"

She shook her head. "No. What did you finally decide to call it?"

"Your idea, kiddo: Winter Ball."

"We've been so busy," Belle said.

"Listen, I'll handle the program," Charley offered. "I'll get it done for nothing. We've . . ." He found it his turn to pause in mid-sentence. "The agency has got plenty of people who owe us favors."

"Well," Sally said thankfully, "that takes care of that. Can you?"

"Consider it done."

"Good. Now then, I'm worried about the menu. It's got to be super-luxe. But on the other hand, I hate to stick the Splendide with too much—I mean, things like caviar would be very expensive."

"I don't think you should bother yourself with these minor things," Belle said. "Hell, Abdul could send over a planeload of caviar and it wouldn't even show on his petty cash accounts. Or send Charley Hopper to Montana to catch 3,000 trout. He'd love that. Charley?"

Markman's ears perked up. "You a fisherman, Charley? God, I'd like to go with you on that mission."

"Come on, cut it out," Sally said irritably. "Belle, talk it over with Archy, will you?"

"Dear, I wish you *would* stop worrying about the details," Markman said sharply. "Archy can handle all that."

"All right, all right! What item am I on now?"

"Coming up on item five," Markman said sourly.

"Yes, the entertainment," Sally picked up. "I gather Rolly Starr was devastated by that girl's murder. Belle, you've got to make sure he doesn't slack off. A lot of people will say yes, then let you down."

"Yes, Sally," Belle said patiently. "I'll see Pat Hyman. She'll put the arm on him."

"And item six, and the last I can think of," Sally said, her face drawn. "Tom Glenn is narrowing down his list of candidates for our award. He ought to have a nomination in early November. He agrees with Leonard it should be an American. You'll have to have a meeting to confirm his choice."

"Okay," Belle nodded. "It sounds like everything is organized. No big problems. Stop worrying!"

But Sally continued to fret. "I can't figure out whether we should formally excommunicate Marjery Cannon or just let her fade away."

Markman said, "Forget her. She'll fade away."

"Does Gregory know about this between her and Mauery?" Belle asked.

"Probably. Don't you know how that little couple operates? Except now, she's bitten off something dangerous. Nobody fools around with Mauery," Markman said.

"Madeleine must still be warm," Sally said wickedly. "It didn't take him very long to find a replacement."

Markman shifted uncomfortably, but Sally didn't notice. They talked for a moment of Sharon Peters marriage to Frank Woodley and Markman shook his head.

"Mauery'll never forgive that either," Markman said.

Belle lost track of the conversation. She turned to look at the ocean. It was a cloudless day and a cool breeze off the water had cleared the coastline of smog. Far down the bay, she could see jets pulling into the sky from the international airport. Leaving, flying into the unknown, the great beyond. Cooper. She remembered for a second, painfully. Then she allowed herself to speculate longingly on how convenient it would have been had she and Charley flown away again. Closer by, circling cormorants set up their flight pattern, too, searching the sea for food. Spotting the glint of a fish, they would fold their wings back in perfect aerodynamic efficiency and plunge down, pulling out with a frantic beating of wings the instant they had the fish and were no more than a few millimeters in the water. The birds were so awkward, yet so beautiful, fulfilling a basic need, hunting for their food. The sight was enough to jolt her back to reality.

"Gorgeous," Belle murmured.

"Isn't it?" Sally responded. "Tell me, how's Susan settling in?

"She seems happy. I talked to her a couple of nights ago, to tell her about Martin."

"She didn't come back?"

"No, I didn't see any point in it."

"I agree," Sally said.

Charley had not agreed. It had seemed to him that Susan should have returned for the funeral and memorial and Belle could understand his point of view. But he didn't know the full story yet; perhaps she would never tell him. Belle had argued it would have been no more than a gesture, unimportant to her. Susan had her own life now.

Markman observed, "This must create a hell of a mess for you, Charley. Is it true there wasn't any will?"

"Yeah," Charley said soberly. "It was typical of Mart to leave all the loose ends flying. But he always operated that way."

"The epitaph," Sally remarked icily. "Martin Cooper, a hell of a guy, but he left loose ends."

"Yes," Charley said shortly. Belle knew he might have replied more sharply. "That's about it."

Sally ended the morbid conversation by saying she needed her nap.

"Darling," she said to Belle, "you will keep me informed, won't you? And I want you to tell Archy I won't have chicken on that menu and it's got to be sit-down. I hate chicken and I hate buffets."

They drove back to the Cooper house above Angelo Drive so Belle could pick up a few clothes and her car and also have a word with Mrs. Atkins, who had not gone to the memorial either.

The three of them sat for a while in the breakfast alcove.

"Charley," Belle asked, "do you want to go through his desk or anything?"

He was shocked. "God, no, Belle! It should be locked up. At least, I think everything should be locked up."

"Frances," Belle said, "could you do this? Would you mind? Pack his clothes in boxes upstairs? I don't know if I can give them away, but that's what I've got in mind."

"Sure," her housekeeper said. "And what else?"

"Just hold the fort, I guess. Move the maid into the main house. I know you don't want to be alone. I don't want to stay here, Frances, you understand that?"

"Yes, of course. Then . . . what shall I do? Will you be needing me?"

Belle realized what was bothering her. "Are you kidding, Frances? Of course, I will. Good God! What did you think?"

They both broke down and started to cry.

"Hey," Charley said, "hey, come on, you two."

Belle followed Charley to his house in her red Jaguar, the car Martin had bought her. As soon as they were inside, she stripped off her black dress, stripped to the buff, and took a long shower. She would never use that dress again. She put on the jeans and shirt she'd been wearing in Montana.

Charley was in the living room when she came out. He'd changed to a pair of slacks and sport coat, and his shirt was open at the neck.

He stood up. "Belle, I've got to go. I hate to leave you now, but maybe you need some time on your own. I've got to get to the office. Hell," he said disgustedly, "the clients are all jittery and the staff is jittery and so are the accountants and the lawyers. So am I. I've got to find out what I have to do."

"I'll be okay," she said. "And I do need a few hours. You're right. I guess I should call the lawyer, too. Should I stick with him now?"

"Sure. He's okay and you know him. The dimensions have changed a little, of course."

"Go on, Charley," Belle said. "I'll be waiting for you."

When he'd gone, she sat down on the terrace and closed her eyes, letting the friendly heat from the late October sun soak through. She was tired and she dozed.

Chapter Twenty-Five

At first shaken by the news of Cooper's death, Pamela Renfrew at once set about seeing what there was she could salvage from the debris of their business association. Cooper had sold a block of ten acres in the San Fernando Valley during the summer and that deal was still pending. A buyer's deposit had been paid and Pamela was still sitting on the check, which she had never banked, thinking Cooper might forget about it in the context of the larger sum.

She was at her desk in Beverly Hills looking over the Cooper files. It did not take her long to conclude that, no, there was nothing she could get out of this. The tax people, lawyers, accountants, would be nosing around like beagles and it was a violent tax offense to finagle figures or documents concerning a deceased.

Shit, she thought to herself, not a nickel. All she could hope for now was to be paid for her services, professional services that is, in this last transaction, and her expenses. These, she could certainly jack up, but even that could be tricky.

Shit, it was not that she needed money. It was more the principle of the thing. She had put up with Cooper, too. Yet, she thought disgustedly, Widow Belle, whom he hadn't banged since May or June, would get the residue. It was not fair, not at all fair.

Still . . . She had gone with Abdul to London, and then to Paris, and had been treated like one of the royal family: the hotel suite, the food, the vintage champagne he wished her to drink despite his own teetotalism, new clothes. And in the process, she had nailed down three or four new clients who, like Abdul, were vitally interested in moving money to the last place in the world of safe refuge, the United States of America. These men were not Arabs, since Abdul steered clear of his own countrymen doing business in the West. They were an Italian, also of minor royalty, two Spaniards, and a German. Pamela had not gotten it quite clear what the little group did in Europe. But it apparently had to do with oil, airlines, and hotels. They'd all had dinner together several times in both capitals: she and David, the Spaniards with two expensive call-girls, the Italian count, the German and his tough blonde wife who looked like she must have graduated from Hitler College.

But all were intrigued with the idea of buying a house with a pool and four or five wetbars in Beverly Hills, especially if the pedigree could show it had one been owned by one of the greater stars.

Christ, Pamela thought glumly, it was these people who were driving California real-estate prices so high a good American couldn't afford to buy a house anymore, unless he was a record producer, singer, Mafia godfather, or drug pusher.

The comforting thing was that David was taking care of her. Not with cash on the line, but in goods, services, travel, and a sense of international notoriety. But no green dollars. Pamela had to keep working to earn her walking-around money. She'd told him so, couching her argument in other logic than that of green money.

"David, you don't want me to get bored, do you? You're away so much. I'll travel with you or I'll be waiting for you when you come back. But I've got to keep active. Otherwise, I'll just get fat."

That was the best argument. Oh, no, he wouldn't want her to get fat.

In London, he'd bought her dresses and shoes, and in Paris couture clothes and expensive leather. But, although she tried her best, hinting and cajoling, he wouldn't buy her jewelry, negotiable gold, silver or stones. David did not like a lot of jewelry. He preferred her skin bare.

Shit, she thought, there was always some problem or other. But, all in all, she was not doing too badly. She'd told her real-estate agency that she'd be in and out, traveling a lot, and that she'd be devoting more and more time to international clients. That seemed to suit them well enough.

She was sitting at her desk, smoking a cigarette and contemplating her life when the call came from Charley Hopper.

"Pamela?" His voice was curt. "We're going over Cooper's affairs. Money affairs, that is. You'd better prepare a list of all his real-estate deals . . ."

"For you?" she demanded. She was not taking any shit from him either.

"No, for the government. They'll be getting to you—soon, I should think."

"Nothing happened in the last few months."

"They're talking about the last few years."

"Shit," she said angrily, then thought she'd best be more politic or they'd even do her out of her commissions. "How—how is Belle?"

"She's bearing up."

Yeah, Pamela thought, she should be.

Pamela drove her white Seville back to Abdul's house at six P.M. He had been out all afternoon, talking business at the Century Plaza Hotel, and had just returned.

"I've started looking for houses for your friends," she told him warmly. "See how I serve you? Do you think they're really serious?"

"Of course," David said cleverly. "Every time the dollar drops on the foreign exchange market, they become more serious than before."

"Well, I guess we may as well try to keep some of the money here."

"You don't approve, my little white princess?"

"As long as I get my commission, I approve heart and soul."

Abdul laughed softly. He slipped out of his soft Italian shoes and then his suit, an expensively tailored silk job. He loosened his tie.

"Ah, Pamela, my white princess, you are so mercenary. Come, my dear, let us go in the pool for a moment, then make love under the olive trees."

"David, it's getting a little chilly out there for that," she muttered. She didn't like to be tagged a mercenary, any more than he would have liked her to call him a greasy little Arab. "Are you going to bring a loaf of bread and jug of wine?"

He laughed uproariously. It had tickled him when she'd first read him Omar Khayyam.

Pamela began her strip, doing it the way he loved best. She took off her shoes, then sat down to remove her panty-hose, showing him the white of her legs, her thighs, a subliminal glimpse of her thick bush. Christ! Then she squirmed out of her dress. Yes, she was getting fat. Finally, she came close to him so he could loose her breasts and press his face in her cleavage. She felt the pressure of him against her legs.

"David," she said luxuriously, "you know, a girl in this country has got to take care of herself. It's not like I live in a harem."

His shoulders shook again with merriment. She put her arms around him to quiet him and felt his juice running down her leg. She moved him back toward the bed, thinking she would somehow avoid going outside and sticking dried leaves in her ass.

"Ah, my great bundle of flesh," he was muttering, "you would not survive the harem. My wives are for children; you are for relaxation."

"Here, David, let me see. Yes . . ."

She had him again.

Pat Hyman still could not believe it about Marcia King and Daisy, even after Daisy had called her from Hawaii. The story, according to Daisy, was that Marcia intended to move her decorating business to the islands and Daisy was to be her assistant. Pat laughed to herself. It just showed how little you really knew about people.

She and George had been at the Cooper memorial service. George had decided that going was the intelligent thing to do for business reasons and to underline the fact that, of course, the Hymans were well enough placed to have been great pals of the advertising mogul and his wife, Belle, not that it mattered now.

After George went back to the studio, Pat got out her little Fiat and drove into Beverly Hills. It was time for her weekly session with Boris the Magnificent. She parked up the street from the Swiss Cafe, had a drink there, and then, toward six, strolled the few blocks to Boris' exercise place.

He was waiting at the door, almost eagerly, she judged appreciatively. Boris seemed to like her and he appeared to enjoy making love to her as much as she liked having it.

Boris slammed and locked the door. She followed him to the exercise room, where it had become their practice to wrestle on the padded floor, she resisting, then giving in to his muscles. Boris was wearing a baggy sweat suit. With a smile, he slipped out of it. He was already erect and, she thought fearfully, enormous. Staring at it, she took off her clothes and faced him.

"What will we practice today?" she asked with forced gaiety.

"Today," Boris said, "we will do push-ups and push-ins." His eyes were darting at her. He even tweaked his mustache, not shy at all about his stand. "Come, Mrs. Hyman, let me show you."

"Why don't you call me Pat? Always Mrs. Hyman."

"It is not good to become too familiar with clients, Mrs. Hyman."

Boris lifted her—he could have done so with one arm—and pressed her against his chest. Between her legs, she felt his projection angling up at her, wet with anticipatory excretion. He slipped easily inside and she let out a yell as he penetrated fully. She wrapped her legs around his waist, letting herself fall backward on his hands. He marched her around the room, like booty captured in a foreign war, then began to jog in place, every movement of his legs plunging him more joltingly into her.

"Christ," she moaned, "put me down. Gently, please."

He dropped to his knees on the mat and eased her backward so that her legs slid up on his shoulders. In this posture, he filled her, worked at her vigorously until she came, shaking with delight.

"Jesus," she sighed.

"More?"

"Just jiggle around in there for a minute or two. Take it easy on me."

"Close your eyes," Boris commanded, "and think of the ocean surf pounding on the shore."

"Yes . . . yes . . ."

Pat concentrated on his revived stroking, for he had not come yet. Then he did, with a sharp intake of breath, but went on nevertheless, willing himself to continue, taking no backtalk from his body. Oozing with his liquid, Pat thought of the sea, the pier at Malibu, its supporting piles shot in the water and anchored in the deep sand. There was a buzzing in her ears and numbness crept over her as her body collected the wherewithal for another straining orgasm. She was panting, so engrossed in the mental image of their coupling that when the bright light exploded outside her eyelids she thought at first it was part of the experience.

But almost instantly, she realized a picture had been taken.

She opened her eyes. Ten feet away, crouched on the mat, there was another man, barefooted and with a mustache that might have been the twin of Boris'. He was holding a Polaroid camera in his hands, and he began to laugh.

"Son of a bitch," she snarled.

At that, Boris pulled out of her and hopped to his feet. "I would like you to meet my friend Samuel."

She lay there, still breathing hard, now with anger as well as interrupted desire.

"Clever son of a bitch, aren't you?"

"Mrs. Hyman, please, it is nothing. I merely like to keep pictures of my satisfied clients. You have heard it said a satisfied client is its own best recommendation?"

"Yes, I've heard that. Two faggots making their living . . ."

"No, no, Mrs. Hyman. Sex is sex. Would you like—I will take your picture with Samuel?"

"No, thanks," she said coldly. They had got her good and proper, she realized, and now she had to get out of it. She got up and indifferently dressed. Her pocketbook—Boris held it clutched in his arms. "Give me that," she said. "How much do I owe you?"

"Five hundred dollars, Mrs. Hyman," Boris said.

"What! You're nuts! Last week, it was fifty."

"But today, it is $500, Mrs. Hyman. All my satisfied clients pay me $500 per week. But isn't it worth it? A massage, a fuck, and two showers once a week? I have high overhead here."

She understood. She would pay the $500 or the picture would become as famous around town as the Mona Lisa.

"I don't have the cash."

"A check will be all right. Your credit is good, Mrs. Hyman."

"Oh," she said wryly, "how nice."

She wrote a check for the $500 and made it out to Boris the Magnificent.

"I will see you next week, Mrs. Hyman, at the usual time? In the usual place—your pussy?"

"How could I turn you down, Boris? And Samuel?"

She thought it over fiercely on the way home. This was not to be suffered. Not from somebody named Boris the Magnificent. It was too much. Even the purest business deal turned to shit.

She called Morris Mauery at his Camino apartment. Luckily, he was still home, for he had gotten in the habit of taking Marjery Cannon out for early dinner most nights. Now, there was something else. That pushy little bitch had somehow, and Pat could never understand how, managed to insinuate herself into Mauery's life at almost the very moment of Madeleine's death. But who was going to say anything to Mauery?

And better Marjery than her. Pat wondered how she liked it. More than Marjery had bargained for, she shouldn't wonder.

"Morrie," Pat said very timidly, "I've got something to tell you, and maybe you can give me some advice. I get a massage once a week at a place called Boris the Magnificent here in Beverly Hills. I was in there this afternoon and Boris and another guy, his assistant, I gather, put the arm on me. I had to play along or they might have hurt me. I think . . . they have . . . a picture. What do you think I should do, Morrie?"

Mauery laughed thinly. "Pat, you should be more careful. Wait a minute. I'm thinking. I'm also a little out of breath. I just finished screwing Marjery Cannon."

Pat, to her delight, heard a muffled exclamation in the background.

Mauery muttered, "Can't go to the cops, I guess. I'll tell you what, dear. Don't think about it anymore. I'll take care of it. Will that be all right?"

"Gosh, Morrie," Pat said, "I'd be ever so grateful."

Marjery was very angry. How dare he? Christ, it would be spread all over town. It would be too much, even for Gregory. Gregory didn't object to her extracurricular activities as long as they were discreet and brought in a little financial dis-embarrassment, as he called it. But Jesus, what if the news were blown all over town? What then?

Mauery hung up and sat, his muscular back quivering with outrage.

"Those little bastards," he grunted, slamming his fist in his hand. "They can't get up to that, not with friends of mine!"

"Morrie, damn it," Marjery protested, "you can't say things like that to people I know."

"Shut up," he said, turning on her irritably. "What's the matter? I'm marrying you."

"You're what?"

"I said, dopey, that I'm marrying you. Jesus!" he stormed. "Get a divorce from that asshole Cannon—right away."

"Yes, Morrie," she said.

Marjery collapsed within herself, and sank down in the bed. She had not reckoned on this. She didn't know that she wanted to be married to a man like Mauery. Having a little fling, a good time, was one thing. But marriage? Mauery was scarcely what Marjery pictured as her Prince Charming. He was not old California. He was a Jew, and a ruffian. Besides that, he was cruel in bed. He drained her of life and spirit, shattered her conception of carefully laid plans. He frightened her.

Ignoring her, Mauery dialed a number he obviously knew by heart. It rang only once at the other end.

"Flynn?" Mauery barked. "I need some advice. There's a massage guy here locally that's acting up, pressuring a friend of mine. Yeah, blackmail, looks like. I'm at a loss, Flynn. But I thought you might know how to handle it. Don't go alone. He's got a pal. Yeah, it's a place called—Jesus!—Boris the Magnificent. Well, I guess he needs to be told very straight, yes, very straight, that we don't go for that kind of shit in our town. You can handle that, Flynn, can't you?"

Chuckling with satisfaction, Mauery turned to Marjery. He put a big, callused hand on her left breast and pinched the nipple.

"It's true, isn't it, Marjery? Beverly Hills is not the kind of place that puts up with rotten shit like that, is it?"

She shook her head worriedly, knowing she was a witness to some kind of hit order.

"You're hurting," she said.

"Sorry. Look, let me ask. I hope this is not an embarrassing question. But look, did you ever think of getting some silicone put under there?"

He flipped the bottom of her breast with his finger.

"I didn't know they were so bad," she said miserably.

He shook his head. "They ain't good, Marjery. Look, I like women with big knockers. Your ass is fine. But the knockers . . . What about it?"

"All right," she said.

"Good. Now start the divorce proceedings with Greg. I don't think he'll fight it, do you?"

Again, she shook her head. He didn't know how funny that was.

Mauery lay back against the pillows. "Jesus, you know, Marjery, there's always something needs to be done, taken care of. You know, Marjery?"

Bertha was wearing her sourest smile. It pulled her lips toward her aquiline nose and made her eyes stare at him mockingly. And, for all he knew, she was trying to be pleasant.

"Well?" she said.

Sheldon had told her he had something important to say. He was determined to go through with it. He had no choice.

"What I have to say is that I'm leaving you."

Bertha's mouth popped open. She was not ready for it, because they hadn't recently quarreled. Her eyes melted and took on that wounded-doe expression she always used so effectively when he, angered beyond endurance, turned on her.

"You can't mean that," she said.

"I do mean it, Bertha," Sheldon said. "I mean it."

"You've said it before," she pointed out sardonically.

She had already regained her composure, thinking she could ride this out, too.

"This time," Sheldon said, "it's a fact. I've been to my attorney and he's filing the papers. You'll find the terms to your advantage, I think."

Having said this so bluntly, he felt himself in control. There was nothing more that he had to say, or needed to say really.

Bertha began to cry. Bertha cried in a very unusual manner. Her eyes did not flicker. She merely stared at him, disbelievingly, and tears appeared from nowhere. Suddenly, her cheeks were wet.

Calmly, but still crying, she said, "Is that fair? After fifteen years?"

"I think it's fair enough."

He had decided he was not going to tell her about Camilla, the child, nothing. It was not necessary. It was none of her business.

"You don't love me anymore, that's it," Bertha said.

Hell, he thought desperately, what a thing to say. Of course, he didn't. If he did, he wouldn't be leaving.

"No, I guess not."

She was so self-centered it could not occur to her that he might love someone else.

"I don't love you," she said.

Ha, he thought, big news. He did not flinch. "All right . . ."

"You found out I have somebody else!" she cried.

"No, I didn't know that, Bertha. And, Bertha, I don't care."

"You bastard!" she yelled, her first sign of real reaction, the tears being something else. "I want the house."

"You get the house. I get the paintings, not all of them but the best of them. You get the furniture, except the things I have from my mother."

"Your mother! Who wants that junk?"

"Never mind," Sheldon said calmly. "You'll get a cash settlement, big enough that you won't need alimony. You can have the cars, except for the Rolls."

"What about my memberships?" Her face was red. But she wouldn't leave anything to chance.

"They'll be paid through the end of next year, including your Amazing Blue Ribbon." He knew her involvement in Mrs. Chandler's Music Center was the most precious of her social treasures.

"What about the Palm Springs house and the place at the beach?" she demanded.

"I want the beach. You can have Palm Springs," he said, knowing the list by heart.

"The apartment in New York?"

"If I'm not there, you can use it." He thought, what else? "The charge accounts. You take yours over the end of this year."

"How will I survive?" Bertha wailed.

Darkly, he said, "You'll survive. Get yourself a good accountant and don't let him steal from you and you'll survive very nicely. Don't forget you were surviving very nicely before you met me."

He was reminding her of the past and that always hurt her more than almost anything else he could mention.

Her face turned white and she began to shake with fury.

"Yes, I will survive," she screamed, so loudly she might have aroused the servants if they hadn't had their own splendid quarters on the other side of the garden. "I was something before I met you."

"Yes, I know you were, Bertha," Sheldon said quietly, but she knew what he was thinking.

"Sheldon," Bertha screamed again, "I was not a whore. I was a cashier at the Bunny Rabbit Ranch, not a whore. I was an executive."

"A madame."

"Not a madame, goddamn it," she shrieked furiously. "How dare you say that? You are an infamous lout. I've always said so."

"I know you have," he said. "You've reminded me of that over and over."

Her face was flushed, straining. She was trying to impress her identity on him.

Voice shaking, she said, "You resent me, Sheldon. And I know why—because I've found God. I'm born again. And you're not. You're nothing but a fucking heathen, Sheldon."

"Turtledove," Archy Finistere said, "we'll be moving to the Splendide in two weeks. At first, we'll have to make do with two rooms."

"Two rooms?" Lou said. "Archy, why don't we move to a good hotel?"

She laughed heartily and squeezed Archy's balls. She could not be angry with him now. Things were going so swimmingly for Lou Finistere. She was quite crazily in love with the new hotel. It was going to be magnificent, so modern, with none of the problems attached to the aging Camino. She had her mezzanine office, headquarters now for the December ball. She was going to be a power in her own right and on a salary of her own.

"Turtledove, you're a great lady," Archy sighed, "Won't it be exciting, our new life? A challenge, an adventure?"

Archy rolled heavily on his side and played with her rolling breasts. He suckled one, then the other, then again the first, his pointed beard causing her to giggle. She felt him, ever so slowly, pulling himself toward erection. This did not happen so often, but talk of the Splendide was curiously stimulating.

"Can't you just see the front entrance of the Splendide," Lou whispered, as if telling a story to a little child, "the portcullis gleaming with a thousand lights, the marble inlay around the doors, brass knobs burnished bright. God, Archy, visualize the lobby, thick with carpeting, wood shining, the little cubbyholes for all the keys."

"Ah . . . ah," Archy grunted, "beautiful . . . beautiful . . ."

Straining, Lou heaved him over and wrapped him in her legs, manipulating him into her.

"So wide and spacious," she murmured. "I'm talking about . . . the corridors. The polished lamps, the chandeliers, such a wide bank of humming elevators, the upper floors, the roof garden with a view of the whole Los Angeles basin."

She could hear his back creaking as he weaseled around inside her.

"And the ballroom," she continued, "the gleaming kitchens, the bars and sparkling crystal."

"Yes," he muttered, "and the shops on the lower level, the beautiful pool, the tennis courts. Ah, the wood-paneled closets."

"TV sets in every room, and the little refrigerators stocked with miniature bottles. Aaah . . ."

God, she thought, talk of the hotel was having the same effect on her as it did on Archy. She was conscious of rising fever. A flush spread across her chest and along her ribs to her thighs. She began to buck.

"Archy . . . God . . ." she moaned. "My elevator is leaving for the penthouse . . ."

Archy beat frantically against her, lifting and dropping his hips in supreme effort. Lou pulled his hairy chest against her breasts. She hugged him with her legs and slowly felt the void between her legs fill, then close as she climaxed. And Archy succumbed. That was the best way of describing his orgasm. His beard fell on her throat and he whispered, *"Mon Dieu."* He was wilted with sweat.

"Oh, Archy," she breathed. "That was . . . super."

And it occurred to her then, frighteningly, that she would be all right so long as Archy was. She had to keep him in good health and satisfied, at least for a couple more years, until she had dug herself securely into the Splendide.

Jurgen Ehrlich would be, for her, a formidable opponent, if opponent he became. She really had to pay more attention to Jurgen, talk to him, compliment him on his work and his appearance, as uncouth as he sometimes was, in short, to ingratiate herself with him. For, chances were, one day Jurgen would be offered the management of the Splendide.

"Archy . . . Archy," she said, "no sleeping here."

"Yes, turtledove." He pulled away, exhausted.

"Archy, don't go to sleep yet. I'm going to get your vitamins."

Jake Cox was alone, sitting upstairs and running Daisy's old movies. She had been a superstar of his silents, yes indeed, and now Jake almost wished he'd put in the necessary sound equipment to make them "talkies." It might have been a serious lapse on his part but still, he hadn't ever really wanted to eavesdrop. Voyeurism, he reminded himself, was by definition limited to sight and should not, ethically, include sound. He did not want to know anything about the late Mr. Cooper's business deals or family problems. Just watching Cooper and Daisy perform was treat enough. His imagination supplied the dialogue.

Jake was sorry now he'd sent that one film of Cooper to the lawyer. His pride of product had caused him to get carried away, and now, with Cooper dead, the film probably wouldn't be seen by anybody else. If he'd had the nerve, he would have called the man and asked for it back.

At the moment, Jake was running and re-running the one starring Daisy and her chum Marcia King. As disgusting as it was to watch over and over, he was looking for some clue. What Jake had been thinking all day was that Marcia was somehow some kind of transvestite. He simply could not accept any evidence that Daisy was kinky, for if it turned out she really was, then Jake would have been completely deceived and he did not like being deceived. He ran the film through again, but there was nothing he could see that brought him any closer to the truth—or that could convince him that Marcia was not really a man. Bolstered by the rationalization, Jake helped himself to more brandy and resumed his place on the couch.

Daisy and Bill Murray, starring Daisy. Produced by Jake Cox. Director of Photography, Jake Cox.

Murray was in side view, panting, as he tried to satisfy the star.

Jake's left hand stole across the plush cushions toward himself. Ah, he asked, who was this quiet stranger infiltrating the defenses? Creep . . . creep . . . and grab.

Daisy and Marcia, far from the maddening crowd, were dining on the beach at the Royal Hawaiian Hotel—not exactly on the beach but on a terrace laid about twenty yards from the lapping water of the lagoon-still ocean.

Both were wearing long white, loose-fitting muumuus. Or were they tutus, Daisy wondered. Marcia's earlobes were afire with rubies, and her mouth was painted bright red, the color of the sweet berries from the interior of the island. Daisy, not to her great pleasure, had had her blonde hair shorn down to short curls like Marcia's. Marcia had insisted it would be cute if they were look-alikes: they might have been twins of a German father and Spanish mother.

They were eating mahi-mahi, the renowned Hawaiian fish, and drinking with it a bottle of imported wine.

"Are you happy, sweeties?" Marcia asked her, fixing her eyes fondly on Daisy.

"Ever so," Daisy replied. "I feel so clean."

They hadn't heard about Martin Cooper until that morning, then discussed the tragedy only briefly—how terrible and all that, poor Belle . . . baloney . . . and what would she do? Then Daisy had forgotten about him until tonight.

Cooper had not been a bad man. The few encounters Daisy had had with him had not been all unpleasant, until that last day. Daisy felt now that she'd known he was in for it, doomed somehow. Too bad. But not worth sweating about.

She had been reminded of Cooper again by a man she'd seen at the bar, a tall man with blonde hair, bold eyes, thick lips, and an athlete's ease of body.

Sometimes, and it seemed more often these days, Tom Glenn felt as though he'd reached the end.

It was eight P.M. and he'd just finished the last of his appointments. He was sitting, finally alone, in his office, wondering what it was he had to do next. Surely, there was something he hadn't finished; there always was.

He moved from his desk to a soft leather couch on the side of the room and put his head back against the wall to rest a moment. Here, in this position, he sat his most nervous patients, he taking a seat on the other side of the coffee table strewn with magazines, medical journals, and lighter reading.

The patient now, he began to ask himself the salient questions.

Number one, why had he ever become a doctor in the first place? Because it had seemed the right thing to do. He could have been a priest or a minister, for as a youth he had felt a certain mission, a desire to serve, to help. But why in Beverly Hills, of all unlikely places to set up a practice? Because he had drifted there after getting out of the service and, even then, this rich enclave within the bounds of Los Angeles had seemed like a lucrative spot to do his work. And lucrative it had been. Glenn was a rich man now—not because he had gouged his patients, for he had not, but because he had been so well advised on good investments and because, as a bachelor, he had worked most of the time and scarcely ever went on vacation and, thus, had had plenty of money available for buying land and securities.

So now, he told himself, he had made it. He had arrived. He was sought after by the rich and the mighty of the movie world, the music world, the business world, and the world of inherited California money.

Glenn removed his glasses, rendering himself so nearsighted that he could barely see where the soundproof ceiling began. He laughed to himself. He had everything, and at the same time not very much. His only joy, only comfort really, was the friends he'd made. Madeleine Mauery had been one of these and she had tried to take advantage of him. She had begged him to help her die. And that was something he could not do. However, that last afternoon: the vitamin injection. Had it been too much for her? She had seemed all right. But he had been a fool. He had not listened to her heart before applying it. And, even more the fool he, he'd included within the vitamin dosage a miniscule amount of speed, an amphetamine, merely to improve her spirits, to lift her from deep depression. Had that done the deed after all? It was not beyond the bounds of medical ethics for Glenn to have given her this small dose of the drug. Any physician would have prescribed an antidepressant.

Ha! And now, so it seemed, Mauery was bringing a malpractice suit against him and would try to take away his money. Christ, Glenn told himself, that was excessive. Nothing untoward would be discovered. If anything, he should have been congratulated for keeping an old lady alive past her reasonable expectancy, given the fact she had a very bad heart.

No, this was Mauery's way of saying he controlled the world, that even death could not occur without his permission.

Sometimes, Glenn wondered how he had the strength to bear it all.

And Sally Markman. This was the one who hurt him most. Sally had been a patient, and friend, for years and now she was dying. There was no question of that. He doubted whether she would survive even until her party. After the month of soaring hope, while she was in a brief period of remission, she was again in decline. Her only hope was her own courage, for cancer, people agreed now, was a matter of the spirit. A moment of depression was enough to bring the monster out of dormancy. Once set in motion, like an iron-clad juggernaut, it took a gigantic effort of the will and spirit to stop it. That was the problem.

Glenn had easily come to the conclusion that the recipient of the research award had to be someone doing landmark work on the base cause of the disease, in susceptibility, not merely in who the victims were, but in an immunization process, that could be introduced early on, before a likely victim had even a first symptom.

Glenn had found such a scientist: Dr. Vincent Richardson, a man who worked with a team of specialists at a Chicago hospital. But he hadn't attempted to contact Richardson, not yet. First, he would have to go before the ball committee. He had to get in touch with Belle Cooper.

Ah, Belle, one of the original survivors. A soft lady, but tough, too. She had had a trying time, and this he knew from Sally. First, she had had to live with Cooper and then she had to deal with the shock of his death. Fortunately, Glenn had not known Cooper well, but what he did know of the man, his death—the manner of his death—was not surprising.

Glenn wondered why Cooper had done it.

Glenn himself had thought often enough of suicide. He had contemplated the act, debated with himself about it. At times, it seemed the painless way, if the coward's way, out of the unreasonable demands of life, a simple reply to life's essential meaninglessness.

God knows, the means were available to him right here in the office. He had only to unlock a cabinet, draw a glass of water, and say goodbye. There was no chance of slip-up.

But it was impossible. Too many people were dependent on him. What would they say to this highest form of selfishness, of disloyalty? Glenn smiled anxiously to himself. He was stuck, trapped. Cooper? Evidently, his had been a different case. Nobody had been dependent on him. Perhaps that was the unkindest rub of all.

He rose from the couch, put his glasses back on, and removed his jacket. Perhaps he would go to the Polo Lounge for a drink. It was a lively place and could lift his mood. And who knows? He might meet the girl of his dreams—he had not met her yet. Perhaps he should get married. Work was his sublimation, but he was at the point where he'd had just about enough of that.

He thought of Maude Mannon. He was younger than she was, although not by that much. He liked her hearty, down-to-earth manner, her slightly raucous view of life and its outrageousness. Next time she was in town, he'd ask her out to dinner. If that, by some strange quirk, proved to be comfortable, well then . . . He could never hope to match Maude's resources, but he was financially secure enough to avoid being called a fortune-hunter.

Yes, he thought more cheerfully, off to the Polo Lounge. But first . . .

Glenn rolled up the left sleeve of his shirt and went into the examination room. He took a sterile hypodermic out of the cabinet and a vial of his vitamin mix from the refrigerator. Sighing a little, for he did not like giving himself shots, he pushed the needle into his arm and compressed the plunger. There! In a minute, he would begin to feel physically better, too, as Madeleine Mauery had. This would keep him going, keep him bright-eyed and optimistic, through the evening. Then, a small downer before bed, and a little pepper-upper in the morning.

Doctor, he smiled to himself, treat thyself.

Chapter Twenty-Six

Belle dressed very deliberately in a nut-brown Chanel suit and, her one concession to widowhood, a black silk blouse. Then she drove her red Jaguar down the hill again, the morning after the memorial service for Martin Cooper.

As she approached the Splendide, she could see, even from a distance, that the new hotel was making great strides toward completion. Already, a hotel flag had been hoisted on the roof; it was dark green and sand-colored.

Belle parked on Little Santa Monica, outside the construction site, then inquired at the gate how one found the mezzanine. A foreman directed her through what seemed like a staging area for an invasion, jammed with trucks and crates.

"You'll have to go around back, miss. Through the ballroom, up the steps to the lobby, then another flight to the mezzanine offices."

Miss? That was a comforting salutation.

The ballroom was finished now, aside from carpeting. The huge chandeliers had been hung, and the space seemed less cavernous. Up in the lobby, an enormously long, polished front desk had been installed across one wall and shelves and cabinets and pigeon holes for mail and keys. She stopped to look. Men were in the offices behind the front desk, working on telephone cables. The paint was beautiful, she thought, subtle, sandy brown on the walls, deeper brown on the wood trims and fittings. And the smell was pleasant, of new wood, paint, and varnish.

Ringing telephones and voices directed her to Lou Finistere's office.

Inside, Lou was on the telephone, talking crisply to the manager of a local hotel. Sharon Peters sat at another desk, the latter covered with long typewritten lists of names and addresses. Camilla Young was standing with Pat Hyman at the window; they were watching the activity down below.

Belle crossed the room and bent conspiratorially to kiss Sharon on the cheek. "Congratulations, you rascal," she whispered.

Sharon grinned and put her finger to her lips. Then her face became very serious. "Belle, I'm sorry."

Pat and Camilla turned.

"Belle . . . yesterday," Pat stammered. "Didn't want to bother you. George and I . . . "

Belle held up her finger. "Thanks. Don't say anything. It's past."

Lou hung up her telephone and stood up. "Belle . . ."

Again, Belle shook her head. She did not want to get into the whole condolence bit. She was amazed for a second how cold she felt about it and, admittedly, how relieved she was it was past. There was no way she could assume a pretense of grief.

"Well, girls, how's it going?" she asked.

They were probably as relieved as she was not to talk about Cooper. But there was something else bothering them.

"Where's Sally?" Lou asked. "We haven't seen her for a week. Is she sick or something?"

Uneasily, Belle replied, "No, no. I went out to see her yesterday. She and Bernard have both had that blasted flu bug. She should be back in a few days."

"Did she tell you that intolerable bitch Marjery Cannon tried to screw up our room reservations?" Lou demanded.

Belle nodded. "Not extremely helpful, was it?"

"Not the way it's going," Sharon said proudly, laying her hand on her guest lists.

"Any RSVP's yet?"

Excitedly, Sharon said, "You wouldn't believe it. The invitations have only been out a week or ten days but we've already heard back on the telephone. We've got something like 200 acceptances."

"That is very good, isn't it?" Belle asked.

"Good? It's great. Fantastic," Sharon cried. "Especially since we haven't actually promised anything yet in the way of First Ladies, governors, and so on. Word gets around, thanks to Suzy and Madame Westmoreland."

"What about Rolly?" Belle asked Pat Hyman. "Sally is worried about Rolly."

Pat made a thumbs-up gesture. "He's got it pretty firm: the main event, our singers, as expressly requested by one of the First Ladies. That's his gimmick. Each First Lady, theoretically, gets to pick out her favorite entertainer. So, plus the popular stuff, we'll have a classical act: Rolly's dickering with Menuhin and Horowitz. A dancer: maybe Baryshnikov. The operatic: Beverly Sills, or that caliber, if we could pull her out of retirement. A tasteful comedian. Rolly says if he'd had more time we could have made it a TV special straight from the Hotel Splendide in Beverly Hills. Next year, that's what he'll shoot for: to get Sinatra or Hope to put on a special direct from the benefit party. How's that? I forgot. Orchestra: Harry James and company."

Belle sighed. "My God, if that won't pull people, what will? But we'll have to pay stars like that."

"Sure," Pat said, "and they turn around and pass the check back to Norman's foundation. At least, we hope they will."

Belle sat down on the corner of one of the desks. She was wondering how Sam Leonard would feel about turning the event into a TV special for airing under the aegis of Cosmos Cosmetics. It could be hellish good publicity, she thought.

"Harry James . . . I used to dance to him in college. Well." She shook herself away from reiminiscence. "I guess by now you know I'm working for Sam Leonard: Cosmos Cosmetics. Sally must have told you that Sam has offered us a lot of help."

Pat said, "Darling, I'm green with envy. A line of makeup called Belle."

Belle nodded, feeling embarrassed. "Lucia Montonya will set up a makeup clinic here in the hotel the ball weekend. All on the house of Cosmos." She paused, then anxiously added, "I hope you are all going to agree it's okay. In return for his help, Sam wants to introduce the line at the ball. It'll be tasteful, I assure you."

Sharon stepped forward, putting her hands on Belle's shoulders.

"Listen, Belle, not only is it okay, it's perfect. We need

cosmetics, and why not a line of cosmetics named Belle?"

"I don't want you girls to think I'm crassly commercial."

"Bull," Lou exclaimed, "when do I get to try it out?"

"Soon as I get some samples in. So, by rights, Sam should pick up the tab for the orchestra and some other incidentals. Sally told you he's going to establish a grant of his own to pay the research prize every year?"

"Listen," Lou said, even more emphatically, "if Sam Leonard is ready to spring with that much loot, it's all his."

Lou seemed to express their complete approval. Camilla shyly interrupted to say she'd spoken to Sol Laykin of Laykin et Cie. Sol was designing a silver piece for the women guests, along the lines of Sally's December Group pin, and tie clips for the men. "And Marcia Lehr is working up a ritzy gift, which, as it happens," Camilla said, "I'm chipping in to the cause."

"Christ," Pat said, "there won't be any room for eats on the tables."

"It'll be all right," Belle said. "We can't put all the stuff on the tables ahead of time. That creates too much commotion. We don't want people stealing cosmetics from each other and fighting over it. And we definitely don't want to put silver things out before anybody is in the room. Things like that have a habit of disappearing. What we'd better do is have the cosmetics and the silver pins at the door when people leave. We'll have an extra stub on the ticket: they trade the stub for the party gifts. We're planning to present the Belle cosmetics in very spiffy black satin totebags."

"Very smart," Pat said wisely. "I can't tell you how many times my party favors have been swiped by my friends when I got up to dance."

Lou fidgeted, trying to add something else. "We're getting locals to host brunches Sunday. We've got about twenty houses lined up."

"Now," Belle said, "*that* is good. It'll round out the weekend."

"Got to keep them happy," Lou said cheerfully, "so they'll come back next year."

"Another thing this genius has arranged," Sharon said, "is for Archy to host a cocktail party at the Camino Friday night. Then there's a bunch of dinners lined up."

"Most of them will have a lot of friends here," Belle agreed.

"Saturday," Pat Hyman said, "they'll want to go shopping. And the guys will go out to play golf, or tennis. So, everybody should be bright-eyed and bushy-tailed for Saturday night."

"Uh-huh, good, good," Belle said. "So, you don't think we have to get together with Rolly?" she asked Pat.

"We should take him out to lunch a couple of times—to stroke him. I think in early November, then again around Thanksgiving. Rolly does love to be stroked."

"Okay," Belle said. "Now, as for me. I've got to go to New York for the April in Paris Ball. But that's for only a couple of days. Then I'll be back here until party time. You can put me to work any way you like."

Sharon said, "I guess I'll be going to New York with you. Maude's going to be there. We want to talk up the affair a little. Norman is arranging a couple of luncheons and so on."

"Well, that's terrific," Belle said. "And I'll arrange for you all to meet Sam Leonard."

"While the rest of us are slaving away, eh?" Lou said, smiling.

Lou had quite obviously turned into the work-horse of the group. She had lost her initial shyness before the Los Angeles crowd and had taken very naturally to the organizing job.

"You can work us to death when we get back, dear," Belle said.

"One other thing occurred to us," Camilla said. "Fashion. You've nailed down the makeup aspect. I've talked to some of the local designers, like Galanos, Jean Louis and La Vetta, and they like the idea of setting up boutiques here in the hotel over the weekend. Best is, they promise they'll contribute to the cause anything they make above their cost."

"That ain't so bad either," Belle said.

Pat Hyman laughed gleefully. "Who says women couldn't run a war better than men? But, my darling, the *pièce de résistance* of our report: I guess you don't know that Bernard Markman has put together a committee of the big industrialists and corporations: whatever we raise, they'll match. How about that?"

Belle whistled. "My God. He didn't say anything."

"Sally doesn't know. He swore us to secrecy."

She understood. She understood completely. And did

not say anything else. A knot of pain rose in her chest. Her eyes misted, Belle took a minute to look around the office. Someone had had the invitation blown up to poster size and it was taped to one wall. Bits of polite graffiti had been scrawled elsewhere. Finally, she cleared her throat. "What about some lunch? I have in mind taking you all to the Bistro Garden."

"Sorry I can't make it," Camilla said.

For the next two hours, Belle heard more of the startling tale of Daisy Cox and Marcia King. Pat Hyman next dropped the news that Bertha and Sheldon were splitting.

"You know the background, of course," Pat said. "No? I'm amazed. It seems Sheldon is leaving Bertha for Camilla, our young helper."

Again, Belle was astonished. But there was no reason to be surprised. Mergings or abrupt partings were quite the norm for this part of the world. What caused eyebrows to raise was a marriage that lasted five or ten years.

"Well," she said, "what can I say? Camilla seems in good spirits."

Lou ventured, "Would you say she . . . perhaps . . . is beginning to get a little chubby around the waist?"

"My God, I didn't notice. Do you suppose . . ."

Pat nodded wisely. "Yes, I do suppose."

Belle bunched her lips. "Well, good for her. That'll make Sheldon happy. Probably exactly what he needs."

Sharon nodded vigorously. "Poor guy. Imagine living with that old sour-puss."

"Now, Sharon," Pat chided her sardonically. "Charity, charity. Seems to me at one time the little birdies were saying . . ."

Sharon sat back, flustered. "Never mind about the goddamn little birdies."

Pat laughed. "Okay, skip it. Our other problem area seems to be Priscilla and Bill Murray. I don't think Priscilla is going to be much help. She's having trouble with Billyboy and she's in a hell of a mood."

"Okay, okay, don't overwhelm me," Belle said. "What about Bertha?"

"She's bearing up, but it's obviously kind of tough when she and Camilla are in the same room," Lou said. "Although, actually, I'm not so sure she knows it's Camilla.

What we've done to avoid confrontation is to put Bertha in charge of the care and feeding of First Ladies."

"Good," Belle said, "and what about all the governors?"

"They," Sharon said efficiently, "are in the hands of Carlotta Westmoreland. She's told us not to worry about it. I think she intends to push her editorial causes on them all day Saturday. She says they don't know it yet, but actually they're coming to L.A. for a political seminar."

Belle chuckled. "Carlotta is very hot right now about water resources and nuclear power."

"For or against?" Pat asked.

"For water conservation programs up and down the western states, against any more nuclear plants until they're better designed."

"And also," Sharon said sarcastically, "for solar energy, tidal electric plants, and perpetual motion."

"Now, Sharon," Belle said, "everybody's got their causes."

They talked for a while about numbers. They had no doubt they'd get their 1,000 couples, but, to be on the safe side, Belle suggested they slip a couple of items to the press to the effect that so many acceptances were being received that they anticipated being sold out in another couple of weeks.

"Well," Sharon observed, "that probably is true, you know. It's going to snowball. But the ballroom can comfortably hold a couple of hundred more if it goes that well."

"No tent?" Belle said. "How disappointing."

Pat laughed. "You must be a frustrated circus performer. Just as well, Belle. We'd need a special dispensation from the fire department for a tent. Right, Lou?"

"Yeah, I gather so. Anyway, it'll be a lot easier to manage without a tent."

"But, my dears," Belle said, "where are we going to serve before-dinner drinks? We absolutely cannot let them into the ballroom before the proper moment. Can we get 2,000 people into the lobby and the foyer of the ballroom? The other big rooms downstairs might not be ready. Yes, we might need a tent for an hour of drinks. Can the fire department object to that?"

Glumly, Lou said, "I understand they can get very sticky. I hope to hell it's a warm night."

"In the beginning of December?" Belle said. "It might be raining."

"Jesus," Pat said, and they silently considered the matter.

"I guess we'd have to pay for four or five fire marshals to watch the thing," Lou said.

"That would be out of Sam Leonard's budget," Belle said.

"The thing is," Pat interjected, "these people are going to be expecting the works—the whole enchilada, as we say—and they should, at $2,500 a couple."

"Yeah," Sharon said happily, "we should net nearly five million if you count in the matching donation."

Belle whistled. "Beautiful. But now, has anybody had the brilliant idea of opening a bank account for all that money?"

"Sally did it last time she was in town," Sharon said. "You're in charge of it: in trust for and all that."

"All right," Bell said. So Sally was delegating that job, too.

"How far do you think we can get with five million?" Pat Hyman asked.

"At least to Hawaii," Lou said dryly.

Belle smiled. "For five million, we ought to be able to do considerable building."

"And labs?" Pat asked. "Equipment? That stuff is horribly expensive now."

"I know, I know," Belle said. "It's discouraging, isn't it? Do you think with five million in the bank we could borrow another ten?"

"What's obvious," Sharon said, "is that we need a banker in with us."

"What about Doug Donohue?" Belle suggested. "How's he getting along? He might be the very man. Has Doris offered any help?"

"Not yet." Pat shook her head. "Too preoccupied. But Doug is coming along and Sally opened the account in his bank. This might give him something to do that's not backbreaking."

"I'll talk to him," Belle offered. "Sometimes I think we get too ambitious. That's all Sally's fault. But there's another thing I've got on my mind, and that's seating arrangements. You remember reading about last year's

April in Paris Ball? Apparently there was practically war over the seats, all the little ladies sneaking in and rearranging placecards so they'd be with their pals, throwing table numbers on the floor? It was complete chaos. We'll see how it goes in New York this year," she said to Sharon. "But that's one thing we're going to have to be very, very careful about, particularly with all these First Ladies and governors here. Security is bound to be tight as hell, so we can't possibly allow any shenanigans with placecards. The doors have got to be closed tight 'til they march in."

"Well, that's certainly agreed," Lou said, tight-lipped. "We'll have guards on the doors."

"By the way," Sharon said, "speaking of New York. Brownie McLean is coming. Norman talked to her. And she's bringing a load of her Palm Beach friends."

"Naturally," Pat said. "Would she miss this?"

"Where are our First Ladies going to stay?" Belle wanted to know."

"At the Camino," Lou replied. "We thought that'd be best, also for security purposes. The suites are reserved. The governors are going into the Beverly Hills Hotel, which we thought they'd enjoy." She winked. "It's a little more swinging there."

"And they're paying their own way," Sharon said. "The only room tabs we're picking up are the First Ladies'."

"And Sam Leonard pays that," Belle said, winking back at Lou.

At the Splendide after lunch, Belle searched for Archy Finistere and finally found him alone in the new kitchens. Archy did not hear her come in behind him. He was standing in the middle of the kitchen, hands clasped behind his back, beard jutting forward, rapturously gazing at the elaborate layout of bright new stainless steel: stoves, ovens, grills, food warmers, yards of cabinet space already stacked with china.

Belle cleared her throat.

"Turtledove?" he murmured. He turned and saw her, a surprised and embarrassed look crossing his face. "Well, Belle. Hello. Oh, ah, Belle, we were sorry about Martin."

Belle patted his arm. "Not to worry, Archy. I wanted to talk to you about the menu for the party."

"Oh, yes . . . yes," he said absently. "We should get together with young Jurgen Ehrlich on that. Isn't this kitchen a beauty?" He led her around for a moment, opening and slamming refrigerators, walking her into the large freezer, hammering his fist on heavy wooden cutting boards. "It's super-modern and absolutely efficient," he said proudly. "They consulted me closely on the design."

"I'm impressed," Belle said quietly. "But the whole hotel looks beautiful."

"No, it's still but a shell," Archy corrected her. "Now it needs guests. Then you'll see, it'll come to life, take on a life of its own with blood running through its veins and arteries."

His face glowed.

"What's the timetable?" she asked.

He knew it by heart. He stared up at the ceiling, pursing his lips and drumming the tips of his fingers together. "I know where we're at from moment to moment. We're laying the carpeting on the top floors. When that's done, the furniture goes up, then we hang the drapes. We work our way down. The carpeting in the ballroom and lobby goes in just as soon as they're finished getting everything upstairs. The restaurants we're letting go until after the party. You'll see, we'll be in very good shape." He stopped to recollect something, then chuckled. "It looked for a minute like we were going to have some union trouble. I had a very nasty phone call from Morrie Mauery. Don't let this go any further, Belle. I'm telling you because you're a friend of Norman's. I called Norman in New York, and that's the last I ever heard about it. I guess Norman has a certain amount of influence."

She nodded, chuckling, too. This was true. Norman knew people in high and low places. She had never questioned him about his contacts, but he had them everywhere. With a matter like union problems, Norman would have known exactly where to go.

"Archy," she said, "tell me something. We're going to be using something like 200 tables. Where do you keep all that stuff?"

He laughed fondly. Obviously, this was the sort of academic question he loved to answer. "My dear, there's tons of space under this building. The parking garage holds 500 cars, but there are also dozens of storerooms, not to mention an extensive wine cellar. Then staff rooms, locker rooms, showers. It's a city in its own right, Belle. You're talking about a hotel with nearly 900 rooms."

"Phenomenal," she said, flattering him, "the things I don't know anything about."

"But why should you?" Archy cried.

She nodded. "Well, we can say it again, Archy. The Splendide is going to be splendid."

Archy barked with husky laughter. He put his arm across her shoulders. "Yes . . . yes. And there's one thing I'd like to say to you, Belle. My youthful wife is having the time of her life. I'm very grateful you've made her part of all this."

"We couldn't do without her, Archy," Belle said.

Before leaving again for New York, Belle got together with Doug Donohue. She had never known him very well and remembered him as a chubby, bustling man. He was much thinner now and he moved carefully. She explained that the committee was expecting a continuous flow of money from ticket sales and asked him how they should handle it. Donohue advised her that the essential thing was to get the in-coming money into the bank on a daily basis because interest mounted up every twenty-four hours.

"You see, Belle," Donohue said. "If you don't break ground 'til February or March, you'll already have three months interest built up. On your five million or whatever at seven or eight percent, you'd be making yourself another $100,000 or so in the interim. That'll pay for a lot of bricks."

Donohue said it was startling to him that they could plan on raising so much in the first go-around. And then to repeat it every year? Outstanding!

"But we'll not raise that much every year," Belle said.

"Still, if you can take in a million a year, you could service a big building loan, something like this. Well, you'd deserve all the tax breaks you can get."

She hesitated. "But isn't that an awful commitment to carry, Doug?"

"Not if you're sure of the thing. I don't think a million a year is an awful lot."

"Well . . ." She obviously couldn't speak for the group. This was a matter of high committee decision. "I think you'll be talking to Norman Kaplan. He'll be president of the December Foundation supporting the center."

"Norman would understand all the financial intricacies," Donohue said.

"Ah, you do know him."

"I know of him," Donohue said. "We'll be happy to do business with you people, Belle. And, God permitting, Doris and I will be at the party."

Belle flew to New York with Sharon and Frank. Charley couldn't get away, not even for the weekend. Due to Cooper's death, things at C.A.A. were still in fragile shape and Charley had to be on the spot at all times. Belle thought about that on the airplane. There would be many separations from now on. She would be traveling extensively and it was obvious she couldn't expect Charley to drop everything to be with her. And, likewise, she knew Charley would not expect her to do any less for Leonard than she had contracted for.

Kaplan met them at the airport. They would be staying at his East Side apartment.

"I asked Maude, too," he said in the car, "but that funny lady is staying up on Fifth Avenue somewhere."

Kaplan had a surprise for her. Susan was waiting at the apartment. She would be going with them to the April in Paris Ball. Norman had arranged a date for her, with the son of a banker friend. Belle had not seen her since before the Cooper unpleasantness. Already, she thought, astonished, the girl looked older, more . . . what? Sophisticated? Belle did not like to think so and she hated the idea of it. She felt the warmth and softness of Susan's body through a collegiately proper wool challis dress.

"Are you all right?" Susan demanded.

"All right? I'm fine. I must say, you're looking very eastern. You know Sharon; this is Frank Woodley."

"Frank Woodley, the jock," Kaplan butted in cheerfully.

Kaplan had met Frank on his last visit to Beverly Hills. Although so dissimilar in look and character, the two got along well. Perhaps it was their view of the world that drew them together. Woodley's humor was broad and biting, Kaplan's pixieish and bitchy, but they thought alike.

Frank shuffled his feet and smiled. He took Susan's hand and held it. "A daughter like this? You didn't tell me, Belle."

Sharon shoved him. "You're taken, buster."

"Well, sit down," Kaplan said. "I'm going to arrange drinks."

He pranced out of the room and, in a moment, returned,

followed by his butler Thomas. Thomas was carrying a bucket of champagne and a tray of glasses.

"Belle," Kaplan said, "I've got some German beer for you."

"No, no," she said. "Charley says I've got to be more sophisticated. I'll have the champagne."

"Oh, my, oh, my," Kaplan said sardonically. "Sophisticated now?"

"Mother," Susan said, "that's alarming. I'm worried."

"Shush." She saw Susan was dying to ask her about Charley.

"Well," Kaplan said, when they were all sitting with their glasses, "tell me, how's Sally?"

She'd known the question would come. Was there any point in concealing the truth? No. She shook her head.

"Not well. I was out to see her a couple of days ago."

Susan did not move. She sat, rigidly, listening to her mother.

Kaplan's face fell. "No? When she was here, she seemed marvelous."

Slowly, Belle said, "She's in a wheelchair now, Norman."

"No!" Sharon gasped. "What the hell! I didn't know that."

Belle nodded. "I'm sorry. We've kept it a secret. Sally is very ill."

"God," Sharon sighed. "I suspected something was wrong when she stopped coming to town."

"I knew all along," Susan said softly. "She never said anything—and you didn't—but I knew this summer."

"I'm sorry, Susan," Belle said. "It's . . . the way she is. She doesn't want anybody feeling sorry for her."

"Good God," Kaplan said mournfully. "So, what do you think, Belle?"

"I don't know what to think. She looked terrible, weak. But, there's one thing. The spirit is still there."

"Spirit is half the battle," Frank said, "if you're talking about what I think you're talking about."

"Yes, that is what we're talking about," Belle said.

"Damn," Sharon muttered, "of all the rotten luck."

"But," Kaplan cautioned them, "we're still keeping it under our hat, right, Belle?"

"Yes. It's just between us, among ourselves."

Sharon said, "So that's what's behind the party? She put

the money up for that land, didn't she? I understand things better now."

The talk of Sally depressed them.

"Well," Kaplan finally said, "I've arranged for us to go out to dinner. Does anybody want to change?"

Sharon and Belle shook their heads. They recovered a little in Kaplan's car, en route to Lutece, a French restaurant not far from Kaplan's apartment house.

"Listen," Kaplan said. "Sally wouldn't want us moping, let's try to remember that."

So, determinedly, they proceeded to have a good time, first toasting Sally Markman with more champagne, then closing the restaurant at 1:30 in the morning.

They discovered the next night that Maude Mannon had somehow managed to get Tom Glenn into town to escort her to the ball. She brought Glenn with her when they gathered again at Kaplan's apartment for drinks.

Glenn looked sheepish but chuckled wispily, almost excitedly, at their surprise when he came into the room.

"Well!" Kaplan exclaimed. "Well! Maude, you might have told me. I knew you'd arrange some kind of a date, but such a distinguished man! Maude, indeed! Well, our table is complete. The Leonards, the Woodleys, Susan and Jack, me and Belle . . . and Maude and the doctor. I don't know why I go to such trouble for you out-of-towners. In fact, I don't really know why we're going to the blasted ball. It ain't what it used to be, you know, since Claude Philippe died. Since then, the thing has been shambles-ville."

Kaplan was speaking of the man whose inspiration the April in Paris Ball had been. Philippe and the late Elsa Maxwell had begun putting on the extravaganzas nearly thirty years before, as an annual salute to the city of Paris.

"Norman," Sam Leonard said when he and Sylvia arrived, "why are we doing this? I know why. Because we have to show the flag. In my case, the Cosmos flag."

The ball was being held, as usual, at the Waldorf. Traffic outside was so chaotic they got out of Kaplan's car a block away and walked to the hotel. Inside, it was bedlam. They fought their way to the anterooms, where drinks were being served, and then succeeded in reaching the ballroom, this awash with tinsel and glitter, But the costume was the thing at the April in Paris Ball. Many of the women, to mark the occasion, were in French couture clothes, exclusive from the best of Parisian designers; others were wearing copies of French couture, of course; and still others were dressed like clowns. Again this year, the seating was pure anarchy—the very thing they had to avoid at all costs in Beverly Hills. People were milling around in the ballroom, looking for their tables, often finding their tables misnumbered or their places already occupied. A man trying to serve as master of ceremonies was screaming for calm. Belle saw a fistfight on the other side of the room. Men were shouting in fury, and women screaming. Some couples stormed out in anger.

"Shit," Leonard growled, "is it worth it, Norman?"

"Not really," Kaplan said, "but I promised Brownie we'd come."

"We'd be better off at Nedick's," Leonard grumped.

Frank Woodley stood a head higher than Kaplan and Leonard, happily surveying the fracas, one arm protectively around Sharon and the other on Tom Glenn's arm. Glenn looked dismayed, but he was guarded on the other side by Maude Mannon, who fiercely pushed toward their table near the front.

"They should film this," Frank said. "You can always use good mob-scene footage. Sharon, little lady, anybody comes near you, I'll flatten them. You, too, Tom and Maude. Hey, make way there! Make way for the important people!"

He pushed a man gently aside. The man whirled furiously, but taking one look at Frank, he got out of the way.

"Calm down, you men," Sylvia Leonard commanded. "Especially you, Sam. Behave yourself like a human being."

They found Kaplan's table and ejected two squatters, Kaplan squalling at them in his high-pitched voice.

"Goddamn it, Sylvia. I always behave like a human being. What the hell do you mean?"

"I mean, you're a mean-tempered man," she said serenely. "Why don't you behave with some aplomb?"

"What the hell is that? Listen, you tiny twerp, you're lucky you got me out of the apartment for this."

Sylvia retreated to black silence, then switched her attention to Glenn. It was impossible to hear what he was saying in this din.

"Where's Charley?" Leonard demanded. "I was expecting him tonight."

"He can't get away," Belle said, shaking her head.

"I can imagine . . . since . . ." He did not finish the sentence. "Should I say I'm sorry?"

"Not necessary," Belle said coolly.

Leonard grinned maliciously. "Do you know what you were saved, Belle? Did you know some smart-assed lawyer was after me for a deposition?" He leaned closer, whispering in her ear. "About your sinful activities?"

Belle blushed. "I'm sorry, Sam."

"No matter. Not the first time that's happened to me. I told him I didn't know anything, didn't see anything, and, in general, that they could go to hell. But I guess that's all past tense now, Belle."

"Yes," she said tensely, aware Susan was conscious of her discomfort.

Leonard put his hand on her wrist and stroked. "I've talked to Charley on the phone. The two of you have done a hell of a job, Belle. How's the fabulous woman?"

"Sally?" She turned her eyes on him. "I don't know how long she'll last."

Leonard nodded, closing his eyes. "I figured that. You know, it shows." He gripped her wrist harder. "You've done your best, for everybody, Belle. Realize that."

It was Kaplan who became restive first. He was annoyed with the service, the continuing hubbub for, even as dinner was being served, some people were still looking for seats or standing at the back of the back of the ballroom, loudly complaining.

"A fiasco," he muttered. "We could get out of here. What do you say? We could trickle away, one by one."

"Anything's better than this," Leonard agreed.

"Oh, wait," Kaplan said, distracted, "I've got another piece of news. We're going up to the Carlyle afterward to hear Bobby Short. And, you know, I've talked him into coming out to play for the ball. I finally got bright."

"It's an awfully big room for him," Sharon said.

"He can handle it." Kaplan said. "I've seen him do the same in San Francisco."

On the other side of the table, Maude was uncharacteristically quiet and, at her elbow, Glenn smiled his mysterious and weary smile. When she was not eating, Maude hung tightly to his hand.

"Tom and I want to dance," she announced.

"Then, for heaven's sake, go dance, darling," Kaplan said.

"Come, Tom."

Smiling shyly now, Glenn helped her up and they moved to the crowded dance floor. Maude drew Glenn firmly into her arms.

Belle asked Sharon, "What's with that twosome?"

"Looks like number six to me," Kaplan cried merrily.

"Sharon, don't say anything to Tom about Sally," Belle said. "He must feel like hell."

The evening ended, as it had begun, back at Kaplan's apartment. Susan said goodbye to her date and went off to bed. She had to return to Princeton early the next day. The Leonards stayed for a moment. Maude and Tom Glenn decided they'd leave, too. Maude said she was very "tar'ed," and she seemed agitated. Belle wondered what was in store for Tom Glenn and, whatever it was, whether he could weather it.

Frank unbuttoned the vest of his evening suit and pulled off his black tie.

"What about a quadruple brandy, Normy?" he asked.

"I'll bring the bottle, you sot," Kaplan said. "Ladies? What'll you take?"

"Would you mind terribly much if we had some more of that very sophisticated champagne?" Belle asked.

Chapter Twenty-Seven

By the end of the first week in November, 500 acceptances for the Winter Ball had been received, each accompanied by a check for $2,500 made out to the December Foundation.

Following Doug Donohue's instructions, Belle had been visiting the bank every day to make a deposit. But it wasn't until she made the trip before lunch that day that she realized they'd passed the first million.

The meeting of the inner circle with Dr. Tom Glenn was taking place in the afternoon, and when Belle announced the figure, rather breathless with excitement herself, Archy decreed celebration. Champagne, Archy said, was in order.

But when Tom Glenn appeared, in a mood even more cheerless than usual, he had something to say that put a damper on their enthusiasm. His voice was ordinarily lost in a crowd, but today he had their undivided attention, particularly when he reported why Sally couldn't be with them.

"She's in the hospital. I've just come from there."

Carlotta Westmoreland softly said, "Send her our best wishes. I hope . . ."

"Tests," Glenn said briefly. "But now you'll want to hear my report."

He told them about Dr. Vincent Richardson of Chicago and why he believed Richardson should be their choice for the first research award. If they approved, he said, he would contact Richardson immediately. There was no dissent. They murmured approval in subdued voices. Glenn promised he would go ahead.

Then he rose and excused himself, saying his day was very busy.

Bertha Moore was first to speak after he left. "Well, I hope Sally is all right," she said. "It wouldn't do . . ."

"She'll be fine," Belle said sharply.

They had not been able to keep Bertha away from the meeting. But Belle thought, it might be all right, for Bertha seemed to be in an unusually good mood. Camilla had flushed brightly at the sight of her, looking more attractive than ever. She was wearing a loose-fitting smock.

Another not-very-welcome member of the committee was Marjery Cannon.

"*She* had the nerve to come," Sharon whispered to Belle.

Marjery sat placidly, smiling as though none of them were aware of what was going on in her life. But possibly she could afford to be complacent. She was wearing a new Pauline Trigere suit and she moved her right hand in such a manner as to draw attention to a heavy stone glinting on one of the fingers.

It was a welcome distraction when Archy opened champagne and served them.

"My dear ladies," he boomed jovially, lifting his glass, "today is a day of triumph. One million dollars! Isn't that a fabulous feat! To you! And to our absent leaders: Norman and Sally. Especially to Sally," he said gravely.

Carlotta Westmoreland added, "I do toast you girls. You've done a swell job. I am, frankly, amazed."

"Now, Carlotta," Pat Hyman admonished, "you should know women can do everything better than men."

"Yes," Carlotta grinned, her face red, "except for one small thing . . . Archy, your hotel is also going to be a triumph."

"It's being whipped into shape, dear lady," Archy said, not very modestly, his chest puffing out. "Lou and I are moving in next week. We're recruiting our staff, and my friend Jurgen Ehrlich has commenced his basic training."

As she'd arrived that morning, Belle had witnessed the unloading of a truckload of wine and liquor, this under the personal supervision of Mr. Ehrlich. He had been standing with a clipboard in his hand, checking the cases off the back of the truck at an unloading bay at one end of the underground garage. And, after lunch, as they peeked into the ballroom, Belle and the girls had watched Jurgen drilling a platoon of waiters, his heavily accented voice echoing hollowly as he harangued them. Then he began a personal inspection of each man.

"Christ, he's like a Prussian drill master," Pat Hyman had murmured.

Now, at the conference table, Belle had her own check list. "How's the room situation?" she asked Lou Finistere.

"We're fine . . . now," Lou said, glancing acidly toward Marjery. "Two-thirds of the acceptances so far are local so we don't have to worry about them. The easterners are beginning to come through. My plan is to use up our rooms in the other hotels first, because we'll have a lot of flexibility here. Archy . . ." She gazed for a moment dispassionately at her husband, who was standing with a champagne glass in his hand and a smile fixed on his face. "Archy would prefer to keep occupancy at the Splendide as low as possible. As well as it's going, there could always be a problem with help. But, if pressed, we'll have to make do. And hope for the best. How many rooms, Archy?"

"Lou, if need be, I expect we'll have 200 rooms available."

"If we *are* pressed," Belle said, "that's good leeway to have."

She continued through the rest of her agenda: entertainment seemed okay, although she reminded Pat they still had to take Rolly Starr out for lunch or drinks. There was no need for them to concern themselves about either the layout or particulars of decor; this was being handled by Finley-Gibbons Flower Fashions.

The menu: strangely, this had been the subject of a good deal of dickering back and forth. But then, with the news that David Abdul was indeed undertaking, as his private gesture, to have a prince's ransom of Beluga caviar flown in from Fauchon provisioners in Paris, the elements of a gourmet dinner fell quickly into place. They would lead off with the caviar, served in generous quantities in potato shells; next, fresh asparagus with hollandaise; then, a clear turtle consomme; this to be followed by thinly sliced filet mignon, charred outside, tender within; a palate-cleansing sorbet made of pure pear juice; finally, endive salad with Brie.

Archy promised a special dessert: it would be specially created by the hotel's French dessert and pastry chef and called Bombe d'Hiver, in honor of the Winter Ball.

Wines and champagne were being contributed by one of the big importer-wholesalers and other booze by the Splendide Corporation.

Belle recited the final menu, which now was to everyone's satisfaction.

"Bobby Short will be playing the minute everybody sits down," Belle said. "He breaks for Norman's introduction of the master of ceremonies. Murray Korda and his violins will stroll the ballroom during dinner. Bobby briefly again for dessert and coffee. And then we get into the entertainment, finally the presentation to Dr. Richardson, with more picture-taking. Finally, dancing to Harry James and then good night all. How's it sound?"

"Outstanding," Carlotta said, "especially Bobby Short. He's my favorite of all time."

"Courtesy of Mr. Norman Kaplan," Belle said. "Now, Archy, before I forget . . . Lucia Montonya's here for a purpose today. We want to create a Cosmos Cosmetic makeup clinic here in the hotel for all day Saturday and maybe again Sunday morning."

Archy snapped his fingers. "*Pas de probleme*, madame. We will put it right in the Splendide beauty salon. Plumbing and sinks are in. Just down the hall from the boutiques."

"That should do," Belle said. "What do you think, Lucia? " She bent her head in Miss Montonya's direction.

"We'll have to get in chairs and furniture," Lucia said.

"No problem, dear lady," Archy said.

He was guaranteeing everything, Belle realized, but could he be trusted to deliver? At some point, she conceded, she'd better have a word with Jurgen Ehrlich to make sure he understood and agreed to all the logistical arrangements.

"Well . . ." Belle inhaled deeply and looked at all the faces, hoping she hadn't left anything out. "Anything else?"

Bertha Moore raised her hand. "I do not for the life of me see how you are going to do 1,000 faces in one small place on Saturday."

"*Dieu!*" Archy's face paled. "Do you think they'll *all* come?"

Lucia smiled, her cheeks even chubbier with professional assurance. "No, certainly they won't all come. But you're right, I'm going to need a brigade of cosmeticians. But we'll have a lot available from the Cosmos office here, and I'll simply hire whatever freelancers I need. Remember," she smiled confidently, "there's no shortage of cosmeticians in Beverly Hills."

"But how many women could you actually handle?" Belle demanded, now worried about that aspect of the organization.

"If I have thirty working, is there room for that many on the premises, Mr. Finistere? Yes. I hope so. Well, with thirty, we should be able to do 500 or so. We're not going to give them a complete face, I don't think, just the highlights—show them our line, 'Belle.' " She smiled craftily at Belle. "How it works. How terrific it is."

"But," Bertha insisted, "they're all going to want to come in the late afternoon, if possible, just before they get dressed."

"Well, that *won't* be possible," Lucia snapped, "that's obvious, isn't it? I think what must be done is this: when you send out your final information telling 'em where they're all going to be staying and all that, insert a note advising that a Cosmos—or 'Belle'—clinic will be available for quick brushups and makeup jobs. But on a first-come, first-serve basis. And if they want to, they can call this number here in advance and make an appointment. Somebody will have to keep a roster." And Lucia was making it clear she would not be sitting in the office taking reservations. "Also, it occurs to me that it would make all the local salons happy if you'd list the major ones close to the hotels, or in the hotels. Give me that list, and I'll make sure they all have a supply of 'Belle' products available. Actually," Lucia said, pleased with herself, "I have to compliment myself. That's an excellent idea."

"Sure," Bertha scoffed bitterly, "if this whole thing is going to be geared to promoting Cosmos Cosmetics. Very commercial, if you ask me."

This was what Belle had been afraid of. She colored and felt their eyes on her. It was up to her to answer.

"Bertha," she said icily, "we agreed to accept Sam Leonard's offer. He's putting money up to help us. We agreed that the women will be delighted to have a quick facial. It is *not* the first time a thing like this has been done."

"Well, I won't come," Bertha barked.

"Nobody's asking you to," Lou Finistere said angrily.

Bertha glared until Carlotta Westmoreland gently said, "Mrs. Moore, it is not a matter of national crisis if we have a beauty product in on our act." Bertha dissolved, her anger turning to embarrassment. "One must remember that an undertaking like this must have its commercial aspects, otherwise, it gets no place," Carlotta added.

Gently, Camilla observed, "Some of these people travel with their own hairdressers."

The remark set Bertha off again. "Oh, yes," she sneered, "is that so? I'm afraid I don't know many women who trot around the country with private hairdressers."

Camilla blushed. "It was not meant as a really serious observation. But I do know some women who do."

"Nonsense!" Bertha snorted. Her eyes turned balefully on Camilla. "Or has Sheldon already hired you your own beautician?"

Jesus, Belle thought furiously, out of nowhere, a showdown had materialized.

Camilla flushed more deeply and her hand shook as she

placed her champagne glass on the table. "I have nothing to say to you," she said.

"I should imagine not!" Bertha snarled. Her face had narrowed to dark fury.

An embarrassing hush descended upon the room. Archy looked confused. Belle swore to herself. She glanced at Carlotta; the old lady's lip was drawn down at the side in disgust. Belle understood Bertha might feel rotten and vindictive, but she should have had the grace not to show it. Belle ignored the tension as best she could.

"Lucia seems to have the right idea. Do we agree to put that little memo in our last mailing, Sharon?"

"Right on," Sharon said smoothly.

Marjery Cannon, undismayed by her own low popularity rating, unconsciously switched attention away from Bertha and Camilla and, naturally, toward herself.

"Placecards?"

"We're doing them as we go along," Sharon said, "and slowly working up a seating plan as the money rolls in."

"I'm sorry I haven't been much help lately," Marjery said, her stiff face in a little-girl pout.

"Well," Belle said, "it's never too late to help. And we're going to need all the help we can get from now on. For one thing, we're going to need people on the telephone here all day long."

"I'll volunteer for that," Marjery said.

Yes, Belle wanted to say, and gum things up again. But they passed over Marjery to Sharon's seating strategy: where the First Ladies and the governors would be placed, and who would be seated with the dignitaries.

They could count on more meetings like this, Belle told herself tiredly. And the matter of the press: fresh news items were needed on both coasts. True, they had 500 and more acceptances, but now was precisely the time *not* to slack off.

"Bertha," Belle said, to show there were no hard feelings, "will you contact the *Times* and try to get a peppy item in the social columns?"

Grimly, Bertha nodded. But she understood they wanted to get her out of the line of fire.

"Carlotta, another item in the *Record*, please?" Belle said.

"Naturally, naturally," Carlotta said. "As soon as I hear from Tom Glenn that the Richardson thing is set; I'll write it myself and you can be very sure it'll run." She grinned. "That's the least I can do."

"But don't forget you're going to be taking care of our friends, the governors," Belle reminded her.

"That's a snap," Carlotta said.

But Bertha was not ready to relent. Her attack came from a different direction this time. "Mr. Finistere, are you *sure* your staff is going to be up to this?"

Archy was acute enough to know he had them all on his side when it came to Bertha. He made a petulant face and pawed his beard.

"Dear lady, if I say our staff will be ready, it will be ready."

"I know," she said archly, "that Mr. Ehrlich is doing his best to whip all those Mexicans into shape. But it must be a tremendously hard thing."

Archy's face stiffened and his eyes went blankly stubborn. He was not going to be browbeaten by this woman, particularly as Lou was beadily watching to see what he would say.

"Mrs. Moore," he said impatiently, "Mr. Ehrlich *and* myself are training the staff. Let me remind you, I have been in the hotel business for quite some years. I believe I know my business. Pray, don't concern yourself about it any longer."

Bertha frowned at her hands, knotty-veined, on the table in front of her.

"Bertha," Belle said soothingly, "I think that's the least of our worries. We have other things to talk about." She thought what else there might be. "Decor. Are you happy about it, Darling?"

Darling Higgins had not spoken yet. Now she announced, "Flower Fashions is preparing a plan right now. I'm not worried at all."

"Good," Belle said. "So we won't worry about it either. But we are concerned about cocktails. I can't see how we can do it in the lobby. Your Esplanade Room won't be ready yet."

Archy threw up his hands. "I don't have the answer to that."

"So you don't have all the answers, Mr. Finistere," Bertha snipped.

"Mrs. Moore, I never claimed to have *all* the answers."

Again Belle wondered what Bertha's purpose was in

badgering Archy. "All right, all right," Belle said. "I'm back to my idea of a tent. Isn't there some way we could put up a tent outside the lobby? Straight out of the cars and into the tent?"

Archy nodded, then shook his head. "I don't know. It's feasible, of course."

Darling Higgins calmly said, "Has anybody thought of having cocktails in the garage?"

"Grubby," Sharon said.

"Harry and Fred could turn it into a palace," Darling said.

Belle nodded. "Not a bad idea, actually. Don't the stairs go down there?"

"Yes," Archy said doubtfully.

"It would be grubby," Bertha sniffed.

"Jesus Christ, Bertha," Pat Hyman exclaimed disgustedly. "Try never to be positive about anything, will you?"

Bertha's eyes fired up again and her lip quivered. "I'm so sorry," she sneered. "I guess one should never try to be realistic."

Marjery piped up, "Bertha, there *is* a big difference between realism and pure obstreperousness."

"And you just shut up!" Bertha said furiously.

Suddenly, Belle had had enough of it. She stood up.

"All right, *ladies*," she said sternly, "let's leave it at that, shall we? God, this is like a meeting of the U.N. Security Council. Darling, please do ask Flower Fashions about your idea for the garage. Bertha, you *will* talk to the *Times*? Sharon is going to include the info about the makeup studio. Let's please try to remember that we're half way there. Now, let's quit for a while, all right?"

Chapter Twenty-Eight

Belle could not stop thinking about Sally. That was one reason she'd found the meeting, the bickering, so onerous. When she got back to Charley's place, she managed to reach Tom Glenn at Cedars-Sinai Hospital.

"How is she, Tom? Can I see her?"

"Well . . ." He stopped and she could feel his despair. "Not today, Belle. I don't know when. She's . . . very weak. I don't know what to tell you. We're consulting now. We have an idea—last ditch. But . . . I don't know what to tell you."

"Tom, will you let me know?"

"Of course I will, Belle," he said, his voice rushing at her.

Morris Mauery was receiving Gregory Cannon at his apartment at the Camino. Receiving was the right word for it. Mauery, just back from lunch with George Hyman, was sitting in his easy chair by the TV set, Cannon standing before him, his hands clasped in front of him, as if protectively, over his crotch.

"Cannon, what have you done about Glenn?"

Flustered and embarrassed, Cannon said, "Nothing, Morris. I don't think there's anything there. Expert opinion is that Glenn . . ."

Mauery interrupted him cruelly, waving a thick finger. "Don't give me that expert opinion shit, Cannon. Everybody knows she croaked twenty minutes after he saw her. He *must* have done something to her."

"Not according to . . ."

"Never mind that according-to horseshit either. I want the suit brought, whatever's in it. Cannon, don't be a moron. Don't think I'm after money, because I'm not. I'm after that creep, that doctor, always messing around here. Are you aware Madeleine left the son of a bitch some of her money?"

Cannon's mouth parted childishly and he smiled coyly. "I didn't know that."

"Shit," Mauery spit disgustedly, "all these broads leave Glenn money, you asshole, and then they croak. Does that ring any bells in your empty head?"

Cannon blushed and tried to interject wounded words to the effect he didn't need Mauery's case. Mauery laughed mockingly and again lifted his finger for silence.

"Leave that be for a minute," he said. "You know something else, I think—I want your wife, Gregory." He said it flatly, unemotionally, as if he were informing Cannon that he wanted to buy his house in Pacific Palisades. Cannon began to stutter brokenly. "Shut up, asshole! I'm taking your wife," Mauery said. "Didn't she tell you that you're getting divorced? Not that it matters. I've got her already, in case you didn't know. Didn't she tell you I've been fucking her every day since Madeleine died? Jesus! She's a secretive bitch, isn't she? You would agree that divorce would be best, wouldn't you, Gregory?"

"No!" Cannon cried. "No! I don't agree. I love my wife. I'm not turning her over to you."

Mauery smiled, for he had all the cards in his hand. And it gave him a great deal of pleasure to put such a man as Cannon into a position of no-exit. Self-righteously, Cannon drew himself up, trembling, and tried to look brave. Nervously, he smoothed his sleek black hair.

"Gregory," he said softly, "try to see it my way. I want her. And I'd be doing her a big favor. And you." He let the words sink in for a second. "I've had some people looking. Well, you stink professionally."

He watched as Cannon's face melted away from stubbornness. His eyes misted over. "But . . ."

"But?" Mauery roared, putting the climax to the intimidation. "Don't but me, Gregory. I'm giving you the facts of life. There are other things. I mean, you don't like broken bones, do you?"

Silently, petrified, Cannon shook his head. His body wavered, wobbled, and he looked as if he might faint. He didn't faint. Rather, he collapsed on his knees in the middle of the floor, in front of Mauery.

"Please," he gasped, "you can do whatever you want, Morris. I'll agree to anything. But, please, have mercy on me. I don't want to be ruined. I don't want to be hurt. Please . . ."

Mauery regarded him with loathing. At least that bum Frank Woodley was a man with some balls. This guy, he told himself scornfully, was a scumbag.

"Get up," he said, "and get the hell out of here."

Weakly, Cannon dragged himself off the floor and stood up. His face was ashen. He gave Mauery one last, pleading look, then hurried out of the room.

When Marjery arrived after her meeting, Mauery told her the good news. "Your husband was here. He says he wants a divorce."

Daisy got in from the airport in the early afternoon that day. She unpacked her things and put them away, then fiddled around the house.

"How's Cocky?" she asked Flora.

"Terrible," Flora said. "He ain't been himself since you went away."

"Well, he'll be all right now."

Flora winked at her. "Didn't work out in Hawaii, did it? I didn't think it would. You're just high-strung. You get carried away, honey."

"True," Daisy admitted.

Marcia had been very perturbed, to put it mildly, when she'd discovered Daisy in bed with that blonde guy from the bar at the Royal Hawaiian. Showdown time: the result was Daisy's departure from the enchanted islands.

"You cut your hair," Flora said.

"It'll grow back."

"It's poolman day," Flora remembered. "You knew. That's why you came back today, ain't it?"

Daisy smiled angelically.

Floyd got to the house at two. By ten minutes after, he was upstairs in her bedroom, pulling off his shiny jeans, and at 2:15 they were deeply engrossed on Daisy's bed.

"You miss me, Floyd?" she asked.

"Yeah. Where you been?"

"Little trip to Hawaii, Floyd. Now, let's see . . ."

Daisy placed him sideways on the bed, calculating that

the sideview, or silhouette, of his engorged dick would make a perfect setup for the camera. And she didn't have to concern herself now about her hair getting in the way. She applied herself to him, sliding the length of it into her mouth, along her molars and back toward her tonsils. Floyd began to moan. There was something about poolmen; maybe it was because they were always in the great outdoors. As she manipulated him, he seized her breasts in both hands and pulled at them, dragging her upward. She shifted him again so that his feet were pointed at the camera, then eased herself down on him, knowing that the full act of entry would be faithfully recorded. When he was completely inside her, she arched backward, her face at an angle to show the camera her enthrallment. He gripped her buttocks, and forced her down, panting and thrusting, his hips jerking up, until she came and he into her like a heavy truck. Daisy climaxed in a burst of flame, yelling at the top of her voice. God, she had missed this, and, actually, she admitted to herself, Marcia had been dead wrong about her. She was not at all bisexual. Jake was saved.

She was waiting for him in the library when he got home, as usual, at 6:30. Jake showed not the slightest bit of surprise, or relief for that matter.

"Good evening, my dear," he said.

"The drinks are made."

Jake nodded and belted down the first of his martinis, his only indication of any feeling. She poured him the second and he picked up his clarinet and began to play.

Pausing, removing the reed from his lips, he asked, "Do you think I'll ever be as good as Benny Goodman, my dear?"

"Better," Daisy murmured, "you'll be much better."

After the usual dinner, which Jake wolfed absentmindedly, they went upstairs.

"And what might we have tonight, my dear?"

"I think you'll like it very much, Jake," she said.

Today's film was rather lengthy. After all, it was a double bill, her homecoming present for him, with two acts and two climaxes.

"Isn't that the poolman, Daisy?"

"Yes, but I thought you'd find the angles interesting."

"Umm," he murmured thoughtfully, "uh-huh. Not bad at all. Normally, I don't feel comfortable with you and servants together. But, Daisy, it's ever so much better when your hair is short."

When Darling Higgins got home, she received the surprise of her life, for Ellsworth was cavorting in the pool with a girl, a dirty-looking girl with long black hair and, as Darling observed when she came closer, a pimply face.

"Hi!" Ellsworth sang out. "Meet Delores. We're having a little frolic in the pool. Want to come in?"

"In a minute," Darling said.

She went back in the house, through the kitchen and out to the garage. She opened a gallon of red paint and carried it to the edge of the pool. As she could plainly see, Ellsworth now had Delores up against the steps at the shallow end and he was screwing her there. Darling walked toward them. Ellsworth was giggling, screaming something about going "straight." Delores, ravenous, lay under him, her head back and her eyes closed.

Darling up-ended the paint can and poured it all over them.

"Darling!" Ellsworth whooped in alarm, "what the hell are you doing?"

"I'm painting you red," she said calmly.

Delores began to bleat. The paint soaked her black hair and ran down her face and droopy tits. She gagged and gasped, for she'd gotten most of it. She shook Ellsworth loose and leaped up, scrambling on her hands and knees toward Darling.

Darling completed the paint job just as Delores reached her, then slammed Delores across the head with the empty pail.

"Get this slut out of my house, Ellsworth," she ordered. "This is not common decency. And you better get your ass out of here, too."

Camilla told Sheldon she couldn't go on like this. She was finished with the committee. She couldn't face Bertha again. She was not going to lay herself open to another such head-on confrontation.

"Camilla . . . Camilla, it's nothing," he said. "Pay no attention. She's always like that."

"Not with me, she won't be," Camilla said. "Besides, Sheldon, look at me." She climbed out of bed and stood at his side. Her belly was big, rounded with child. Lovingly, Sheldon ran his hand over the mound, then lifted his head to put his ear next to her smooth, distended skin. "You won't hear anything yet," she told him gently. "What can we do, Sheldon?"

"Let's get out of town. Let's go to the beach or New York."

"And then?"

"And then, as soon as we can, we'll get married."

"Where else could we go? I want to be far from this place, and these goddamn bitchy women."

"Europe?" He threw out the suggestion. "Why not? You could have the baby in Europe. Then it could have a dual nationality."

"Yes," she nodded, but discouragedly, "but what do I do with my kids?"

"You hire a full-time nanny—or we bring them with us."

"But they're in school," she objected.

"We'd be gone maybe three months. That's not so long. Maybe they shouldn't be around when the baby comes. They might get confused."

Camilla considered it. The idea of just leaving was very attractive.

"My mother—I guess I could leave them with my mother."

Sensibly, he said, "We're going to have to tell your mother sooner or later. Why not sooner?"

"You're suddenly so brave," Camilla said, smiling. "All right, let's go down to Palm Springs then and see her."

"Will she be angry, do you think?" He frowned. "She'll object to me, I suppose. Me a Jew and you a staunch WASP."

Camilla shook her head. "No way. She'll know you've got money. That's very important to her."

Sheldon scowled blackly. He was sensitive about his money and he disliked having it mentioned in the same context as shining love.

"Hell . . ."

"I don't want you to think my mother is a grasping woman," Camilla told him. "But money makes a lot of difference to her. If you've got it, it makes you pretty much okay, whether you're Jew, Catholic, or WASP, black, brown, white, or red."

"Well . . ." He was pensive for a moment, then he chuckled. "God, I'm lucky I'm marrying you, not her. We'll drive down tomorrow."

Gregory Cannon decided to kill himself. That was the only way out of it for him. He could not live without Marjery and, at the same time, the final scene with Mauery was his supreme humiliation.

He was praying as he searched for her sleeping pills. "Our Father, who art in heaven," he mumbled, "you've got to forgive me this as you forgive all else . . ."

He rummaged in her medicine closet, in her cosmetics. Then it occurred to him that Marjery never took sleeping potions.

Damn it, he thought helplessly, there was no other bloodless and painless way to do it. Gas? Hell, the kitchen was completely electrified. He could hang himself, but he admitted he'd never have the nerve to kick the chair away and leave himself dangling.

"Our Father who art in Heaven . . ." he repeated. Oh, hell, there was no way.

Gregory went downstairs and crouched on the floor alongside the coffee table, holding his head in his hands and swaying. He was weeping silently and without tears. He rested his head on the coffee table, then slowly thumped his head on the wooden edge. Damn! Damn! He bumped his head harder, then harder. The thud, the dull pain, jarred his brain, knocked it against the back of his skull. He could do it this way, simply batter himself into insensibility. Bang! He cracked down harder and stars popped out behind his closed eyes.

Whack! Gregory, dizzy, fell over backward and lay stretched out on the floor, his arms and legs spread in a posture of crucifixion.

They'd find him there, like that, he thought numbly, crucified without benefit of cross or nails.

Bertha Moore was showing Jurgen Ehrlich her home and Jurgen behaved so obsequiously that one might have assumed that he'd never been in any form of habitation except hotels. He sighed and wheezed approvingly and held tightly to her hand as she led him through the fifteen rooms, one at a time.

"I won't be keeping most of the art," Bertha murmured. "I can't stand it anyway."

"There is much art in the world," Jurgen observed cleverly. "I prefer mountainous scenes to abstract art."

Bertha stopped in the upstairs hallway outside her bedroom, hers because Sheldon almost always had slept alone at the other side of the house.

"Archibald Finistere is an old fool," she said.

"Ah . . ." Jurgen put his fingers to his lips. "He is my superior."

"Sure," she said bitterly. "He got you over here so you'd do all the work while he preens himself in front of the committee ladies. I don't think he's got the faintest idea what goes on at the Splendide. I want you to be chief of the hotel, Jurgen, not that senile, old fool."

"Sssh, *schatz,*" he whispered.

"And that wife of his," she continued disagreeably, "that Lou Finistere, with her tight sweaters and big tits. She lords it over everybody. But I've seen better than her, believe me. When we're married . . ."

"Married?" His red, pointy face gaped.

"Of course. You love me, don't you?"

"With all my heart, *schatz,*" he proclaimed.

"Then please stop calling me *schatz,*" she said darkly. "I know what it means. It means 'cutie' or 'hot stuff' in German. I want you to call me sweetheart or darling. *Schatz* is something you'd call a . . . woman of uncertain virtue . . . a . . . prostitute."

He was shattered. "No, no, sweetheart. It is not."

"Sweetheart," Bertha said grimly. "Now, I want to show you my bedroom."

She pulled him inside and immediately put her arms around him. People might have considered her to be an irritable and often impatient woman, but she was, she knew, much more than that. The proof was her bedroom: it had been decorated in extremely feminine fashion. It was blue with white highlights. Little white bows had been tied on all the bureau pulls and there was a nude on the wall facing the bed. The sheets, when she pulled away the cover, were navy, decorated with little white cupids. And she had a bidet in the bathroom, still not so common in Beverly Hills. This she knew from close inspection of other people's bathrooms.

"It is beautiful, sweetheart," Jurgen trilled.

His hands were at her dress, groping between her legs, and she felt his slender hardness against her.

"Jurgen," she whispered, "let me . . ."

"Fornicate, yes, please . . . sweetheart."

It was not a meeting Pamela had been looking forward to, but there was no way she could avoid it.

A butler opened the door of the Leonard apartment at the Waldorf Towers and ushered herself, David, and Norman Kaplan inside. It was a business visit, strictly business, that had brought her to New York with her lover. Leonard, through Kaplan, had become something of a close friend of David's despite their different religions.

"One world," David had hissed.

They stood in front of the fireplace until Leonard hustled into the room. He was dressed in a three-piece gray suit. When he caught sight of Pamela his eyes twinkled maliciously.

"Good evening, good evening," he said. "Nice to see you. Come, sit down. Sylvia will be out in a minute."

"Sam," Kaplan said, "this beautiful lady is Pamela Renfrew."

"Of course," Leonard exclaimed heartily. "Pamela and I were together at a party once, during the days of the unfortunate Martin Cooper. Do you remember, Pamela?"

"Yes, certainly," she said, smiling distantly.

If he dared to say a word, she told herself, she'd kill him. Did she remember? What a question. Yes, she remembered throwing herself at him, undressing for him, doing everything but handstands, only to be mocked and made to feel fat and ugly.

"Sam, it was your kind self that put me in touch with Pamela," David said softly. "She sold me my house."

"Of course," Leonard said. "That's right. I'd forgotten. It did work out then?"

"To a perfection," David said warmly, touching her hand.

Pamela ordered a vodka martini and hoped the butler would make it a big one. How things had changed for her since that party, since Cooper. Leonard couldn't be in any doubt that she had become Abdul's mistress. It would have been obvious from the way he caressed her hand that she laid for him. Leonard's sharp little eyes lit on her, bubbling over with the realization that she did everything this smooth Arab wanted of her. Did Leonard regret now that he'd turned down the blowjob of his life? Probably. But she understood better why he had refused when Sylvia Leonard came into the room. Sylvia was dressed in a billowy caftan that fully covered her little body, but her head poked out of the top like an artillery piece in camouflage. Sylvia ruled this man and that was obvious. Pamela thought sourly that Sylvia must be one of the world's smallest ball-busters.

"Sylvia, you know these gents," Leonard said. "Now, meet Pamela Renfrew, a lass from the Golden West."

Mrs. Leonard looked her up and down, powdered face analytical. "How do you do?" she said.

Now, Pamela realized with a shock, Leonard had very possibly told Sylvia about her. The little bastard. Christ, this was embarrassing. But David did not seem to pick up the momentary tension.

"I've heard, Miss Renfrew," Sylvia said, "that you handle only the most expensive houses in Beverly Hills. Do you sell many?"

Charley came home at five. He dragged in the door, shaking his head. "Tough, tough day. Belle, beloved one, please make me a heavy bourbon and water and I'll be your slave forever."

He flopped down on the couch in the living room. It was too cold to go outside. Belle made the drink in a big glass, chock full of ice, added a large lemon twist, and brought it to him. She knelt beside him and kissed him.

"I'm your slave, too," she said.

"Belle, do we have to go out tonight?"

She nodded. "I promised Doug Donohue we'd be at his table. Charley, you were in the Air Force. You should be pleased."

"That was a while ago, slave. And don't forget. Donohue was a full colonel and I was only a lowly second-lieutenant."

"But a hero, nevertheless," she said. "It won't be a late party. I'm pooped out, too, from my afternoon with the squabbling ladies. And . . ." Her voice dropped. "Sally's in the hospital. I'm depressed."

"Oh, Christ! What happened?"

"I don't know. Tom Glenn was not very reassuring. He said she's very weak. Charley, let's go to bed."

"Yes," he said, his eyes steady, understanding.

"Let's go to bed right here," she said. She put her head on his chest and stroked his body. She began to undress him, feeling a frantic need to make love, then and there. She slipped quickly out of her clothes and got beside him on the couch. He smoothed her skin, nuzzled her breasts, kissed her throat. She put her fingers on him and felt his warmth beating, her own desire quickening in the pit of her stomach.

"Please, Charley . . ."

They shifted and he moved between her legs, and slowly she eased him inside her. Her tension began to dissipate. They did not move. The warmth of their coupling spread through her. She closed her eyes and sighed, then moved slightly beneath him, drawing him. She clamped her legs around him and rocked him on top of her body.

"Charley," she said. "I feel so desperate. I need it. I feel so wanton. I'd like to do this for the next twelve hours. Come on, delight me. Come on, handsome."

She crushed him with her arms, pulled with her hands, the fingers spread widely across his back. God, she might have scratched and drawn blood so fiendishly did she want him to thrust, even hurt her. The tempo of his movement picked up to searing excruciation. He was perspiring. Their skin electrified at each contact, until he reached the end of his control and ground down with short, sharp thrusts. And she felt his body begin to tingle as the nerves jumped up and down his back and his thighs. She was thrilled, sensing that her body was completely his, huge and throbbing from her toes to the nape of her neck. She began to climax, softly, then more fully until her whole body shook with the force of it, and Charley came, dissolving her into a sweet breathless darkness.

"Oh, my," she cried, "oh, my, my . . . my . . ."

The guard down below announced Morris Mauery, and Sharon was at once frightened out of her wits. But Frank was calm about it. He told her to have Mauery sent up, that there were a few things they might as well get settled once and for all.

But they hadn't reckoned Mauery would have a companion. To Sharon, it looked like the same man who'd trailed them on the road to Palm Springs.

"Hello, Sharon," Mauery said, his face straight and hateful, "meet Flynn."

Frank began to laugh. It was a strange and annoying time for him to be so lighthearted, Sharon thought, when she was frightened, very frightened.

"Hey, pal," Frank exclaimed softly, "we've met before."

The stocky man called Flynn nodded curtly but did not speak.

Mauery turned on Woodley. "Pack your shit," he ordered.

Frank kept smiling. He stood lightly, on the balls of his feet, grinning in a manner Sharon knew would infuriate Mauery. She spoke firmly.

"He's not leaving here, Morris," she said flatly. "Frank and I are married. He's my husband."

This news startled Mauery. And clearly he was very annoyed he hadn't known.

"You son of a bitch," he snarled at Woodley, "so you were after her money, you two-bit stuntman asshole."

"Same to you, ugly man," Frank said pleasantly. But he was not smiling any longer.

"Flynn," Mauery muttered.

"You're packing your shit, like the man said," Flynn said.

"Says who? You? I flattened you once and I'll do it again."

But Flynn did not let him close enough for that this time. He pulled aside his coat and yanked out a gun.

"This says so," Flynn said.

"Bullshit. You wouldn't dare shoot that thing off up here."

Mauery grunted. "Maybe that's so and maybe it's not, smart ass. Don't try my patience. Get him, Flynn."

Flynn began to edge toward Woodley. But he was very cautious. At the same time, he could not allow Mauery to see that he was afraid. He jammed the muzzle of the gun toward Frank's stomach. Frank avoided him, drifting from side to side.

"Come and get me, punk," he said gently.

The tone of his voice should have frightened the life out of Flynn. Flynn was not going to shoot, this was clear. He lifted the gun and swung it wildly toward Frank's head. For an instant, it seemed he had managed to whip Frank's face, for Frank put up his hands in a crazy gesture and suddenly was whirling toward the floor. His legs kicked out in front of him, but even before he had made contact with the rug, there was a sharp, cracking sound and a scream of pain. Flynn spun around, his gun arm flailing. A shot went off, deafening, and Sharon was conscious of the shocking smell of burnt powder. She staggered to the side.

It was not immediately evident that Mauery had been hit. When she looked around, Mauery was still on his feet, a bemused expression on his face. An instant later, his face was covered with blood. He gave out, his body dropped, crumpling, toward the floor and she realized a deep furrow had been cut across the top of his head.

Flynn, poor man, had dropped the gun. He writhed on the rug, clutching at his knee, still screaming.

Frank was already on his feet. He didn't touch the gun. He kicked it away from Flynn.

"Shit," Frank said disgustedly, "I didn't mean for that to happen. Goddamn it, Flynn, you clumsy ape, I think you've just executed your boss. Did the order come down from Chicago, or where?"

"You dirty cocksucker!" Flynn shrieked. "My knee is busted."

Ignoring Sharon for a moment, Frank said, "That's right, Flynn. Let that be a lesson to you. Never fuck around with an asshole stuntman. You want to know how I did it? No? Well, I'll tell you anyway. You can think about it over the next few years. See, I just fall like a sack of spuds, but in the process I catch you with my left toes behind the ankle and kick like hell with my right foot. It's leverage, Flynn. Didn't you ever take physics?"

Flynn moaned piteously and turning his head to see Mauery, he began to vomit.

"Sharon," Woodley said, remembering her, "get the hell out of here. Call the police and the medics."

He stood idly, smiling at Flynn and still speaking to Flynn in a sympathetic voice. Sharon hurried out of the room and shut the door.

In the kitchen, she held fast to the sink, swaying. But she managed to control her nausea. When she was breathing less frantically, she got on the phone.

The dinner was finished and coffee was being placed on the tables when one of the organizers of the Air Force dinner-dance got to Belle at the Donohue table.

"Mrs. Cooper? There's an important call for you in the lobby. Can you come, please?"

"Yes." Her knees began to shake. "Don't move," she told Charley. "I'll be right back."

"Important" phone calls in the middle of a party were enough to frighten anyone to death. Susan . . .? For some reason, it had not occurred to her it would be about Sally until she heard Glenn's voice.

He could hardly speak. "Belle . . . She slipped into a coma. We've done everything we can, Belle . . ."

"I see," she said mechanically. She realized he wanted her to tell him what to do next. "Tom, I promise you, she's not going to die."

"Medically," he whispered, "medically, she doesn't have a chance. It's all through her, Belle. It's gotten to the liver. Medically . . ." He repeated the word. It sounded like a curse.

"Charley and I are coming right over to the hospital," Belle said.

Chapter Twenty-Nine

This was the crisis. Glenn was sitting with Bernard Markman in a lounge outside the intensive-care area at Cedars. If it were possible, Glenn looked to be in worse shape than Markman, who was slumped in a chair, his eyes closed, face white, his hands folded over his bald head.

They came in silently and sat down. Glenn's lips quivered when he saw them but Markman did not open his eyes.

Belle did not often pray, but now, sitting there in the

long hours before dawn, strung-out ganglia of speculation squirmed in her head. To think the simple truth, there was life and then there was death. Life: a few hours before she and Charley had been making agonizing love, bodies taut and alive, all this as Sally struggled with her body, laboring to keep it functioning as the disease swept forward, victory and unconditional surrender in sight.

She was dozing as first light, gray and cold, filtered through the blinds of the room. Glenn was sitting as before, erect and thoughtful, his eyes, almost glazed, fixed on his slender hands.

Belle came instantly awake when a nurse entered the room and bent to whisper in Glenn's ear.

His face was puzzled, then elated. He jumped up. "Come with me, Bernard . . . Belle . . . Charley."

The four of them hastened down a silent corridor and Glenn opened the door of Sally's room. Belle and Charley hung back hesitantly as the other two approached the bed. The space between was cluttered with all manner of equipment.

"Sally," Markman murmured.

"Hello, husband."

Belle barely heard the faint voice.

"Sally," Glenn whispered. "Sally . . . We're here. Belle is here, too."

"Belle . . . Where is she?"

Glenn motioned for her to come to the bed. Holding back a torrent of tears, she came close and took Sally's hand.

The face was terribly drawn and tired and the lines connecting eyes, mouth, the chin were deeply vivid. As usual, the eyes were startling. They did not sparkle, but they were strong and comprehending.

"Never say die," Sally sighed. "How long have I been asleep?"

"All night," Markman said. "You've had a good long rest."

"Christ!" The voice was more powerful. "I'm hungry. What about something to eat?"

Glenn was shaking and his voice was wet with emotion. "We'll arrange a big breakfast for you."

"Good," she said, closing her eyes luxuriously. "That was a hell of a good sleep. I traveled. I think I've been all over the world and then some." She opened her eyes again and stared thoughtfully up at Belle. "I'll be out of here in a couple of days."

"Of course you will, Sally," Markman said soothingly.

"I'm not kidding," she snapped. "Stick around and have breakfast with me, Bernard. You don't have to go to the office today, do you?"

"No, no," he said. His eyes were astonished. He couldn't figure it out. Brashly, he said, "I'll just tell I.B.M. they'll have to wait."

She chuckled wanly.

Belle didn't break down until she and Charley were outside again, in the corridor. Then, she put her head on his shoulder and began to cry, almost uncontrollably. He stroked her back, quietening her.

Glenn came out next. He was delirious.

"I do not understand it. I do not understand it," he kept saying. "I thought—I thought she wouldn't last the night. I do not understand it."

"I do," Belle said. "I understand it. It's her. She came through it. But how?"

Glenn couldn't answer. If he had, he would merely have repeated that he didn't know.

They went home and slept until ten that morning. Then, feeling marvelous, Belle got dressed, said goodbye to Charley, and drove down to the hotel.

This was when she heard Mauery was dead. Pat Hyman, manning the telephone, hung up quickly, her face drawn from a sleepless night, for George had been among the first who had heard.

"Sharon won't be in today. Sharon can't come in today," Pat began to sputter. "Jesus! This is horrible . . . fantastic . . . unbelievable."

"What, for Pete's sake, Pat?"

"God! You don't know, do you? Morris Mauery was killed last night. Killed dead. It seems impossible. He was so close to George. He was shot, killed dead."

"Pat—Pat—what the hell are you talking about?"

Pat was blubbering with excitement. "Mauery went to Sharon's apartment last night with a man with a gun. There was an argument, a fight. The man was going to shoot Frank Woodley. Instead, he shot Morris Mauery, right between the eyes."

Belle sat down with a thump. She frowned, trying tc

reassemble her thoughts. Jesus! Life in Beverly Hills was becoming almost too exciting. She had known Mauery only to say hello to and had heard only bad things about him.

"Sharon and Frank?" Her words stumbled.

"No, no, they're in the clear. Frank was defending himself. Son of a bitch, Belle, I didn't even know they were married. Morris was apparently totally pissed off at that. The mean fucker was trying to chase Frank out of town."

"And that's all there is to it? As simple as that? Unbelievable."

She remembered Archy Finistere's story about the threatening phone call from Mauery, that Norman had somehow taken care of that problem.

"The unbelievable part," Pat said in a hollow, awed voice, "was that it seemed to be accidental. If it's accidental that your own hitman kills you instead of the target . . . Well, Jesus Christ, Belle, I never expected Morris Mauery would be killed accidentally."

"Good God, good God," Belle said faintly, passing her hand across her forehead. "Pat . . . I don't know. We're supposed to have lunch with Rolly today. Are you up to it?"

"Up to it?" Pat replied almost hysterically. "I wouldn't miss it. I want to hear what Rolly's heard."

Rolly Starr was in a state of near nervous seizure when they met him at Ma Maison. He thrived on horror and tragedy. His long frame was agitated, his cheeks bright red, and he was drinking glass after glass of white wine.

"Incredible . . . quite marvelously incredible, ladies!" he exclaimed as they sat down. "But he was indestructible, Pat."

"So he led us to believe," Pat said dryly. She had recovered.

"What does George say?"

Pat shook her head. "Nothing. He's in shock," which was not true. But she was not going to tell Rolly what George had really said. With a world-weary smile George had muttered something about good riddance and then asked a rhetorical question: Who would he deal with now to get his work done? No, no word of sadness or regret from George, and here she had always considered George almost unnaturally fond of Morris.

"Heavens!" Rolly cried, "we've had nothing lately but one violent death after another. Oh God!" Dramatically, he flung his hands over his face. "Belle, God, I'm so sorry. I'm so rotten. Forgive me?" Belle did not change expression. Wordlessly, she nodded. "But it's all so ironic," Rolly went on, undeterred, "ironic enough to stand the test of the silver screen. Could there be, do you think, any connection between Morris Mauery and the late, luscious Jane Farelady? What an unutterable, delicious irony that would be."

"I can't think how," Pat sniffed, "since he's been boffing Marjery Cannon with such dedication."

Martin Cooper, she mused: George had not been especially busted up over that fatality either. Pity, George had remarked, seeing a beautiful Silver Cloud destroyed.

Rolly straightened up to alert full height. "Maybe I'll start looking for a script." He patted his fat lips with his napkin. "I've got just the girl to play Jane. Her name is Rita Ruggles. She's a real sex bomb—if anything, more of a sex detonation than Jane." He giggled immoderately. "I believe she screws like a mink."

"Rolly, really!" Pat said. But the observation delighted her. She also appreciated Belle's apparent discomfort at the callous bantering about Jane Farelady. Martin Cooper, she understood, had probably been banging that, along with everybody else, before his untimely and premature departure from the land of the living. But why should Belle care? She was already firmly linked in every way with the divine Charley Hopper. Balls, Pat thought viciously, it was nothing much more, all of it, than a game of musical chairs, or musical beds. She and George were nature's own survivors. She loved George for that, if nothing else, for the fact he was cynical and so realistic.

Rolly finished his bottle of wine and ordered a bottle of Ma Maison house champagne. He toasted them boisterously.

"This is a celebration more than it is a wake," Pat noted sourly.

She was thrown into a brooding, intospective mood. Her concern now must be whether or not, and how, Mauery and his hitman, this Flynn, had guaranteed the silence of Boris the Magnificent. Mauery was not around now to enforce an injunction on Boris. Was she going to get a phone call? Had they gotten the picture away from Boris? She had to think they probably had. Morris had been efficient, if, in the pinch, unlucky.

Rolly was bubbling so excitedly that now and then Pat felt a spray of spittle light on her hands.

"And how is that dear lady, Sally Markman?" Rolly demanded. "I've heard she isn't well."

Belle said, "She's a lot better, Rolly."

"Such a marvelous woman," Rolly gushed. "And I've done my damndest for her. Everything is signed, sealed, and delivered."

"Rolly," Belle said, flatteringly, "you've done magnificently."

His chubby face beamed. "I mean, God, it's going to be the best show any of these yokels have ever seen in their entire life."

"A hell of a lot better than that turgid April in Paris Ball," Belle said. "I think we should do something right now for our entertainers, to show we're counting on them."

"Just buy their books," Rolly crowed sardonically. "They've all got them on the stands now. Send cigars, a few joints . . ."

"No, no, Rolly, be serious. What about something in the way of flowers?"

"Not flowers," Rolly said expansively. "Send something impressive, substantial—a tree. Something along the lines of a baby redwood."

"Now, Rolly, Rolly," Pat cautioned him in motherly fashion.

"All right," he sulked. "Since you're so chintzy . . . I'll tell you what I got the other week—a beautiful espaliered dwarf pear tree. They're beautiful, put against the side of the house. Every time you eat one of the pears, you think of Adam and Eve—I mean the Winter Ball."

"Done," Pat said. "We'll get Darling to take care of it. She's Mrs. Jolly Green Size Three."

Rolly began to whoop wildly again. "Haven't you heard about Darling? No? Oh my God—it's so lushly rich! She and that husband of hers, that whore. Darling caught him poking a lady in their swimming pool. She poured red paint all over them, stained the pool beyond redemption. Darling is leaving Ellsworth. In fact, she's kicked him out and thrown all his clothes in the garbage can. Darling is going straight. It's unbelievable! That's what I *love* about this place: *everything* is so unbelievable!"

* * *

Thye kissed Rolly goodbye over and over and then Belle drove Pat back to the Splendide.

Nothing had changed. The hotel was the scene of unrelieved noise and confusion. Trucks were being unloaded, driven off, more trucks arrived, and so on and on.

Archy Finistere and Jurgen Ehrlich were standing inside the open front doors of the lobby, rubbing their hands, slapping each other enthusiastically on the back, and talking at the top of their voices.

"Ladies! Ladies!" Archy cried when he saw them, "you are witnessing the last acts. Today the carpets are being put down in the ballroom; upstairs, the beautiful drapes are being hung. We are receiving the last furniture, furnishings, glassware, china, silver. We have arrived! Jurgen, my boy, I think of you as my very own son!"

Ehrlich was practically jumping up and down with excitement. At this last compliment, his eyes, already red and weary, flooded with tears. He seized Archy's hand and kissed it.

When he recovered sufficiently to talk, he burbled, "Mrs. Cooper, several huge boxes have arrived for you. I have sent them upstairs to your command post."

"Ah," she said, smiling at them. "That'll be my stuff from Cosmos."

Archy had clasped his hands behind his back now and he followed the bustle in the lobby like an admiral in civilian clothes. He looked a bit like a bearded version of the atom-submarine innovator Hyman Rickover. Or a pin-striped Admiral Nelson on the bridge of the *Victory*.

For a moment, he diverted his attention to say, "And what do you gels say to the death of Morris Mauery? A shocking affair, what?"

"A tremendous shock for us all," Belle said quietly.

Archy grinned. "Yes, yes, wasn't it?"

Their feeling of closeness, camaraderie, was shattered now by the unexpected appearance of Bertha Moore. Bertha marched down the steps from the mezzanine and strode toward them, rather like a military personage herself.

Without prelude, she announced, "Mr. Finistere, I have to say that the toilets are not working properly upstairs."

Archy reeled back as if she had struck him, and Ehrlich reddened with anxiety.

"Mrs. Moore," Archy stuttered, "don't you understand—water pressure is not yet at its full?"

"It is sickening," she insisted, "it reminds me of a mining town in Nevada. Moreover, sir, your waiters are nothing better than Mexican peasants, a bunch of stupid clods."

Archy's face turned white, then red with fury. He pivoted on one heel and marched away.

"Mrs. Moore," Ehrlich said bluntly, his face apoplectic and quivering, "may I respectfully suggest you leave the management of the hotel to the managers?"

"Yes," she snarled. "Then, manager, manage thyself!"

Belle wondered if Bertha had suddenly gone utterly mad.

"Bertha, you're making problems again," Belle cautioned her. "I think you should go home and rest."

"I am going home," Bertha raged, "and I may not be back—ever."

"Whatever grabs you, honey," Pat drawled viciously.

Bertha turned and left them, her back rigid with anger. Ehrlich looked miserable, embarrassed, violently angry.

"Mr. Ehrlich . . . Jurgen," Belle said apologetically, "I'm sorry about that. We all are so impressed with what you're doing here."

"Thank you," Ehrlich said, but his mind was far away. "It is not something that concerns me very much."

Disconsolately, he walked away from them and they continued upstairs. Men were putting carpeting down on the stairs and in the hallway.

Pat observed, "Seems to me Mrs. Moore has popped all her buttons."

Belle shook her head. "I just hope Lou doesn't ever hear her talk like that to Archy. She'll cut off her . . ."

"Balls, yes, that's right," Pat said laconically.

But Lou had already had a dangerous dose of Bertha. She was fuming and started yelling when they came into the office.

"She's gone, Lou," Belle said soothingly. "She's on her way home."

"That no-good bitch," Lou raged. "If she makes one more peep, I'm going to slug her. Bitching about everything."

"We know," Pat said, "Forget her. Screw her."

"That's what she needs," Lou said, "a good hard screwing. And not only that, I had a phone call from Camilla and she won't be in anymore. That big 'c' has scared her away."

"Jesus!" Belle said disgustedly. "See that. One bad apple . . ."

Just as she said the words, she noticed Marjery Cannon standing in the doorway.

"Bad apple?" Marjery said levelly. "Is that me? No . . . you couldn't be talking about me like that. I'll take over whatever Bertha was supposed to be doing."

Her arrival reduced them to an embarrassed silence. What could one say to a woman who had just lost a repulsive lover? Should it be condolences or congratulations?

Marjery looked at them squarely and smiled a little. "I know what you're thinking," she said impassively with about as much emotion as there was on her frozen face. "Morris is dead. And so what? You think I care at all? I don't, not at all. I was never going to divorce Greg and marry him, whatever you think. I was scared of him and scared of what he'd do to Greg if I put him off. I was playing him along and, mercifully, he's been taken care of. Christ!"

Marjery did her best to cry for them. The carefully built lines of her face trembled and her makeup cracked. She managed to close her eyes for a second but that was obviously an effort.

Pat Hyman surmounted this impasse with what seemed a very cruel observation: "In that case, duckie, you'd better toss that big ring in his coffin."

Marjery stopped in mid-tear and cast a haunted, disbelieving look at Pat. Then she began to laugh, honking with derision.

"The fuck I will! I paid for that!"

Belle sat down, covering her face with her hands. She couldn't believe this exchange. They never ceased to amaze her, these good women, one and all. Goodhearted, yes, in a way, but they were capable of such startling crudity, nastiness, even viciousness. Her committee, she thought, yes, good God, her committee.

When she looked up, Marjery had collapsed, still laughing, in Pat's arms. And Pat was laughing, too, although she made a comical face at Belle.

Marjery abruptly stopped. She stepped away from Pat and gruffly asked, "What is it you want me to do?"

But before Belle could adjust her mind to reply, Sharon Peters came into the office. This was cause for hush to fall over them, then instantly to spiral Marjery into another spasm of near-hysteria.

"Sharon! Darling! Sweetheart!" Marjery screamed. "God! My lover tried to kill you. I'm so sorry."

Belle began to moan to herself, as this incongruity piled on the other. A bad dream, she thought. But what Marjery had said was true: it was a simple fact. Morris Mauery had been ready to kill Frank Woodley and Sharon.

"Ladies . . ." She tried, ineffectually, to stop it.

But Marjery was determined to have her drama. "Sweetheart!" she lowed. "I'm glad you got him. I'm glad. I'm happy."

It was Pat Hyman who had the right medicine. She slapped Marjery across the face. "Jesus Christ, Marjery! That's enough. You goddamn fool! Shut up! Shut up, I say."

Sharon said nothing. Marjery's wailing had stopped her in the doorway.

Marjery collapsed on the floor. A racking cry burst out of her and she beat her temples with her fists.

Belle stood up. It was abundantly clear that now was the time to visit the bank.

"Our Father who art in heaven," Gregory Cannon was praying to himself. "I humbly thank Thee for Thine most personal intervention on behalf of your poor servant, Gregory Cannon."

He chortled to himself. Gregory was standing at the window of his office, staring down into Wilshire Boulevard.

And what an intervention it had been, just what the doctor ordered.

He was very fortunately placed, for just as he was going to turn away and have a nap on his leather couch, a dirty green Cadillac bashed head on into a gleaming white Rolls. There was a loud crash which he heard distinctly even through the carefully sealed windows. Boy, he thought, what a beauty. He watched as the two drivers, unhurt within the weight and build of the two heavy cars, opened their doors and hit the street, already screaming and waving their arms.

Now, which of them was at fault? The Cadillac had been

turning left, and the Rolls had taken advantage of the yellow caution light to turn right. Collison. Hmm, he thought, it was a toss-up. But a case, yes, it was a case for Gregory Cannon, fighting defense lawyer—or, who knows, counsel for the plaintiff.

He rushed out of his office.

"I've just witnessed a terrible accident," he muttered to his secretary. "I'll be back in a few minutes."

It was about four P.M. that day when Norman Kaplan came into the committee office with David Abdul.

"Surprise! Surprise!" he cried.

Belle was very pleased and relieved to see Kaplan. And she was dying to tell him about everything that had happened. The stories would delight him. "Norman, am I ever happy to see you here."

Kaplan gathered her jovially to his heavy chest. Abdul kissed her hand.

She could almost feel the force of Abdul's lust when he spotted Darling. Darling looked, as Sam Leonard would have said, ravishing. Her red hair was ablaze, her face so innocent and girlish, very simply made up. Darling was in a gay and outgoing mood. She was dressed in white with pearls at her throat.

"Ah . . ." Abdul wheezed softly, "it is Mrs. Higgins . . . Darling? A wonderful name."

"We met at that luncheon downstairs," Darling said merrily, "don't you remember?"

"Yes, of course."

He and Norman had come to the hotel for an inspection and Abdul was very pleased. Very, very pleased with everything, he said. He remained to talk to Darling when Belle pulled Kaplan out into the hallway to tell him about Sally.

Kaplan was perplexed, then cautiously elated. "Does it mean she's shaken it off, Belle? Is that possible?"

"Tom mentioned something about a drug, a last-ditch try. I'm praying she'll be all right now. But is it possible? I don't know."

"I was praying on the airplane," he said seriously.

"Norman, you are going to stay now, aren't you—until the ball?"

"Yes, I'm here now until the ball. Sam will be in early in the week."

"Do you think they'd like to stay in . . . my house? I'm not living there now, you see. You do see!" He smiled shrewdly, revealing his sharp little teeth. "Mrs. Atkins would be pleased to have somebody there."

"Ask them. invite them," he suggested. "I've already invited them to be my guests. I don't know, Belle. He always likes the Beverly Hills Hotel." He placed his hands on her shoulders and looked into her eyes. "I understand you've been having more high drama out here."

"Jesus," she breathed, "I can't begin to tell you. Wait 'til tonight. You'll come up to Charley and me, won't you?"

"With pleasure. I talked to Susan before I left yesterday. She's in good shape. Her marks are good so far."

"Norman, what would I do without you? Norman, what would I *ever* have done without you?"

"Without me, my lovey darling, you'd be doomed," he chortled.

Abdul heard Pamela trying to get in the front door, her key scratching in the lock which had been changed only a half hour before. Then, there was a period of silence as she evidently stopped to wonder why her key no longer worked. She had to know he was here, for his Bentley was parked in the courtyard.

She began knocking, then pounding on the door.

"David? David! David!" Her heavy and, in extremis, loud voice boomed.

Abdul got up and walked into the entry. He was smiling to himself. The things outraged women got up to.

"David, are you there? Are you all right? David, answer me. I'm going to call the police!"

He did not want that. He put his mouth up to the crack where the double doors met. "Please don't bother me, Pamela. I'm very busy."

She shrieked in alarm, then disbelieving fury. Her vocal cords stretched toward panic-alert. Abdul had the check ready and he'd left it on the side table in the entry. Although the doorjam was tight, as tight as a maiden's sweet slit, he thought lasciviously, he managed to slide the envelope underneath. He heard her gasp, then the tearing noise as she ripped it open.

"Son of a bitch," she shouted, "buying me off. Goddamn you!"

Softly, he hissed, "Go away now, Pamela. I owe you no more."

He could hear her snorting, almost neighing, in frustration. But it would be of no possible use. He had made up his mind and the check signified the end of the chapter, payment for service rendered. Abdul always paid his way. If she used the money properly, she would be on her way to becoming a rich woman. Inside, he had put a clever note, something he had learned from that old German financial wizard Hjalmar Schacht: "Work hard and save your money, Pamela!" Perhaps he wouldn't have been so hard on her if he had not begun to hear the stories—from Sam, from Norman, and lastly from Darling Higgins. Pamela was a grasping mercenary, a revolting creature. And increasingly fat, bloated really. Ugh!

"Goodby, Pamela," he whispered.

"David, David." Outside, her voice was lower now, pleading. "Let me in. I want you. I want to suck you and fuck you. Don't you want that, my sweetest little sheik?"

"No, Pamela . . ." he whispered.

Then, alarmingly, she began to shout again, offering the same ministrations in a strident voice that was sure to echo through the neighborhood and give him a bad name here among his new friends.

When she quieted a bit, he said, "Pamela, go away and stop this—or I will let Hildegard loose."

Hildegard was the Doberman he'd bought to watch the house when they were away on their travels.

"Jesus!" She was crying now. He could visualize the tears coursing down her crude cheeks. "All right . . . all right . . . you fucking Arab."

Smiling sadly with yet this new indication of the calumny of Western attitudes, Abdul slithered softly in his bare feet back to the living room and Darling Higgins. She was stretched warily like a deadly cat across the tiger skin, which, in turn, was thrown carelessly on top of a room-sized Persian carpet.

Her eyes were flooded still with smouldering desire. She smiled, the tip of her red tongue caught between her teeth. She had heard enough to know that Pamela was a thing of the past and that she, Darling, was the thing of the present and future—well, at least near future.

Darling's body was so white, not outrageously white and sickly like Pamela's but a deep, resounding, pearly white which was the opposite, the complement, of the red hair. The body was like the body of death and eternity, at the same time the body of life and aching present desire. She was desire. She was copulation. Her breasts were smaller and taut against her chest, not floppy and disorganized like Pamela's or his wives'. The manicured, closely trimmed pubic hair was like the last green on the most perfect golf course. What a course to play about! Her belly was muscled, her thighs lithe and well-exercised from all her riding. She was like the rider of an Arabian horse. She *was* the Arabian horse ripe for the riding.

And Darling lay in waiting like a cat, and as he approached she closed her thinly lidded eyes, opened her mouth, and her scarlet tongue lolled out.

"Darling," Abdul whispered.

"David, give me your love. Come . . ." She held up her arms, so white and female they seemed to have no bones in them at all, and lilted them like a ballerina. The bush of red hair at her crotch surged imperceptibly, or nearly so.

He lowered himself beside her, putting his brown skin against her whiteness. This was possibly, Abdul thought, the most thrilling thing that had ever happened to him. Women were always available to him: those not attracted to him on the grounds of simple fascination could be had for money. But, in his longish life, he had never had women so easily as they could be had in Beverly Hills. Here, a man like himself had merely to smile, sigh, and whisper a few words of flattery.

Abdul was enough of a philosopher to know that anything that might happen here was without substance, that real life lay in his homeland. Yet he marveled at this country. In particular, he was astonished by California and, even more specifically, he found it hard to believe the hedonism of Southern California. But the pinpoint of his amazement was Beverly Hills. It was like an island drifting in space, totally separate from the rest of this country; surely, if there were catastrophe, Beverly Hills had no right to survive. This party they were organizing—it was not only a hobby, a way to pass the time; it was a cause, their offering to the gods, their puny justification for being alive. Idly, Abdul wondered if this spoiled and pampered society had the power within it to regenerate. It was said by many, including the Marxists, that democracy had reached its twilight and that this degeneracy was its manifestation. Abdul wondered. It was a matter of some concern to him, for one needed a place to play, a place to put one's money for safekeeping. The morality of the society—that meant nothing to him.

At least Darling Higgins did not come to him out of greediness, for, as he understood it, she was one of the richest of the Beverly Hills ladies. She was here because she liked his brown skin as much as he was thrilled by her whiteness. Abdul began to feast on her body and she to devour him, until both were shaking with convulsions of passion. Abdul held her off until she began to cry out for him, to clutch and pull, to beg for him to transport her to the holy future, until she could not even form the words to beg for him. Only then did he engulf her. Ah, he thought, these California men, they knew nothing. But how could they hope to match him? He had been trained and engrained with the mysteries from the earliest possible age; his father had seen to that. For in his country, drinking coffee, carrying on protracted business negotiations, and making love were the only accepted occupations for a man.

Abdul sighed to himself as he made love to Darling. Her receptacle was like a tiny cut in the earth where smugglers might have stored their booty. Within, the one precious jewel. She would never be the same again, he complimented himself. And with her finely tuned body, she was more receptive to his expertise than brutish Pamela had ever been.

"Princess Darling," Abdul murmured. Even his voice brought a response of extended physical exertion.

"Prince David," she whispered, her voice uneven.

Naturally, she was in ecstasy.

Then Abdul began slowly to realize that Darling was doing things to him that he had forgotten about. Her body was like a machine into which he had plugged his life force and Darling was now in the process of extracting from him very vital substances.

Chapter Thirty

The last week of November brought with it weather so unseasonably warm in California that there were many last-minute efforts from the rainy and freezing East, Southeast, and snow-bound Middle West to break into the finalized party guest list. But Sally decreed they would not deal with any more RSVPs beyond the magic figure of 2,000.

Even then, Sam Leonard demanded and got an extra two tables. He had determined at the last minute, and despite Kaplan's injunction during the summer, that he would send the *Jetsetter* to freight in a contingent of Parisian Beautiful People. Thus, Sam argued, the ball would gain a bit of royal luster to add to the republican (with a small "r") presence of the former, and they hoped, present First Ladies.

"Belle," he said over the phone from New York, "tell that little martinet Kaplan I'm paying for it, so what's the diff? We'll have a prince and princess, two counts, two countesses, and one pair of illustrious freeloaders. Look, honey, I'm not particularly crazy about these characters, but they do attract press coverage. And that can't be bad."

There was no arguing with him. The Paris contingent would be placed in spanking-new suites at the Splendide and they would hope for the best. Sam had also anticipated Belle's suggestion that the event might be useful for future Cosmos TV use. Three cameras were to be installed in the ballroom by an independent producer under contract to Cosmos; Cosmos would pay the entertainers, and it was devoutly hoped the latter would turn over their paychecks to the December Foundation.

* * *

The days wound down. The Gibbons-Finley Flower Fashion crew moved into the ballroom on Tuesday. It was then the committee understood the extent of Darling Higgins' floral ambitions. First of all, floor to ceiling trellises would be constructed at the rear of the room to conceal serving areas and TV camera points. Gibbons, Finley, and Jurgen Ehrlich agreed on a plan for the tables: These would be grouped in wedge-shaped clusters, each to be serviced by its own contingent of waiters. The food would be served in efficient and hot condition, and quickly. Waiters would disappear immediately after big coffee samovars had been put on the tables.

Centerpieces for the tables were to be low and sprawly so as not to obstruct vision. They would be simple, yet elegant: red and white roses and peonies mixed in rhinestone-jeweled holly.

"The party colors," Darling murmured, "pink, red, and white. The colors are to suggest Christmas and to flatter us all."

"Flatter your red hair, Darling," Pat Hyman pointed out.

"Peonies?" Belle said. "Where are you getting peonies?"

"Harry ordered them from North Church, New Zealand," Darling informed them, rather smugly. "That's the only place they're blooming this time of the year. He's going to weave them into the trellises with thousands of bunches of baby's breath."

"Jesus," Pat said, "outstanding. When they take a fix on that *and* the caviar they'll know they've arrived."

"Darling," Belle said, "are you sure? This is going to cost a bloody fortune."

Darling shrugged. "My dear Ellsworth can afford it, darlings."

"And then what?" Pat asked.

Darling smiled cleverly. "Outside, topiary sparkling with Paris opera lights, which should be very beautiful. And tell me what you think of this: We're getting eight-foot white balloons and Christmas trees to float on top of them, all decorated with opera lights and flowers. The whole ceiling arrangement will be anchored and connected by Italian-silk streamers. The stage will have banks of pink, red, and white with full-sized evergreens behind the band, also laced with strands of peonies and roses. How's that grab you, ladies?"

"Jesus, Darling," Pat sighed. "It sounds just great. But, my God, can you afford it?"

Darling chuckled. "That little sweetheart, dearest Ellsworth, is going to pay the whole bill—although he doesn't know it yet. But aren't you going to ask about the garage? Well, we—me and Harry and Fred figured out this has got to be completely different in decor from the ballroom, so the garage is going to be done completely in white, carpeting, chairs, tables with just holiday foliage in csystal containers. They'll not have a clue they're in a garage. Then up the steps to the entre floor and into the ballroom and Zowie! a whole new ambiance. From an ice palace to Versailles. Personally, I think it will be great."

"When do our friends the Peonies arrive from New Zealand?" Pat inquired stoically.

"Saturday morning," Darling replied. "At least, they better or Harry's in big trouble."

Belle smiled. "I have no doubt they'll get here. They wouldn't dare not get here."

"Correct," Darling said, "they would not dare to risk the wrath of Darling Higgins.

"Quite a scene," Pat remarked, coolly puffing on a long cigarette. "David Abdul's Iranian and Russian caviar gets here on the red-eye Friday night and Darling Higgins' pink peonies Saturday morning. Impressive. We better make sure and let the press know the logistics."

"Not such a bad idea, Pat," Belle said. "Why don't you see if they'd like to send a photographer to the airport?"

As much as they might like to joke about it, out of nervousness and tension as the Saturday night approached, it would be a terrific scene, Belle told herself. A master stroke for the tables was Sally's decision to go with Marcia Lehr's specially ordered Lalique crystal favors in the shape of the phoenix, rising from the ashes: the ancient symbol of resurrection and eternal life.

Particularly appropriate, although few people knew it.

Sally made the trip in from Trancas Wednesday morning. Belle would never forget the fact of her recovery—or, Belle thought realistically, what seemed to be recovery, at least a second remission. There was no denying she was thin as a rail and her face terribly worn. But the fact she was there, still with them, and had driven herself in from the beach—that was simply remarkable. Belle thought it had to be a dream. Sally had died and somehow been resurrected. Was it blasphemous to think so?

On her first day back, she did not intend to stay long, but in the end she took Belle, Lou, Sharon, and Marjery to lunch at Jimmy's. It was warm enough to sit outside.

"Girls," Sally said warmly, "I can hardly believe it. We've made it to the end . . . and, at last, I'm well enough to be here with you."

"We've been worried about you," Marjery said.

"We've been worried a little bit about *you*, Marjery. Are you all right now?" Sally responded.

"I'm fine," Marjery said breezily. It was as though she'd passed through a serious illness, too. "I feel like I'm back in the fold."

Belle pondered this. It was as simple as that, was it? They all understood, accepted Marjery's lapse. Hell, it could happen to anybody—was that the reasoning? A very superficial arrangement of life and society, she thought glumly. Still, there was no reason not to forgive Marjery and welcome her back, she supposed.

"Our only major concern now," Belle said, "should be picking up all these First Ladies and getting them into town and keeping them happy. Everything else is as much under control as humanly possible."

"And Bertha's out of the picture?" Sally asked.

"Yes, and Camilla, too."

Sally smiled. "So I hear. The fortunes of war."

"Well," Marjery said, "it so happens we've figured out the First Lady business. I'm going to meet Mrs. A. Priscilla Murray has Mrs. B. Darling, believe it or not, is taking on the redoubtable Mrs. C."

"A, B, and C? What is this?" Sally demanded.

"Security," Belle said. "We've already had our instructions from the Secret Service. We're not to refer to them by name."

"The press?" Sally asked.

"They're not to be told when the women arrive. There's going to be a press reception at six o'clock Friday night at the Camino."

"And they've all promised to come?" Sally demanded. "More the wonder."

"Yes," Belle said, "and Maude is bringing Mrs. D personally. As you know, Carlotta will be in charge of the governors. As many as get here Friday will be at the reception, too. There should be at least three of them at the ball."

Sally nodded somberly. "My darlings, it's almost too much for me to absorb. And I hope you'll understand I can't promise much now except to present my emaciated body on the night of nights."

Lou Finistere answered emotionally for them all. "Sally, that's all you've got to do." Pausing, she wiped her eyes. "Sally, I can't tell you how much this has meant to me, working on this . . . with you . . . for you. I feel like, I don't know, that I've really accomplished something."

"Now, now . . ." Sally was close to tears and, for a second, they were all on the edge of weeping. "Girls, girls, don't take emotional advantage of a sick old lady."

"Sick, hell!" Sharon scoffed, "you're as right as rain now, ducky. Sally, I must say my word. I'm a happy woman and you're the best—I think you're the best woman I've ever known."

Belle smiled at Sally. There was nothing she could add.

"You goddamn rascals," Sally said gruffly. "Cut it out now."

Friday was as warm as Monday had been, warmer if possible. Warm wind from the desert and a high pressure area to the west in the Pacific pushed the L.A. temperature into the eighties when, according to the paper, it was forty-something in New York with snow predicted.

Try as they did to hold it down, the committee had been forced over the 1,000 couple mark by another forty couples.

It was then that Archy put his foot down: one more table, and he was quitting, leaving his profession, his wife, and going to Tahiti where, with his French background, he could always open a small cafe.

Belle went with Charley to the press reception, which was to be followed by Archy's cocktail party in the biggest of the Camino's upstairs rooms. The local TV stations had come out and those affiliated with the national networks had promised extensive coverage, well justified if one considered this could be the biggest gathering of former First

Ladies until the next inauguration or state funeral. The Los Angeles newspapers and magazines had sent writers and photographers.

The room was swarming with security, easily distinguishable from the press by their neat suits, button-down shirts, and communications earplugs, their blank, watchful eyes.

The First Ladies did their duty, and they were good at it. Led by their assigned guardians—Darling, Marjery, Priscilla and Maude—they drifted through the crowd, pausing to shake hands and to answer questions. They posed for pictures individually and in twosomes, threesomes, and then, toward the end, gathered for group pictures, which took a good twenty minutes to bring off to the satisfaction of the photographers.

There were no formal speeches. To conclude the media event, Marjery mounted a podium at one side of the room and took up the mike. She said there would be only a brief announcement: The December Foundation at this moment had in its coffers more than two and a half million dollars—they'd agreed not to give the exact figure—and construction of the women's cancer center was to begin in the spring. Questions . . .

Where was Sally Markman? Pictures were definitely needed of Sally Markman, at whose initiative this whole project had been started. What was the final amount of money needed to complete the center? More than fifty million, Marjery replied, but it was hoped this initial drive would bring in ten million, what with the Winter Ball, additional grants, matching donations, and help from national foundations. Was the committee confident it could reach their final target? Without any doubt, Marjery said vigorously, and Mrs. Markman, who could not be with them tonight, would be available for all the pictures they wanted the next night at the Beverly Splendide.

Belle gripped Charley's arm. The fact was Sally was home at the beach, resting up for the final ordeal. Despite her show of strength earlier in the week, she was still very weak. The trip to town had tired her. She could not squander her limited energies on the preliminaries.

After the press reception, they went upstairs briefly for Archy's party, now getting a chance to shake hands and have a few words with the prominent guests. Kaplan had joined Priscilla and Mrs. A. Belle had meet her before, in the old days in New York, and they talked breathlessly for a few minutes. Maude had come in with Mrs. D and Tom Glenn.

"Tom," Belle said, after the introductions had been performed, "have you talked to her today?"

"Yes," he nodded. "She'll be fine."

Maude had formed a Texas triangle—Mrs. D, herself, and Charley—and the three were laughing about something or other.

Sharon and Frank Woodley came into the room with Sam and Sylvia Leonard. Sharon was hanging tightly to Frank's arm.

"Ah," Kaplan said, "our hero!"

Frank smiled a little grimly. "Didn't plan it that way, Kappy."

Belle chuckled. Somehow, Woodley had dug out Kaplan's schooldays nickname.

"Kappy . . ." she murmured.

Kaplan made a face. "Rascal . . . Frank, what'll happen to that man Flynn?"

Woodley shook his head as Kaplan explained to Mrs. A what they were talking about.

"I hope they put him away for a while," Woodley said, smiling wryly for Kaplan and Mrs. A. "And I hope they advise me when he's getting out."

Leonard very seriously said, "You must show me that trick some time, Frank. It could be very useful at board meetings."

Belle's friend from San Francisco, Shiela Brown, and her contingent had arrived in town in the late afternoon after what had evidently been an uproarious trip. They were still in a boisterious and smug San Francisco mood.

Archy presided over a wine-tasting table at one end of the room, cajoling and urging the guests to try and compare California cabernets with French bordeaux while Lou, in a tight-fitting and revealing black cocktail dress, roamed about in a high state of excitement.

Eyebrows lifted at the entrance of Darling Higgins and David Abdul. Darling looked very pleased with herself. Her small, fair face was jaunty and she transmitted a daring wink toward Belle. Belle was momentarily startled: Did Darling somehow consider her a co-conspirator?

She chuckled to herself, for Abdul seemed to be moving in a sort of daze. Ha, Belle thought, Prince Abdul had perhaps discovered that Beverly Hills ladies were sugar and spice and everything nice, but that there was an inordinate amount of spice in the concoction.

"My friend David seems to have found a new love," Kaplan grunted.

"Seems so," Belle replied. "His old love was . . ."

Kaplan glanced at her carefully. "Someone you know—that cowish creature called Pamela Renfrew. He was in New York with Pamela just recently. They were introduced by Sam Leonard."

Belle frowned. But it was all past now. "Pamela certainly gets around."

"It looks," Kaplan said waspishly, "like she's been dealt out."

Charley said softly, "Ten to one, those two just got out of the sack."

Archy Finistere pounced on Abdul, clapping him on the back with such force Abdul looked as if he might collapse. Darling smiled.

"Darling," Belle said, "you look wonderful."

"I am wonderful," Darling replied.

Rolly Starr hustled into the room with several of his stable of Hollywood notables and made straight for Belle and Darling.

"You sweet things!" he exclaimed. "You look like princesses tonight."

"That's what I feel like, too," Darling said.

"What *have* you done with Ellsworth?"

"Dumped him," Darling replied. "Rolly, do you know David Abdul?"

"No!" Rolly cried, as if thunderstruck. "Mr. Abdul, the man who's given us the Beverly Splendide?"

Belle let him get away with it. She didn't remind him that Abdul had been at their first luncheon meeting at the unfinished Splendide.

Pat Hyman made a rare appearance with her husband George. George looked out of place and his smooth, tanned face was dejected. Possibly, Belle thought, he still hadn't recovered from the death of his friend. Pat seemed determined to rub it in—she led George directly to Frank and Sharon Woodley, kissed Sharon heartily, and introduced them.

Rolly was asking Abdul if he'd ever considered investing in the picture business and Abdul was declining softly.

Shaking Frank Woodley's hand, George muttered, "I hope you'll always be on my side, Mr. Woodley."

Frank smiled carefully. "Always," he said.

Then George made almost the same suggestion to Woodley as Rolly had made to Abdul, that they should meet some time and talk about the movie biz.

Sam Leonard took Belle by the arm and drew her aside. "I've booked a big table up at the hotel. We'll go there for dinner. I thought us, you and Charley, Kaplan and his noted friend if she wants to come, Sharon and her killer, Abdul and his gorgeous pal. Anybody else?"

"Sure, Maude and Tom. Maude's 'noted' friend will probably disappear right after this. She's looking a little . . ."

"Yes," Leonard said. "Belle . . ." He seized her shoulder and kissed her on the mouth. "You've seen the ad in *Vogue*?"

"Could I miss it?" She kissed him back. "It's beautiful."

This was the beginning of the campaign, introducing Belle—a sophisticated woman, a sophisticated product for the woman of the world.

"I was floored," Leonard said happily. "And that's only the beginning. You and Charley—you make some team! But your work is only starting."

"I'm ready," she said.

"Charley?"

Belle moved her shoulders. "We're talking about wrapping up the agency when the estate is settled."

Leonard nodded. "That'd be smart, Belle. You know, once one of the principals in a two-man partnership like that is gone, the thing changes so much you might just as well start all over again."

"Charley thinks we could sell out to some of the associates. They've got their own accounts."

"Right. All you got to do is change the name. You and Charley should keep a small stake, throw them business when you can, make use of them when you need 'em. And Charley could concentrate on Cosmos . . . and you. Hey! Who's that pulling at my arm? Oh, it's Sylvia. Hello, Sylvia. You're such a little squirt I didn't see you there."

Sam grinned at Sylvia. She kicked him sharply in the shins.

Chapter Thirty-One

"After this is all over, in a couple of months," Sally said, "I'm going to get a face job, my husband. I hope you're not going to mind."

Bernard Markman shook his head and smiled calmly. "And then," he said, "we're going on a long trip, a good vacation after all these years. Sally, what's happened to all the time?"

"It's flown away," she said sadly.

They had watched a spectacular winter sunset in the west, a solar furnace quenched in the horizon fourteen miles away in the deep Pacific and leaving behind a crimson glow, another preview of the end of the world.

"Like the boys pissing on the campfire," Sally commented mischievously.

Bernard nodded, hardly listening. He was too used to hearing her iconoclastic cracks. It became immediately chilly. They went inside for a simple meal of heavy soup, French bread, and a bottle of stout red wine.

"Earthquake weather," Bernard remarked. "Whenever it's hot like this in December and January, everything starts shaking."

"Or typhoon," she grinned.

"Maybe both, and the continental shelf slips into the sea, retribution for all our sins," he said.

"What sins? The sins of the lush life?"

"Yes. God's revenge on the sybarites," he murmured, then went off on a tangent. "We'll go to Tuscany to start with. I love Tuscany. I was there during the war." He put his hand on hers. "We'll eat pasta and drink that hard Tuscan wine and walk in the vineyards . . ."

"Of the Lord?"
"No, just the vineyards."
"Listen, handsome," Sally said, cutting to the bone, "I want you to quit worrying about me. I'm feeling a lot better, you know."
He pressed her hand. "You don't absolutely have to go to that ball tomorrow."
Sally laughed. "Are you kidding? That's a date I'm going to keep even if you have to carry me there on a stretcher."
"Well," he said, irritated at her stubbornness, "after that you've got to promise that you'll rest."
"I promise. Then the face. I'm already bald as a coot and I hate it. But I can do something about the face."
"That man in Palm Springs," he suggested, "we could go down there."
"Precisely," Sally said. "But do you think the hair can grow back?"
"Anything is possible. You've already proven that."
Sally smiled gently at him. She really did love this man, still such an overgrown schoolboy. And she knew all about him. Had he really changed so much? He was hers again, as he had been in the beginning.
"Husband," she said, "let's go to bed. I have an overwhelming desire to make love to you." He looked doubtful, so she said, "Don't worry. Whatever it is, it's not catching."

Pamela Renfrew was cruising the streets in her white car, on the lookout for that Bentley of Abdul's. She was not sure what she'd do if she were to spot it. All she knew was that she was very angry and in a vindictive mood. How could he have thrown her over so easily, so cruelly? Shit, wasn't she ever to have any real luck in life? She had been misused by so many men she must go down in the records books as a victim. Just when she'd been on the verge of success, her hopes had been blown into a thousand smithereens. She had counted on going with Abdul to the Winter Ball, counted on thumbing her nose at all those social ladies, the snooty, snotty rich and mighty who had always treated her so patronizingly: Belle Cooper, angelic Belle, the great Sally Markman, Marjery Cannon who, it was said, gave even better head than she, Pamela Renfrew . . . and the likes of men like Kaplan and Sam Leonard.
Pamela had been at the Polo Lounge for a couple of drinks, which she had hoped would calm her; instead, they

had made her more angry and frustrated. She'd been so absorbed in her own misery that when the time suddenly came, she hadn't made it to the ladies' room in time and she had wet her pants. The hell with it. She'd simply stuffed them in her pocketbook and now she was driving bare-assed, the whirl of air from the air conditioner playing on her thighs and making her horny. She needed a man and quickly, and preferably a little one she could crush in her legs and squeeze to death just as she should have that rotten little A-rab.

She passed that other Arab mansion on Sunset Boulevard. It was empty but floodlit, the copper roof caved in where it had burned. Outside, nothing had harmed the statues, painted garishly with black pubic hair and red-tinted nipples, the cocks orange. Christ, they would never find a buyer for that place now.

There was nobody for her. She thought for a second of driving to the airport and flying to Las Vegas, picking up one of those high rollers. But no, she couldn't go to Las Vegas without any pants. Why couldn't she find love? She was ready to give it. She could have loved Cooper to death if she'd had the opportunity. And then it had been too late. If she had said yes that afternoon of his last phone call, deserted Abdul ahead of a last humiliation, Cooper would still be alive.

Pamela drove home. She closed the garage, but before she got out of the car, she pulled out her little automatic. She was not going to be surprised and raped again without a fight.

But all was quiet. As she closed the kitchen door and turned on the light, the phone began to ring. With her luck, it was probably an obscene phone call, she thought bitterly.

It wasn't, however. It was the German man Schall, whom she'd met in London with Abdul. His accent was heavy, harsh, but the voice eager and ingratiating. He had just arrived in Los Angeles and, as he had told her in London, was interested in property. When could he see her? How was his dear friend, David Abdul?

"He's out of town," Pamela said. "You can see me tonight, if you wish. Please come to my home. I have all my real estate information here with me. I'd come to the hotel, but I'm waiting for a very important phone call."

"Yes. Good. I will come."

"And your wife, too, of course."

"My wife does not accompany me."

All the better. She gave him the address. He said he would be there as soon as he could find a cab.

Well, she thought, more cheerfully, things were looking up after all. Pamela went upstairs and took a quick shower. She dabbed perfume liberally under her ears, at the cleft of her bosom, and then, thinking Germans were fond of heavy weather and strong odors, she shoved some in her navel and on her thighs. She dressed in a pair of tight slacks, leaving aside the panties again so there wouldn't be any marks between her body and the smooth fabric, and a loose blouse, which, without a bra, showed the lift of her breasts and the shadow of her nipples.

Pamela smiled at herself. She couldn't recall ever having had a German lover. But this time, there wouldn't be any fooling around. He could try it once. If he liked it, then he'd sign a contract that would be just as binding as a buyer's offer. And there would also be a down payment, a good-faith advance.

Daisy and Jake silently watched Daisy's latest cinematic triumph. But Jake was not so very pleased.

"First the poolman," Jake observed grumpily, "and now a Japanese gardener? Daisy, your cast of characters is showing more inventiveness, I agree, but a good deal less distinction."

She protested, "It's very thin these days, Jake. Maybe it's the weather." Then she suggested something she'd been thinking about all day. "Why don't we ever film ourselves doing it? Wouldn't that be a novelty?"

Jake shook his head. "That would seem like . . . incest, my dear."

"I want to," she said. "Come on!"

"Well . . ." He was shy. He shook his head, but her position in the household was more influential nowadays. She took his hand and insisted, and dragged him off the couch to the bed. Jake remembered that the weight of their bodies activated the camera. He giggled and clucked reluctantly as she pulled off his Mandarin robe. It was all but impossible for her to arouse him.

"Would you maybe feel better if you were wearing a mask, Jake?"

"Perhaps."

It was an inspiration. Daisy dug around in her bureau and found a black mask she'd worn to a costume party once upon a time. She put it on him.

"You look like the Lone Ranger, Jake."

He laughed breathlessly and looked in the mirror. But it worked. The disguise turned him into a maniac, a sneering, grunting monster, and finally he made love to her in a manner he had never before achieved. Curiously, Daisy was almost satisfied, and knowing that made her cheerful. When they finished, he could not wait to run the film. Keeping the mask on his face, he watched gleefully.

"Beautiful," he exclaimed, again and again. "That's me and it isn't me. Who is this mysterious stranger taking this wild lady in his strong arms and forcing her to passionate love? It is Zorro!" he exclaimed. "It is the Scarlet Pimpernel! Is he in heaven or is he in hell, that damned elusive Pimpernel?"

"Easy, easy," Daisy cautioned. "Why didn't I think of this before?"

"My dear," he told her, his eyes fierce behind the mask, "henceforth, with my martini and clarinet, I will have my mask. I will wear it every night."

"Flora will think you've gone nuts," she said. Hell, she told herself, it was true: Jake was completely bananas. He'd probably want to wear it to the Winter Ball.

Jurgen Ehrlich stood at the entrance of the ballroom watching the Flower Fashions people festoon the room with silk streamers, place trees and position pots and vases around the trellises, on the stage, and outside. Tomorrow, the fresh flowers would be added to complete the marvelous transformation.

Stiffly, he did an about-face to march erectly up the steps to the lobby. The hotel was being turned into a paradise for that one night: Saturday. It was astonishing for him to watch the Finley people work. No job seemed too big for them to undertake. Upstairs, 100 rooms on the third and fourth floors would be occupied. The Splendide was already carrying its own weight.

But he had a problem: Bertha Moore. She had been so unmannered, so rude to Archibald Finistere that he was shamed. He could not abide that. He was faithful to his captain. If Mr. Finistere had told Jurgen to jump off the roof he might well have done so. No . . . Yes, he had made up his mind there would be no marriage of himself and Bertha Moore.

The lobby still smelled deliciously of paint and new wood, of fresh and unsoiled carpeting. All the paraphernalia of hotel efficiency was in place behind the long desk—windows for the cashiers and the machines to handle every known credit card. Keys hung neatly, like soldiers, from the bottoms of the pigeonholes, the small property of whomever had rented the room.

Perkins, head porter, was standing at his post, already dressed in the tailcoat that would be the uniform of his exalted office.

"Well, Mr. Perkins, all is *in ordnung*, yes?"

"All in order, Mr. Ehrlich," Perkins said, not disturbed Ehrlich had let slip the German word.

Unfortunately, Bertha chose that moment to call him.

"Jurgen," she said severely, "I've been waiting dinner for you."

Muffling his voice behind his hand so Perkins could not overhear, Ehrlich muttered, "*Schatz*, it is impossible. I will be up and working all night."

"Jurgen, didn't I tell you? I don't like that word."

He ignored her objection, for it was a perfectly good word. "It is impossible," he said firmly.

"But I want to see you," Bertha wailed.

"Perhaps . . . I will be there for a few moments after midnight."

"Not until then?" she said mournfully.

"That is correct, *mein schatz*." He underlined the words.

Slowly, she said, "All right . . . I'll be waiting."

Ehrlich did not say anything else. He hung up the phone. Perkins was watching him without expression. Perkins, Ehrlich understood, was the perfect hotelier: speak no evil, hear no evil, see no evil. Briefly, that meant Perkins never talked.

Ehrlich cracked his knuckles with satisfaction. Whatever he did with Mrs. Moore from now on would be on his terms. He would make her understand that she should never have embarrassed him in front of Mr. Finistere.

Chapter Thirty-Two

Saturday dawned brightly to brilliantly clear blue skies. It was slightly chilly, but the weather remained so dry that everyone that morning was complaining of sinus, coughing, sneezing and even nosebleeds.

"California—the home of the sinus condition," Pat Hyman grumbled energetically as she and Belle met at the hotel.

"Never mind," Belle said, "the easterners won't notice. This sun is everything they've ever hoped for."

Acitvity in the ballroom was no less hectic than it had been Friday night. In the remaining hours until balltime, completion of the decoration proceeded with mathematical precision. The ceiling was finished: Christmas trees decorated with hundreds, perhaps thousands, of tiny opera lights floated magically atop balloons like clouds among the chandeliers and silk streamers. Additional arc lights had been installed to light the stage for the TV cameras; the Flower Fashions crews were working with sound and light technicians, covering the equipment as much as possible. Tables, still bare of tablecloths and settings, were in place. A dozen young men were lacing the background trellises with greenery. The last act would be to weave the floral color scheme into the green—the red and white roses, and pink peonies, which had arrived on schedule at six A.M. and were now outside being revived from jet lag in tubs of cold water—and then to place the centerpieces. Gibbons and Finley were both there, scuttling calmly around the room, overseeing the last of the work.

Downstairs, the garage was finished: It was pristine white and gleaming. The cocktail area had been closed from roof to floor with white canvas; against this, stark green trees stood out impeccably. Dozens of small tables, white-clothed and mirror-topped, and white garden chairs had been placed in groupings. Ten mirrored bars had been set up and the cement floor had been covered with white fire-retardant carpeting.

"My God," Pat exclaimed. "It's fantastic. I like it almost better than upstairs."

Jurgen Ehrlich joined them. He was roaming restlessly. His eyes were tired and watery from lack of sleep. It had been a rough night, for the Splendide was being put to its first test. One hundred rooms and suites on the upper floors were occupied. The demands on the new staff were obvious. Ehrlich had personally seen to breakfast; as the hotel restaurants weren't open, the entire load fell on room service.

Despite his weariness, Ehrlich fluttered his hands with enthusiasm.

"We will prevail," he cried, almost too excitedly. "It is a miracle. My men are a marvel. I am overjoyed, ladies."

"It *is* a mircle," Pat gushed, "thanks to you, Jurgen."

"Ah, dear lady," he spluttered, seizing Pat's hand and kissing it. "Such a joy, this family of ours. In the next years, we will always remember this moment, standing here, on the morning of December the second."

"Before the deluge," Belle said.

Ehrlich didn't get it. He marched away, absently, forgetting them.

"Do you think it is before the deluge, Belle?" Pat asked quietly.

Belle shrugged. It was a depressing thought. "I don't know," she said. "Sometimes, it seems that . . . Look, all this, all the money that's being spent, all the money people are spending to come here. Sometimes, I wonder, Pat. Maybe I didn't get enough sleep last night. I was thinking of the trillion things that can go wrong today. It just seems as though, when you put on a spectacle like this . . . that some horrible catastrophe has to follow . . ."

"I know what you mean," Pat said morosely. "We're not very cheerful, are we? I was thinking the same thing, that people will look back. They'll say, 'Remember the Winter Ball? That was the last big party before the . . . earthquake of . . . or the last blast before the revolution . . . or the last gala affair ahead of the catastrophe of . . . the war of . . .' "

Dryly, Belle added, "Or before the famine . . . fuel crisis . . . or . . ."

"Anyway," Pat said, putting her arm around Belle's waist, "they won't be able to say we didn't live it up, will they?"

This was the last chance they had all day to have any sort of conversation, serious or otherwise.

Lucia Montonya and her cosmeticians were in action. Tables had been set up, mirrored and decorated, and already Lucia was working on a dozen early customers out of brightly labeled jars and bottles and vials of "Belle" cosmetics. The labels were simple but extremely elegant, Belle thought: her silhouetted profile in the center, dark red script "Belle" across the bottom.

Lucia seemed very pleased. "We're going to do land-office business. Sam is going to be pleased and, for once, I'm really going to earn my keep."

That was a peculiar thing for her to say. Belle was surprised. It had never occurred to her before that Sam might be keeping Lucia Montonya.

"Lucia," she said, passing the statement, "it's marvelous."

"And so is the product, Belle. You should be proud as a peacock."

Across the hall, the local designers were showing their couture models. There had been a few sales already, so early in the morning.

"What else can we do?" she asked Pat.

"It's in the hands of the gods," Pat said.

Sally arrived with her husband just before lunch. They had been given a suite upstairs and it was there they all ate. The chefs had made light omelettes and a huge green salad. Archy opened champagne and poured it himself. Ehrlich passed around the glasses.

"Ladies and gentlemen, here's to you," Archy said. "With this, we have set sail."

Bernard Markman stood up. "Archy, to you and the Splendide. Long may it thrive."

After lunch, the lobby became active. The men were coming back from golf and tennis dates, the women from their shopping expeditions. Others were streaming in to take advantage of the "Belle" makeup clinic, impressed that it was being administered by the famous Lucia Montonya and even more by the fact that the fantastic new line, "Belle," had already been announced in *Vogue* and *Harper's Bazaar*.

Sam Leonard looked in at four P.M. and he and Belle visited Lucia.

"Lucia, my lovely," Leonard said, "how are we doing?"

Lucia kissed him lingeringly. Why, Belle asked herself, hadn't she ever caught on to this?

"They love it, Sam," Lucia said.

"You see, Belle," Leonard beamed, "you're a hit!"

"No less than I expected," Belle said. "Now, what about a look at the ballroom?"

Leonard whistled when he saw what had been accomplished. "Christ, this is something else. I never dreamt it would look so good. Abdul and Kaplan have really put something together. I wish I'd known. I'd have invested some money myself . . . even though Abdul is an enemy of my people." He grinned self-effacingly.

Belle remembered another detail. "We're keeping the 'Belle' bags upstairs until much later. After everybody is inside the ballroom I'll have them placed on the front desk—everybody'll get to pick them up when they leave, along with the Laykin silver pins."

"Smart," he said approvingly. "The price of silver being what it is, somebody could make a bundle heisting the stuff. You better make sure a security guy is posted inside after the doors are closed—and locked. You've got to watch it like a hawk. Another thing, I hear it's quite possible some character is going to try to sneak a rival line of cosmetic crap in here. We're not going to let them get away with that, are we, Belle?" She took note of his warning.

Harry Finley declared the ballroom finished at five-thirty, and Belle went upstairs to her room and took a shower. She sat in a bright red pair of panties and bra Charley had bought her for good luck and made up her face with her product. It looked good; it was her. Leonard was right. Jimmy Galanos had designed a red sheath, which she would wear with ruby earrings and necklace, red shoes . . . red everything. When she'd finished, she inspected herself in the mirror. Wow! she thought, you are a knockout, lady.

Belle was combed out and ready for action at 6:30. Remembering Leonard's warning, she went directly to the ballroom.

Leonard had been so right. At the garden entrance of the ballroom, a man was passing out boxes of Arabian Nights, or whatever that cosmetic was, and the waiters, not knowing any better, were already plopping it down on the tables.

She was furious. What nerve!

Her voice crossed the room so loudly that the man leapt back.

"Get that stuff out of here, you! You're not putting that on the tables."

The man recovered enough to grin. "Who says so?"

"I say so." Belle strode between the tables to get to the other side. "I'm one of the organizers of this ball and we're not having your stuff here."

"Bullshit! Cosmos doesn't own this ball."

"Cosmos *does* own this ball," Belle said angrily, "and you're not putting that stuff on our tables."

"You're Belle," the man said. "I recognize you."

She was momentarily startled. "You do? All the better then. We've got this exclusively. No, tell these waiters to get it off the tables. You should be ashamed of yourself, taking advantage of them. Do it now, or I'll call security, and we've got plenty of that around, I can tell you."

He hesitated, faltering. "I'm just doing a job."

"I realize that. But you can tell your boss it didn't work. You've got five minutes to get that trash out of here."

"Trash?" He laughed. "I'd like to hear you say that to Spiro Angelicus." He fumbled in his vest pocket. "Here's my card. When you get your thing going, I'd like to talk to you. I'm a hell of a merchandiser." He turned to the waiters, who were standing around uncertainly. "Okay, you guys, pick all that shit up and put it back in the boxes."

"And don't leave any behind," Belle said.

"And don't leave any of it behind, you guys," he ordered.

She waited until she was sure she'd seen the last of Arabian Nights, and took another look at the ballroom. It would be her last private moment. It was marvelous; yet in five or six hours it would be all over, the carefully executed decor already obsolete. Belle wondered if anvone would ever dare repeat this party, whether they, the December Group, would do as well next year. Belle didn't want to know how much it was costing Darling Higgins: for the ballroom, the garage, and even, she had just discovered from Finley, individual floral arrangements sent to all the out-of-town guests.

Belle made sure the garden doors were securely closed and locked. But she had no worry now. As she was crossing the room to leave, security men came into the ballroom. There were six of them and they began a close inspection.

"I'm surprised you weren't here sooner," she said to their leader.

"We should have been. Slip-up. I didn't know they'd finished working in here."

"If a man tries to get in the back door with cosmetics, please throw him out," Belle said.

The man looked amused. "Have no fear."

Archy was in the lobby when she came up, performing his own last-minute inspection. Banks of flowers had been laid along and on top of the check-in desk, against the walls, and on each side of the entrance, forming a pathway to elevators and the wide steps leading to the ballroom and garage.

Archy was dressed in a sharply pressed black double-breasted tuxedo with a big black bow tie and cream-colored, resplendently ruffled shirt. Gold cufflinks glinted at his wrists; gold studs shone on his shirt front.

"Mr. Finistere, I believe . . ."

"Belle!" He rumbled with laughter. "You look—how should I say it?—breathtaking."

She kissed him on both cheeks. "French style, Archy, for good luck. But please . . . if you haven't thought of it, which I'm sure you have, we must have a picture of the ballroom before it's destroyed. It's beautiful."

"All in the works, Belle," he said. "Have no fear, *ma cherie*."

Charley arrived a few minutes ahead of schedule. He looked, for Charley, unusually elegant. He was tall and handsome in black tie and black velvet dinner jacket, decorated with a red carnation boutonniere. He saw her from the doorway and stopped dead in his tracks, staring at her so admiringly that she started to laugh.

"Holy cow," Charley yelled, "is this my date?" He came up to her and took her hands in his. "It is. Man! Dignified but sexy, gracious but wanton."

She continued to laugh. He was reminding her of what Sam Leonard had said that night at the Bistro so long ago.

She whispered, "Wanton, is it? You'll see, my dear fellow, when this is over."

He stared into her eyes. "Belle, when this is over, we're going away for a few days. My schedule says we've got nothing to do before Christmas. Therefore, we're going to Acapulco one week from today, that is to say December 9. We've got to be in New York on the sixteenth. What say to Christmas in New York?"

"Could we?" she cried. "That would be marvelous."

"I thought it would be a good idea. Maybe we could even see a little snow for a change."

Charley held her there for a moment while he dug into his pants pocket. He handed her a small box. "This is something I thought you'd like."

Belle opened the box. Inside, on a bed of satin, there was a cabochon ruby ring, its domed, convex stone polished to a mild luster and surrounded by small diamonds. The red of the ruby, deep but not faceted, glowed. Belle slipped it on her finger, the third of her left hand, and wagged the hand at Archy.

"Heavens," Archy exclaimed, "that is a handsome ring. Good Lord if it's not."

Belle put her arms around Charley, caring nothing that they were in the middle of the lobby and in full view of half the world.

"Charley," she whispered, "it goes with my underwear."

He chuckled. "It's nothing binding, just something I felt like giving you. It's an antique ring and I fell for it."

"Thank you, Charley. I love you," she said in his ear.

Maude and the girls arrived with their protégées, the former inhabitants of the White House, promptly at 7:30. They swept into the lobby flanked by secret service men and went straight to the elevators. Belle and Charley stood with Finistere, waiting for the governors. They came in two cars, out of the first of which climbed Carlotta Westmoreland. Squat, red-faced, and white-haired, Carlotta was dressed in a heavy, beaded, gown with a throat-high bodice.

"Come along, fellas," they heard her say.

The governors followed her obediently. Carlotta winked at Belle.

A black, chauffeur-driven limousine pulled up under the porte-cochere. David Abdul, Norman Kaplan, and Frank Woodley stepped out. Frank's wife was already upstairs.

As usual, Kaplan was puffing with energy. Abdul smiled quietly and shook Archy's hand. Fingering his neat black mustache, he nodded silently as he looked around.

"You go on upstairs," Belle told Woodley. "Eighth floor."

Gergory Cannon entered the hotel by himself. He looked nervous and said hello in a jerky voice. Pat Hyman, trailed by George, was next and then Archy's good friend, the other veteran Beverly Hills hotelier, Hernando Courtright, and his wife, jovially sauntered in. He looked around admiringly.

"Archy," Hernando barked brusquely, "you scoundrel, you've done it again. It's magnificent. I'm proud of you, my boy."

Archy laughed delightedly, hugging himself. "He calls me 'my boy' because he's six months older than me. Go straight up to the eighth, Hernando, and they'll point the way. I'm proud you're here. And no peeking behind the scenes."

Glenn came with the Leonards and a fat, balding man of medium height. Somehow, Belle had pictured Dr. Vincent Richardson as tall, with a research-worn face. Richardson looked more like an overworked and coronary-prone insurance company executive. But Leonard nodded approvingly to her. He was plainly much impressed with Glenn's choice.

With Bernard Markman at her side, Sally stood serenely in the center of the room, a glass of wine in one hand. She had dressed for the occasion in a Norell pearl-gray dress. She looked wan, it had to be admitted, but in full control. Again, Belle was thunderstruck by the marvel of her recovery, or at least the grip she had on herself. Tonight, eyes shining, this person might have been the Sally Markman of six months ago, when she had conceived the idea for the Winter Ball.

The First Ladies stood in a semi-circle around Sally; the governors, two senators, and several congressmen in Carlotta Westmoreland's command close by. Sam Leonard and Sylvia were keeping an eye on their French group; the latter were plainly impressed, although, joking and chattering among themselves, they tried not to show it. Waiters circulated with drinks and Belle noted with some emotion that the two hoteliers, Archy and Courtright, arms over each other's shoulders, were at the window. Archy was pointing off to the west, toward the Beverly Wilshire.

Tom Glenn was introducing Vincent Richardson to Sally, then the First Ladies, the governors. Leonard stepped forward, hands in the pocket of his jacket. He cleared his throat.

"I'd like one short word," Leonard said quietly. "I'm Sam Leonard and I'd like to say that my wife Sylvia and myself are immensely proud to be part of this gathering. We're proud, too, of Dr. Vincent Richardson here and exceedingly fond of Dr. Tom Glenn, who brought Dr. Richardson to us."

All eyes turned to Richardson. His jowly face flushed; he looked to Glenn for help. Glenn shook his head, smiling; Maude slipped her hand through the crook of Glenn's arm.

Richardson mumbled shyly, "I'm not used to this sort of thing. I can only say I was totally surprised and pleased when I heard from Tom Glenn, and now I'm thrilled, overwhelmed."

"Bravo," Carlotta Westmoreland chirped. She turned on her flock. "You politicians had better take note that everything happening here tonight is happening without benefit of taxpayers' money."

Naturally, on cue, they laughed and shook their heads, letting everyone know they were completely in Carlotta's power.

Then Sally spoke up: "While we're in this small group, let me express my appreciation to everybody. You're all helping us realize our ambition and make our dream come true. Thank you to the women who've helped organize this, thanks to all the people who have come such a long way to be here. Thanks to Vincent Richardson for the work he does, and for being what he is. But remember one thing: the Winter Ball is an annual event and we'll expect you all again next year."

"And," Kaplan announced sonorously, "we will *all* be here."

Belle gulped. He meant Sally.

"Belle, Belle, where are you?" Sally said. "Come over here. My dear friend, Belle Cooper . . . You may have seen her pictures in the magazines by now."

Sally put dry lips to Belle's cheeks. "Susan called, just an hour ago," she murmured. "To wish me—us—luck."

"I'm sorry she's not here."

"Hell," Sally waved her hand. "She'll have plenty of time for her own charities, later. So here we go, kiddo."

This was the last moment of quiet for the rest of the evening. When they went back downstairs, the lobby and the entrance were bedlam. Photographers were working busily and now demanded what they had been waiting for: pictures of the First Ladies, with Sally, with the governors, pictures of Sally with her committee and with the Leonards, and Richardson, and so on, in infinite variation. Guests were streaming in and the lobby was jammed. The traffic was directed to the garage level. Although it was very crowded, it worked . . . Just before nine, it was decided to throw open the ballroom doors. Captains, waiters, pointed people to their tables . . . It took fifteen minutes to get everybody seated and waiters at each station began pouring champagne as Bobby Short played the piano.

When the hubbub had somewhat subsided, Kaplan got up from their table and went to the stage. He took the mike.

"Ladies and gentlemen . . . ladies and gentlemen, pray silence for just a moment. My name is Norman Kaplan and it is my honor to be president of the December Foundation, which we are dedicating tonight, along with this beautiful new hotel: the Beverly Splendide. Mesdames First Ladies, governors, senators, congressmen, your beautiful ladies, all honored guests from near and far, welcome to our cause. Now, it's my pleasure to introduce to you our master of ceremonies for the evening, a man who, as they say, needs no introduction."

And so it went, smoothly, rapidly. There were no hitches. It was, Belle thought, a miracle.

Norman, as he should be, was in a state of almost sensual excitement. He maintained a constant patter of talk with his date for the evening, the redoubtable Mrs. A., treated the whole table to words of praise for everything: himself, the wine, the service, the beautiful women, the stunning men. David Abdul smiled his secret smile. Sally clutched Bernard Markman's hand. Nearby, Leonard, Glenn, Richardson, the French count . . . prince . . . princess . . .

The waiters, schooled and drilled by Ehrlich and now almost seasoned veterans after a day of experience in the new hotel, white-gloved and immaculate in their Splendide uniforms, whipped among the tables with Beluga caviar, heaps of it in small potato shells, then offered a sour cream topping; ice buckets of frosty vodka appeared magically . . .

The first course was cleared from the tables speedily. Korda and his violins provided musical background, restrained and conducive to conversation. Next, the asparagus, the soup, the main course of delectable filet, sorbet, and then the endive and cheese. When it came time for the Bombe d'Hiver, two dozen waiters carried it into the room amid a fanfare of violins. Jurgen Ehrlich personally led this parade, holding a marshal's baton and directing the dispersal of each waiter to his assigned table. Ehrlich stood in the center of the dance floor, marching in place, his red face thrown back, hupping loudly. He was grinning wildly.

"Good God," Belle said to Charley, "I think this is what Jurgen has been waiting for. This is the high point."

Kaplan was giggling immoderately. "Believe this," he exclaimed. "Jurgen Ehrlich is a fable. Were we wrong to steal him away from Switzerland and then the Camino? I don't know anybody who could whip a bunch of waiters into such shape in such a short time."

Short returned to the stage for more of his Carlyle Hotel favorites . . . Master of ceremonies took over again . . . TV cameras whirred and one crew with a portable camera panned across the audience; the smiling faces would be dubbed in again and again if the production ever came to final screening form. The singer . . . the ballet . . . the opera . . .

The acts followed one on the other with clockwork precision, no hitches, no delays. Belle knew Rolly Starr was backstage, directing it all. In his way, Rolly was a genius, too, she thought; as much as people might knock Hollywood—its strange life styles and unusual inhabitants—when it came to something like this the place was unmatched. Nowhere was such a strike force of talent assembled; nowhere else, the expertise to make best use of it.

Then, suddenly, it was time for the presentation to Richardson.

The principals went to the stage: Richardson, Sam and Sylvia, Tom Glenn. Norman escorted Sally.

Belle had been expecting it: a shrinking in her throat, a clutching at her heart. It was the emotional climax of the evening, at least for her. She gulped and got her handkerchief ready. She took Charley's hand and murmured, "I'm going to cry."

"Go ahead," he said. "Me, too."

But she was not alone. Mrs. A. was already dabbing her eyes. Norman must have explained everything to her.

Kaplan took command again, as president of the December Foundation. He read Richardson's biography, as the doctor stood shyly, his fat chin perched on his hand. Tom Glenn gave a soft account of the important current work Richardson and his team were doing. Finally, Sam spoke, repeating at slightly greater length what he had said upstairs.

Kaplan resumed. "Now, Mrs. Sally Markman . . ."

When Sally came forward, Kaplan put his arm around her from one side and Leonard from the other. Then came what is called a standing ovation. For some reason, people who would not have recognized Sally in the street understood this was due her. They stood and the applause went on and on . . . until Kaplan raised his arms, calling for quiet.

Sally said only two sentences: "I thank you all for what you've done to help. I thank everybody from the bottom of my heart!"

Belle was crying now and, glancing at Charley, she saw his eyes were wet.

"Now, now," Kaplan shouted, "please . . . Dr. Richardson, your time has come."

The plaque was small and bronze. Richardson took it nervously, almost dropping it. He shook hands with Leonard and Kaplan, then kissed Sally.

He had trouble speaking. "I won't—can't say much. You've heard enough about me already. I'm very proud—for myself and my associates." He turned slightly to look at Sally, then Leonard. "I wish I could tell you tonight that we can see the end of our fight against this disease: cancer." He pronounced the dread word forcefully, as if telling them *Fear Not*. "I can tell you," he went on simply, "that we're on the trail and that we will get there . . . with the help of people like yourselves who are willing to face the facts." He took Sally's hand and then concluded solemnly in the dead silence of the room, "So, I thank you in a personal way, for myself, and I thank you for all the people around the world who are on our side. Thank you."

Richardson stepped back, nodding acknowledgment of the applause.

A comedian jumped up from one of the front tables, a long cigar clamped in his right hand. Jauntily, and so carelessly that it should have seemed completely spontaneous, he made for the stage, exclaiming loudly, "Doc, we love you. But what have you done lately for ingrown toenails?"

This spun down the emotion, the tension of the moment. When he had finished a mild roast of guests, entertainers, and the VIPs, he asked all of them to group on the stage: the First Ladies, the governors, and assorted other politicians, the entertainers, Sally, Kaplan, the Leonards . . . Photographers, loosed from behind barriers outside, rushed inside for ten minutes of frenzied picture-taking . . . and so ended the formal part of the evening.

Belle sat with her hand in Charley's. They had done it, but now, all at once, she felt emotionally drained, exhausted. Yes, somehow they had pulled it off and, looking around, she took pleasure from the glow of fulfilled, happy faces. Often, such a party as this one ended in letdown, anticlimax. But these people, all 2,000 of them, were satisfied: they had participated, been entertained, delighted, and impressed. Catharsis—it was not easy to achieve in a party of this size. An indication of success was that they did not jump to their feet and head for the door . . . dancing had begun.

Leonard bent to murmur in her ear, "They loved it, Belle. It's a good piece of work."

Sally and Bernard Markman bore down on them. Belle stood up and put her arms around Sally.

"Belle, my love, thank you," Sally whispered.

"No, thank *you*," Belle said. "How are you holding up?"

"She's a tiger," Markman said, beaming.

Sally kissed Sam Leonard and hugged him. "You are a great man, Sam," she said. "I love you."

"And I you," Leonard said softly.

"Hey! Come on, beautiful, enough of that," Markman commanded. "Let's have a dance."

As they moved toward the floor Leonard dabbed at his eyes. "Shit, Belle, I'm too hardhearted to be thrown by a thing like this."

"Yes, you are . . . not," she said.

Kaplan was helping his friend, Mrs. A., from the table. "Madame," he said, "let us dance."

"Charley?" Belle asked. "Dance?"

"Go on, you oaf," Leonard barked, "before I take her."

They squeezed through the crowd. Charley put his arm around her and they moved slowly to the music.

"I dance like a dead-beat," he grumbled.

"I don't care if you do. I just want to move a little."

Maude and Tom Glenn eased up beside them.

"Honey," Maude said, "wasn't it marv'lous? Wasn't Tom a winner?"

Glenn grinned enigmatically. "I'm speechless."

They danced away and Belle asked, "What are they playing now, Charley?"

He shook his head. "Something Glenn Miller . . ."

"Yes, it takes me back," Belle said. "Life is funny, ain't it, Charley?"

Chapter Thirty-Three

"Well," Sheldon Moore said, looking at his watch, "it must be just about over."

It was nine A.M. in the morning in St. Moritz. They were having breakfast beside the bedroom window with its view of the snow-capped mountains.

"And we missed it, Sheldon," Camilla said, "and, you know, I don't care."

Comfortably, even smugly, she patted her stomach. Sheldon already looked ten years younger. They had been taking long walks in the clear air, tramping through the town and up the lower trails, not yet overladen with either snow or skiers in these pre-season days. Their hotel was snug and cozy and Camilla was happier than she'd ever been in her life.

Sheldon whacked off the top of his second soft-boiled

egg and doused it with salt and pepper. "Want some more coffee?"

"Yes, please, just a half cup." Camilla looked skyward, toward the horizon of mountain tops. "Where do you think we'll be this time next year?"

"Anywhere you want to be."

"Maybe back in L.A.," she said thoughtfully. "Next year, I'll help Sally. I feel bad I ran out on her."

"You didn't run out. You were there almost 'til the end. And she had plenty of helpers." He poured her coffee and took her hand. "Today, I'm taking you down to that store and I'm buying you a new parka—a big one."

Sally and Bernard Markman were back upstairs in the Splendide suite by one in the morning.

"Well, husband," she said joyfully, "what about another glass of champagne?"

"Not for me, baby. I've had enough."

Sally merrily commenced to hum: "After the ball was over . . . Sally took out her glass eye . . ."

"Please . . . no singing."

She continued: "Stood her peg leg in the corner . . . and hung up her false hair to dry . . ."

"Sally, goddamn it!"

She laughed. She felt very well. Somehow, something had happened. The pain, a dulling presence just a couple of weeks before, had lapsed into an occasional reminder of a twinge, and tonight she had not been bothered by it at all. But, in fact, she was very tired and she didn't really want another glass of champagne. It had been a strain. But a good night's sleep, ah, and there was no reason why she shouldn't sleep the sleep of the angels.

"Sit down a minute over here, kiddo," she said.

She led him to the long couch by the windows. Ahead of her, she could see the lights of the hills; Hollywood, Beverly Hills, West Los Angeles, the crest loping toward the sea in the west.

Bernard said, "It was a good party, my dear."

"I know. It's amazing how well it went."

"Are you completely pooped?"

"Tired, not pooped. Actually, I feel fine and that's the truth." Then she said what she'd been planning to say. "Husband, I don't know what's going to happen, whether

I'm going to be all right now, or not. But I am satisfied."

"You're going to rest up," he said, "and then we're going away."

"Yes . . . yes! Will you please listen to what I'm saying? I've had a good time with you, a good life. I couldn't have been any better off, any luckier. I mean that, Bernard."

He nodded sheepishly, embarrassed, and she wondered at once if he knew something about her that she didn't. "Sal, I haven't been so great . . . I've never given you enough time . . . I was always too selfish."

She held up her hand. "We've lived," she said. "We made it through. You're perfect for me; you always were. Now, let's go to bed. Unzip the back of my dress, please."

She undressed in the bathroom, conscious of her various aches and pains. But they were muted tonight. By the time she'd slipped into her nightgown, she was overtaken by an extreme languor. She was well and truly ready to end the day, the hectic night. Sally eased between the sheets and, as she waited for him, she drifted weightlessly down the steep, winding path toward sleep. She was smiling to herself. What she had told Bernard was the truth. She had been lucky. Her life was good and now she had done something that would always make her remembered. She was fortunate in her best friends, like Belle. She loved her husband.

Sleepily, she was barely aware of him coming to bed, of his weight beside her, his hand on her shoulder, a light kiss next to her ear.

"You're a hit," she heard him say.

"You're a smash . . ." Her words dissolved between thought and expression as she dissolved into sleep. Then she was washed by images, of Bernard, the ocean, the sand . . .

By 2:30, the Splendide was quiet. Bertha expected Jurgen would come soon. She had not gone to the party. What, how, by herself? she had demanded of him. Bertha had slipped into the hotel at ten P.M. and had come upstairs to his room. She had been waiting there four hours now, first in front of the TV set, then in bed reading a copy of *Time*. At midnight she had taken a bath, had oiled and perfumed herself. She would be ready for him when he arrived, she calculated, somewhat wearily wondering what life was really all about. Here she was, full circle, waiting for a man in a hotel room.

She slipped on a pair of black stockings, a black garter belt, and then a black negligee, all of which she'd been carrying in her pocketbook. She sat down once more in front of the TV set and crossed her legs. The legs were still very good, long and slender.

Bertha waited. She sat quite still, waiting.

There was a noise in the hallway. She ran to the door. Jurgen was outside, talking to someone. She heard a woman's voice and realized, to her horror, it was that bitch Lou Finistere. Jesus, they were saying good-night. Bertha bounded back across the room and flicked off the light. She was standing, silhouetted against the window when he came in.

"Schatz?" he whispered.

"Here," she replied softly.

He turned on the light and saw her. He grasped, *"Donnerwetter!"*

"Come here, Jurgen," Bertha said. She let the negligee fall to the side, showing him stockings and garter belt. His eyes bugged incredulously, for he was shocked. She had never acted so whorishly with him, or with Sheldon, for that matter. "I have an empty spot for you, something warm and tight."

His intake of breath was sharp. He was carried away. He came at her with ferocity, but her own lust was the stronger. There would be no doubt in Jurgen's mind that he had transported her; she groaned and thrashed about on the bed, finally raking him down the back with her fingernails. His male ego would be inflated to bursting.

"Jurgen, my God," Bertha exclaimed in haunted, panting tones, "oh, my God, Jurgen. You're incredible."

"Ja, schatz," he muttered, covered in perspiration, humping all the harder.

Whatever Lou Finistere was up to with Jurgen, this would make him forget it. This was the best screw he was likely to have in his whole Teutonic life.

Bertha grinned to herself. In a way, it was nice to be back in the saddle again . . . Sheldon. She could have spit. Sheldon had taken that girl off to Switzerland. Well . . . she had Switzerland inside her right here.

* * *

Gregory Cannon made himself a final scotch and water and went upstairs. Marjery was already in bed. Gregory was feeling marvelous, full of himself. The party had gone so well. Marjery had been one of the stars of the evening and he, basking in her reflection, had personally met two First Ladies and two governors.

Life was looking up. His bill to the estate of Morris Mauery had been sizable, for hours devoted to Madeleine Mauery's death, but there had been no demur from the executor, a swarthy man from the Middle West. They were anxious to close the estate.

"Hi," he said, when he came into the bedroom.

"Hi, I'm asleep."

"Would you like a little sip of scotch and water?"

"No."

He was not put off. "Would you like to play doctor and nurse?"

"Shut up," she said, "and turn off the light."

Darling Higgins and David Abdul had slipped away while everyone else was still dancing, and they were together in the jacuzzi at the end of the pool behind the house Abdul had bought on the hill.

"Princess Darling," he murmured.

Her breasts were covered to the rosebud nipples in the swirling hot water, her head was back, and her red hair fanned across the tile.

"Prince David," she said.

Abdul took a deep breath and ducked under the water. He put his face between her legs, his nose against the soft lips of her puckered holy of holies. Her hips rolled with the gesture and she seized him by the hair to pull him up, kissed him with the knowledge that he was hers, and moved to gather him within her. They made love in the water, the water jets playing over their bodies; his tanned form from his millenium in the desert, hers bleached by the sunless northern skies of her ancestors.

But it was all the same, Abdul sighed to himself: men were men and women were women. He knew what he was going to do: he was going to give her a baby, for the time had come for the first of the brown-skinned and red-haired Arabs. It was called the melting pot here in this country and he was going to add his touch of spice to the pot. Thinking of the analogy of the pot and the stirrer, he stirred. Darling was going to give him a son as red-headed as Lawrence of Arabia.

Lou Finistere could not sleep. She lay on her back beside Archy, hands folded under her head, and went over in her mind the passage of the Winter Ball. She relived each moment of it, moment by moment.

Archy was snoring heavily, snorting, gulping, and whistling.

He was a mastermind, no doubt about it. But the strenuous evening had taken its toll of him. She had danced with Archy and then, carried away, Jurgen had invited her to the floor. He was a scrawny figure of a man, but he was wiry and there was a certain gentleness to his touch. Toward the end, Archy had wandered away, saying he would check the front hall and then go upstairs and Lou had lingered with Ehrlich until the last of the guests had left the hotel or gone upstairs to tuck in. Jurgen had seen to the removal of all the glasses and silver, and only then was Lou ready to say good night. Outside his room, for she would continue on down the hall to hers and Archy's suite, she gave Jurgen a lighthearted kiss to show how grateful she was . . . for everything. She had felt his gasp of pleasure as she pressed her breasts to his chest and his start of surprise as she playfully stuck her tongue in his mouth. He had seemed so overcome that she pulled away and quickly said good night.

Ah, yes, Jurgen, she thought to herself. Jurgen was one she'd keep simmering on the back burner.

Pat Hyman sat silently as George babbled about good old Morrie and the clumsy way he had met his end. George had had too much to drink, but he had insisted on a last one before they went to bed.

"Of course," he was saying, "Morrie was showing signs of senility, I thought. Maybe it's just as well he went at the beginning of the downside and not when he was in full decline."

"George," she finally said, "enough about Morrie. He was a pig."

"Son of a bitch," he mumbled, "a hell of a way to talk about a friend."

"I'm going upstairs," she said.

Life went on. The party was over. What in the hell, Pat asked herself listlessly, was she going to do tomorrow?

They said good night to the Leonards in the lobby of the Beverly Hills Hotel and finally it was time to leave and get some sleep.

"See you in New York the middle of the month," Sam summed up. "Belle, thanks for everything."

"Well, we're off," Sharon said.

"Maude, come see us," Sylvia Leonard said.

"On our honeymoon," Maude promised, putting a hold on Glenn's arm.

"We'll all be in New York for Christmas, won't we?" Belle asked.

"Yes," Leonard said optimistically, "can we all meet in the big city for Christmas? Or, I'll tell you what: We could take the plane and fly over to the boat."

"Ship," Sylvia corrected him acidly.

"Where I come from, Sylvia," Sam snapped, "it's a boat. A ship is what you get in the Navy."

"Dummy, anything over a fishing boat is a ship."

"What the hell do you know? Every time we go out, you get seasick and it doesn't matter if it's a boat or a goddamn ship."

Finally, Belle and Charley were in his car and the car was pointed in the direction of his canyon.

"Charley," Belle said, "I want to get undressed and sleep for a week."

"That's exactly what you've got—one week. And then we're going to Mexico."

As the road climbed, they saw a red glow in the sky at the top of the hills.

"Looks like there's a fire over there somewhere—on the other side of Mulholland," he said.

"It lights the sky," Belle said. She thought for a minute, then pounced. "Charley, do you think sinfulness is beautiful?"

"It keeps people young, that's for sure," he said.

"Then you don't want to solemnize our arrangement?"

"I didn't know there was such a thing as solemnizing sinfulness."

"Maybe if you make a pact with Lucifer," she said.

"Which agency is he with?" Charley asked lightly.

"Lucifer and son. You know, they do a lot of Beverly Hills accounts."

"Oh, yeah, I've heard of them. They're hell to do business with . . ."

"Okay, Charley," she murmured happily. "I can see you're determined to be flippant. Listen, Charley, I'm asking you once and only once. Do you want to get married?"

He didn't answer immediately. Slowly, he drawled, "Do I get any time to think it over?"

"No, Charley, no time to think it over."

"Yes."

"You mean yes you want time to think it over? Or yes you want to get married?"

"The latter," he said. "What about you, Belle?"

"Affirmative."

"Well, then, that's a double affirmative," he murmured. "Would you like to give me a kiss?"

"Positively."

He laughed and that was it. "About time," he said.

"Charley . . ." There was nothing else she could think to say.